Compelling Interests

To Adina —

Yours for life,
Jessica Shaver Renshaw

Author of Best-Selling *Gianna: Aborted and Lived to Tell About It*

Compelling Interests

JESSICA SHAVER

© 2006 by Jessica Shaver Renshaw. All rights reserved.

Pleasant Word (a division of WinePress Publishing, PO Box 428, Enumclaw, WA 98022) functions only as book publisher. As such, the ultimate design, content, editorial accuracy, and views expressed or implied in this work are those of the author.

No part of this publication may be reproduced, stored in a retrieval system or transmitted in any way by any means—electronic, mechanical, photocopy, recording or otherwise—without the prior permission of the copyright holder, except as provided by USA copyright law.

Unless otherwise noted, all Scriptures are taken from the New American Standard Bible Copyright 1960, 1962, 1963, 1968. 1971, 1972. 1973, 1975. 1977, 1995 by THE LOCKMAN FOUNDATION. Used by permission.

ISBN 1-4141-0629-7
Library of Congress Catalog Card Number: 2005910343

The State does have an important and legitimate interest in preserving and protecting the health of the pregnant woman...and it has still *another* important and legitimate interest in protecting the potentiality of human life. These interests are separate and distinct. Each grows in substantiality as the woman approaches term and, at a point during pregnancy, each becomes "compelling."
——Roe v. Wade, January 22, 1973

The appellee and certain *amici* argue that the fetus is a "person" within the language and meaning of the Fourteenth Amendment....If this suggestion of personhood is established, the appellant's case, of course, collapses, for the fetus' right to life would then be guaranteed specifically by the Amendment.
——Roe v. Wade, January 22, 1973

Dedication

To all the heroes
of this second Civil War,
especially those
who are still determining
how it will come out.

Table of Contents

Acknowledgements	xi
Characters in order of appearance	xv
PART 1: 1940–1960	17
PART 2: 1965–1973	33
PART 3: 1973–1982	81
PART 4: 1982–1985	119
PART 5: 1986	167
PART 6: 1987–1988	199
PART 7: 1989–1991	245
PART 8: 1992–Sometime in the 21st Century	293
Postscript	337

Acknowledgements

More than thirty years ago when I stood frustrated at the kitchen sink and asked, "Lord, is a journal all I'm ever going to write?" this book immediately began unfolding in my mind. I thank God for answering that question and for the years of rich research He has provided since then, for the amazing ways He exposed me to the views of activists on both sides of the issue.

I am also grateful for:

Rebecca Younger, Bonnie Beardslee and their staff at New Life Mothers Home in Long Beach, California. **For pouring out your lives in this ministry I offer not only my gratitude but all the royalties from this book.** For local heroes Bev and Bob Cielnecky, Al and Judy Howard, Vi and Pat Griffith who have similar ministries to women with unwanted pregnancies and for heroes like them all over the country.

Joan Andrews, for her openness in sharing her life with me even down to details such as watching a sunset through chipped paint from a prison cell window. Her family, William, Elizabeth, Bill, John, Susan, David and Miriam. Richard Cowden-Guido, for permission to quote from Joan's published letters. The memory of Charlotte Susu-Mago, on whose sacrifical life I based Gwen Nakashige. Lana Clarke Phelan's public and moving

Compelling Interests

talk about the experience which led her to help get Roe v. Wade legalized. I based some aspects of Seely Tucker-Thomas on her.

The opportunity to give my book *Gianna: Aborted and Lived to Tell About It* to Dr. Edward Allred, the doctor who aborted Gianna, and for his extended phone call to discuss her abortion with me. I appreciate his honesty and willingness to make public his views as an abortionist.

LaVonne, Lynn, LaGard, Elizabeth and all the others who helped with research, including the many women who talked to me about their abortions. Gianna Jessen, born alive after a saline abortion and her birth-mother Tina, each of whom shared with me their incredible story. Sandra, Jim and Robbin, who told me what it was like to be arrested at a pro-life demonstration. Those who described to me their suicide attempts.

Helen and Jack Graham, who hosted the Unitarian-Universalist meetings, with Gerre, Norene, Bill and Ruth, Diane, Audrey, Kathleen, Virginia, Jackie, Sandy, Marvin, Connie, Margaret and Troy, Dave and Judi, Nordie, Christine and Rick, all determined to find common ground.

Resources I relied on, including:

Roe et al. v. Wade, District Attorney of Dallas County, United States Reports, Vol. 410, October term, 1972

Aborted Women: Silent No More by David C. Reardon

Aborting America and *The Silent Scream* (with American Portrait Films), Dr. Bernard Nathanson

The Abortion Handbook for Responsible Women, Lana Clarke Phelan

Abortion Questions and Answers, Jack and Barbara Willke

Giving Sorrow Words: Women's stories of grief after abortion (as well as her many articles), Melinda Tankard Reist

The Scarlet Lady: Confessions of a Successful Abortionist, Carol Everett

The Woodland Hills Tragedy, S. Rickly Christian

You Reject Them, You Reject Me: The Prison Letters of Joan Andrews, Richard Cowden-Guido, ed.

All the books of Margaret Sanger

Acknowledgements

Planned Parenthood: A Practical Guide to Birth-Control Methods

Our Bodies, Ourselves, Boston Women's Health Book Collective, 1976

Woman's Body, An Owner's Manual, 1981

Books, articles, films and radio broadcasts on abortion by Francis, Edith and Franky Schaeffer, Charles Colson, Jim and Shirley Dobson.

Tilly, Frank E. Peretti

I'll Hold You in Heaven: Healing and Hope for the Parent who has Lost a Child through Miscarriage, Stillbirth, Abortion or Early Infant Death, Jack Hayford

A Time to Heal and *Forgiven and Set Free* (with Susan Ficht) and *A Post-Abortion Bible Study for Women,* Linda Cochrane

Completely Pro-Life: Abortion, The Family, Nuclear Weapons, the Poor, Ronald J. Sider.

Editors: John Fried, who printed my first articles on abortion in the Long Beach Press-Telegram. My beloved mother Barbara Reynolds who read the first draft and believed there was a book in it somewhere. Carole Gift Paige who taught me how to bridge into fiction. Frieda, Jane, Margaret, Marjorie, Mary and others in the Third Wednesday writers' group. Athena Dean, founder of WinePress Publishing, who didn't push. Project Manager Tim Noreen and editor Georgia Varozza for their patience. (Whenever you're ready, I have a 650-page version of this book available.)

The prayers and practical support of both my husbands, Eric Shaver who slipped into eternity in 2002 and Jerry Renshaw. When the only hard copy of this manuscript disappeared and the back-up diskettes were blank, I mourned but thanked God, reminding Him the book was His to do with as He pleased. Through Jerry's perseverance in finding and restoring the entire book from files saved in obsolete software, God resurrected it. I love you, Jerry.

Those of you who helped whom I have forgotten to include. Write me at lil.shaver@verizon.net. If this book goes into a second edition, I'll be sure to credit you.

Compelling Interests

Those of you willing to listen to your counterparts on the other side.

My spiritual family who have prayed and are still praying for the impact of this book on you.

Characters in order of appearance

Cecile Tucker-Thomas (Seely), author of manual on self-abortion
Gwen Nakashige, liaison for adoptions
Joan Andrews, pro-life Catholic
Liz Tewksbury, Cecile's assistant, feminist lawyer
Richard Michaelson, M.D., abortionist
Julius ("Caesar") Guy, obstetrics student at University of California at Irvine
Pat O'Connor, Julius' roommate
James Weatherill Weiss, US Supreme Court justice
Ester Guy ("Dove"), Julius' wife
Stephanie Lancaster, adopted child
Artyce Lancaster, Stephanie's adoptive mother
Laurel Sandoval, nurse
Mariana Hernandez, sidewalk counselor
Tasha Akatellia, pregnant woman
Bobbie Porter, teacher, Women's Studies, Cal State Anaheim
Cindy Hodge, arsonist
Ann Lawson, nursing student at Cal State Anaheim
Noel McAllister, student at Cal State Anaheim

Part I
1940–1960

EL PASO, TEXAS—"You're pregnant." Removing his glasses, the obstetrician glared at Seely Thomas. "What did y'all go and do a fool thing like that for?" His eyes, now naked, were weary and pouched.

Crouched in the chair on the other side of his desk, Cecile started to answer but her mouth was dry and no sound came out. This man had delivered her son—had delivered *her*, sixteen years ago. She had no more freedom to think independently under his stern, paternal gaze than a mouse had in a boa constrictor's cage.

Dr. Ward raised a thick finger and pumped it at her in disapproval. "Mrs. Tucker, I warned you about this!"

Seely clutched her pocketbook with both hands, the knuckles losing their pinkness. Her wide blue eyes gazed anguished into his, as if beseeching him to change the results of the test.

"I—"

He interrupted her, speaking slowly and deliberately, his eyes narrowing slightly under heavy brows that were still brown, although the shaggy head above them was nearly white.

"It's been—what, not even three months!"

Compelling Interests

"I know," said Seely, swallowing, her voice small but as clearly Texan as his. She shifted uneasily in the chair. "I know we ha'en't paid for the first one, Dr. Ward, but—"

"Never mind the first one! I told you another one could kill you! Didn't I tell you not to get pregnant?"

"But you didn't tell me how not to!"

The doctor studied her drained face for a moment: the soft child's lips and cheeks, the skin as yet unlined by the anxiety in her expression. A kerchief hid all the dark hair but her tightly rolled bangs.

"You remind me of my granddaughter." He shook the thought aside, replaced his glasses, picked up a pen and scribbled something on a pad of paper. Tearing off the sheet, he handed it across the desk. "Well, I'll try to see you through it."

Seely knew the storm was over. It took courage to risk arousing it again.

"Can't you—we—do somethin'?"

"No." His frown made her shake. "I told you not to get pregnant!"

Cecile walked back into the waiting room and blinked a little at the sunlight flooding it.

"Are you all right, Miz' Tucker?" asked the nurse behind the counter. She wore a crisp white uniform, with her name on a badge above the pocket. Her blonde hair was in a net, tucked under a perky white cap.

"What?"

"Are you goin' be okay, honey?" There was genuine concern in her voice. She asked more quietly, "Y'all pregnant again, aren't you?"

Seely turned slowly and spoke as if dazed. "How could I help it? Am I just supposed to tell him no every time, the rest of our lives?"

The nurse glanced over her shoulder and motioned Seely toward her with a forefinger. "Take this," she said. She wrote an address on the back of a blank envelope. "Don't you tell anyone who give that to you."

Seely's hand reached out mechanically. "What is it?"

"You know. You'll need fifty dollars. Don't let them charge you more than that."

Seely looked down at the words. "Mexico?"

Part 1: 1940–1960

A noise made her glance beyond the nurse, where a door was opening. As the doctor stepped into the room with her, the nurse straightened and said stiffly, "No, we don't fill prescriptions here. You have to take that to the drugstore, Miz' Tucker."

Seely knew better than to say more.

TOKYO TO HIROSHIMA—As the Japanese countryside whizzed past, Gwen Nakashige found the rhythm of the train mesmerizing. The even sway of the cars as they rounded terraced hills, the regular *clackety-clack, clackety-clack* of the wheels on the tracks, the predictable whoosh of steam as the train jerked to a stop at each platform.

Beyond the soot-gritty windowsill, Gwen Nakashige could see narrow dirt roads with men stripped to the waist carrying baskets of rocks, pounding them to pebbles with mallets, filling the many potholes. And rice fields—tier upon tier of inch-deep lakes dotted with seedlings, each mirroring more stair-stepped hills beyond. She had to absorb the view in quick mental snapshots; it alternated with the reflection of her own face in the darkened window as the train plunged into tunnels.

It was 1951. She and Ken had flown to Japan as guests of the American military, still occupying the country, so Ken could spend several months as personal interpreter for an American general in Tokyo.

They had gone by prop jet, the seemingly endless flight punctuated by a refueling stop in Alaska. She remembered how men had forced the plane's door open to the Arctic night, how the coziness of the cabin had suddenly been invaded by penetrating cold, blown in on hurricane-force gusts of wind and snow.

Gwen and Kenichi—always Ken after the first introduction—had watched curiously as men in heavy parkas and gloves exchanged crates and luggage, yelling vainly over the howling storm. They could see glistening faces ringed in fur. Beyond them, the light fell away to blackness.

The general had been pleased with Ken's services and now the couple was free to travel south for a two-week vacation, all the way down the underbelly of Honshu, to meet Ken's relatives in Hiroshima. The general had arranged for them to have a private compartment on a train appropriated

Compelling Interests

by the occupation forces. Delicate chrysanthemum designs were embossed into the gold fabric wall covering—

"Are you sure you're not pregnant?" Ken's voice brought Gwen back from her reverie. She glanced at her husband in the velvet seat opposite hers and realized he had been studying her for a long time. He was smiling.

She gathered her red hair together at the back of her neck and let it go again self-consciously. "What makes you think I am?"

"They say pregnant women have a glow…"

"It's probably just the sun glinting off the race paddies." Gwen leaned forward and batted him playfully on the knee. "Ken, I'm 42. We've tried so long, I don't think I'd know how to glow. My glower's burnt out." Love and humor transformed her otherwise bland face: a little too round, a little too flat, a little too white.

"You'd radiate," he said. He moved over to her side, put an arm around her and pulled her close enough to kiss.

Tired, Ken and Gwen turned in early that night. Moments later, a distressed young Japanese man with close-cropped hair and an immaculate conductor's uniform knocked at their door.

He spoke apologetically in Japanese.

"What's the matter?" Gwen whispered to her husband.

Ken asked the man a question she couldn't understand and at the answer, inclined his head slightly and said, "Hai," which meant he was agreeing to something. The moment the conductor disappeared, Ken's eyes crinkled even more narrowly than they did naturally, his mouth curved upwards and his brown cheeks filled with air which burst out in a hoot of delighted laughter.

"What in the world?" Gwen was mystified. "What did he say?"

"He said, 'Please don't turn out the lights yet. Other people are not ready to retire.'"

She looked blank.

"Apparently this coach is a special one made for the emperor. When our lights go out, all the lights in the entire car go out! The conductor said, 'When the emperor wants to sleep, everybody has to sleep.'"

Part 1: 1940–1960

Gwen laughed with him, laughed till her eyes watered and she had to hold her sides.

"We don't dare turn the lights out," she whispered at last. "We'll have to leave them on all night."

"'When the emperor wants to sleep, everybody has to sleep.'" Ken repeated in a most proper, official voice. "I love it." He shook his head, still chuckling.

"I love *you*, 'Emperor' Kenichi Nakashige," said Gwen contentedly, settling back into the curve of his arm. "There's one thing about being married to you. It's never boring!"

They found the city of Hiroshima recovering surprisingly fast from its devastation of six years before. The epicenter of the atomic bombing was now a Peace Park, with only the skeleton of one domed building remaining. A recently-constructed cenotaph shaped like a covered wagon was in the middle of the flat, treeless park; it held the names of those killed, Ken's uncle explained. Some of his distant relatives were among them; they themselves had lived outside the city and hadn't been affected.

Gwen loved Ken's family, even though they had no common language. After a few days, his school-aged cousins summoned enough courage to touch Gwen's hair and ask if it was real.

"They've only seen American G.I.s," the uncle told them, through Ken. "You are the first American *woman*."

"And a redhead!" Ken added in English. Everywhere Kenichi and Gwen went on foot, children would gather to follow them. Thin and runny-nosed, the girls with identically bobbed black hair and dresses too big for them, they would gather curiously to stare at her, elbowing each other and pointing. Gwen heard murmurs of *"Gaijin!"* (Foreigners!) *"Gaijin da yo!"* When she smiled at them, they giggled and scattered, only to be drawn irresistibly back.

The couple had no imperial compartment on the trip back to Tokyo. The train was so crowded, it looked as if they might have to stand the entire trip.

"Don't lock your knees," Ken warned. "I've read that the guards at Buckingham Palace keel over when they do that."

Compelling Interests

The train was slowing, pulling into a station. On the platform, Gwen could see gaunt men with large trays balanced by straps around their necks, piled with *obento,* delicious lunches of sushi and sour pickles in boxes made of thin bamboo strips, and little pottery teakettles of steaming tea.

"*You* want to try ordering dinner this time?" Ken asked in her ear.

Gwen nodded. "Sure. Piece of cake. Piece of *rice* cake, I guess I mean."

She steadied herself against the train's rocking and threaded her way slowly toward the door, but people were six deep there and she couldn't get close enough to a window to catch a vendor's eye. So she tried what she had seen others do, holding up pastel paper currency and calling out "box lunch" in Japanese.

The response of those around her was startling. Impassive faces suddenly riveted their attention on her, arms grabbed her and before she knew what was happening, she was being bodily lifted and propelled through the crowd, which made way for her. Finally, someone opened a narrow door and thrust her inside. She found herself alone in a room the size of a closet.

She didn't come out for a long time and when she reached Ken again, she looked sheepish and her face was as bright as her hair.

"What happened to you?" he demanded. "I was getting worried! And where's our *o-bento?*"

"*O-bento!*" Gwen repeated, clapping a hand to her forehead. "Oh, no wonder!"

"No wonder, what?"

"I tried doing what I've seen other people do, you know, calling out my order and hoping someone would pass it on, with my money."

"Yes."

"Instead, a bunch of people grabbed me and started pushing me through the crowd toward the doorway."

"What in the world—?"

"They took me to the door of the bathroom and insisted I go in!"

"Gwen! Why?"

Part 1: 1940–1960

"I stood in the bathroom asking myself that, afraid to come out—and now I realize that instead of '*o-bento,*' I'd been calling—" she lowered her voice to a whisper, "'*o-benjo, o-benjo!*'" Gwen started giggling.

"Oh, Gwen! 'Toilet!' That's the best one yet!"

"Better than telling your family they were wonderful carrots, instead of people?"

He put his arms around her, while the Japanese around them pretended not to see.

"Being married to *you* isn't boring, either."

When they got back to Maui, Gwen went to her doctor and found out why she had been feeling queasy on the flight home. Ken was right. She *was* pregnant!

LEWISBURG, TENNESSEE—Joan Andrews' heart was beating so hard it made her chest hurt and she was ashamed of her fear. She got a better grip on her lunchbox with one hand and Susan's hand with the other. Was it to give courage to Susan or get courage from her? Joan wasn't sure, but she knew that she should be the brave one. Susan was only ten and she was a whole year older.

Would the big boys be waiting for them out behind Belfast Elementary School again today? Reality cut her hopes short. Of course they would. That's where they changed buses to go on to the high school. But maybe they wouldn't wait today. Maybe Friday was enough, jeering and taunting and throwing Joan's book bag in the dirt. Maybe they knew now that they couldn't make Catholics cry.

But what if they tried again? Could she stand up to them? Could she keep them from hurting Susan? She knew she could whip the boys her own age; she'd had to do it more than once on the playground during recess. But high school boys?

They came within view of the school and she felt her whole body sag with relief. No bus, no boys. She'd kept Susan walking so slowly that the

Compelling Interests

buses must have come and gone. She imagined the boys milling around, making jokes, nudging each other, and passing around a cigarette for quick, secretive puffs. When the little girls didn't show up, she could picture them climbing onto the next bus, the last one taking a last discreet drag on the cigarette, his eyes narrowed against the smoke as he stood on the steps, looking around, before he flicked the butt away.

Joan could almost feel their disappointment and she found herself able to forgive them. They probably weren't really mean, any more than her older brothers Bill and John were. Probably each one of them wasn't so bad, if the other guys didn't—

Just as they reached the corner of the school, Joan's heart lurched. She could hear a bus pulling up right behind them. She tried to hurry Susan across the back of the building but she could hear the bus brake on the gravel and the door squeak as it opened. There was a babble of young voices and the thud of feet. Now the elementary kids were catching up with them. Maybe they'd make it—

"Hey, Catholic babies," called one voice.

"Don't turn around," Joan whispered—but it was too late. A tall figure in jeans, his shirttail out, one fist curled, had overtaken them and was blocking their way.

"You didn't say good morning," he said, his eyes darting toward the other boys gathering around them. One side of his mouth seemed to be smiling, but his eyes weren't. Neither of the girls said anything. "Are Catholics too rude to say good morning?"

"Good morning!" squeaked Susan, in a voice that was mostly air. Trembling all over, Joan moved closer to her and squeezed her hand tightly. *Catholics aren't rude*, she wanted to say. You're *rude!*

But she could only watch, her dark eyes lifted apprehensively to the high school boy's chest. She didn't dare raise them farther.

The boy was circling now, taunting. "Tomboys," he said. Joan was acutely aware of the fact that she and Susan wore pants but had no time to wonder why Mama didn't dress them like the other girls. "So Catholics are tomboys, eh?" He leaned suddenly into Joan's view and as he talked, she could smell tobacco.

Part 1: 1940–1960

"Go ahead and cry," he breathed. "Catholic babies! You know you want to!" Behind him, looming tall as telephone poles, the others snickered.

We're not babies! thought Joan. *Catholics don't cry!*

Susan's small voice surprised Joan. "Our Papa's the principal here and we're going to tell on you!"

Maybe that was a mistake. The boys closed in menacingly and one of them in the back called, "Liar!" while the one closest to them hissed, "Oh, you're gonna snitch, are you? Gonna tell your da-a-ddy?" he asked.

Then of course Joan knew they couldn't tell. The honor of the entire Roman Catholic Church lay heavily on her thin shoulders.

Why did these boys keep picking on her? What had she done to them? Why did they think it such a bad thing to be Catholic? Mama and Papa were Catholic and they were the nicest people she knew—

Just then, the fist in front of her blurred and connected with her stomach. Joan collapsed in on herself, the pain so great she could only writhe helplessly as she heard him slug Susan. She was dying, oh, she was dying, she was going to throw up, she couldn't breathe—he was doing it again!

Joan heard moaning and gradually realized it was hers. She lay doubled up on the ground, her head spinning, hugging her stomach and struggling for breath. There was a kind of ringing in her ears, far off, and her whole body burst into a cold sweat in her attempt to stay conscious. Susan! She had to help Susan! Everything seemed—far away and cloudy.

She felt Susan's hand find hers and together they climbed unsteadily to their feet, adjusted their backpacks and looked at each other, but said nothing. Susan's face was white as chalk. Her eyes had tears in them. Joan kept her own lips caught tightly between her teeth. She wanted to hug Susan but she didn't dare. She knew they would both start crying for sure if she did.

"Come on," Joan said, picking up her lunchbox. "We'll be late."

Susan and Joan were quiet in class that morning, but they were always quiet, and no one asked them any questions. Joan had a hard time concentrating on long division. Her stomach ached. If this was part of what it meant to be Catholic, then she would have to live with it. But she was

Compelling Interests

angry at herself. She should have said something! She should have defended Susan! Then she began to feel angry at the boys.

She knew she was supposed to forgive them and maybe she could forgive them for what they did to her, but they had no right to treat her sister like that! Even though she knew Mama and Papa and the priest would be shocked, she couldn't forgive them for hurting Susan and *she didn't even want to try.*

Immediately, she felt guilty. Of course she had to try. Mama said you had to forgive your enemies.

Even Miss Hunter? a voice somewhere deep in her asked.

Joan thought about that for a moment. Miss Hunter had started it, really. Well, she had. She told the whole fifth grade, with Joan sitting right there, that Catholics were "closed-minded." Closed-minded, that's what she had said. She said some other things, too, things about the Pope just being a man and something about a "'quizzition"—Joan wasn't sure what that was.

Once she had called Catholics *"fantical"*—at least that's what it had sounded like. She'd asked Papa and he said the word was "fanatical" and asked her why she wanted to know. But Joan just said it was a word Miss Hunter had used in class. That wasn't a lie, even if it wasn't *all* the truth.

She sighed. She would have to forgive Miss Hunter. Maybe even the boys in her class. But the big boys, big as grown-ups, who would hit little girls? Besides, they made fun of the Catholic Church and that was wrong. But Miss Hunter had made fun of it, too, and you weren't allowed to even think that a teacher was wrong. It was all very confusing. Why did it have to be so hard to be a Catholic?

No, it was wrong to think that. Mama would tell her it was an honor to suffer for Christ and that if it was hard, she would be blessed for standing up for Him.

But she hadn't. She hadn't said a word or stood up for anybody. Not even Susan. Susan at least had said something. *But I'm a coward,* Joan told herself. *I've always been a coward.*

Part 1: 1940–1960

Well, maybe it counted a little that she hadn't run away. Maybe she and Susan had proved that even when they are persecuted, Catholics stand their ground. Even when they get punched in the stomach, hard, five or six times, and are left gasping for breath, tears pricking hot behind their eyes, Catholics don't cry.

Not until later.

"Mary, Mother of God," Joan sobbed into her pillow that night. "You know how I feel. You know what it's like to be a girl and not be understood. People must have hurt your feelings, too. Please don't be ashamed of me for being a coward and make me braver tomorrow." The cool glow of the Madonna by her bed was reassuring. There was a mother figure in heaven who could go to Jesus on her behalf and persuade Him to go easy on a little girl who meant well, who longed with all her heart to please Him.

Summer finally came and it was wonderful to be out of school. Joan was twelve, a year she would remember all her life as her most formative one.

It was the perfect day for a picnic—warm with just enough breeze to keep the day from feeling muggy.

It had started out as a pleasant family outing. The Andrews family, including Cindy, had all squeezed into the Buick and headed for their favorite spot along the river. Although the Duck River was deep and treacherous and most parents made it off-limits to unsupervised children, its beautiful grassy banks held secluded nooks, perfect for picnics.

Joan helped Papa spread the faded red-checkered tablecloth on the ground and anchored its corners with bowls of potato salad, jars of dill pickles and plates of sandwiches. John and Bill raced down to swim in the safe, shallow part of the river near the picnic area and Mama settled herself cross-legged on the grass with baby Miriam where she could watch them. Susan had taken David by the hand and gone off to look for blackberries.

Their cousin, unfamiliar with the warnings Joan had grown up with regarding the river, wandered up the embankment. Joan didn't see Cindy lean over the cliff to stare fascinated at the water surging past with deadly speed. But she did hear the splash and the simultaneous yelp of surprise as

Compelling Interests

the girl toppled into the cold water—a yelp which turned to partial, blood-curdling screams as she fought for her life against the strong current.

By the time Mama leaped to her feet, Joan had shot like a streak up the bank and dived in, disappearing into the raging river.

John and Bill caught the commotion out of the corner of their eyes, their cousin being swept toward them, floundering, tossed and worried by the churning waters, her eyes terror-stricken.

John sized up the situation in an instant. He swam rapidly to shore, struggled up the bank and heaved a fallen log into the current. By the time he had dived in after it, Bill had reached the log. Together they braced themselves as the chest-deep water pushed against their legs. One at each end of it, they forced the log into the current and balanced it with all their strength as the frightened little girl was swept toward them. Joan was nowhere to be seen.

Cindy grabbed frantically at the log and flung a wet arm and leg over the rough bark. Only then did Joan bob up beside her, gasping. She was so weak the boys had to sling her across the log and hold her there as they pushed it to shore.

"She dived in," Elizabeth Andrews told her sons when she had helped them pull both exhausted girls up the bank. "She knew Cindy can't swim."

"But Joan can't swim, either!" protested John.

"She was in the river before we knew what was happening," said the usually quiet William.

John looked down at his little sister in awe. Clutching a towel around her shoulders, her thin body looked small, hunched on the grass. She was trembling more with delayed fear than with cold.

"How did you do it, Joan?" he asked.

"Under her— Held her up— Held her—ankles," Joan panted.

"She got under Cindy and held her up on her shoulders so her head would be out of the water," William interpreted. He shaped what he was describing in the air with his lean hands as he talked.

"That was brave, Joan," said John admiringly. "You could have drowned."

Part 1: 1940–1960

"I knew—I was going—to die," whispered Joan, "but—you have to do something." She looked up at him, her smile shaky because her teeth were chattering. Strands of dark hair dripped across her eyes. "You have to try."

"Joan!" The sharp cry pierced the air and Joan, in her room, realized with a shock that it had come from Mama, somewhere downstairs. She raced down the stairs, calling, "Mama? Mama? Are you all right?"

Mama was in the kitchen, wearing an apron over the figure that was just beginning to show her pregnancy. She half-sat on the kitchen stool and she seemed to be panting, one hand to her abdomen.

Joan looked at her, frightened. Mama had never cried out like that.

"Mama, what's wrong? What can I do?"

"I'm having pains, Joan," gasped Mama. "Call the doctor! I think—my water broke."

"Oh, no, Mama—the baby?"

Mama didn't answer. All her attention was focused inside.

As Joan started to dial Dr. Peterson's, glancing worriedly at Mama between each number, Susan came in. She sized up the situation immediately. "You'd better lie down, Mama!" There wasn't anywhere to lie but the bench they all sat on for meals—which was too narrow—or the floor. "Thank goodness I just mopped it this morning!" Mama panted.

"Oh, for goodness' sake, Mama," scolded Susan, though her voice sounded anxious. "You should have called me! You shouldn't be mopping—" Each of the girls took an elbow and helped Mama off the stool.

Mama eased herself to the floor. "I mopped my way through five pregnancies and never had a—Ooh!" Her moan scared Joan in mid-sentence and her own voice faltered. "Right away, please, Dr. Peterson!"

When she hung up, she went to Mama and knelt beside her.

"Oh, Mama, I wish I could help!"

"I'll be all right—but the baby—"

Compelling Interests

She seemed to have a kind of convulsion. Joan started to lean down to put her cheek to Mama's but Mama shook her head. "I'm having a miscarriage, I think," she said. She seemed calmer now, although her forehead was damp. Joan took a corner of the apron tied around Mama's waist and wiped it gently.

By the time the doctor arrived, the baby had already come, in a transparent, wet sac. Mama wiped tears from her eyes and tried to get up to greet him, but he motioned her back down. The girls stood back soberly as he felt her abdomen through the print dress.

"Dr. Peterson," Mama tried to say lightly, "I asked Joan to call you. I guess I should have asked her to call Father Michael instead. I'm sorry we put you to the trouble."

"Mrs. Andrews, it's never any trouble. I'm sorry there isn't anything I can do."

Father Michael came later. Mama let the girls help her wrap the baby in a tiny, soft blanket that had been Miriam's and place him on the kitchen table. Joan gazed wonderingly at the still, wet body, reached out a finger and gently touched the infinitesimal hand. Only three months along, yet he was perfectly formed.

They named him Joel and Father Michael baptized him and then blessed a corner of the yard for them to bury him in.

When the boys came home from work, one of them dug the hole while the other helped Papa make a coffin only a foot long. Joan placed Joel in it and each of them cut off a lock of their own hair to place beside him. Papa covered the coffin and tacked it down and after placing it in the hole, they each threw in a handful of dirt and said a prayer for him. Miriam and Joan were crying. Whenever Joan prayed for her family after that, she always included Joel.

Part 2
1965–1973

EN ROUTE FROM HONOLULU TO LOS ANGELES—During the first six-hour leg of the flight, as the 747 headed eastward from Tokyo, the sun had risen and set in record time—and now it was yesterday. They had just taken off again, this time from Honolulu, and the moon was already up. She glanced out the window. The airport rushed by, then the tops of palm trees, then there was nothing but sky. Gwen Nakashige wondered if she'd ever get used to the miracle of air travel in the '70s.

The stopover in Honolulu hadn't been long enough for her to go home to her apartment on Kapahulu Street and check her mail. But she'd be back in a week, after she'd met with the adoptive couple and had a chance to go to Anaheim and visit her niece. *I haven't seen Annie for three years—and kids change so much between three and six.* It still felt odd to be a great-aunt.

She sighed. *I wonder how many more times I can do this.* She felt wearier than she had after many of her previous flights. *Jet lag seems to be affecting me more than it used to,* she thought, rubbing her eyes. *Of course I'm 64. I suppose that could account for it.* With stiff fingers, she rearranged the tiny bundle on her lap, then searched her soft white hair for sliding hairpins.

Compelling Interests

The 747 circled and leveled off, leaving Oahu behind like a crumpled topographical map on a desk which stretched to the horizon. As the plane banked, Gwen caught a glimpse of the crescent moon. It would be overhead by the time they reached Los Angeles.

She peeked between the folds of blanket in her lap. The baby was sleeping, his brown face serene, the tiny epicanthic folds smoothed over the closed eyes.

The young woman next to her had been gazing out the window. Now she spoke playfully.

"Well, back to the real world," she said with a soft pout.

"What?" asked Gwen politely, glancing from the tanned hands and brightly-painted nails to the pretty face, framed in bleached hair which turned up perkily at her shoulders. Mid-twenties, she guessed.

"Vacation's over. Time to leave Paradise and get back to reality." She smiled at Gwen. "How long were you here for?"

Gwen, who had taught high school English, winced in spite of herself and smiled. "Twenty-five years."

The woman twisted in her seat to stare at her. "You *live* in *Hawaii?*"

"Honolulu."

"Wow! Do you ever get used to it? How can you bear to go to sleep at night? Aren't you afraid you'll miss something?"

Gwen's eyes twinkled. "I force myself."

"Do you, like, have luaus all the time and stuff?"

"Every meal except breakfast. I got tired of having to go out in the back yard every morning and dig up my corn flakes."

The woman tapped Gwen's hand lightly. "Oh, you're *teasing* me!" She thought a moment. "Were you born in Hawaii?"

"My husband was. On Maui."

"Was it exciting for him, growing up there?"

"I guess he really didn't know it was supposed to be. It was just—normal."

"But I mean, all those palm trees and pineapples—You can have pineapple for breakfast every day if you want to, can't you? That was the

Part 2: 1965–1973

hardest decision for me the whole time I was here. Every morning, which should I have—papaya or pineapple? Do you have any children?"

"I had a daughter—" Gwen's voice drifted off momentarily. "She died at birth," she added and busied herself with the bundle on her lap. Why was she sharing this with a stranger? Somehow it seemed important that someone know. Suddenly, from the bundle, came a tiny cry.

The woman next to Gwen looked astonished. "What was that? Why, you have a baby in there!"

With hands which looked years older than her smooth and pleasant face, Gwen tenderly unfolded enough of the hand-crocheted blanket so the woman could see the little brown face and tiny fists, no bigger than kukui nuts.

"It must be brand-new!"

"Born Monday," said Gwen proudly.

"Girl?"

"Boy."

"Is he yours?"

Gwen laughed and shook her head. "No, he isn't mine. I'm just kind of the go-between."

The woman, stroking one of the baby's hands, looked at her blankly.

"There are couples I hear about who can't have children," Gwen explained. "They pay my way to Japan to bring back babies whose mothers don't want them. This one is going to a couple near Los Angeles."

Her seatmate's face was registering shock. Her pretty mouth fell open and her eyes stared. "Japan?" she mouthed. Her voice lowered to a conspiratorial whisper. "Are you one of those black-market people?"

Gwen laughed. "No, I'm afraid it's all perfectly legal. I don't steal them or sell them. I just arrange for them to be adopted."

"Oh," said the woman, as if she weren't quite sure whether to be relieved or disappointed. "So this is some little Japanese baby that is being adopted by an American family?"

"That's right."

"Why don't they adopt an American baby?"

Compelling Interests

"In most of the cases I hear about, either the husband or wife is Japanese. I happen to have contacts in Japan because my husband was Japanese and had relatives—"

"Your husband was Japanese?" Then, "Did he die, too?"

"Yes."

"Do you speak Japanese?"

"Some. We spoke English at home because he was *nisei*—second generation. He grew up in the States. The first time he ever went to Japan was in 1951. He had relatives who lived near Hiroshima and we went over to meet them after the Second World War. We couldn't go there *during* the war, you know, because the United States and Japan were on opposite sides." Gwen thought she had better clarify that, in case the young woman had gaps in high school history as well as in English.

"Whose side was your husband on?" the woman asked bluntly.

"Ken? America's, of course," said Gwen. "This was his country. But because he was of Japanese ancestry—" she sighed, "he had to go with all the other *nisei* to a relocation camp in Arizona. Naturally I went with him, because we were married by then," she added.

"Was it like the ones in Germany?" the woman asked, wide-eyed.

"Like the concentration camps? Oh, no. The people who rounded us up weren't cruel, just afraid. In fact, some of them were very apologetic." She seemed to be talking more to herself now. "Anyway," more briskly, "the war ended and we finally got permission to visit."

Gwen found herself describing to the attentive girl next to her what post-war Japan had been like—as impudent as the children who held out their hands for chewing gum, as timeless as the gray-bearded priests chanting in the temple.

There had been 5 ½ million living in Tokyo in 1951, only half what it was now. Even then it was hard to believe that one more person could crowd into those streets full of impatient taxi drivers, skillfully evasive bicyclists and impassive pedestrians.

"They were all so polite to us," she said. "The only person I ever heard express anger against Americans or even bring up the war was some drunk that bumped into us on the Ginza one night."

Part 2: 1965–1973

How could she describe how strange and wonderful it had all been? Mt. Fuji—ethereal from a distance, homely and barren underfoot. The Imperial Palace, with swans cutting quiet swathes through its surrounding moat. Boys in school uniforms—the Japanese loved uniforms—with tall wooden clogs on their feet. A little girl in a thick, padded kimono coat big enough for two, jumping rope with an even smaller girl asleep on her back, the tiny head bobbing wildly.

It was such fun to go with Ken, to meet the relatives they'd only heard about. She described how, at the end of their two-week visit, she had struggled to express her gratitude for their hospitality in Japanese. His relatives had burst into giggles, hiding them unsuccessfully behind the sleeves of their kimonos. "I *meant* to refer to 'all you people'," said Gwen, "but it turned out I had called them all carrots!"

Her new friend smiled. "You have so many neat stories! What an interesting life! You are really lucky."

Yes, she was lucky, Gwen thought. Lucky and lonely. She had been to Japan so many times since that first trip, but most of them without Ken. Every time she went, the memory of him possessed her more than any other.

It had been such a good marriage, even if it hadn't been easy. The hard times had only brought them closer. The war. The relocation camp. The difficulty of starting over after the war, at least until Ken realized that his knowledge of Japanese customs made him invaluable to the American occupation forces. The loss of Bess—

Bess's death was what had started it. Gwen had never forgotten how the baby had looked in the tiny coffin, so pale for being half oriental, with that shock of black hair which had been plastered down at birth but stood out as soft as a dandelion's spikes in death.

Alive throughout most of the long labor, the baby had emerged at last with the cord around her neck. Remembering, Gwen felt tears spring to her eyes and she bit her lip.

It was the knowing that Bess had been *alive* in the womb, the certainty that what was there before birth was *life,* that had motivated Gwen after her husband's death to seek meaning for herself by finding homes for

Compelling Interests

babies nobody else wanted. Since 1948, abortion had been available in Japan throughout pregnancy; it had taken Gwen nearly four years to cut through the red tape and get permission from Kagawa Memorial Hospital to arrange adoptions for Japanese mothers willing to carry their unwanted babies to term.

She knew that for each baby she placed in a home, thousands would never draw a breath. She knew her efforts were only a token. But it didn't matter to Gwen. Every baby was precious to her. Each one was Bess all over again.

Her seatmate didn't ask any more questions. *Maybe I blew her circuits,* thought Gwen with amusement, but she was grateful. She closed her eyes. *Bess.*

She must have slept after that, because it seemed only minutes later when a voice roused her. "Look," the young woman was saying. "Los Angeles."

Gwen dabbed her eyes and peered through the thick glass. She forced herself to speak cheerfully.

"L.A.'s smog has such a terrible reputation," she said, "but the smog in Tokyo this morning was a lot worse. Or should I say," she went on, eyes twinkling, "that the smog in Tokyo *tomorrow* morning was worse."

Her new friend smiled at her kindly, but without understanding. Ken would have understood.

SAN FRANCISCO—As Cecile pushed through the heavy wooden doors of the medical school and stepped out onto the porch, the pounding of a hard rain and the smell of wet dirt assaulted her senses. Subconsciously, she fought their intrusion. She had enough on her mind without unsolicited stimuli from outside.

On the porch she hesitated, letting groups of women part to go around her and down the steps. The downpour blurred the shapes of cars in the lot across the campus. She peered at them dispiritedly without seeing them.

Part 2: 1965–1973

All this way for three days of nothing, she thought. As if sharing her opinion of the conference, gusts of wind had torn one of the posters from a pillar where it had been taped and hurled it face up on the glistening pavement: Conference on Reproductive Rights, March 26-28, 1965.

Overpopulation. Birth control. That's it. Not one helpful thing on abortion, at least nothing American women can get hold of. African women, maybe. Indian women. But nothing definite, nothing positive, no hope for us American women.

Unbidden, the memory was there again. In her mind's eye, she watched herself climb into the taxi, gripping the handhold in the door for confidence as the car sped down the darkened streets of Juarez. She saw the taxi pull up at a storefront and wait as she drew herself slowly out of the back seat, doubling over even while she handed the driver the pesos. She saw the car leap away before the furtive woman behind the door answered her knock.

But if the quarter century since then had softened the terror, why were her short nails trying to dig into the palms of her hands and why was she holding her breath to keep from screaming?

The dread. The blood. The sobs of pain, of relief—and then of anger. As hard as she had worked to suppress the memory, if she let it, it was all still as raw after twenty-five years as these shafts of rain ricocheting forcefully off the pavement at the foot of the steps.

As it always did, resentment flooded in on the heels of the memory. There should have been someone she could have talked to. A woman had a right to a safe, legal solution to an unwanted pregnancy. No girl should have to go through that kind of fear and humiliation, ever.

She took a long breath and studied the stream of women bent beneath their umbrellas, hurrying to their cars. If the conference had been a waste of time, why wasn't she following them? What was this tension which, like a taut rubber band, held her immobile when she strained to go? *They have no answers,* thought Cecile. *Nobody has answers. Why go home? There aren't any answers there, either.*

She felt in her purse for a tiny packet, folded into strips of soft clear plastic. Pulling the pleats apart, she struggled to cover her short, gray-

Compelling Interests

flecked hair with the bonnet which resulted and to tie its ends under her chin. She aimed her umbrella at the steps, pressed the release and shook it open. *Do I really think abortion will ever be openly discussed, much less permitted?* she thought bitterly. *That would be too good to be true.*

Gripping books and papers in the crook of her left arm, Cecile pulled the umbrella close to her face and made a reluctant dash for her car.

In the middle of the street, standing huddled on the divider, was a woman in a bright yellow mackintosh and a sou'wester and boots, handing out what appeared to be leaflets. It was hard for Cecile to be sure, through the condensation fogging her glasses. As she hurried by, the woman thrust one of the rough mimeographed sheets at her. Clumsily, Cecile transferred the umbrella to her left hand, grabbed the paper and added it to her wet armload.

She didn't reach Long Beach until after midnight, aching with the strain of eight straight hours of driving, anger a very real presence beneath her disappointment.

John stirred and half-woke as she turned on the closet light, kicked off her shoes, and tugged her dress over her head.

"How did it go?" he asked dutifully.

"Rotten." She didn't feel like talking.

She didn't feel like sleeping either, she realized. Leaving her dress where it had fallen, she turned off the light and padded in her slip and nylons back to the kitchen, where she had dumped the damp pile of papers on the checkered oilcloth.

I can organize my notes, she thought. *The guy from India wasn't bad.* She fumbled for a cigarette in her purse, flicking on the gas burner to light it. She took a deep drag as she sat down and the acrid smoke made her squint.

"Repeal abortion laws." The title of the sodden leaflet she had been handed in the rain caught her eye. Suddenly it didn't matter that the leaflet was crumpled, colorless, printed on cheap paper.

"A woman's body tells her when a pregnancy is wrong," Cecile read. "For the church or the state or anyone else to dictate to a woman that she

Part 2: 1965–1973

must carry within her a fetus she does not want—an endoparasitic growth threatening her health, her sanity, her life—is slavery at its cruelest."

This is it! thought Cecile. *This is what I've been looking for!* She sank onto a chair and read the words again. Yes! Yes! This was what she had been trying to put into words for twenty-five years. *Women know. Women should have the right to choose.*

She lapsed into thought, periodically reviewing the crudely printed document until she had nearly memorized it. "Abortion laws are sexual discrimination laws. Male physicians, male legislators, male-dominated religions are refusing women the self-evident right to custody over their most personal possession, their own bodies."

She felt as if she had discovered womankind's Declaration of Independence and Emancipation Proclamation all in one. She held it as if it were inscribed on parchment and sat thinking until dawn, one cigarette after another burning down to her fingers. When Cecile finally went to bed she had an envelope ready to mail, enclosing her two-dollar membership fee in an organization which she had never heard of before, Reproductive Freedom for All Women, and sending for every pamphlet they had, at a dime apiece.

The bed creaked as she climbed in next to John and said aloud, as if he had just asked his question and was still awake to hear the answer, "The only person with guts enough to say anything worth listening to was a woman standing in the middle of the street in pouring-down rain."

During the next six months, Cecile was in frequent touch with the group of five women who, as it turned out, comprised the total paid membership of Reproductive Freedom for All Women. In September, she got a call from San Francisco. Three more women had joined and they wanted someone representing RFAW to come speak to them in Albuquerque. The organization couldn't afford to fly someone down. Cecile was closer than they were: would she be willing to go?

She'd never spoken in public before but somebody had to speak to this issue, she decided, and why not her?

She took her navy blue skirt, a white blouse with little blue flowers on it and a long navy blue jacket that she hoped would hide about ten

Compelling Interests

pounds. Maybe it was too dressy but she was anxious about the talk and the outfit was comfortable and familiar. She had worn it often enough to work at the library.

She didn't think she should stay at a motel with John's latest construction job so tenuous, so she planned to drive straight there and back. If she left directly from work, even with Friday night traffic out of the city she should just make it by the meeting the next morning. Lots of black coffee and a few catnaps at the side of the road should get her through.

The group met at a small college at ten o'clock Saturday. Seven women showed up, grouping themselves around her on folding metal chairs. Cecile looked at the faces fixed expectantly on hers.

I had 16 hours driving to plan this talk and I can't even remember my own name, she thought nervously. She heard her voice, surprisingly calm, welcome the group and start to introduce herself. *They aren't so threatening,* she thought. *They're just hungry for information. I can give them that.*

"You can call me Seely," she told them. "Before I tell you about our group and its objectives, I'll tell you a little bit about my own abortion." She touched her throat. "It's hard to get that word out," she laughed. "I've never talked about it before." The women chuckled with her.

"I got married when I was fifteen and we lived in El Paso. Ten months and three days later, I had my first baby. I didn't know anything about giving birth—anymore than I had known anything about periods or sex or pregnancy—and there wasn't anyone to tell me.

"I was in labor three days and gave birth to a tiny, jaundiced baby you could hold in your hand. My doctor told me, 'Don't have another one or you'll die.'

"I asked him how I could keep from having another one and you know what he said? 'Stay away from your husband.'" The attentive women around her shook their heads sympathetically.

The memories were flooding back. Three months later she was pregnant again—pregnant and "scared spitless." She told about going to her obstetrician, who still hadn't been paid for the delivery of her first baby.

"I told you not to get pregnant," he scolded her.

"But you didn't tell me how not to."

Part 2: 1965–1973

"Well, I'll try to see you through it," the doctor said grudgingly.

"Can't we do something?" she pleaded.

"No. I told you not to get pregnant."

She told how she finally managed to get the address of a Cuban midwife in the outskirts of Juarez, who wanted fifty dollars for an abortion.

"By the time I saved and borrowed enough money, I was four months into the pregnancy," Cecile told the women. "The midwife packed something inside me and told me to go home and wait. Three days later—" Her voice wavered. Cecile was surprised to find herself wiping away tears. She took off her glasses.

"Three days later, I began heavy contractions. We were having dinner at my sister's. I was bleeding. I had a fever. The pain was so severe I had to leave the table. I locked myself in the bathroom—and found—that I was—there was a tiny limb protruding. I panicked. I used toilet paper to stuff it all back inside. I told them, 'I've got to go. I'm sick. I'm going home.'"

The women listened, their own eyes glistening with tears. One was crying unashamedly.

"It was dark," Cecile went on in an unsteady voice, "but I took a taxi back to the midwife and she—she put me on a gurney and cleaned me out and then she—held me and said, 'Honey, did you really think it was so easy to be a woman?'"

She couldn't say any more. Her shoulders were heaving, her breath was coming in great sobs, muffled by her boxy hands. Tentatively, one of the women stood up and came to her, leaning over to give her a tender hug. Two or three more approached, one kneeling in polyester bell-bottoms to offer her a Kleenex.

The tenderness only made Cecile cry harder. "I felt so—so *abandoned*," she managed to gasp. "It was so frightening. I didn't know anyone—"

When she was able to catch her breath and dry her eyes, Cecile tried to laugh at herself. "This is embarrassing. I didn't know this was going to be a therapy session," she said. Another sob escaped her in spite of herself. "I thought *I* was coming here to help *you!*"

Compelling Interests

"You *are* helping us," said a middle-aged woman, who had dark circles under her eyes and a puffy, sad face. "I went through the same thing last year. I haven't dared tell my husband. I haven't dared tell anyone till now." Her voice had become very soft. "It helps just to be able to talk about it."

The serious young woman who had knelt to offer Cecile a Kleenex had quietly retaken her seat. Now she tucked her straight black hair behind her ears, swallowed, and spoke in a tight voice. "I wish one of you could help me. I'm pregnant." She wound the strap of her purse around two fingers.

Present reality thudded into place for Cecile. What had been then for her was now for this pale woman. It was, after all, why Cecile had come—to prevent her own nightmare from happening to anyone else.

"Tell us about it," she said, realizing as she did so that she was stalling for time.

"My name is Liz," the woman was saying. "I'm twenty-three and I have two kids. My husband was filing for divorce when I found out I'm pregnant again. I told him but he left anyway. I don't want another child. I don't know how I'm even going to raise the two I have. Besides, having his baby would bring back too many painful memories. I just want to get on with my life, the sooner the better."

"I don't know Albuquerque," said Cecile. "Does anyone here know who she could go to? Do you?" she asked, turning to the woman with the circles under her eyes.

"I went to my aunt. She gave me the name of some quack about a mile from here. I wouldn't recommend him. He charged me five hundred dollars and I had to go to a hospital for a D&C afterward because he botched it."

The pregnant woman was still waiting. Had they no more to offer a woman now than they had had in the '40s? Cecile thought quickly and was about to speak when Liz added, "I'm Catholic so I can't have anyone know."

"Does your family doctor know you're pregnant?" The anger she so often felt at the deceptions women had to resort to was rising fast within her.

Part 2: 1965–1973

"Yes."

"Okay. Go to a doctor who doesn't know you—out of town, maybe—and have him insert an IUD, what we call 'the loop', in your cervical canal."

"Isn't that to *prevent* pregnancy?" Liz asked uncertainly.

"Yes. But if you're already pregnant, it can bring on an abortion. Just don't tell him you're already pregnant.

"Or," Cecile went on, speaking briskly and with more assurance than she felt, "try to fool your own doctor into thinking you are having a miscarriage and finishing the job for you."

"How?"

"Buy some calves' liver and rub the blood where it will look convincing. Or bring a urine sample from a friend who isn't pregnant so he'll think the fetus is already dead and he'll clean you out.

"If you go out of town—I don't know about New Mexico rape laws but if you can pretend you've just been raped, you may be able to get a legal abortion. Be sure you act like you've been raped. Tear your clothes, scratch your arms, mess your hair up and talk incoherently. Practice your story ahead of time. It helps if you claim he was black, or it was your father or something."

That led to a long discussion and when the meeting was over, Cecile was drained. She started for Long Beach and had gone only ten miles when she knew she wouldn't make it without sleep. She pulled into a crummy-looking motel, rented a room with her last $8 and slept around-the-clock.

A week after she reached home, she received a postcard from a Liz Tewksbury. It said simply, "Seely, I did it. I'm free and I'm profoundly grateful to you. If I can find a job and an apartment for me and my kids in Long Beach, I'm moving. I want to help you pass the word."

No one took a vote; no one offered her a salary; no one even put it into words, but from then on, Cecile was assumed to be Southwest Director for RFAW. Still shy at first about confiding her own experience to strangers but driven by conviction, she spoke again and again, until she had blanketed five states with urgent appeals for legal abortion.

Compelling Interests

ST. LOUIS, MISSOURI—After one semester of active involvement in anti-Vietnam protests, fasts, and prayer vigils at St. Louis University, Joan Andrews found herself disenchanted with the peace movement. She called her parents in Tennessee.

"Papa?" Joan asked, reassured by the sound of his voice. "Can you come get me? I want to come home."

"I'll never say no to that offer," her father responded. "We've all missed you."

He drove the old Buick up from Lewisburg and pulled up in front of Father Rogers Hall. She saw him from her window and when she ran downstairs to hug him, the white hair, the rough shirt, the faint, familiar scents of the farm and his quiet voice were comforting.

"How is Mama?"

"Fine."

"And the boys? Any word from John?"

"They're fine, too. Susan and the younger two can't wait to see you." He anticipated her next question as she opened her mouth.

"The horses are fit as ever."

He picked up her suitcases and she hurried to get the door for him.

"Maybe it isn't college," she said thoughtfully, falling into step with him as they walked together to the car. Papa said little but he was listening. She could always count on him for that.

"Maybe it's me."

As she spoke, her father lifted her battered suitcases into the back seat, revealing his tanned, muscled forearms where his sleeves were rolled up. He could have been forking hay over a fence to the cows, the gesture was so right for him. Cramped into the front seat, gripping a steering wheel, was not. He was more at home on the tractor.

Joan let herself in next to him. "I don't know, Papa. I want so much to do something that will make a difference, but it never seems like enough. Maybe I lost heart when I heard that Bill and John had both been drafted and that Bill has to go to Vietnam. That depressed me.

"You know, Papa, to a lot of the students here, the peace movement is just—oh, not a game, exactly, they're very sincere about wanting to stop

Part 2: 1965–1973

the war but—I don't know—it's like *we* have to stop it. Ourselves. I don't believe we can do anything without God. I don't want to judge them, but it seems kind of—prideful."

Papa drove, directing the car toward Nashville. "That's not judging them," he said.

"Then I got to thinking," Joan went on, confidentially, "maybe I'm just a coward. I've always been a coward, Papa.

"Remember when I was six and you and Mama wanted me to start Belfast School and I wouldn't go until Susan was old enough to go, too? I don't know why you let me get away with that, Papa, but I'm so glad you did. I *couldn't* have gone alone. I *couldn't*. I would have died.

"And the next year, when Susan was old enough, we both went and I remember we stood at the teacher's desk and she asked me my name. And I got so scared I couldn't speak and I was too scared even to run away. I just stood there. And Susan answered for me, real quick, 'Her name's Joan.'

"Oh, Papa, I couldn't even say my own name! I don't know what I would have done without Susan. She spoke for me all through elementary school."

Papa glanced at Joan and smiled, the wrinkles friendly and the blue eyes tender. "You're no coward, Joanie. You fought the other kids when they made fun of the church. And you took all that abuse from the high school boys. If your mother and I had only known what they were doing to you—I wish you'd told us, Joan. You shouldn't have had to go through all that."

"Well, I hate to say it, Papa, with you the principal there and all, and I'm sure she had some reason for her prejudice, but my teacher caused it. She really had no right to speak that way about Catholics, right in front of the whole class. I *was* a coward, too, Papa, because she was mocking the faith and I didn't say anything. I just felt so sad inside.

"That's probably why the boys, the ones my age, anyway, teased me all the time. They called Susan and me liars and cheats because we were the only Catholics in the school. I did have it out with them during recesses, though!" she said with satisfaction, her deep-set, dark eyes glowing at the memory. "I must have spent every recess dirt-fighting the boys.

Compelling Interests

"I couldn't fight the teacher and I couldn't bring myself to fight another girl, because they all wore dresses, you know, Papa, and somehow, it didn't seem right to get them dirty—" She broke off. "Why did you let Susan and me wear pants?" she asked. "No one else did and that was another reason I guess we were treated different. We were the only tomboys."

Papa didn't answer. Joan assumed he didn't know either and she lapsed into silence. She didn't want to talk about what the big boys had done to her. Her thoughts reverted back to her heroes, men she had been reading about recently.

After a while she said aloud, "That must be why I admire brave people so much—because I'm not. I read Dostoevsky this semester and I thought how awful it would feel...to be shut away from your family in a dark cell. I could never bear that. It would be so scary.

"And those men who helped to rescue Jews from the Holocaust. I did a paper on Raoul Wallenburg. He was a real hero, Papa. He risked his life to save Jews. Why didn't the others rise up, Papa? How could the people not rise up?"

Her father shrugged, but sympathetically, Joan thought. That's how Papa had always been. "You're sure a talker," he had said once. "You're always thinking about something." But the way he said it, it was like he admired the quality, like he enjoyed having his mind stirred to consider things beyond the pattern into which his own thoughts fell.

All the pressure of deadlines and her anxiety over world problems eased as they bypassed Nashville and neared Lewisburg. They passed the community hospital and the International Harvester dealer and crossed the railroad. The next farm was theirs. Right at the edge of the city limits, it was 225 acres of pasture and forest, of cows and horses.

Home. That was where she belonged. Maybe all of her agitation had a perfectly simple explanation. Maybe she was just plain homesick. How she had missed Mama! Mama was a safe haven from the world. Joan knew that in her absence, Mama prayed late into the night for her protection, and not just for Joan, but for Bill and John and Susan, the other grown children, and for David and Miriam, whose arrivals eight and ten years after Susan's birth had delighted them all.

Part 2: 1965–1973

Joan looked over with grateful eyes at her father, his rugged hands on the wheel, his concentration on the road ahead. She had missed Papa, too—that self-effacing, versatile man who had earned a law degree from Vanderbilt University and worked for the legal department of Bell Telephone in Nashville, leaving that job to become teacher and then principal of the 125 students at nearby Belfast School. Now he was a cattle farmer. Was there nothing Papa couldn't do?

At home, it was safe to be Catholic. Being Catholic was a *good* thing there. Every night since they were tiny, Mama sat in her rocker between the boys' bedroom and the girls' bedroom and said the rosary with them. Every Sunday the Andrews family shared Mass at the mission church in Lewisburg.

Joan's heart leaped as the white frame farmhouse came into view. From somewhere, the June breeze wafted to her eager senses the subtle odor of wild onion.

She loved the earthy smells, sounds, and sensations of the farm: the firm back of a horse responding to the pressure of her knees, the clouds of choking dust that rose from the horses' sides when she whacked them and let them loose to graze. The familiar cycles of sheep-shearing, plowing, disking, seeding, raking, and baling were sources of her greatest peace.

I want to spend my life here, she thought. *I want to raise horses and break them and breed them.* She smiled at herself. She knew she wouldn't make any money at it. She was no businesswoman.

Someday God will bring me a husband, a wonderful Catholic husband, and we'll have a big family. She did not stop to wonder how she would meet this man, tucked away as she would be on her parents' farm. God would bring him and until He did, she would remain pure for him.

But the important thing was, she was home.

Cecile wasn't sure when she decided to write a book, urging women to demand the repeal of abortion laws. Once she made up her mind, she wrote it in six weeks, most of it with two fingers on her Smith-Corona at

Compelling Interests

the cluttered kitchen table, tears of rage streaming down her face. She no longer had to clear the table for meals; John had gone. Before she kicked him out she had reclaimed her maiden name and joined it to her married one—Tucker-Thomas. She didn't bother to change it again.

The rest of the manuscript she wrote by hand, while riding with Liz or waiting in doctors' offices, when the ideas were like great waves pounding the shores of her mind, too many to capture even in her fastest personal shorthand.

It was the crystallization of all the turbulence and passion of the last three and a half years, nights spent listening to women talk tearfully about their sense of enslavement and despair, days spent trying to arrange deals with doctors who knew that women's desperation and need for secrecy made them easy marks for exorbitant sums of money.

Liz knew Spanish—enough, anyway. Cecile studied the medical aspects and Liz the legal ramifications of abortion, even enrolling in law school, and together they arranged to smuggle women over the border, where in filthy rooms above a garage or a bicycle shop, Mexican doctors did the bloody business for $600.

Some of the women were propositioned before they got off the makeshift operating table. Others came home with blood poisoning, hepatitis, anemia, uterine inflammations, or cervical scarring that meant they would never conceive another child. Some paid for an abortion and came home broke, only to find themselves still pregnant.

Humiliation and horror—that was what women were willing to endure to be free of an unplanned pregnancy. That was all Cecile and Liz could offer them—an experience they would struggle to keep out of their conscious memories and out of their nightmares for the rest of their lives.

It was three A.M. in late January of 1969, when Cecile and Liz finished editing the 142-page manuscript they knew could put them both in prison. Cecile had long since given up worrying about that. There wasn't anything in the book they hadn't said at their meetings, meetings to which they had invited local police, medical professionals—and reporters, who spread their words across the country.

Part 2: 1965–1973

"Liz," said Cecile wearily, "it's done." She held the manuscript in her lap and stared at it. "It's done and I'm scared."

"Scared? Of jail?" Liz stopped gathering the scattered pages of their rough draft to look at the older woman.

"No. I'm scared that some panicky sixteen-year old will read it and won't see that we are saying, 'This is what *not* to do!' Liz, we have been so specific, a young woman could use this as a how-to manual on self-abortion."

"But Seely, you said we had to. Some of them are trying those things! We have to tell them the dangers!"

"But what if they don't *see* them as dangers?" said Cecile, removing her glasses and fingering them restlessly. "What if they only see them as opportunities?" Her tired eyes were troubled. "I was one of them, Liz! A terrified kid who didn't know what pregnant even was and who sure didn't know what to do about it. This isn't just telling them how to fake out a doctor. We're describing things that could kill them—coat hangers, knitting needles, lye! What if they start an abortion and can't get to a doctor in time? What if—"

"Don't be so hard on yourself, Seely," said Liz, reaching out to cover Cecile's hand with her own. "Two doctors went over every chapter and you've got a disclaimer at the beginning—"

"*I* wouldn't have read any disclaimer when *I* was pregnant," said Cecile. "I wouldn't have paid attention to anything but what would get me *un*-pregnant."

She pushed back a lock of graying hair with a firm hand.

"I don't like having to be a criminal, Liz, just because I believe women should have a right to custody over their own bodies. I wish to God the day would come when abortion would be legal and this book would be obsolete!"

From a trickle, it would become a stream. Printed underground, the *How-to Book* would be passed from hand to hand by women in every corner of the country. The Catholic response was harsh but Cecile wasn't upset by it.

Compelling Interests

"In order for them to criticize us, they have to quote us," she told Liz. "They're disseminating our information where we never could have, farther than we could have dreamed."

Between 1969 and 1972, Cecile and Liz would send 5,000 women to the back alleys of Tijuana, dozens more, the rich ones, to hospitals in Japan. For all their time, they made only five dollars per woman.

CHICAGO—Dr. Richard Michaelson reached his room at the Drake Hotel just as the phone rang on the nightstand.

"Richard?" came Carter Mackay's voice. "You've got to come downstairs. We're losing them. They don't care what a cynical old reporter thinks. They need to hear it from a physician."

"No 'How's the weather in New York?' No 'Happy Valentine's Day'?" Richard asked grandly.

"Sorry, Richard, this is serious." Mackay's voice seemed creased with worry.

Michaelson unlatched his suitcase and flipped it open, unpacking with one hand as he listened. His questions were curt.

"Is Seely here?"

"Yes. She's supposed to speak in a few minutes, but I don't think even she can make much headway with this crowd. The moderates have got the WomanPower people to agree to therapeutic abortion, the kind of thing they got a couple of years ago in California—rape, incest, mother's life. That's not enough, Richard. You've sent enough women to Puerto Rico and Sweden to know that. Unless we get all the restrictions lifted, you doctors will be tied up in endless committee meetings quibbling about whether each particular case is justified."

"WomanPower? That new national women's organization? I thought WomanPower was all Leninists and lesbians."

"It runs the full feminist gamut. There are political radicals and lesbians but there are a lot of garden-variety liberals, too. The point is—" Mackay was sounding a bit exasperated at having to explain, "we can't afford to have them vote until we've convinced them to go for total repeal."

Part 2: 1965–1973

Michaelson, at six-foot-five a formidable presence with a rumbling voice that commanded attention even over the phone, was nevertheless soothing when he chose to be. He chose to be now.

"What's the most vocal group against us, Carter?"

"Oh, the Catholics. Easily. Richard, the Catholics are our *only* enemy. They're bankrolled by that monstrous reactionary hierarchy which has opposed all progress down through history."

Michaelson had heard it all before. He spoke with a trace of affection. "Carter, if you talked about the Jews that way, you'd be lynched as an anti-Semite."

"The Catholic anti-abortionists down here are calling themselves 'pro-life' and 'pro-family,'" Carter was saying. "They're all nine months pregnant and they've brought baby carriages—You've got to come down, Richard. You can't imagine what a zoo it is with seven hundred angry, sweaty women with placards shaking their fists and yelling obscenities at each other."

"Let Cecile talk and then call a break," said Michaelson calmly. "Announce that a special workshop will be held during lunch in a separate room—can you get another room? If not, use the lobby—for pro-family women interested in preserving restrictions in abortion laws. Did Liz come with her?"

"Yes."

"Good. Liz can chair it. I'll come down and talk to her." Michaelson hung up abruptly and if he had been an ocean liner, his passage down the hall to the elevator would have left smaller craft rolling wildly in his wake.

Liz Tewksbury was coming across the lobby as he stepped out on the ground floor and he noted with approval that she was dressed more smartly than she had been when Seely had introduced them at one of the public forums at which both he and Seely had spoken—in Long Beach, was it? Or San Diego—although her long black hair, now cropped short and shaved at the neck, was a bit "masculine" for his taste.

She spoke first, stretching out a tastefully manicured hand which he engulfed in one of his own. "Dr. Michaelson?" She was in her late twenties now, still intense but seeming more settled than she had been.

Compelling Interests

"I'm glad to see you again," she was saying. Her voice was warm and assured. "I took your advice—Do you remember you told me I should go to law school? It isn't Harvard but it will give me the credentials I need to fight for repeal in the courtroom—if I pass the bar next year."

"I remember," he said, with evident pleasure. "Good for you! We need lawyers."

I was right, he thought. *She's going to be one of our best. She's sharp, aggressive—One of these days she's going to rip the opposition to ribbons.*

Aloud, he said, "Liz, I need a big favor. I want you to lead a workshop for delegates against abortion."

She searched his eyes. "*Against* abortion? What's the catch?"

"Take as long as you wish," he said, significantly. "Do whatever you like with them. Let the anti-abortionists talk out all their problems. Meanwhile, we're going to be proposing the establishment of a committee to lobby state legislators for total repeal." He paused slightly. "You may have to miss the vote," he said carefully.

"Stall?" she said, understanding at once. "I can do that."

"I knew you could," he said. "We'll see if we can get you on the committee."

He was still looking for Seely—women were pouring out of the conference room, so he knew she had finished speaking—when he passed Liz again. She had buttonholed a homely college girl with stringy hair which was probably blonde when clean. The girl wore a dirty University of Chicago sweatshirt and leaned, ankles crossed, against a planter full of artificial ferns.

"What's your name?" Michaelson heard Liz ask.

"Bobbie Porter."

"Bobbie, could you make a couple of signs for us?" Liz already held big sheets of white cardboard, he noted with approval.

"Sure." Bobbie uncrossed her ankles, which were bare between her torn jeans and dirty tennis shoes.

"Write 'Pro-family Workshop,' with an arrow pointing toward the lobby. We need them right away."

Michaelson smiled. Fish in a barrel.

Part 2: 1965–1973

As Michaelson strode to the podium, Cecile suddenly knew what the big man reminded her of. As a child of three or four, Cecile's parents had taken her to a restaurant in El Paso where there had been a stuffed polar bear in the entry, standing on its hind legs in a glass case. Cecile had gazed up and up and up to the chest and then the nose and the top of the bear's head with the same awe she was tempted to feel now, gazing at Richard. She had been trying to put her finger on that analogy since she first met him four years ago.

The rest of the women obviously felt awed, too. They quieted as if his very size gave him credibility.

Michaelson spoke to the issue bluntly. "The notion that controlling reproduction is somehow inherently 'sinful' is rubbish and it is destructive. It grew out of fear on the part of certain superstitious religious systems, fear that a reduced birth rate would deprive them of income and followers.

"Here are the facts. Fact: overpopulation is a greater threat to the human race than nuclear war. Fact: women who are forced to bear children they don't want and can't care for are likely to abuse those children. Unless we allow women the right to all forms of birth control, including abortion, which is simply surgical birth control, the blood of those victims is on our heads.

"Fact: women are dying by the thousands every year because they are deprived of access to safe and legal abortions. Five to ten thousand women each year die at the hands of back-alley butchers. Because women are denied access to legal abortion in early pregnancy, many of them are into their second or even third trimester before they are able to find a doctor to terminate the pregnancy. Their blood, too, is on our heads. I, for one, am not going to have it on mine."

The women were beginning to override some of his statements with applause. Many were bouncing their signs rhythmically up and down and a low chant of "Pro-choice! Pro-choice!" began to swell from their midst.

Cecile could hear Michaelson's voice reverberating around the room. "It is *humiliating* that women who want to abort have to come up with some excuse that will pass a medical committee's approval. Abortions should be permitted for *any* reason that the woman involved feels is

Compelling Interests

legitimate. Modified abortion laws are nothing but a farce. Abortion should be legal for *any* woman for *any* reason at *any* time. *Repeal!* That is the *only* non-discriminatory legislation that is fair. Repeal all abortion laws!"

"Repeal!" the women echoed. "Repeal the laws!" They were on their feet, cheering wildly. "Repeal!"

Michaelson nodded to Carter Mackay, who took over quickly, and the vote was nearly unanimous. Forming a committee was the obvious next step. By the end of the session the delegates had agreed to form a twelve-member committee, to be called, of course, REPEAL. Half of the members would be men, including, as they had planned, both Michaelson and Mackay, plus a token black, a pro-choice Catholic and a liberal Protestant minister, to placate any residually religious among the feminists.

The founder of WomanPower would be on the board of REPEAL, though her hands were full with her own organization, just three years old. Tucker-Thomas and Tewksbury would take charge of the west coast.

That evening at the Pumproom, waiting for their steaks, Michaelson said contentedly, "Now we should be able to lean on the New York legislature."

"Richard," asked Mackay thoughtfully, fingering the stem of his martini glass, "where did you get those statistics on maternal deaths?"

Michaelson was silent.

"Richard," Mackay said again, "how many women *really* die every year from illegal abortions?"

"Official figures? Under forty," said Michaelson. He sat back, filling his side of the booth. "Unreported? Probably a couple hundred."

"Just curious," said Mackay. "Cheers."

IRVINE, CALIFORNIA—"Come to New York with me, Caesar," Pat O'Connor urged, his ruddy face peering over the edge of the top bunk at his roommate, who was sprawled with uncharacteristic informality along the couch, enjoying the lull between the last final exam and the chaos of commencement.

Part 2: 1965–1973

Julius Guy just smiled. He had long ago succumbed to the nickname, since Pat was determined he have one. Anything was better than Julie.

"Come on, Caesar, we'd be good together." Pat's eyebrows, each a bushy circumflex, were asking Julius a question as hopefully as a dog sitting up. "Michaelson is the best in the business and if abortion is legalized in New York, we could be millionaires by the time we're out of residency." His boyish shock of red hair was tousled and his blue eyes so earnest, it was hard to resist him. Women couldn't.

As usual, Julius let Pat talk without committing himself one way or the other. It was one of the things that had helped their friendship work through these last two years of medical school. Pat dreamed out loud and with great energy. Julius enjoyed listening languidly to his dreams—he was perpetually amused at Pat's unbounded enthusiasm for life—and then did as he pleased. When what pleased Julius coincided with what Pat had suggested, he let Pat wonder whether his powers of persuasion had had anything to do with it.

"Think of it, Caesar! With a pregnancy, you're tied down to a seven- or eight-month commitment, all those check-ups and then delivery itself.

"But abortion—it's all over in what, twenty minutes? No unsolicited phone calls in the middle of the night from women complaining about edema or wondering if they're in labor. No messing around with a husband in the delivery room. You're in and out and collecting your fee. I love it."

"New York winters, O'Connor? The only ice I ever want to see is something carved as a centerpiece for the Sunday buffet at the Chez Cary." Julius spoke lazily, his dark eyelashes grazing his cheeks. His little sister had always complained about Julius getting the dark curly hair and the long eyelashes. He kept his hair cropped short because he found the curls frivolous—and because he didn't want to confirm his image as Caesar.

"Why not stay out here, Pat? It's already legal here and there are plenty of pregnant women on the West coast, too." He gave Pat a wry smile. "You should know."

Compelling Interests

Pat grinned down cheerfully. "Aw, come with me, Caesar. I'll let you dust," he teased. "I'll let you wipe down the shower walls."

Julius reached for the closest thing at hand—a tennis ball—and heaved it good-naturedly at Pat. O'Connor ducked and the ball bounced harmlessly off the poster of a Ferrari 410 SuperAmerica behind him.

That was the other thing that made their relationship work. Julius never took Pat's teasing seriously. After two years as his roommate, he was used to Pat's stories about him.

"I don't dare get out of bed at night," Pat liked to tell every new ear he could waylay. "If I even get up to go to the bathroom, Caesar will have made my *bed* by the time I get back." He would run his fingers through his unruly hair. "He's so compulsive that when I eat cookies in our room, he follows me around with a broom and dustpan. *Seriously.*"

Pat would clap Julius on the back and somehow in spite of the undignified treatment, Julius managed to maintain the professional poise that he seemed to wear naturally.

"Mr. Meticulous here—" Pat would tell whoever would listen, whether in one of severe Dr. Pinchot's chemistry labs or at a bar in town, "is so *organized* that when we were all moving into the dorm in September, you know—" if they were in a bar, he would stop for a swallow of beer, "he was so *organized* he had everything put away before I could get all my stuff out of the car.

"I mean, here I was with suitcases in each hand, another one under each arm, my registration papers in my *teeth*—" he would demonstrate, "in a torn undershirt and shorts, all sweaty. And Meticulous here—get this—arrives *after* I do, brings up matched luggage, unpacks, hangs up all his pants, transfers these neatly folded shirts and underwear to his drawers, makes up his bed, sheets, blankets, and bedspread, has his books—including *Gray's Anatomy,* of course—in order on the desk with a brandy snifter of mints and a little, bitty bar of soap just *so* on the top of the dresser.

"I'm panting like a fool, junk everywhere—I won't even *find* my *socks* for a *week*—and Caesar is standing there, perfectly composed, not a hair out of place, asking me if I mind if he puts up Porsche posters. Would

Part 2: 1965–1973

you *believe* it?" He would poke whoever was sitting next to him. "I mean this guy's unreal."

Julius Guy took the ribbing in stride. Despite aptitude tests in high school which indicated that his greatest strengths were in business, he intended to become a surgeon and he kept their room—or at least his half of it—as sterile as an operating theater, dusting furtively with an old sock when Pat was in class.

He could afford to weather minor ridicule, he told himself. The very fastidiousness, precision, and efficiency that Pat mocked were going to make him one incredible doctor.

WASHINGTON, DC—REPEAL won its first victory. Within a year, the New York state legislature swept aside all restrictions on abortion. Pregnant women from across the country hastily stuffed a change of clothes into overnight cases and converged in New York City to camp outside hospitals offering legal termination.

In Washington, a federal judge had ruled the previous fall that the DC anti-abortion law was "unconstitutionally vague," and abortions were now routine. Catholics there read of the New York ruling and as incensed as they were at it, they were more incensed with their own bishops—not, as Mackay was, because the bishops opposed the idea of abortion, but because they weren't opposing its practice.

"They've issued the most anemic statement I've ever read," exploded one 44-year old man to his son. "And listen to this. A reporter asked one of the bishops if he will organize efforts to repeal New York's new murder-on-demand law or to defeat legislators who voted for it. You know what his answer was? 'Oh my, no!' Can you believe such spinelessness? 'Oh my, no!'" He snorted and tossed the *Post* aside.

"The bishops have surrendered. There's no point in looking to them for leadership in this thing. Who is going to have the guts to stand up for what's right?"

His son studied him with a long, thoughtful look. "Us?" he asked simply.

Compelling Interests

Within two weeks, volunteers had offered to join them—volunteers from New York and Pennsylvania, from Dallas, Philadelphia, and Detroit. They threw down their gauntlet—by registered letter—to five DC hospitals, demanding they stop performing abortions.

When none of the hospitals responded, the Catholics held a press conference. One reporter was openly hostile. "How dare you speak of yours as the 'Christian position' on abortion when you know perfectly well there are lots of Christians who disagree with you?"

The demonstrators-to-be were blunt. "We believe anyone who defends the morality of taking innocent life forfeits his right to the name Christian."

By nine o'clock on the morning of June 6, people began gathering at Stephen Martyr Church for a special Mass. Four priests led a procession into the church: a white priest, a black priest, a Mexican, and a Chinese. There was a flock of altar boys and a contingent of the Sons of Thunder, a new Catholic youth group: young men in khaki, wearing red berets, rosaries around their necks, carrying papal flags. All took their places in the sanctuary. There was a blast of trumpets and the Mass of the Holy Innocents began.

Out of the mouth of babes and sucklings, O God, you have fashioned praise because of your foes.

The Church prays...

O God, the martyred innocents bore witness to you this day... Destroy in us the evil of sin, so that our lives may bear witness...

The Word of God...

Death has climbed in through our windows, it has entered our palaces, to destroy the children from without and drive young men from the streets... Herod is going to destroy the Child... A cry was heard in Rama, wailing and loud laments. It was Rachel weeping for her children and refusing all consolation, because they were no more...

The Innocents sing...

Our soul has escaped like a bird from the hunter's net. Had not the Lord been with us...they would have swallowed us alive when their fury was inflamed against us... Our soul has escaped.

Part 2: 1965–1973

The worshipers pray...

God the Son, born of Our Lady Mary, broken and murdered on the Cross, take into Thy Sacred Heart these little children, broken and murdered under the scalpel of white-hooded executioners... Burn our land and ourselves of all iniquity. Lord hear us!

The Sacrifice...

THIS IS MY BODY, THIS IS THE CHALICE OF MY BLOOD...

Communion with the Lord of History...

Tantum ergo Sacramentum, veneremus cernui...Genitore Genitoque, laus et jubilatio...

The Christians go forth...

Lord of all we bow before Thee... All on earth thy scepter claim... Holy, holy, holy Lord.

As the crowd left the church they picked up signs outside the entrance. Some of them also carried crudely fashioned wooden crosses, and this wave of crosses, red berets, placards, banners, and flags rolled down the sidewalk toward George Washington Circle, a long city block away. As the vanguard of the line reached the circle, its end was still forming in front of the church. Passers-by stared at the procession, friendly, but curious. They had not seen Catholics parading in the streets before.

Three hundred Catholics grouped in a semi-circle around the statue in the center of the small park. On horseback, George Washington faced the University Hospital Clinic, where his nation's children were being aborted.

At the base of the statue, speakers fired the crowd. One was a woman, mother of three, visibly pregnant with her fourth. "I have never taken part in a demonstration before," she said, "and I hope that I will never have to again. But I am feeling life inside me so I *must* be here today."

A man in his forties thundered forth next. "America—land of the scraped womb! You are about to abort your future because you are daggering to death your unborn tomorrow....We take upon ourselves this morning, and we swear not to lay it down in our lifetime, the Holy Cross of Crusade against the enemies of life and its Creator... *Viva Cristo Rey!*"

Compelling Interests

The crowd roared back the new cry—*Viva Cristo Rey*! and holding their crosses aloft, all headed for the clinic.

As they approached, the young security guard inside hastily locked the front door. Before he could cut them off at the side door, one of the men jammed his wooden cross into the opening and stepped through, explaining that the group was there to plead for a moratorium on killing. Other demonstrators surged in behind him. The security guard yelled "You're crazy!" and as he aimed a can of mace at the crowd, the man in front reached out to deflect his aim.

Now the first policeman arrived: large, white, middle-aged, out of control. He charged down the stairs and into the vestibule with his Billy club swinging. He knocked one protestor to the floor, beat him with his club about the head and on the arms. His lunging entry had pushed the group against the inner door. The glass cracked, then shattered.

Within minutes, five of the Catholics were handcuffed and clambering into a paddy wagon, charged with unlawful entry, destruction of property, and assault.

In the Central Cell Block in downtown Washington, someone showed them a copy of the *Washington Evening Star*. They had made the front page: "Catholic Militants Attack GW Office in Abortion Protest."

On June 10, the demonstrators held a press conference to tell the media the other side of the story regarding the criminal charges. The city editor of the *Star* said the paper was "not interested."

The rescue movement had begun.

In Lewisburg, Tennessee however, at least one Catholic knew nothing about New York's ruling, nothing of the protest it precipitated in the capital. Joan Andrews, whose name was to become synonymous with the rescue of pre-born babies, who would be the role model for all non-violent actions against what she would call the "killing centers," did not yet know that rescues were necessary.

WASHINGTON, DC—Backed by the rising sun, the familiar facade of the Supreme Court building was still in shadow as James Weatherill Weiss guided his car through rush hour traffic along Constitution Avenue. Later

Part 2: 1965–1973

in the day the winter sun would reflect from the white marble in such brilliance it would give headaches to admiring tourists.

Less than two weeks till Christmas, Jim thought. *If I have to be cold, I'd rather be standing to the top of my waders in some tributary of the Colorado, braced against the current.* He drove around back and pulled up to the guard hut.

"Good morning, Mr. Justice!" the man on duty called out cheerfully. Jim acknowledged the greeting with a smile, lifting two fingers from his temple in a casual salute, and drove down the ramp into the underground garage.

As he eased his Pontiac into the space marked in stenciled block capitals, "J. Weiss" ("J" for Justice, not for James), Jim reviewed the day's schedule.

The critical cases, of course, are Roe and Doe, he thought. *Like it or not, we have to deal with whether a woman has a constitutional right to get an abortion and whether a doctor has the right to perform one without state interference. No more quibbling over jurisdiction.*

Still, he dreaded coming down on one side or the other. If deciding whether the right to privacy applied, if that were all that was involved, the Court could evaluate the case solely on the basis of the Ninth or Fourteenth Amendments. There were precedents for extending the right to privacy implied in the due process clauses of the Fourteenth Amendment to specific activities: Griswold v. Connecticut, for example, which permitted married couples to use birth-control devices.

In Eisenstadt v. Baird, the case they had just ruled on, they had voted to allow the distribution of contraceptives without a license. In doing so, the Court had recognized "the right of the individual, married or single, to be free from unwarranted governmental intrusion into matters so fundamentally affecting a person as the decision whether to bear or beget a child."

Not that he felt comfortable extending privacy to cover abortion, but precedent wasn't what was bothering him most. Behind Roe v. Wade and Doe v. Bolton were sticky ethical and medical judgments—and worst of

Compelling Interests

all, political ramifications. He knew the issue was an inflammatory one at both ends of the political spectrum.

Jim rode the ancient elevator to the first floor and his footsteps echoed on the golden marble of the Great Hall. The massive bronze doors wouldn't slide open to the public for another hour.

Forty-four feet overhead, the dingy ceiling was swallowed up in gloom, its once-bright gilding dimmed with age. Jim knew that the Chief had just scheduled the Court's first refurbishing since its completion in 1935. New paint and better lighting would make a big difference.

As one of the newest—and, at 50, one of the youngest—members of the Court, Weiss had been assigned a small room in the front, with a view of the Capitol dome above the bare trees. Two of his clerks had spacious offices near his, each with its own complete law library; the other two were housed upstairs. They rotated every few months.

Hanging up his overcoat and settling into the swivel chair behind his desk, he reviewed the opinion of the district court. The case itself was a simple one. It involved a young woman residing in Dallas County, Texas—single, pregnant—who wished to terminate her pregnancy by an abortion "performed by a competent, licensed physician, under safe, clinical conditions." Texas law permitted abortions only if the mother's life were endangered by the pregnancy; this condition did not apply to "Jane Roe," as she called herself. She was suing the Dallas County district attorney, Henry Wade, challenging Texas criminal abortion statutes as unconstitutional.

It was not in the brief, but Roe had made it widely known that her pregnancy was the result of gang rape. It took an effort on the Justice's part not to let that influence his evaluation. A woman's right to abort a pregnancy resulting from rape was to Weiss an absolute one. This case called him to consider the merits of aborting any pregnancy.

At stake were a multitude of issues. If the Court were to allow Roe's abortion merely because she wanted one, it would open the door to abortion for any and every cause—from medical necessity to mere convenience.

Part 2: 1965–1973

The arguments in favor of such a law cited as a primary right the freedom of all women to decide the course of their own lives, with particular reference to their own bodies. Yet this freedom, with its questionable Constitutional basis, troubled Weiss for several reasons.

For one thing, *no* one had complete freedom to do with one's body as one pleased. The Court had refused to recognize an unlimited right of this kind in Jacobson v. Massachusetts and in Buck v. Bell.

Also, he felt that in this day of multiple forms of birth control, most women were free to choose not to get pregnant in the first place.

Third, he felt that a woman was morally obligated to protect the life—or potential life—within her, since it was totally dependent on her. The idea that anyone could choose to decide whether another human being should live or die was abhorrent to him. He was having a similar problem with Furman v. Georgia, a current case that involved capital punishment, but did not involve innocent life.

And fourth—

"Mr. Justice?" He had left his door open and now Pete Olsen, one of his clerks, was standing uncertainly in the doorway.

"I'm sorry to interrupt your thoughts, but you asked us to meet with you at nine?" It was a question.

"Oh, yes. You're all here? Come on in."

They gathered in chairs around his desk, three men and a woman, all graduates of prestigious law schools, all his to command for a term. It was up to him to put them at ease. Despite their breezy camaraderie, clerks never totally lost the sense of awe he read in their eyes and bearing when he shook hands with them the first day. A word, a frown from him, and they would sit up straighter and kill the quips.

"I want some feedback on Roe," he told them, tilting back in his big black leather chair. Jim knew Roe v. Wade was a first-round draft choice so he had turned the research over to all of them, letting them work out among themselves who would do what. "Where do the medical experts stand on abortion? What about the Hippocratic Oath?"

Compelling Interests

"The Oath has gone through a number of revisions," the lone female clerk offered. "Many current versions don't include the phrase about 'not aiding a woman to procure abortion.'"

"The AMA, the American Psychiatric Association, and Public Health seem to be coming around," said Pete.

Jim touched his fingertips together in a gesture he had once criticized as pretentious and vowed privately never to make.

"Is a fetus part of a woman's body or not?" he challenged them. "What do you think?"

"No," said a beefy but earnest clerk with glasses, a shock of hair in his eyes. "A baby is a separate individual with its own distinctive personality and physical characteristics—hair color, eyes. It can have a blood type incompatible with the mother's. If their bloods mix, it can kill her." He gestured to show he was taking the example to an extreme. "If the baby's a boy, what does that make the mother—bisexual?"

The others rolled their eyes, exchanged glances.

"Okay," said Jim, leaning forward. "Let's go with that. Suppose the fetus is *not* part of the mother. Suppose it is a separate entity for a time contained within, deriving nourishment from and protected by the mother's uterus. Does that mean a woman must be a captive host to another being she never wanted in the first place?"

"No," said the woman. "That's mandatory motherhood. That's slavery."

"What kind of mother will that woman be?" he asked.

"Abusive," said the woman, her bluntness reminding Jim of his wife. "Women forced to raise children they don't want are more likely to reject and neglect them."

"Evidence?" demanded Jim.

"Common sense," she shot back—respectfully.

"I'll admit," said the Justice, "if legalizing abortion could lower the incidence of child abuse in America, that alone would justify the decision in my book."

As they wrestled with the issue, Jim tried to place himself, as a man, in the position of being required to host, nurture, and raise a child to

Part 2: 1965–1973

adulthood—a 20-year prison sentence, at best. If he would fight against such a sentence for himself, how could he shackle women with it, even if they were uniquely designed to carry a baby to term?

He hated this kind of slippery, ambiguous case. Why wasn't the law clear-cut and straightforward, as it had been at Yale? True, it had been complex. There had been judgment calls that he and his classmates had argued in the dorms till dawn. Maybe the difference was that those cases, from the viewpoint of a law student, all seemed so theoretical. This one involved real people with real dilemmas. And he was expected to do something about them.

A sound cut into his thoughts. For a fleeting instant, he was still back in school. Then he realized it was the buzzer signaling 9:45, time to assemble for the first oral argument of the day.

"Class dismissed." He grinned.

As his clerks filed out, Jim smoothed his thinning hair and gave a critical squint into the mirror behind his desk. Then he let himself out into the corridor, his mind working. In his dark business suit, he was indistinguishable from a tourist, except that he traversed corridors marked "Private." Few visitors recognized him as one of the country's most powerful men.

The issue of abortion should never have come before the Court in the first place, thought Jim. The key question—whether the fetus was a person—was one for biologists and obstetricians, maybe even clerics and philosophers—not for lawyers!

In the testimony before the lower courts, judges had heard women tearfully describe mutilation at the hands of what they termed "back-alley butchers." Jim Weiss was grateful that he had only to listen to lawyers summarizing the arguments gleaned from these presentations, but the emotion and drama were present nonetheless.

Licensed physicians from the state of New York, where only last year abortion had been legalized in cases where the mother's psychological health was endangered, had testified before the lower courts that yearly as many as 5,000-10,000 women desperate for abortions were dying at the hands of greedy incompetents in Sweden and Mexico.

Compelling Interests

There were vivid descriptions, some of which had to be tempered by judges for the sake of propriety, of women attempting to self-abort with coat hangers, knitting needles, and caustic chemicals.

He found himself puzzling over this. *Why would so many women—two million per year according to the radical Cecile Tucker-Thomas—hate a child they had conceived so much that they would resort to measures which threatened their own life?*

He reminded himself that he and Bev lived a very sheltered existence, between the Supreme Court, their house in Virginia, and the family homestead in Colorado. Obviously, the social set in which they moved was far different from that in which pregnancies were so unwanted a mother might seek to destroy her own progeny.

Yet, he had no sure idea which way to vote. He and six others—two new justices had been appointed but had not yet been sworn in—held power over the destinies not only of untold numbers of women but of untold numbers of human beings not yet born, not even conceived. What he would do today—hold thumb up or down—would supersede all state laws.

He could, by his vote, reaffirm fiercely guarded criminal laws against abortion or he could expand the hard-won exceptions to those laws to make every case an exception.

Such power ought not to be allowed seven fallible human beings, Weiss thought, opening the door to the conference room. *Especially—in the case of abortion, at least—to seven men.*

Punctuality characterized them all. According to time-honored custom, the men shook hands all around, donned their black robes and waited behind the red velvet draperies for the Crier's gavel.

"The Honorable, the Chief Justice and the Associate Justices of the Supreme Court of the United States! Oyez! Oyez! Oyez!"

The audience—a cross-section of middle America—stood in silence as the justices strode into the courtroom and took their places.

Although he could have contented himself with the bench memo summarizing the lower court's rulings, with an analysis by his clerks,

Part 2: 1965–1973

Weiss had chosen to study all the briefs himself. Among the arguments presented on behalf of those who favored the legalization of abortion had been testimony from doctors as well as references to judgments rendered in the past, from British common law, British statutory law, that kind of thing. Almost whimsical, Weiss felt, were the quotes from great philosophers throughout history—Hippocrates, Plato, Galen.

As he had when reading this testimony, Weiss felt uncomfortably out of his field as the petitioner made the first presentation. He had the distinct feeling that not being an expert on history, as he knew he was on the law, he was at the mercy of those with a political agenda and that just as many authorities and statutes could probably be marshaled to support a position *opposing* abortion.

When it was time for the appellee's half hour, Brother Kildare, a liberal committed to legalization, made the appellee look like a fool. Jay Floyd, Assistant Attorney of Texas, had barely begun presenting the state's case when Kildare interrupted, "When does an unborn fetus come to have full constitutional rights?"

"At any time, Mr. Justice," answered Floyd. "We make no distinction. There is life from the moment of impregnation."

"And do you have any scientific data to support that?" asked Kildare.

"Well, we begin, Mr. Justice, in our brief, with the development of the human embryo, carrying it through to the development of the fetus, from about seven to nine days after conception."

"Well, what about six days?" pursued Kildare. The audience chuckled.

"We don't know."

"But this statute goes all the way back to one hour."

"I don't—Mr. Justice, it—there are unanswerable questions in this field. I—" Floyd was flustered at the laughter around him.

Weiss felt irritation at Kildare's flippancy. This was serious. In allowing abortion, would they be depriving unborn persons of their constitutional

Compelling Interests

right to life? *If there are unanswerable questions,* he thought, *we should give the fetus the benefit of the doubt.* In any case, Kildare was out of line.

It looked like the vote would be 4-3 in favor of legalization although the Chief was against it and Weiss was inclined to be so also. Even though he knew that the four in the majority would use the delay to pressure him to join in the opinion, he felt relief when the justices agreed in conference to have the decision put over.

Still, Jim felt uneasy about Stevenson's reason for recommending a delay:

"We are about to hand down a decision regarding striking the death penalty," Stevenson pointed out. "It seems impolitic to permit abortion at the same time. The juxtaposition of the two decisions if we rule for them will look as if we are allowing convicted killers to live and sentencing innocent babies to die."

Is that what it would look *as if we were doing?* Jim asked himself, *Or is that what we* would *be doing?* In any event, with this case tabled, he didn't have to worry about it yet.

EN ROUTE FROM HONOLULU TO TOKYO—This time it was a DC 10. The trips were blending in Gwen's memory now so they were as one, each vignette captured for all time. The swans were always rippling the reflections of the bare cherry branches. Ken's cousins were always tittering into their sleeves.

In freeze frame, she was still elbowing Ken and exclaiming, "Look at the two-headed girl!" her wonder melting again into amusement as she realized that the ample quilted jacket enfolded two sisters.

She felt in the pocket of her purse for the aerogramme she had received the day she came home from surgery, took it out and laid it on her lap. She would wait to unfold and read it over. Just taking it from her purse had been effort enough for the moment.

Part 2: 1965–1973

The ache in her bones never let up now. The drone and vibration of the plane should have been soothing. Instead, she wanted to jump up and pace. It was all she could do to keep from squirming, seeking a more comfortable position that she knew didn't exist.

Giving her thoughts free rein gave her the only relief possible now. She let them drift. Snow. Snow and howling wind and darkness. It was Sitka again. Men interminably loaded and unloaded the plane through the huge cavity right in front of her.

Snow. It was blowing now through a different door. What was it? Where? She remembered: the train from Hiroshima to Tokyo, that exhausting 17-hour ride the last winter before Ken had died.

Gwen had been pregnant with Bess, although she didn't know it yet. She had watched wistfully as a father held his toddler on his lap, amusing him with a whole zoo of colorful *origami*—not just paper cranes, but whales and lions and turtles. There was no seat for the two Americans, not even room to maneuver from the cold doorway to the warmer aisles between the rows of worn velvet seats. So there they stood, grandson of a *daimyo* and great-granddaughter of a Kansas farmer, packed together with thirty or forty strangers. That time, too, though without the moaning wind of Sitka, the snow had blown in through the open doors whenever they stopped.

All those bodies, padded with heavy coats, swaying as one with the motion of the train; all those minds blotting out thought, mesmerized by the clacking of the wheels over the rails, each enduring his own personal pain with the stoic acceptance of the Buddha. For Gwen, it had been the backs of her locked knees—

"We're landing," the stewardess said gently near her ear. "Please fasten your seatbelt."

Gwen felt for the straps on either side of her. Funny that she should think of trains now, while she was descending toward Haneda Airport in a DC10.

She starting reliving that other train ride, the very first one. "When the emperor wants to sleep, everybody has to sleep ..." For the few months they had left together, Ken and Gwen had laughed about that night. In their

Compelling Interests

own home, Ken used to snap off the bedroom lights while Gwen was still reading or undressing, with, "The emperor wants to sleep now."

Gwen's chuckle startled her out of her reverie. The plane's rear wheels bumped, bounced, bumped again. Then the front wheels. The brakes were on, hard. Gwen braced involuntarily against her belt, feeling the mammoth bird shudder to a gentle roll.

Her mind would not stay in the present. The plane's movement took her back immediately to the lurching, screeching stops on the commuter trains, punctual to the minute. She'd ridden on plenty of those, too, then and on later visits. Gwen loved to watch mothers slip the small canvas shoes off their preschoolers so the children could kneel on the seats and look out the windows. The shoes were always placed neatly side by side on the floor, toes out.

She remembered how awkward she and Ken had felt at first when women nursed their babies on the train or when men urinated beside the tracks. Those things had ceased to bother her long before they ceased happening.

She remembered the white-gloved conductresses announcing primly *"Wasuremono no nai yoo ni"*—Don't forget anything—to the masses flowing out one side of the train as other masses jammed in the other side.

In the efficient Japanese way, there was a station attendant (in the inevitable uniform) who physically wedged passengers' backs and legs and briefcases into each car so the sliding doors could close. There was even someone on the platform in charge of collecting and depositing in bins lost change and buttons and reading glasses and umbrellas that were wrenched loose from their owners during the melee of those surging aboard—

A man's coat brushed her arm as he maneuvered his bags down the aisle of the airplane. People were getting off. Well, she could wait. She didn't mind waiting. She felt so tired.

The baby she was going to receive this time—boy or girl, she didn't know yet—was unlike all the previous ones. It was American.

Gwen slowly unfolded the aerogramme and read it again.

"Dear Mrs. Nakashige:

Part 2: 1965–1973

"This summer, I hope you have not been inconvenienced by too hot season. Here in Japan, we recently had our harvest festival of *Obon*." Gwen laid her head back and smiled, remembering the light-hearted parades of young people she had seen skipping down the street during *obon,* beating drums or clapping and singing.

"Thank you for your many kindnesses to Japanese women with embarrassing pregnancies" (there really was no suitable English equivalent for *komatteiru*—"embarrassing" was close enough). "I wish I could trouble you for one more favor. We have a contact with an American woman who came to us in her seventh month for abortion. Although our physicians were willing to perform abortion even this late, I persuaded her to consider adoption, as she was very agitated and seemed ambivalent.

"This lady has agreed to remain in Tokyo and to give birth to her child, if you will find an American family to adopt. Please consider this one more kindness if your age and health permit. We would be most indebted. She is expected to give birth in middle October.

"Wishing you a pleasant journey.

Sincerely,

Shinjiro Mori, M.D.

Director of Obstetrics and Gynecology,

Kagawa Memorial Hospital."

Gwen folded the letter and slid it back into her purse. *An American woman who doesn't want her baby went all the way to Japan to get rid of it—and I'm going all the way to Japan to bring it back for someone who* does *want it.* Maybe fate had a grim sense of humor after all.

She began to gather the few things she had brought—a couple of changes of clothes and the inevitable *omiyage* or small gifts for the friends she would be seeing while waiting for the baby's birth.

One more. She could get this one last baby. The gnawing pain in her bones reminded her of last month's surgery and the doctor's sober, "It's spread too far." This would be the last life she could save. She couldn't even save her own.

Compelling Interests

WASHINGTON, DC—Today. Conference was today. Today he, James Weatherill Weiss, was expected to decide between an unborn baby's right to life—if indeed it had one—and a woman's right to liberty and the pursuit of happiness.

We don't know enough, thought Jim. *We don't know when the fetus becomes a person. We don't know how new technology may affect viability in the future. In a few years, it may be possible for fetuses to live outside the womb at four weeks, or two.*

We can declare the fetus a non-person, not eligible for Constitutional protection, but if medical science ever proves the personhood of the unborn child, Roe's case will collapse and our ruling will be nullified. The fetus' right to life would then be guaranteed specifically by the Fourteenth Amendment.

But what about the woman? He remembered his wife Bev as she had stood by the door that morning to see him off. In all his years on the bench, Bev had never tried to influence his decision on a matter before the court.

Yet this morning, her eyes brimming with tears she couldn't hold back, she had touched his hand beseechingly as she offered him his briefcase.

"Jim," she had begged, "remember the thousands of women who are dying!"

He was still uncomfortable at the memory of her outburst. His judgment had to be based on the facts, not on emotion. He heartily wished the day were over and he, divested of the robe of sovereign lawmaker, could escape via the secret passageway to the fourth floor, where, with his clerks, he could shoot a few baskets in what they quipped was "the highest court in the land."

Because, with only half an hour before he was due in the conference room, he still had not decided which way to vote.

With a sigh, Jim gathered his notes together and moved to the door. It was time. Striding down the hall, he considered his dilemma. To free the woman at the expense of the potential child or to protect the child at the expense of the woman? *Where is Solomon when we need him?* he thought ruefully.

Part 2: 1965–1973

If they were to permit abortion, should there be any time limits? Was the fetus more alive or more human at eight months than at three? The question came full circle to the point at which life begins—something biologists, doctors, or philosophers could not agree on. At that point, whatever it was, whether at conception or at "quickening" or at viability or at birth, abortion would become a matter of weighing one set of rights against another.

Surely, Jim thought, conviction beginning to build, the heaviest responsibility of parenting fell on the woman, so it was her right to choose. If there should be time constraints, they could come out in the writing. Guidelines were all that the justices had the right to offer women, principles which common sense, reason, and human compassion would apply as needed.

He entered the conference room more confident and at peace than he had thought possible under the circumstances.

Chief Justice Browning opened the discussion with scant ceremony. "Brethren, we are considering Roe versus Wade and Doe versus Bolton, two rulings which challenge state restrictions on abortion. Does a woman have the constitutional right to terminate a pregnancy which in her opinion adversely affects her health?

"As you know, I am not happy with unrestricted abortion before viability but I am personally inclined to favor overturning the Texas criminal abortion law because it does not permit abortions in cases of rape and incest. I would vote yes." He turned to the justice next to him in seniority.

"Brother Smythe?" Traditionally, the justices discussed a case from most senior member to most junior, then voted from junior to senior. In practice, as a justice discussed a case, his vote usually became obvious.

"I concur. I think portions of the criminal abortion laws need to be struck down to allow doctors professional discretion. The Georgia law hamstrings doctors by requiring them to submit each abortion case to two other physicians and a hospital committee. That's unreasonably restrictive."

"Brother Kildare?"

Compelling Interests

Kildare's vote was understood. "I would vote to uphold both cases against the criminal abortion laws, based on the right to privacy. Griswold v. Connecticut. Eisenstadt v. Baird. And more recently, Markle v. Abele in Connecticut. The federal judge who struck down Connecticut's abortion law—" he referred to a brief he had brought with him—"stated that the moral positions of each side 'must remain a personal judgment, one that [people] may follow in their personal lives and seek to persuade others to follow, but a judgment they may not impose upon others by force of law.' I would vote yes."

"Brother Stevenson?" prompted the Chief.

Clayton Stevenson spoke vehemently.

"The Court knows my feelings on this. In light of the ambiguity regarding when the fetus becomes a person, I believe we should give it the benefit of the doubt until we have clear evidence one way or the other. I think due process may bear on this issue. It may be that in allowing abortion, we are depriving an unborn person of his or her rights. I'm opposed to that."

"If anything, due process would apply to the woman, not the fetus," the Chief objected.

"The Court apparently values the convenience of the pregnant mother more than the continued existence and development of the life or potential life that she carries. I think allowing abortion on demand will have disastrous consequences in every way. I would vote no."

The Chief spoke again. "Clay, I don't see women resorting to the procedure casually. I think you're overstating the consequences of this decision. States can still control abortions. The Court rejects any claim that the Constitution requires abortion on demand."

The next justice supported both cases. "Abortion in this country was made illegal in the nineteenth century because it was unsafe. Since the invention of antiseptics and antibiotics, the mortality rates for early abortions are lower than those for childbirth. I would favor abolishing abortion laws on the basis of the Ninth Amendment. It's one of those rights not specifically given to the federal and state governments which should be left to the people."

Part 2: 1965–1973

Weiss was next. Only one more vote, providing a simple majority, was needed to strike down all abortion laws across the nation. Of the three justices remaining, Martinelli could go either way and the two new men were unknown quantities. They had both been appointed by the president, who was against abortion. If they and Martinelli voted against the rulings, his own vote would decide the case.

"My brother Weiss?" The Chief was waiting.

Again, he could see Bev standing by the front door, feel the brush of her hand against his. "Jim, remember the thousands of women who are dying!"

He did remember. Louder than necessary, he said simply but firmly, "Give women a choice."

Part 3
1973–1982

LEWISBURG, TENNESSEE—The barn was cold that January morning and so was the metal handle of the milking pail, even through her mittens. The sun wasn't up yet and the ground was frozen beneath her rubber boots. Raccoons had been in the trash again.

Joan Andrews, 25, stood at the wooden door and looked with satisfaction at the gentle brown and white faces of the twenty Jerseys lined inside the barn. But she headed first for the mares.

Ruach was her favorite. Ruach was ¾ thoroughbred, ¼ quarter horse. She and Miriam owned Ruach together. Joan fished in her coat pocket for the pieces of carrot she had saved and offered one to the horse, who took it from her mittened hand with soft lips.

She stroked the mare's nose and moved to the next stall, where Seuter Le Canon, a white Arabian, was tossing her head up and down and whinnying in anticipation. Then to Marya, the red-brown mare with the wide white blaze and the white stockings.

Joan trained the thoroughbreds and Miriam, 14, rode them in local events. One of these days Miriam wanted to enter Seuter in the Point-to-Point race in Nashville and if she did well, maybe they'd try Churchill Downs and Ellis Park, over in Kentucky.

Compelling Interests

Joan moved with easy familiarity among the cows, setting the stool next to the fat belly of Big Mama and taking off her mittens at the last minute so that the touch of her hands would not startle the cow.

Leisurely she pulled the long turgid teats, aiming the frothy milk into her pail. This was the best time of the day, when she could silently review God's goodness and gird herself mentally for whatever the day might hold. Big Mama stamped, shifting her weight.

Steam rose from the pail as Joan carried the warm milk back to the house. Morning milk was always the sweetest. It would taste good on their oatmeal.

The kitchen was warm and bright as Joan let herself in, and it was filled with the fragrance of coffee and the sound of cheerful conversation. Over the years, as the family had swelled to eight, Will and Elizabeth had torn down walls to enlarge the room and now it was huge. Papa kept the open fireplace fed with cedar he chopped himself, from the first cool days of autumn till the warmth of late spring made its heat unnecessary. Even the piano was accessible from the kitchen and Papa played light classical music for them every night.

As the rest of the family gathered around the kitchen table, Mama set the huge pot of oatmeal in their midst and they murmured the time-honored blessing: "Bless us, O Lord, and these Thy gifts which we are about to receive from Thy bounty. Amen." They crossed themselves and Mama started the biscuits around.

After the blessing, Joan opened her dark, deep-set eyes and studied each of the members of her family in turn. How she loved each one of them: her hard-working father and mother; her older brothers Bill and John, out of the Army now and back in college; Susan, a year younger than Joan, and the teenagers, David and Miriam... . Joel would have been thirteen now.

Being together like this would never again give Joan the sense she felt that morning around the table, of being in harmony with the whole world. Not once she heard the news.

"Dad, turn on the radio," suggested Susan.

Part 3: 1973–1982

"That's right," said Mama. "This is the day—" Her voice faded out as the pile of bowls in her hand diverted her attention. Susan finished for her. "They're supposed to decide about abortion."

"They won't make it legal," said Joan with confidence, swinging one foot onto the bench and hugging her knee to her. "Americans wouldn't let them. It's barbaric."

But the first news was troubling. "The United States Supreme Court is expected to rule today to overturn—"

"*Stop* that!" Joan hissed to David, who was mussing her hair affectionately. His wide-eyed look at Mama said, *What's gotten into her?* but Joan didn't see it. "I can't hear."

"—closely-guarded secret since last October, sources within the courthouse believe that state restrictions on abortion at least during the first three months will be struck down—"

Susan said "No!" in a small voice and Miriam covered her nose and mouth with both hands. Joan started praying audibly, as if unaware of what she was saying.

"How could they? How could they?" asked Susan in quiet despair but no one answered her.

It was late morning when the rumors were confirmed. Out of the wooden box, the matter-of-fact voice of someone they had never seen changed their lives.

"The U.S. Supreme Court today legalized abortion-on-demand through the first three months of pregnancy. In delivering the long-awaited ruling on two controversial cases, Roe v. Wade and Doe v. Bolton, the Court ruled that during the first three months of pregnancy, no state may deny a woman an abortion for any reason."

"For any reason!" echoed Joan. She glanced up at the faces around her in anguish. "Oh, Lord, have mercy! Joel wasn't any older—" She broke off to listen.

"In the second three months," continued the anonymous voice smoothly, "a state may require that an abortion be performed in a licensed health facility.

Compelling Interests

"In the last trimester, states may make laws restricting abortion but must permit it in cases where the woman's life or health is endangered. The Court defined 'health' broadly to include 'physical, emotional and psychological well-being, family conditions or the woman's age. In other news—"

Someone switched off the radio but for several long seconds, no one said anything.

Then Miriam asked slowly, "What did they mean about a woman's health? How could being pregnant make a woman sick?"

John leaned back in his chair. "They said 'physical, emotional, and psychological.' That means if having a baby upset her so much that—"

"Why would having a baby upset anyone?" This time Miriam looked at Mama.

"It shouldn't," said Mama, "unless she was having it out of wedlock, which she shouldn't have been having relations in the first place."

"But in the last—trimester, is that what they called it?" said Bill. He whistled through his teeth and winced. "There have been babies born in the last three months of pregnancy that were—" He spread his hands. "That's like a full-term baby, almost."

Miriam still looked puzzled. "If someone was upset about having a baby, why wouldn't she have an—an abortion as soon as she found out? Why would she wait till it's almost born?"

"Don't ask me to explain the reasoning of the Supreme Court," said Bill, getting up. "I've gotta get to work." He stepped over and kissed Mama on the cheek.

"It's because they're men," said Mama softly. "Men don't know what it's like to carry a baby that long. I just don't think any woman would do that."

Joan's mind was still on yesterday's Supreme Court decision as she walked down the gravel path to the gate and tugged open the cold metal mailbox for the Lewisburg *Tribune*. Today there would be a summary of

86

Part 3: 1973–1982

the decision, and with it, the great wave of American indignation and moral outrage that must have greeted it. Surely the decision would be denounced from pulpits, challenged in courts. She expected to read of demonstrations in the streets.

Standing there by the mailbox, her hands turning red from the cold as she held the sides of the newspaper, Joan read paragraph after paragraph, forgetting that her sweater was unbuttoned and the feet shoved into her rough, over-sized shoes were bare at the ankle.

In an interview, a doctor named Richard Michaelson, head of some group called REPEAL, had declared the decision "a victory for women." *Don't they understand? It's a disaster for women!* thought Joan. *And what about babies?* That ungodly women's liberation group, WomanPower, had sent a dozen roses to each of the seven justices who had upheld the decision. There was no outpouring of public rage. There was barely any unfavorable response at all.

At last, her stomach tight with disappointment, Joan folded the paper. Surely tomorrow.

She searched the *Tribune* again the next day and the next but the backlash didn't come. Clinics were opening for business and women were giving them business. Any M.D. could do abortions. Some obstetricians were doubling as abortionists; some had abandoned obstetrics altogether for the more immediately lucrative field of abortion.

Joan decided to talk to her father about it. Papa never said much, but he was a good listener, especially if there weren't a half-dozen other people around. He would have made a good judge, she thought. In fact, he looked like one, so distinguished with all that gray hair. Sometimes she wondered why he had chosen not to become a lawyer after graduating from the university. Probably because he didn't like to argue. And who could blame him? With six children, who could get a word in edgewise?

Joan caught up with him as he was plowing and he slowed the behemoth to an idle to allow her to swing herself up into the cab with him. Once they were in the cab together, she didn't feel like talking. Just being near Papa was comforting and besides, the engine made too much noise.

Compelling Interests

It wasn't until Papa shut the engine off at last and they were trudging back to the house for lunch that she broke the silence.

"Papa, how can a doctor deliver a living baby for one mother and then kill one for another? I've tried and tried to see it from their point of view, but I can't. It seems so awful, so schizophrenic."

She was remembering Joel and wondering if Papa was, too. How could a doctor look at a dead fetus as she had looked at her baby brother and not feel sorrow that all the promise of its future had died with it? How could he think of the baby that would never gaze into its mother's eyes while nursing, as Joan had seen David and Miriam do, of the toddler that would never take unsteady steps, holding to its father's finger—and know that he had taken that life?

"Delivering a baby is so—so life-affirming! How can a doctor who has listened to a baby's heartbeat and has felt it kicking—how can he blot that out of his mind when he is destroying that little body in its mother's womb? Why don't nurses refuse to help them? Don't they feel nauseated?"

"I guess it's like the Nazis," her father offered. "They only see their job as a small part of the whole, so they don't feel responsible."

"But no one is ordering them to do it. And if someone did, they could refuse. They wouldn't be shot for refusing... How can people go against their consciences like that?"

"Well, I don't know, Joanie." Papa paused to turn on the faucet on the side of the house and leaned down for a drink, the rest of the water turning the dirt to mud around his boots. "It's real hard to understand how anyone could do that. It must be like the priest told me once about people's consciences getting seared. If we keep doing wrong long enough, it doesn't bother us any more."

"But what about that *first* time?" Joan persevered. "Wouldn't that bother someone so much, he'd never do it again?"

They were both silent again as they sat on the steps and pulled off their boots. Papa put his beside him and sat for a moment, his hands on his knees. Then he reached out gently and touched Joan's cheek. His eyes seemed to say, "I wish I could make the world the way you want it to be."

Part 3: 1973–1982

Joan's world was simple and God was at the center of it. If God said something was right, it was right. If God said something was wrong, it was wrong. He could set the rules, because He was God. Life was a good thing, because God had designed it and He declared it so. Hadn't their priest said that children are a gift of the Lord, that the fruit of the womb is a reward? A blessing, not a curse—something to be desired, not avoided, something that enriched the quality of life of those touched by that blessing.

Since God was the One who gave life, only He had the right to prevent it or to take it. What if her parents had used birth control, Joan thought, and limited the number of children God wanted them to have? Which ones might not have been born? Which ones could they have done without? Not sweet, outgoing Bill or quiet, intelligent John. Not artistic, warm-hearted Susan. Not intuitive David, the bookworm or gentle Miriam, lover of horses. Joan couldn't imagine life without any one of them.

Of course babies were alive in the womb. When they were both pregnant, hadn't Elizabeth, the mother of John the Baptist, told Mary, the mother of Jesus, "For the moment your greeting reached my ears, the child in my womb leaped for joy"?

Only the deceitfulness of the human heart which their priest spoke of could enable a person to devalue human life to the point where he could destroy the most innocent and helpless of all, could dismiss ethical considerations for crass gain.

Joan's heart ached for the aborted and the aborter alike. God had made clear to His people in the days of Moses, "Today I set before you life and prosperity, death and disaster. Choose life, then, so that you and your descendants may live."

Choose life. God gave women choice but He warned that the choices were not equal. One would result in blessing, the other in anguish. Doctors and nurses and pregnant women who were choosing death were choosing for themselves destruction and separation from God.

Every night Joan said the rosary, as she had since she was a tiny child when her mother sat in her rocking chair between the children's bedrooms and taught it to them. Now, in her prayers, Joan included the babies aborted that day and those who had aborted them. She asked mercy for those who had shown no mercy, because they didn't know what they were doing.

At mealtimes, the family added a new prayer, a prayer for all the babies. "Eternal rest grant unto them, O Lord, and let perpetual light shine upon them."

IRVINE, CALIFORNIA—Julius Guy had met Ester at a cultural function—something to do with Filipino-American friendship—he remembered that it had been held on the Fourth of July. He had gone with a number of other residents from Seaside General Hospital as a favor to the administrators. The Ambassador to the Philippines contributed substantial sums to the hospital.

Ester's father was a minor official attached to the American embassy in the Philippines; her mother, a Filipina, had been gracious and regal in green silk.

He had never voluntarily asked a woman to dance before, had never wanted to, but at some point in the evening, Julius asked Ester to dance. For the first time in his life, he was grateful that his father had forced him to take ballroom dancing—and that some of the skill had apparently rubbed off during the three lessons before he refused to go back.

"You're so petite," he marveled into her ear and she smiled up at him with such contentment and such trust that he felt quite heady. He didn't dare ask, but surely she was not quite five feet, even in her spiked heels. At five-six, he was used to feeling short; next to Ester, he felt gigantic.

And clumsy.

As they danced, she seemed so fragile in his arms that all his muscles were sore afterward from trying to enfold her tiny waist gently and to guide her around the other couples without allowing them even to brush against her. A great deal of his attention was absorbed in being sure he didn't step on her toes; all of her attention, he could see, was riveted on him—on his face, on whatever he was babbling to her.

Finally, he led her from the crowded ballroom into the hallway and they stood flushed, gazing into each other's eyes. The admiration in hers undid him; he knew he had not the slightest reason for believing he looked

Part 3: 1973–1982

any different than he had in the mirror before coming to the party, except a little pinker, but he felt uncharacteristically disheveled and self-conscious, the more so as she drew a fan from her tiny purse and wafted cool, perfumed air onto his hot face.

"Are you warm?" is all she had asked—but the way she asked him! As if she cared. He wasn't used to that in women. Women were colleagues. They opened doors for themselves, they carried stethoscopes or sphygmomanometers, they covered their femininity with sterile white gowns, they were efficient and distant and professional.

He was caught completely off guard by this woman who actually hung on his words, who seemed incapable of evaluating this conversation with a young doctor in terms of whether or not it would advance her own career, who seemed to have nothing better to do in her whole life than gaze at him.

"Ester," he said thoughtfully. "That can't be a Filipino name."

"It is," she laughed. "It's very common. The names of saints are common too."

He reached out and encircled her wrist with his thumb and forefinger. There was room to spare. "You are so delicate, you are like a little bird," he said, and she laughed with pleasure. "A little dove. I'm going to call you Dove."

She was wearing some kind of diaphanous Filipino dress with stiff, elevated puffed sleeves. It was pale pink. He had felt the smoothness of her back through the thin fabric as he danced with her. Her thick black hair was swept up and back from her face. Her eyes were alight, her lips slightly parted.

With a finger she reached up and touched his eyelashes. "So pretty," she said. "Shall I call you 'Beautiful Eyes'?"

She was looking up at him with pure delight and as he gazed down at her, captivated, he thought, *There is something intoxicating about being adored.*

Within six months, her parents were throwing them an engagement party—inviting 300 people Julius didn't know. He moved through it in

Compelling Interests

a daze, doing and saying all the right things and not aware of anything but Dove.

He really didn't like foreigners very much. But if these people spoke with an accent, at least they spoke English, he told himself, and if the faces were foreign, at least they were genteel. Julius could tolerate their customs, though quaint and unfamiliar, because he was in love.

Late that evening, long after dinner, Dove's parents ushered him to the table again. Dove took his hand and said, "*Balut!* You have to try *balut!*"

There were serving plates down the center of the table piled high with what looked like boiled eggs, only larger. Dove took one of the eggs, juggling it from one hand to the other to keep from burning her fingers, and cracked it against the edge of the table for him.

Then, her head tipped charmingly in concentration, she pried off the top of the shell with a pink-painted nail and offered him the egg. Inside, he could see a half-formed bird. He looked at her for explanation.

"Duck," she said. "Twenty-one days old. It has to be exactly 21 days old. In the Philippines, vendors sell them everywhere—in bus terminals, on the streets. At night, you can hear them calling, '*Balut! Balut!*' Because it makes its own broth, we call it 'soup in a shell.'"

He hardly hesitated; love makes cowards bold and the bold reckless.

"How do you eat it?" he asked and glanced around. Some of the men were tilting their heads back and pouring the contents of the shell directly down their throats. The women were more dainty, picking out the boiled meat with their fingers, the bones as soft as those of canned salmon.

"However you want," Dove said.

She clapped her hands in delight as he upended the delicacy and gulped it down and her family laughed approvingly, so it was worth it. He could not have described to anyone what *balut* tasted like, however. His senses were full of Dove.

They were married in 1972, while he was in his second year of residency. He was surprised at how much he enjoyed having Dove to come home to and how easy it was to settle into this new relationship—to share a closet, to smell the fragrance of apples in the bathroom when she had

Part 3: 1973–1982

been in there washing her hair, to change into a robe after work and forget to watch the news because he was watching her cook dinner.

Ester teased Julius about some of his routines—about his habit of keeping his dirty clothes on hangers till he could wash them and of wiping down the shower walls and polishing the faucets after his daily ablutions. Every night he emptied the change from his pockets and added it neatly to the small stacks of pennies, quarters, nickels and dimes on top of the dresser. He knew it was obsessive, but habits were comfortable.

They were both traditionalists. He earned their living. She stayed home—and seemed genuinely contented there, doing her own housework and experimenting with casseroles. She liked to sew and she spent hours turning the small flower bed along the front of the house into a blaze of marigolds, pansies, and California poppies.

He didn't want children but they hadn't discussed the subject when she confided to him that she was pregnant. A few weeks later, before he had given the idea much thought, she miscarried. He was secretly relieved. Dove was not built to bear children. The thought was out of the question.

"I don't want you to have children," he told her. "You are so small, Dove, I'm afraid it would be too hard on you." He didn't ask what she wanted and she never told him.

She may have been content with her role but he was not content with his. Measuring bloated stomachs and answering questions about stretch marks bored him. He knew he was a fine O.B. but he had no bedside manner at all—and no interest in developing one. He wanted to do medicine, not counseling. And he wanted to do something more meaningful with his life.

Anyone—almost anyone—could deliver a baby. Ninety-nine times out of a hundred a well-coached woman didn't really need him. He wanted a specialty where he was needed, where women *couldn't* make it without him.

He thought about what having a baby might have done to Dove and about women like her forced to carry to term a pregnancy that might threaten their own lives. He thought about women who had been raped

Compelling Interests

and about couples emotionally and financially devastated by the birth of a child with severe handicaps.

His motives were not as crass as Pat's had been but he ended up in the same field. Abortion.

Five years later, Julius knew he had found his niche. He had opened a chain of ten clinics, Family Services, in three counties throughout southern California and had bought a 24-bed hospital in Compton, exclusively for abortions. He was now doing 40,000 abortions and grossing $10 million per year.

He and Ester had moved to a large home in Long Beach with room for more flowers—a friend had given her cuttings of something called epiphyllum or jungle cactus and some of her brilliantly colored hybrids were beginning to win prizes.

They also owned a split level in the mountains right on Lake Arrowhead, with a ski boat at the end of the dock and a 270-acre ranch near San Luis Obispo. He had a portfolio of silver and oil stocks and one of the largest stables of quarter horses in the country. He drove a Mercedes 450 XL and owned two airplanes, a Lear jet, which he kept at the Long Beach airport, and a 10-place King Air 200 turboprop, which he kept at John Wayne Airport in Irvine, to travel between clinics.

Unexpectedly, Julius received a postcard from Pat, forwarded from UC Irvine. On the front, there was a photograph of the Statue of Liberty, with a ribald remark in a balloon by her mouth. On the back Pat had scribbled, "Hey Caesar—Deciding to do abortions was the smartest choice I ever made. I feel like the Texan who drilled for water and struck oil. I must have wiped out a whole kindergarten class by now. What did you end up doing?"

Julius was repelled. That was a crude way of putting it—although, if he stopped to think about it, he himself had probably "wiped out" several kindergarten classes. Pat's cavalier attitude toward an unpleasant but necessary job offended him and seemed to drive a wedge between them. For the first time, Julius felt a real dislike for Pat.

Part 3: 1973–1982

LONG BEACH, CALIFORNIA—Stephanie had been tucked in. Twice. Mommy had broken away from her psychology textbooks to read Winnie the Pooh to her and pray with her and kiss her and now she was about to get stern—they both had school in the morning. But Stephanie had one last, almost foolproof delaying tactic.

"Tell me about Aunt Gwen, Mommy, about bringing me on the airplane."

"Maybe tomorrow night."

"*Please?*"

"You know it as well as I do, Steffie," said Artyce, weakening.

Stephanie held her breath, hoping, hoping.

"Aunt Gwen was a wonderful person. She wasn't your real aunt but she loved you as much as if she had been."

Stephanie settled into a cozy position. This was the very best part of the day. Her nightlight gave a warm glow to Mommy's face.

"She called me from Hawaii and said that your mother was in Japan and was going to have a baby in just six weeks. She had names of lots of people who wanted to adopt babies but it was our turn. She said she would go to Japan and bring the baby—that's *you*," said Mommy, giving Stephanie's nose an affectionate poke, "to California for us if we wanted you.

"Of course we wanted you! We sent money right away so she could go to Japan. We were so excited! We got a room all ready for you. We didn't know whether you'd be a boy or a girl, so I didn't know whether to buy *blue* blankets or *pink* blankets. I finally just bought *yellow* blankets.

"*Any*way, to make this short so you can get to *sleep*—" here Stephanie wriggled in protest, "we were so excited the day you were coming, we got to the airport an hour early—and then the plane was late. I didn't think I could stand to wait another minute. We'd waited four years for you!

"Aunt Gwen came off the airplane holding a tiny bundle in a blue blanket. When I saw that blue blanket, I felt a little disappointed. I'd especially wanted a girl! But I thought, Well, I'll love him, anyway."

Stephanie smiled to herself.

"Aunt Gwen put you in my arms and said 'Isn't she beautiful?' and I thought, 'That's funny. Doesn't she know that blue means it's a *boy?*'

Compelling Interests

"I couldn't believe I really had a little girl until I got home and checked for myself!"

"Tell about that flower-thing she put around me," prompted Stephanie immediately.

"Well, when the plane stopped in Hawaii, Aunt Gwen bought a lei—like a flower necklace. She put it around her neck so she could carry you and your diaper bag and her suitcase. When she put you in my arms, she took off the lei and put it around you. And you were so tiny, it went all the way around your feet. Even stretched out, you fit inside that lei."

"Did she ever come back?"

"No, Steffie, she wanted to, but she died before she could. Her niece in Anaheim called to tell me."

"Was I still a baby then?"

"You were three months old. I wish—she would have loved to have been there for your first birthday. And all the ones since." Mommy's voice was brisk again. "She gave us the best present we've ever had."

"Wrapped in a blue blanket," said Stephanie contentedly. That's the way Mommy always ended the story.

"Wrapped in a blue blanket."

As Artyce went back to her homework, joy flooded her heart. As much as she and Dan had prayed for a child, Artyce could not have imagined the power of this tiny brown-haired, brown-eyed pixie to so captivate her heart. A little over five years ago they had never met but now she would willingly die for this mite of humanity. *I am standing on tiptoe,* Artyce said to herself, *on the tip of Maslow's pyramid.*

OMAHA, NEBRASKA—It was a quiet night at the University of Nebraska Medical Center. Laurel Sandoval and another young nurse she only knew as Judy were standing in the hall of the obstetrics wing, casually comparing dates from the night before, when they were jerked to attention by a scream from one of the labor rooms.

"It's the late-term," said Laurel and both women ran to the room where a patient, admitted for an abortion, had been injected with a saline

Part 3: 1973–1982

solution 30 hours earlier. As Laurel flicked on the light, the patient was staring at them from her bed in horror.

"It's moving!" the woman shrieked. "It's moving and crying, like a real baby!"

Judy pulled back the covers. Instead of the dead fetus normally expelled after saline, there was a small baby boy, its arms and legs moving. Laurel was still in shock when Judy scooped up the squirming infant and afterbirth in the loose bedcovers and dashed out of the room.

Laurel didn't know what to say to the woman. This wasn't supposed to happen. As soon as Judy came back, Laurel stepped out into the hall to talk with her.

"Where did you take it?" she asked in a low voice. "The I.C. nursery?"

"I didn't know what to do with it," said the other nurse. "I just stuck it in the utility room. By the sink. It won't live very long, will it?"

Laurel wasn't sure. This was what she hated about having abortions done on the maternity ward. It was too hard on her emotionally. She believed in choice, but this was the last straw. She didn't want to do any more late-term abortions.

People said she'd get used to it—that it wasn't any different from handling parts of a chicken when you made dinner—but she hadn't. Whenever she helped with a D&E abortion, she would have nightmares that she was feverishly trying to hide fetuses from—from whom? She had no idea.

Dilatation and evacuation was just like a D&C, only it was used later in pregnancy, after 12 weeks. The doctor would use a curette, a sharp loop-shaped steel knife to cut the fetus and placenta into pieces small enough to draw out through the cervix. It was the nurse's job to reassemble them, to be sure there wasn't anything left inside to cause infection.

She wasn't the only one who was bothered by late-term abortions, but none of the nurses were sure whether they had the right to refuse to help with one and they didn't want to lose their jobs.

"I think we should tell the head nurse," she said at last.

The head nurse called the doctor, who was clearly disgruntled at being awakened. His advice was passed to the other nurses.

Compelling Interests

"He said to leave it where it is," Judy told Laurel. "He said it will probably die in a few minutes."

Laurel was standing at the door to the utility room, a large closet where bedpans were emptied and dirty linens stored. The baby was still kicking feebly.

"Isn't there anything we can do?" she whispered.

"We can't, Laurel, not after the doctor said not to. We'd get in trouble."

The head nurse came by, glanced past them to the stainless steel drain board with its pile of bedding and said tartly, "It's criminal!"

The girls listened respectfully and Laurel nodded, relieved that someone in authority was acknowledging what she had felt in her heart—until her next words.

"It's criminal for this to happen," the head nurse repeated. "Doctors have no business giving anything less than a fetocidal dose of saline. They're never around when it takes effect. We're the ones who always end up having to deal with this stuff and we don't have the authority to make decisions about it."

"You mean this happens—often?" asked Laurel tentatively.

"Sure. Not here, but probably every day somewhere in the country. There was one a couple of months ago at Cedars-Sinai. There were two in Delaware this spring—the lab guys already had it in a specimen jar before they noticed it was still alive. Why do you think we call it 'the dreaded complication'?"

"The dreaded—?"

"A live baby. If it survives abortion, we have to try to keep it alive—but who wants it? The mother doesn't. She came in to get rid of it. The doctor doesn't. He was hired to kill it. It's a mess," she went on. "It's better if you just let them die naturally—but then there's the risk of being sued."

Laurel felt confused. "If a doctor *does* use a—a fetocidal dose of saline, he isn't sued because the fetus dies, is he?"

"Of course not."

"Then why would anyone be sued if it died naturally?"

Part 3: 1973–1982

"That's my point. If a woman comes in for an abortion, she has a right to a dead fetus. So why sue the doctor if he doesn't try to save it? It doesn't make sense. This could all be avoided," she said irritably, "if doctors would just do what they're hired to do in the first place."

Maybe, thought Laurel on the bus home that morning, she shouldn't wait to see whether it would cost her her job to refuse to help with late-term abortions. Maybe she should just leave. She could go out to California and live with her sister, like they'd talked about for so long. She could get a job with a family planning clinic or something, where they wouldn't do late-term abortions. This kind of thing wouldn't happen then.

During the days that followed the Supreme Court's ruling on abortion, Joan read voraciously. For some reason she did not wholly understand, she was still consumed with passionate interest in the Jewish Holocaust. She studied and meditated deeply on the lives of Monsignor Hugh O'Flaherty, who had fought for the Jews, and Fritz Jaegerstaetter, an Austrian farmer who was beheaded for refusing to be conscripted into the German army in 1943.

"How could the people not rise up in defense of the Jews?" she kept asking anyone who would listen. "How could the people not rise up?"

Her simple way of seeing life enabled her to have a quiet consistency, as powerful as a tree root straining beneath a sidewalk. In many ways, her unswerving focus, her humble audacity, held echoes of her counterpart in France five centuries earlier.

"You have to do something. You have to try," she had told her brother. She was aware of the cost she would incur if she tried to "do something" about the unborn. She lingered again over Dostoevsky's description of prison life and knew, although the knowledge woke her with her heart frantically beating, feeling a strange panic, that the course of action she felt called to take would mean imprisonment.

But how could she not rise up in defense of the unborn? How could she not rise up?

Compelling Interests

Joan was still waiting for someone else to lead a protest against abortion when her younger sister Miriam phoned home excitedly from St. Louis University.

"Joan, it's here! The rescue movement!"

"Rescue movement?"

"Yes! There are Catholics here that have been protesting abortion for nine years—ever since it was legalized in places like Washington, DC and New York. Oh, Joan, it's so good to have people who care enough about the unborn to *do* something. You have to come up and join us!"

Joan and Susan left for St. Louis right after Christmas, and in early March they joined their sister in the doorway of a family planning clinic for the first time in their lives. It was Joan's first rescue and it led to her first arrest. Rather than finding it scary, she found it exhilarating.

By April she was a pro, writing to her brother John of the difference between arrests by city authorities and by county authorities.

"In our sit-in in the city this week, the police read us Miranda. First time for that. We were also charged with resisting arrest as well as trespassing, despite our passive resistance. They don't charge that in the county anymore. The city police also search us. They did strip searching once, but our lawyer hit the roof—now just partial.

"Miriam and I really hope we get home this summer..."

In St. Louis, Joan began going blind in one eye and a doctor told her she had cancer. She had the eye removed on a Wednesday and was back out blocking another abortion clinic that Saturday.

Now Joan's life became an itinerant one. When out of jail, she earned enough at race tracks—galloping and hot-walking and grooming horses—to meet her few material needs and to provide her with a schedule flexible enough for demonstrations and trials. Pro-lifers let her unroll her sleeping bag on the floors of their homes. She carried her belongings in a paper sack, and bought clothes at thrift stores. Privately she referred to herself as a 'bum' and told a friend, "You can get shoes at Goodwill for 10 cents; nice ones..."

When arrested and jailed for blocking a clinic door, she would refuse to pay a fine, would serve her sentence of a day or so and catch a bus for

Part 3: 1973–1982

the next clinic. She saw her family only five or six days a month. From the Baltimore City Jail, she wrote them:

"Jail is pretty much what I expected....This morning I awoke to a fight in the adjoining cell tube. There was yelling and screaming and crashing of chairs, and even metal cots banged about. We called for the guards but they were a long time coming. At first they couldn't break up the fight because, even armed with billy clubs, the guards were afraid to go into the cell. Finally the matron called for help on the wall phone of her station, and the women were put in solitary.

"I like most of the guards. I think they really care, and they try to be as fair as they can. There is a lot of injustice though, coming through the court system...I'd be writing forever if I started citing specific cases. It's pitiful...

"The most touching thing is the number of women who want to pray with us. Despite the horrors, there is such a presence of God..."

She didn't mention the finger broken when a cop wrenched one arm behind her back. Or the fact that she was put into a cell with women charged with crimes ranging from prostitution to murder. Or the lice— Her family would read about those details in the newspaper. The important thing was, two or three women a week were changing their minds about aborting their babies when Joan and her friends blocked the entrances to clinics and that was two or three lives saved.

Yet for weeks after her release, the shock of her jail experience would leave Joan drained. The raucous, continual noise was such a contrast with the quiet of her family's Tennessee farm, and the barbarity around her was so alien to the tender love and mutual concern she had grown up with, that even after she had been freed, she felt dazed. She found it hard to regain the fervor for rescues that she had in the beginning.

From home, she wrote her brother John, who was then in Saudi Arabia:

"It's strange. This loneliness only draws me to a desire to be more removed. To go further away from everybody. I know these feelings won't

Compelling Interests

last forever. And I don't even really mind, although it makes me restless and sad. I do wish I could be free of the sit-ins here in St. Louis so I could take off—somewhere beautiful and fresh and close to nature and winter. Somewhere alone, with a cabin and a fireplace. I want to enjoy solitude..."

SAN FRANCISCO—Cecile Tucker-Thomas, now national director for REPEAL, had moved to San Francisco, leaving Liz still in charge of the west coast. They had gathered around them a nucleus of women who realized that they could never afford to get complacent, never let down their guard. There were reactionary forces out there—not just the Roman Catholics anymore; there were ominous flickers of opposition among the fundamentalists—determined to drag the country back into the Dark Ages.

Cecile spoke out publicly against these forces. Zealots, she called them. Or sexist bigots. They were mostly men, she told women, old religious men who opposed abortion and birth control with arguments such as the "fact" that women were designed to have children, so they had to "cooperate with God" and produce as many as possible.

"The only birth control they permit is the rhythm method and you know the medical term for women who use the rhythm method," she would say facetiously. "Mothers."

The fact was, Cecile told women, it was simply a power thing. Men had power and they didn't want to lose it. If male legislators and corporate heads could keep women chained to their homes through pregnancy and motherhood, women couldn't be a threat to them.

"What are women? Just containers?" she would demand. "If men could get pregnant, abortion would be a sacrament."

Women always laughed at that, but they got her point.

Alone, Cecile sometimes questioned her own statements. But it had to be the men who opposed abortion. Why would women fight against themselves? Against having more rights, greater freedom? Why would they want to stay enslaved?

Now that REPEAL had won and abortion was legal, Cecile thought it was time to change its name.

Part 3: 1973–1982

She suggested calling it Keep It Legal, until someone pointed out that the initials spelled KIL. They finally settled on Keep Abortion Safe and Legal, or KASAL.

Although based in San Francisco, Cecile traveled around the country frequently, sharing what she had experienced in the back alleys of Juarez. Her openness gave other women the courage to admit illegal abortions of their own.

After one of her talks in Los Angeles, Liz introduced her to a woman in her late twenties named Bobbie Porter.

"Bobbie teaches Women's Studies," said Liz.

Bobbie's blonde hair was long, gathered at her neck, her eyes a pretty hazel. She had a boyish figure, accentuated by her tight jeans.

"It's really an honor to meet you, Ms. Tucker-Thomas," said Bobbie, taking Cecile's hand.

"Call me Seely."

"Seely, you're my hero. I heard you speak in Chicago way back in 1970, when KASAL was first set up. Before it *was* KASAL, of course. When I heard you speak, I decided to dedicate my life to promoting feminism. I even changed majors."

"That's quite a compliment," smiled Cecile. "Liz wrote to me about you. You teach, don't you?"

Liz spoke for her. "Long Beach University. One of the best and most progressive programs in the country."

"Keep up the good work," said Cecile.

Orange County was conservative—so conservative that Seely described it as "just to the right of Attila the Hun." One of its newest senators, Nate Marshall, had co-sponsored a pro-life amendment to the California State Constitution and it was important to nip it in the bud.

So Seely and Liz gathered their most aggressive forces and flew to Sacramento. From the day the hearings started, they were in the front row of the Senate committee room, heckling, booing, yelling obscenities. It not only rattled the medical professionals who were testifying but it guaranteed that the opposition would get free airtime on the news each night.

Compelling Interests

They were becoming a force the New Right would have to reckon with. Strategy was everything—being at the right place at the right time, having credibility, attracting media attention, keeping the pressure on.

Liz was playing the part perfectly. As an attorney now, she had the credentials and the attaché case required to get the establishment to listen to a woman. She made the most of her clear complexion and dark hair and eyes. She was letting her glistening black hair grow out, softening the "butch" look which had characterized her till now. She always wore red: a tailored red suit or a vanilla-colored suit with a red blouse and nails to match. She looked good on the six o'clock news.

She was a sharp lawyer, too, with a fierce loyalty to her clients. She only defended women and she picked her cases carefully—precedent-setting cases of sexual discrimination, usually, such as the lesbian who had been kicked out of the Navy and the airline stewardess who claimed she had been fired for gaining weight. Tewksbury won most of them.

On the fourth day, the pressure they were exerting paid off. Maybe it was because they had been roused to real fury by the news that another state which had ratified the Equal Rights Amendment had just reversed its vote. That made five. In spite of the extra time Congress had granted them to get the rest of the 38 states needed to ratify the amendment, they not only hadn't gained a single new state but had lost some—despite their protests that reversals weren't legal—and it looked as if the amendment was going down in flames.

Senator Marshall had referred scathingly to the time extension as an illegal "fifth quarter."

The feminists took their wrath into the committee room with them that morning and were able to interrupt Marshall so loudly that he was forced to stop talking altogether.

It was at that point that Liz Tewksbury, in a red suit, stood up and hurled something at the senator, hitting him across the face. The act was electrifying. Reporters were scribbling madly or speaking softly into their Pearlcorders, describing the pandemonium that followed, without yet knowing what the object was.

Part 3: 1973–1982

Liz told them afterward on the steps of the Senate building. "It was a chastity belt for the senator's wife Marilyn. If the senator wants to prevent abortions, he'll have to prevent sex."

But even that wasn't what made the biggest sensation. His left eye swelling shut, a red welt rising on his cheek, Nate Marshall had lost his temper.

"Get out!" he had shouted at Tewksbury. Then, to the front row, "You dykes! Somebody get them out of here!"

The reporters sat up. Marshall had just written tomorrow's headlines for them. Forever irretrievable, the words were moving out over the airwaves, through the amplifiers, onto the Pearlcorders. Liz and Seely had the satisfaction of knowing they had seriously crippled Marshall's approval rating.

What they couldn't have known, which was better than they had hoped, was that a reporter from a small newspaper in Auburn, northeast of Sacramento, had misheard Marshall's outburst and thought he had called the women "kikes." By tomorrow morning, the senator's secretary would be parrying calls not only denouncing her boss's homophobia but his anti-Semitism as well.

LONG BEACH, CALIFORNIA—"Lydia, here's your lunch. Ask Daddy for milk money, I don't have a cent to my name. Louie, I signed that health form. It's on the table—oh, good grief, would somebody get Tabby off the table? Linda, she's licking the milk out of your bowl! No, it's not cute, honey! Get her off of there! Shoo!"

Mariana Hernandez grabbed her purse and car keys from the counter, nearly tripping over Lisa, who was standing in the doorway to the garage. "Come on, Linda, I mean Lisa, get in the car. Vamonos!" As they trooped cheerfully after her, she muttered, "Why did we ever give all of you names starting with 'L'?"

With considerable grunting and friendly shoving, the four children climbed into the station wagon while their mother hauled up the wooden garage door. She jumped into the driver's seat and turned the key. There was a grinding noise as she shifted into first.

Compelling Interests

Backing out of the garage, Mariana sighed. "I can't put it off any longer. I'll have to get this car into the shop. I'll go straight there, after I drop you kids off at school." The children weren't listening; she didn't expect them to. She wasn't really talking to them.

Or at least she thought they weren't listening. Three blocks from home, Linda, 9, said conversationally, "They all end in 'a,' too, Mom."

"What ends in 'a'?"

"Our names. Well, just the girls' names."

"Tabitha ends in 'a,' too," pointed out 12-year-old Lydia.

"Mommy, doth Tabitha end in 'a'?" lisped Lisa.

Louie said disparagingly, "Lisa, you don't even know what 'end in a' *means*," at the same time Linda said, "That doesn't count 'cause we call her Tabby. Only people names count."

"It does, too," Lydia defended herself. "She's a girl in our family. Doesn't it count, Mom?"

Fortunately for Mariana, they were passing the family planning clinic just then. A tall man paced the sidewalk in front of it, saying the rosary, and she could see another car, covered with pro-life bumper stickers, just pulling up. That must belong to the man who carried a huge sign with the graphic photo of an aborted baby curled up in a pail. Those two were regulars, Monday through Saturday. Mariana wondered how they could afford to not work.

As usual, she called her children's attention to the two-story brown building. "There's the clinic, kids. Let's pray that God will change the minds of the women who go there today." The kids were silent, respectful, while she prayed aloud, eyes open, very simply.

"Dear Jesus, open the eyes of these women. Help them realize what they are doing is wrong and give them love for their babies."

Then Louie asked the question that would change all their lives. "Is that all we're going to do, Mom? If people are really killing babies in there, shouldn't we do something more?"

Lisa lisped in bewilderment, as she did every morning, "Why, Mom—why would a mommy not want her baby? Why would thee kill it?" but this time Mariana didn't hear her.

Part 3: 1973–1982

Do more, her mind said. *Do more. What more* can *we do? Isn't praying a lot?* But her mind pounded, *Do more.*

She *should* take the car to the shop. It might be the transmission. But once the kids were deposited at school, Mariana found herself driving slowly back toward the clinic. She told herself she would just drive by, then, as she got closer, that she would just park up the street from the building and watch to see if any women went inside. If so, she could pray for each one.

She sat at the curb for a while and no one came for a long time. Still, she could not make herself leave. *Do more.*

There was a woman coming now, young, slender, in a gray sweat suit, a sweatband around her head. She had parked in the back and was walking around to the front door. The public sidewalk was separated from the walkway around the building by a narrow row of low bushes.

As Mariana watched, the woman was almost to the glass doors when both men converged on her.

"Repent!" shouted one. "Murderer!"

"God will not hold innocent the one who sheds innocent blood!" shouted the other.

Quickly, head down, clutching her purse to her chest, the woman dashed to the door, struggled with it for a moment and disappeared inside.

Mariana felt a rush of sympathy for the woman. It must be hard enough to come here, hard to make the decision and hard to carry it out, without being attacked for it. She knew the men meant well, she knew they were concerned about the life of the baby. She too believed abortion was murder. So why did she feel like she wanted to push the men with the placards into their cars and tell them to shove off?

She felt anger rising within her. Didn't they have any compassion for the woman? Couldn't they understand what she must be going through?

A black Firebird was pulling into the lot. Mariana saw a teenager in shorts and tank top climb out and start toward the building. Before she thought about it, Mariana was out of her own car and moving to meet her.

Compelling Interests

The men were at the other end of the sidewalk. Mariana hoped they would keep their distance.

"Hello," she called to the young woman as soon as she was within earshot; she had mere seconds to win a hearing, the seconds it would take the teenager to walk around to the front of the clinic. "My name's Mariana. How far along is your pregnancy?"

The woman looked at her and turned the corner. In twenty-five feet, she would be gone.

"Please!" said Mariana. "By the time you miss your first period, your baby's heart is already beating! Please consider adoption!" They were walking parallel now, the shrubbery between them. "Don't do something you'll live to regret!"

The woman shook her head and reached for the door—then paused. She turned slowly and for the first time looked at Mariana. There were tears in her eyes. Mariana couldn't tell whether they were tears of remorse or of resentment.

"Murderer!" shouted the man with the sign.

The young woman's face tightened. She walked inside.

Mariana felt defeated. If only she had had time to sit down and talk with her. Women didn't *know*. They didn't know about the baby within them, about what abortion would do to them, about their other options. Surely, they just didn't know.

The next woman almost passed through the doors before Mariana realized she was there. "Ma'am," said Mariana pleadingly. "Please don't do this to your baby!"

The woman she was addressing was about 25, African-American, with smooth skin, closely cropped hair and pretty features. But what struck Mariana most forcibly was her figure. She was bulging.

"You leave me alone!" the woman snapped at Mariana. "I already got two—and no husband. Nobody's gonna make me have this one!"

But at least she had stopped and was listening. Mariana groped desperately for the right thing to say. "You've got to be at least six months along! Your baby has all his organs now—fingers, toes! He can feel pain!"

Part 3: 1973–1982

"I don't know about that," she said. "All I know is I live with my mama and she says she's not gonna raise a third baby, no matter what. If I come back still pregnant, she gonna throw me out on the street."

"I'm not saying you have to raise it. But your baby deserves a chance to live! Do you know how the doctor will remove him from you? He'll have to use a knife and forceps. Please consider adoption. I know families—and an abortion this late in pregnancy is dangerous for you, too."

"Well, this isn't my idea, you know. I wouldn't do it if I didn't have to. I know it's not right." She was weakening. "That's why I've put it off so long. But Mama didn't give me a choice."

"We can make a choice possible," said Mariana softly.

"It really would be dangerous for me?"

"Yes! Infections, blood clots, blood poisoning. You could die! You can go to the library and verify everything I've said."

The rest of the woman's hardness seemed to dissolve.

"We can help you," Mariana assured her. "I'll do anything I can. My name is Mariana."

"I'm Tasha," said the young woman. "Will you find a home for my baby?"

On Saturday, when she drove to her new job at Family Services, the first thing Laurel Sandoval noticed was that someone had thrown cans of red-brown paint all over the clinic walls. Dr. Julius Guy and Janice Brown, the office manager, were already in the parking lot behind the building, talking by Dr. Guy's open car door.

As Laurel approached, she heard Janice say, "They're getting more violent." She was studying the doctor's face with concern.

The slight, immaculate doctor with the eyelashes Laurel secretly thought were gorgeous, looked concerned too but Laurel noticed that he was controlled.

"We have the law on our side," he said.

Compelling Interests

Laurel came up to them without speaking and they greeted her with brief nods.

"Are you going to call the police?" Janice asked.

"I went upstairs and called them as soon as I got here. They're on their way. I came back down because I forgot my briefcase."

He must have been upset, thought Laurel. In the three weeks she'd been working at the clinic, she had never known Dr. Guy to forget anything.

"Are you going to file charges?" Janice pursued.

"Of course."

"Do you think it was the two men?" Laurel asked.

"No, I don't think so. We never had any trouble like that until the others started showing up."

"How are you going to find out who they are?"

"I already know who they are. I copied down their license plates last week. That Hispanic woman has been here at least twice. She may be some kind of ringleader."

Laurel thought about the five patients that had missed their appointments for the previous Saturday. It was not unusual for one or two patients to get cold feet and not show—but five? She thought they might have been intimidated by the protesters but she didn't want to upset Dr. Guy further by voicing this aloud.

He had taken a sheet of typed paper from his briefcase. "The car is registered in the name of Paul Hernandez. Oh, here are the police. Come with me, both of you. I want you to give them a report, too."

For the past two weeks, Mariana had come to the clinic almost every day, just after it opened. The first Saturday, two friends had met her there and after they bowed their heads briefly and prayed together, they had tried to approach and talk to clients. The second Saturday, a fourth woman joined them.

Part 3: 1973–1982

During the night someone had flung red paint against the building and apparently the clinic staff thought Mariana had something to do with it because she hadn't been there half an hour when a patrol car pulled up.

The four women, who had been attempting to hand out literature, stopped uncertainly and waited on the curb. Both the protesters who came regularly, the tall man who said the rosary and the one who carried the huge picture of the baby in the wastebasket, wandered over when two men in uniform got out of the car.

All six picketers had been more or less lined up along the sidewalk. When the cops stepped forward, the picketers took a step back.

Except Mariana.

"We've had a complaint," said one policeman. "The doctor and some of the clients claim they are being harassed."

"We aren't trying to harass anyone," said Mariana. "We're trying to persuade women—"

"This is private property, you know, ma'am," said the other policeman. "You have to stay off it."

"Can we be on the sidewalk?"

"Yes, but you can't block the entrance to the clinic or to the parking lot."

"Do you know anything about this paint?" asked the first cop.

"No, it was here when we got here."

"We had a complaint about that, too."

"We won't break any laws," said Mariana. She indicated the other three women, who were nodding. "I can't speak for those men. I don't even know them. But we want to let women know—"

"You can hand out your literature if the clients want it but you can't force it on them. Stay off the property. Keep moving. And don't litter."

"Yes, officer," said Mariana. "Thank you, sir."

Mariana was playing dominoes with her children after school Thursday when the doorbell rang.

"I'll get it, Mommy," sang out Linda, who was nearest the door. Mariana heard the door open and after a minute, Linda called her.

"It's some man and he wants you."

Compelling Interests

She lifted Lisa off her lap and struggled to her feet, slipping into her shoes.

She didn't recognize the man at the door. He was holding out an envelope. "Are you Mariana Hernandez?"

"Yes."

Without another word, he handed her the envelope. He was halfway down the walk before she had it torn open.

"What is it?" The kids had gathered around her.

"'YOU-HAVE-BEEN-SUED.'" Louie read aloud, standing on tiptoe to see over her shoulder.

"Whath 'thued'?" asked Lisa.

"It means she must of did something wrong," said Louie anxiously.

"Must have *done*," said Mariana absently.

"What did you do, Mommy?"

"I don't know—Dr. Julius Guy is suing me for $50,000 for trespassing and malicious mischief."

"Is that what you done?" asked Lydia.

"*Did*," corrected Mariana mechanically.

"You said 'done' before."

Mariana wasn't listening. "I don't think I broke any laws. I did what the police told us we could do."

She dialed the other three women. Yes, they had also been served with papers. Fifty thousand dollars per individual and $50,000 per organization. He had named Birthright as their organization, a national pro-life group with an office in Los Angeles.

We're not even part of Birthright, thought Mariana. *And where did he get my name and address?*

Two weeks later, in mid-October, the phone rang—rang five times before Mariana could get in from the clothesline to answer it. It was Tasha.

"I've made another appointment," she said. "I just can't go through with it."

Part 3: 1973–1982

"Oh, Tasha," said Mariana, thinking fast. A neighbor could watch Lisa, who didn't have preschool on Thursdays, and the rest of the kids wouldn't be out of school for an hour. "Where are you? I'll come over."

Mariana had some difficulty finding the house. It was in a decrepit neighborhood where old cars rusted in every front yard and roosters crowed in the distance. Tasha's house needed paint but there were expensive wrought-iron bars on every window and a heavy iron screen door which clanged shut like the door of a vault when Tasha let her in. On a battered, lumpy couch, Tasha cried and Mariana overcame her own shyness and put an arm around her.

"You can do it, Tasha. You've got less than two months. I'll stay with you through the whole thing, if you want."

"But Mama says we can't afford it."

"Let me call my obstetrician. I'll see if she'll let you pay in installments. Maybe our church will help."

"Is there any place I can stay till the baby comes?"

"You can stay with us."

The doctor agreed to waive the upfront fee. "I'll bill you afterward," she told Mariana. "If you have the money, you can pay me. If not, forget it." Mariana's church took a collection and raised the $800 for the hospital.

"The pastor understands," Mariana explained. "He and his wife adopted a baby that would have been aborted."

With only a week's notice, fifteen women in the church gave Tasha a shower—a bed jacket for her to wear in the hospital and a Bible and some toys for her two little boys, Raymond and Rodney. "We want to help make it easier for you to give the baby up," they said.

One of the women drew Mariana aside after the party. "Whatever happened about that lawsuit?"

"The judge threw the case out for lack of evidence. He could tell that whoever threw the paint wasn't part of our group."

"Well, that's a relief!"

"Yes," said Mariana, "but I guess Dr. Guy accomplished part of his purpose. It scared off one of the women who was doing sidewalk counseling—or actually, it scared her husband off and he asked her not to do it any more."

"If you counsel on Saturdays, I can come," offered the woman quietly. "And I think my sisters would, too."

Mariana enrolled Tasha in a childbirth class and attended with her, carrying a pillow and feeling awkward among the other couples.

What must people think of us? she wondered, *Two women—a black and a Chicana—going through Lamaze together?* She didn't even joke about it with Tasha, who was working on her breathing, oblivious to everyone around them.

But Mariana's concerns were ungrounded. No one seemed to care.

That Saturday Mariana counted twenty people gathered in front of Family Services: several women, some couples, two little girls. Most had signs: 'Murder by Appointment Only' and 'Abortionists are Making a Killing.' One little girl's sign said, 'My name is Melissa and I'm a 286-week old fetus.'"

Mariana didn't know most of them, but when necessary, she reminded them to stay on the sidewalk and keep moving. As they strolled from the end of the property on 23rd to the entrance to the parking lot on Elm, she led them in songs popular at her charismatic church.

Back and forth, from one end to the other.

She studied the women entering the clinic. Their faces were set and hard, their chins at a defiant tilt. Not one of them would look at her. They were often escorted by a boyfriend or mother, who glared at the picketers and sometimes yelled for them to mind their own business.

After a long time the patients would emerge from the building more slowly, leaning on the arm of a solicitous mother or lover. Faces drawn, the women were more subdued now, often huddled over, though whether in pain or shame, Mariana couldn't tell.

Here came a young man and woman, looking preoccupied. They shook their heads when Mariana tried to speak to them. Here were two sharp-looking young women, walking swiftly, looking at her with supercilious expressions and ignoring the handouts. Here were a black mother and daughter.

Part 3: 1973–1982

One 19-year old girl, clutching a brown paper bag probably containing a urine sample, had stopped to listen to a pro-lifer describe her regret over her own two abortions.

"There is an organization, you know," the pro-lifer was telling her, "for women like me who feel they were exploited by abortion. It's called WEBA."

A young blond man in uniform was pacing the parking lot, Mariana noticed. Dr. Guy must have hired a guard. When patients came toward the clinic, he went over and planted himself at the front door. He looked utterly miserable.

"Do you agree with what they're doing here?" Mariana asked him.

"Me? Naw, I'm Mormon," he told her. He didn't seem to mind answering her questions. "I've been married four months. My wife asked me if I'd let her get an abortion if she got pregnant and I said, 'If you do, you'd better get a good lawyer, because I'll sue you for divorce.'

"I'm assigned here just for a few days to prevent trouble. When I leave, I don't care what you do."

There were more picketers today than ever, Laurel noticed. She and Janice had gone out to lunch together, and as Janice pulled back into the clinic parking lot, a couple of protesters scooted out of the way. The Hispanic one they took to be the ringleader shouted, "Adoption! Not abortion!," waving a tract at them.

Laurel studiously avoided their eyes but Janice rolled down the window and shouted, "Isn't it enough not to have an abortion yourself, if you don't believe in them? Why do you have to interfere with other people's lives? Can't you get a job?"

The woman she was addressing was short with coarse, wavy brown hair and brown eyes. She looked tired. "I *have* a job," the picketer said, not raising her voice. "Saving babies."

Compelling Interests

At least they were staying off the property, Laurel noticed. The judge had said they had a constitutional right to be on the public sidewalk and to pass out their propaganda as long as they kept moving.

Janice must have been remembering the same thing. "The judge should be here." Janice shoved the Maverick into "park" and jerked the key out of the ignition. "How is any woman going to be willing to force her way through all this? What about *their* constitutional rights?"

She unlocked the clinic's back door, still fuming. "What's it going to take? Having them burn the place to the ground, like they're doing in other cities? They've already thrown paint all over the place. It's only going to get worse, until they've shut down every clinic in the country."

Laurel followed her as she stormed up the steps, only to be met at the top by the benign Dr. Guy. Laurel ducked around Janice and pretended she wasn't listening as he took Janice aside and calmed her down. "It's okay, Janice. Don't let it get to you. Don't waste your time with them. We'll do everything through the courts."

Janice was right, Laurel thought. The women who were brave enough to run the gauntlet of the picketers that morning were upset when they came upstairs. Some of them were angry.

"It's hard to get in here," one complained. "They shove gory pictures in your face and accuse you of everything under the sun. Can't you make them stop?"

"We're trying," Laurel heard Janice say. "Dr. Guy hired a guard. We had some vandalism and he's suing. The problem is, they are allowed to be on the sidewalk, because it's public property."

"Some places back east have staff that go out to the cars and get the women and escort them into the clinics."

"It may come to that," Janice agreed, "but if the women will drive into the lot and come in the back way, they can avoid most of it. We're also going to start mixing up the days we schedule abortions. We'll try to keep them off balance."

To Laurel, she murmured, "Just let them come on the property one time or lay a hand on one of our clients and I'll have them locked up so fast it'll make their heads spin!"

Part 3: 1973–1982

At eleven o'clock at night, ten days before Christmas, there was a knock on Mariana's bedroom door.

"Probably that pregnant girl," mumbled Paul, beside her.

"Which one?" asked Mariana wearily. By now she had personally talked dozens of women into carrying their babies to birth. She had managed to find homes for every one of the "moms" who needed one, either in established facilities for unwed mothers or with private families, although she was having to go farther and farther—Riverside or San Fernando Valley—to find them. Paul and Mariana still housed women in their own home till they were placed elsewhere. Besides Tasha, Paul and Mariana had taken in a pregnant illegal alien just two days before. She was sleeping on their living room sofa.

But this was Tasha. "It's started, Mariana! Can you take me to the hospital?"

Mariana was immediately alert. "I'll be right out."

Riding together, Tasha was excited and nervous. After one period of puffing, as they'd practiced together in training, Tasha said, "Mariana, I've changed my mind. I want to keep this baby. You know, I have this real strong feeling it's going to be a girl. Wouldn't it have been awful to abort the girl I've always wanted? I want to name her after both of us, because we're a team. You like the name Tashiana?" She pronounced it "-ahna," as Mariana pronounced her own name.

"I like that," said Mariana, but warning bells were going off inside her head. How would Tasha, who was living on her mother's welfare, keep a baby? Where would she live?

The delivery room clock said ten. They had been up all night and were dead with fatigue but were still concentrating so hard, they didn't feel it yet. Tasha's forehead glistened with perspiration and Mariana, watching the overhead mirror now instead of the clock, had forgotten all about wanting breakfast. "It's a—boy!" shouted Mariana. "Tasha, it's a boy!"

Once the head and one shoulder were out, the rest of the slippery body had slid easily into the doctor's gloved hands. She quickly suctioned out

Compelling Interests

his mouth and laid him on Tasha's abdomen so she could cut the cord. The baby was crying vigorously.

Smiling behind her mask, the doctor lifted him and held him out to Tasha. Tasha shook her head.

"No," she said softly. "Let Mariana hold him first. He wouldn't be here without her."

Mariana took the tiny, moving baby into her arms, tears streaming down her face. "He's a miracle!" she breathed. "He's our first miracle."

She turned and offered Tasha her son. Grinning through her tears, Mariana said, "You still want to call him Tashiana?"

PART 4
1982–1985

Tasha did not keep the baby after all. She knew it wasn't best for him. Mariana helped her choose an adoptive family from the names kept on file at her church.

On an exceptionally warm Sunday in early January, when DeShawn was two weeks old, Tasha dressed in white lace and took him to church on the bus. Mariana met her there with a hug.

"Go on down front where Paul and the kids are," she told Tasha, hastily pinning a corsage of pink rosebuds on her chest. "I'll meet you there in a few minutes. I've got to run home. I forgot my camera." As she dashed out, she called back, "It'll be right after the announcements."

Tasha and DeShawn sat in the front row, conspicuous because so few blacks were scattered throughout the sanctuary. The women who had given her the shower kept coming up and hugging her until the corsage Mariana had pinned on her ample bosom was a wreck, but Tasha didn't care.

Just as the pastor announced, "We have a special ceremony this morning, something we've never done before," Mariana slipped into the pew beside them.

The pastor described how Mariana and Tasha had met outside Family Services and how the church had taken up a collection so Tasha wouldn't have to go through with the abortion.

Compelling Interests

"Tasha," he said, beckoning to her, "would you bring DeShawn forward now?" As she did, there was a murmur of, "Oh, isn't he darling?" DeShawn's dark hair and skin stood out against his mother's white sleeve; his eyes were tightly scrunched against the light and his tiny lips seemed to be tasting something.

"Some of you women already know Tasha and you've been praying for her and her baby. Well, this is DeShawn!"

Tasha tipped him shyly toward the congregation.

"Tasha has done a courageous thing and it wasn't easy for her. She has decided to give her baby up for adoption. She picked a couple here who have wanted a baby for a lo-o-ong time—" a ripple of affectionate laughter indicated that their desire was familiar to everyone— "and we want to let her present DeShawn to his new parents.

"Clarence and Vonette, would you please come forward?"

A black couple in their early thirties rose, he in a gray three-piece suit; she in navy blue. They moved forward eagerly, the young woman alternately smiling and biting her lip to keep from crying.

"DeShawn's the name Clarence and Vonette chose," the pastor was explaining. "DeShawn Timothy Sedwell."

Vonette's arms were open by the time she reached the front of the church. Tasha extended the tiny baby and Vonette's arms enveloped him. Choked up, she said, "Thank you," looking at DeShawn and then again, gazing up at Tasha, "Thank you."

DeShawn's new daddy was choked up too. Swallowing, he said soberly, "Praise the Lord."

After the service, women crowded around Clarence and Vonette, remarking on DeShawn's tiny fingers and his button nose.

Tasha moved up the aisle alone, her face expressionless. Mariana snapped one last picture and hurried to catch up with her.

"Tasha? Let me drive you home."

Until Mariana dropped Paul and the children off, the crowded van was full of noisy chatter, which made the silence afterward all the more apparent.

Part 4: 1982–1985

When they pulled up at the tract house, its fence sagging, its outside in need of paint, Mariana turned off the engine and said, "This was hard for you, wasn't it?"

Tasha burst into sobs. "I never want to go through this again! I'm going to get my tubes tied!" She looked up in amazement as Mariana, instead of consoling her, threw back her head and began to laugh.

"I'm sorry," gasped Mariana. "Maybe it's all the tension we've been under. We just had that beautiful, touching ceremony—" she gestured jerkily, "and here you are, talking about your plumbing!"

Tasha's face took on a soft pout. "Well, you don't have to get all hysterical about it."

Then she too started laughing and they laughed and cried in each other's arms till they were breathless and their sides ached.

"What are you going to do now?" asked Mariana at last, wiping her eyes.

"I'll tell you one thing I'm *not* gonna do. I'm *not* going to get pregnant!" She thought for a minute. "I think I'd like to finish high school."

"That can be arranged," said Mariana. "Would you like me to go with you when you enroll?"

It was Presidents' Day, and as with any three-day weekend, business at Dr. Guy's clinic was brisk. An obese woman charged up the stairs swearing at the picketers she had encountered on the way in. She demanded loudly to be first and when her turn came, she asked Laurel to pull up the Venetian blinds—"Don't just open 'em, pull 'em all the way up. I want them to know it's my turn!"

She pushed up the window and yelled at the picketers below. "Here I am! See? Here I am, having an abortion! I'm killing a baby!" The rest, mostly obscenities, was unintelligible to the small group below, who had stopped singing and were staring upward in confusion.

Laurel tried to calm the woman down. "I *am* calm!" the woman argued, jerking her arm away. "I feel fine. I've done this before." At Laurel's urging, she lay back on the gurney. "Ten times. This is number eleven."

Compelling Interests

Laurel recoiled. "Eleven times?" She stared at the woman, who couldn't have been over 35. "How could you? I mean, haven't you had any problems from any of them?"

"Never!"

"Why don't you use birth control?"

"I don't know, honey. I just can't be bothered."

Later that day, Laurel was in Janice's office, asking a question about procedure, when Dr. Guy appeared at the door. "Janice," he said, "where are we advertising?"

"Yellow pages, white pages, local papers." Janice looked at him inquiringly.

"Under what headings?"

"Clinics, family planning—let's see, abortion, of course—"

"See if you can come up with some more markets—college newspapers or yearbooks or something—or categories we can add. Maybe you can come up with some," he added to Laurel.

"I'd like to see if we can run about 90-100 through every week."

"Saturday's are already packed," said Janice. "If we do any more business on Saturday, we'll need more help. Laurie has to do prep and recovery and I have my hands full with paperwork."

"That's fine. Maybe a high school girl after school and on Saturdays." He checked his watch. "By the way, I've got the clinic in Lynwood open now and I'm on my way to Riverside to sign the lease there. Have you got the address and phone in Lynwood in case you need to make a referral?"

"Yes," said Janice. She smiled. Laurel didn't see any of her earlier agitation. "How many does that make now? Twenty-one, isn't it?"

"Well, counting the ones around San Diego—and the hospital—22, I think. I don't know." He smiled back. "That's your job. Business managers are supposed to track things like that."

Part 4: 1982–1985

Kim Crnik started working the day before Thanksgiving and it was a good thing, because with the four-day holiday, business was heavier than it had ever been.

"You'll help Laurel in recovery," Janice told Kim, introducing them.

"Just keep an eye on the clients when they're waking up," Laurel explained. "Sometimes you have to calm them down."

Kim was big-eyed but silent.

"It's not *that* bad," Laurel smiled. "I just mean they may cry a little."

All morning, Laurel could hear the picketers chanting below. It was hard for her to concentrate.

Later that day, when all the operations were over and Janice was talking to Laurel in the hall, Kim came out of recovery, closing the door behind her and approached them timidly.

"Ms. Brown?"

"Janice," said Janice. "Ms. Brown makes me feel old."

Kim spoke in a low voice. "Janice, what should I say if—one lady in there said she felt like she'd killed—"

"You don't have to say anything," Janice cut her off. "Or just tell her the procedure's over and she'll feel better about it tomorrow. Oh, and don't ever use the word 'baby.' It makes it hard on them. We refer to 'the pregnancy' or 'products of conception' or 'fetal tissue.' If it ever comes up."

Kim started to leave.

"One thing you should remind them," Janice added. "It's in the printed material we give them but be sure and tell them if they have any problems, to come back *here*. Do you understand? Not to a hospital, not to emergency." Her voice softened slightly. "We do a lot more abortions than they do, so we know more about possible complications. We can handle them better than a hospital could. All right?"

Kim fingered the tail of her French braid and nodded.

"Are there a lot of complications?" she asked hesitantly.

"Nothing you have to worry about. If they have any questions about anything, refer them to me."

Compelling Interests

Mariana had done sidewalk counseling for over a year now. She knew it was effective. She couldn't count how many women had changed their minds about aborting, once they knew someone would help them. So many pregnant women she talked to weren't having abortions by choice, at least not by their own choice. Mothers, boyfriends, or healthcare workers were choosing for them. Mariana found it ironic that the people who advocated choice weren't the ones letting women know they had other choices or making those choices possible.

She knew the counseling was effective, too, because the angry woman who ran the clinic had burst out the door the other day and screamed, "You're ruining our business!"

Tasha came with her when she could, which wasn't often. Since the night of DeShawn's adoption, Tasha had moved back home with her mother and the two boys. She had a job cleaning houses during the day and was taking classes at night, working toward her GED. She seemed much more contented than the defiant young woman Mariana had stopped so many months ago. When she did join them in front of the clinic she was especially effective with women because she could say "I've been there."

There was a rapid turnover of guards at the clinic. The latest one was white, a stocky, kindly-looking man in his sixties. For several days he had been firm, resisting the pro-lifers' attempts to give him literature.

"I'm on duty," he would say stiffly.

One morning, fifty people came to protest and their presence was so supportive, Mariana found herself singing. As their march brought her close to where the guard stood, she had smiled at him. "You look like a grandfather," she said.

"Six times," he said proudly.

"Which one of your grandchildren would you give up?"

"What?"

"If your kids had wanted to abort one of your grandchildren, which one would you be willing to give up?"

"I'm just doing my job," he said.

Part 4: 1982–1985

"Would you have guarded the Nazis while they killed Jews?" she asked. Not accusing, just hurting.

"I fought against them." He started to move away. "I'm just doing a job."

"So were they."

Several hours later, just before she left, Mariana noticed the guard again and it looked to her as if he had tears in his eyes. Spontaneously she stepped onto the forbidden property and reached up to give the taut figure a quick hug. "I know this isn't easy for you," she told him.

When she drove away, he was out on the sidewalk among the protesters, asking them questions.

Sometimes Mariana saw Dr. Julius Guy, arriving or leaving in his gunmetal gray Mercedes. He was slight, fit, tan, neatly dressed, with the longest eyelashes that she had ever seen on a man. When the Catholic picketers saw him, they would shout "Murderer!" Dr. Guy never flinched or paused in his stride.

He seemed like such a nice man, it was hard to believe he made his living the way he did. Someone had brought Mariana an article about Dr. Guy in the Business section of the *Southbay Journal*. The man had an actual franchise of abortion mills.

The article claimed that he prided himself on his ability to do a suction abortion in under five minutes. He was quoted as saying it eliminated 'needless patient-physician contact.' Mariana thought about Dr. Guy's patients and her heart went out to them. These women needed some kind of human contact, some emotional support at a time like this! She remembered the ten-year-old girl whose mother had dropped her off at the clinic with the ultimatum, "Get an abortion or don't come home!"

She remembered the woman who had stopped to chat with her after an abortion, admitting "I'm a Christian and I know it was a sin, but—" thoughtfully, "I don't feel bad about it." Her face belied her words. *Oh, honey,* Mariana had thought sorrowfully, *you'll have the rest of your life to feel bad about it.*

Compelling Interests

This morning there had been a black mother who was almost insane with grief because her 22-year-old daughter had just been taken away in an ambulance.

"They told me I couldn't keep her from having an abortion if she wanted one," the woman sobbed to the sympathetic group gathered around her.

"While I was waiting for her upstairs one of the nurses ran out of the surgery room to the office and got another nurse and I heard her say something had gone wrong, that she wasn't big enough, that they were having to call in the doctor." She mopped her flushed face. "I tried to make them tell me what was going on—Another nurse came out and said she was fine, the abortion was over, the doctor was only going to put in a few stitches."

She began to cry again. "I knew she was lying! They wouldn't let me see her. They said it would upset her. I told them, 'Don't you touch her! Just let me take her home!' but they wouldn't listen. And then the ambulance came—"

Mariana prayed with her. The arrival of the ambulance had shaken her up, too. It was the fourth one in four weeks.

Later, Mariana saw a girl about 17 years old drive into the parking lot and step out, holding a large soft drink in one hand. She had seen her before and she noticed the girl was wearing a badge with the name "Kim" on it. The girl was walking toward the door, ignoring the group on the sidewalk, but she stopped as Mariana approached her and introduced herself.

"Do you work here, Kim?" Mariana asked. Kim sipped her drink.

"I just started. I'm in recovery. I wake the women up."

"How do you feel about abortion?"

"I don't believe in it."

"Then why do you work here?"

"It's a job."

"What do you think about these people picketing?"

She shrugged. "They have a right to be here."

"How does the picketing affect the patients?"

Part 4: 1982–1985

"They wake up crying and screaming when they realize what they've done. I've gotta go."

The following week, some people representing a pro-life group none of the others were familiar with arrived with large signs. One of those who came was a young man, tall and exuberant.

"Let's make faces at the women who come!" he said to Mariana.

She looked at him with distaste. "I think things are hard enough on them already." She tried to walk alone, away from his group, remembering to keep moving. But later, when she was trying to invite a woman in the parking lot to come closer so they could talk, the young man rushed up to ask, "Do you need sign reinforcement?"

She glanced up at his sign, which said, "ABORTION IS TAX-FUNDED BABY MURDER" and winced.

"Those aren't for the women," he said hastily. "Those are for people driving past."

That afternoon, a silver Porsche slid up to the curb. Mariana didn't pay much attention until she realized that an elegantly-coiffed matron had exited the car on the far side, and was heaving eggs—a whole carton of them—at the protesters, one after another. The line of people on the sidewalk halted and watched, open-mouthed, as the woman jumped back in her car, gunned the engine, and sped away.

"She missed us!" gloated the young man who had irritated Mariana before. "At point-blank range!"

A couple who had parked half a block away were strolling toward the clinic, their arms around each other, her head lovingly on his shoulder.

Mariana spoke to the woman. "Please don't do what you're about to do!"

"You don't know what we're about to do," snapped the man who was with her.

"An abortion can hurt you as well as your baby," Mariana pleaded.

By this time they were at the top of the steps. The man opened the door for his girlfriend and turned to fling a mouthful of obscenities at Mariana.

Compelling Interests

"We care about you!" she called as they disappeared inside but tears were stinging her eyes as she tried to recover from the ugly words. At that moment the young man with the "baby murder" placard caught up with her.

"Did you get through to them?"

"No."

"You failure!"

She could only look dazedly at him. She knew before he added, "I didn't mean it" that it was just youthful thoughtlessness, but she didn't need that. He was babbling now, covering up. "I think those are the ones closest to coming around—you know, the ones who are mad. You never know."

Mariana kept walking and praying. Dr. Guy's gunmetal Mercedes drove into the lot and went behind the building.

"I'm going to get his license number," said the young man. "Maybe we can get his address and go picket his house."

They had found out where he lived. Ester met Julius at the garage door almost in tears one evening.

"They were here!" she said. "All afternoon. Chanting and marching and calling. It was awful. I had to stay in the back of the house and I didn't dare go out. I tried to call you—"

"You know how to use the security system," he told her. "Push the red button. You'll have the police here in five minutes. You don't have to put up with that."

"I don't know," she said. "It was so unnerving I couldn't think straight. I tried to call you and your secretary wouldn't let me speak to you. She said you were seeing patients and you'd call me back. But you didn't."

"Don't let them bother you," he said, giving her a brief hug. "There's nothing they can do to you."

"It's so unnerving," she said again. "It makes me feel angry and guilty and scared all at once. What if they try to burn the house?"

Part 4: 1982–1985

"Call the police," he repeated. "I'll alert them if you want and have them keep an eye on the house." He saw that she was kneading her hands. "Honey, good grief. They have nothing better to do with their time than harass us. It doesn't mean anything. We have deadbolts and alarms—"

"They called you a murderer," she said. "I could hear them. They said you murder innocent babies."

"They aren't babies, Ester. They're fetuses. Unwanted fetuses. I'm doing women a favor and it's perfectly legal."

"I know," she said, "but it still makes it sound so horrible."

"I'll take you out," he said. "How about lobster?" He lifted her chin with a knuckle and peered reassuringly into her troubled face.

"I was going to make a meatloaf," she said distractedly, "but I didn't get it in the oven. All that racket—"

"We'll go out, Dove," he said gently. "Get your coat. Maybe we should get away for the weekend."

That night, a dream woke Julius in the darkness of predawn. What was it, exactly? Something about a cat. Yes, he had put a cat in a large Mason jar and put the jar in the refrigerator. He remembered now. He had had to push the orange juice to the back and take out the milk so the jar would fit.

When he went back later to get it out, the cat was rigid. He thought he'd killed it. Besides exposing the cat to the cold, he realized he had screwed the top on without any holes and it couldn't breathe. But he opened the jar and let it slide out onto the floor, and before long the cat revived and was fine.

That was disturbing enough. But there was more. He had taken the same cat and carefully cut it up with his scalpel, putting the pieces on a plate in the refrigerator overnight. This time he knew there was no hope of reviving *them*. In the morning, he had emptied the plate into the sink and run the scraps down the garbage disposal.

When Julius woke, he dispelled the disquieting dream with a hot shower and a cup of coffee, leaving for work before Dove was even up. Whenever there was a slack in the production line at the clinic, he would call his stockbroker or the overseer at the ranch, checking on his holdings. By noon, he'd forgotten all about the dreams.

SOUTHBAY JOURNAL, February 7, 1982—"An estimated 16,500 human fetuses were discovered in a storage container in Woodland Hills on Feb. 4. They were packed in formaldehyde-filled jars stuffed into boxes stacked eight feet high inside the container.

"Some 43 of the fetuses had been aborted more than 20 weeks after conception… from doctors and clinics as far away as San Francisco, Sacramento, and Missouri.

"After opening the container, one of the workers said, 'I saw one fetus with legs 2-1/2 to 3 inches long and the body and head were demolished. I was scared, frightened, and had tears in my eyes.'

"His boss said, 'They're just fetuses, but they sure looked like little babies to me.'"

Mariana put the newspaper down and sat at her kitchen table, thinking. What did the staff of Family Services do with all the fetuses they aborted? She knew that some fetuses were used in stem cell experiments to find cures for diabetes and mental retardation. There were rumors that collagen from aborted fetuses was one ingredient of cold cream—at least in some countries in Europe.

She remembered residents around the clinic who had stopped to thank her for what she was doing. Several of them had complained about the extra trash the business generated.

One woman told her, "I've had to call the Health Department several times. They use those see-through bags, you know, and at night dogs tear them open and spread everything around."

"Anything offensive?" Mariana asked.

"Yes! Bloody paper towels and examining gloves. We've even had rats."

How would someone find out whether they were dumping the fetuses out with the trash—even if she had the time to ask?

Part 4: 1982–1985

The guard, who talked to her freely now and was counting the days until the transfer he'd requested came through, had told Mariana that clinics were exempt from health inspections.

"It's only licensed as a counseling center," he said. "It doesn't need a medical license because first trimester abortions aren't considered medical procedures. And because it doesn't need a license, it's not subject to inspection by state health officials."

Sometimes there were deaths—and lawsuits. At a garage sale, neighbors told her about an abortion clinic she hadn't even known about down on Magnolia Avenue that had suddenly shut down a year ago because three women died there. Mariana drove past to look at it and there were still IV bottles hanging inside and half-drunk cups of coffee on a desk—you could see them through the windows.

If only she had time to follow up on all these things. But she was busier than ever now. It seemed like no matter where she went, Mariana ran into women who were considering an abortion or who had just had one and needed someone to talk to. She was asked to speak at the local Catholic high school and afterward a freshman came up and begged her to help break the news to her parents that she was pregnant. "I was going to get an abortion," she confided, "but what I really want is to have them love and forgive me and help me do the right thing."

More and more, Mariana saw the need to reproduce herself in a full-time staff.

She talked to Tasha about it. "I've been contacting the people in charge of a couple of pro-life organizations, to see if we can come under some other group. Birthright supports what we're doing but they're educational; we're activists. They don't want the association. I think the lawsuits we got made them nervous.

"Anyway, we're going to incorporate separately under the name Lifeline and I wondered if you'd like to be on the board."

"Sure. What will the new group do, exactly?"

"We're praying for a building. We need to have a place where ten or twelve moms can stay." Mariana's voice went from businesslike to euphoric. "We would have two women to a room and each room would be

Compelling Interests

beautiful. We could get church groups to paint the walls, buy new linen and bedspreads. Each church could decorate their room any way they wanted, with homemade throw pillows, plaques or needlework on the walls, and little baskets of toiletries the pregnant women could keep.

"We would have housemothers who are good at counseling, because many of the girls who get pregnant don't have a good relationship with their parents. We would have Bible studies once a week.

"I have two doctors at St. Luke's who refuse to perform or refer for abortions. They are willing to deliver the babies at a reduced fee. And we'll try to arrange with the nearest high school to let the girls take classes there if they haven't graduated. We'll get people in the community to come in and teach them job skills and crafts.

"We could even have a couple of rooms for women who want to keep their babies, so they can stay for a few weeks after the delivery and learn things like changing diapers and taking temperatures."

"That sounds expensive," said Tasha.

Mariana answered cheerfully. "If God wants it to happen, he'll provide the money."

On a rainy January 22, 1983, the tenth anniversary of Roe v. Wade, a handful of stalwart pro-lifers with signs showed up at the Los Angeles County courthouse to mourn the tenth anniversary of Roe v. Wade.

It was Saturday and the streets were deserted, the office buildings locked. There were no passers-by to read the signs.

The protesters—a pitiful representation—stood dismally in the grassy square across from the courthouse. Their shoes stamped the grass to dirt and the rain turned the dirt to mud. The downpour chilled and subdued them. Men and women selling buttons and bumper stickers and books under a makeshift awning hugged jackets to their chests and tried to keep their feet dry, while their customers, hair wet and hands blue, clustered at the tables in a desultory way, less to look through the materials than to avoid the heaviest of the showers.

Part 4: 1982–1985

Finally, aware that their protest had gained for them only the possibility of pneumonia and that it had made not a whit of impact on the city, they trudged to their cars across the soggy ground, no longer bothering to avoid the puddles, and drove slowly, single file, out of the parking lot, leaning forward to peer through steamy windshields pelted with raindrops.

What possible effect could so few have upon a whole nation? How could the hole in the dike be stopped when the whole dike was crumbling?

That week, Joan Andrews wrote to her brother John, "My time in jail wasn't too bad, and in fact one police officer sneaked a rosary into my cell. He wasn't even Catholic… The contrast is great between various police officers. Later in the week when I was arrested in Bridgeton for blocking doors at an abortion chamber, one of the arresting police officers went into a rage when I refused to walk out, and he locked me in a stranglehold by the neck and demanded I walk out. He kept choking me and almost got hysterical. Finally he just dragged me out because I wouldn't submit. He cursed and raged all the way back to the station. I always remain silent in the face of rage unless I am asked a direct question.

"My throat and jaw was bruised for more than a week."

Stephanie had never had a man for a teacher before. She was so anxious for Mr. Johnson to like her. Somehow it seemed important to be able to please a man. Daddy wasn't home much anymore and when he was, he and Mom were always arguing. She didn't know what she could possibly have done to make them mad, but she felt like she must have done something.

When Mr. Johnson assigned the 6th grade class project for health, Stephanie's heart sank. How could she ever do that? She could never ask Mom or Daddy to help her with it. No one in their family ever talked about things like that.

Compelling Interests

Even though she wanted Mr. Johnson to like her, she put the project off all week. Other girls and boys brought their list of contraceptives available at their local pharmacy; one boy even brought a box of condoms his father had loaned him.

"My dad said, 'Just don't use them,'" he joked as he showed the class.

Mr. Johnson nodded approvingly. "Not yet, right?" he amended. "You're a little young."

He reviewed what he had taught them about the various types of contraceptives. "As you have found out, there are a number of different methods of birth control available. When you start having sex, you will want to choose the one that's right for you."

He took a small square foil package out of the box of condoms on his desk and tore it open. Inside Stephanie could see something flesh-colored. Mr. Johnson was blowing it up like a balloon. When it was impossibly big, he stopped blowing and held it up. "One size fits all," he joked. The boys nudged each other and made obscene comments.

Then Mr. Johnson got serious.

"Some people—maybe even some of your parents—are old-fashioned or religious and may not approve of birth control. In this day and age, that view is no longer practical. Or responsible. Without birth control, you could conceive a baby—and how many of you feel ready to become fathers or mothers? No, of course not. Using birth control is part of being mature about sex."

He picked up the whole box of condoms. "Don't leave home without them," he joked, pretending to slip them into his back pocket.

After class, Mr. Johnson came by Stephanie's desk, as she had known he would.

"I haven't seen your list yet, Stephanie."

"I know," she said faintly. "My mother was kind of too busy to take me to the store."

"Would you like a few more days?"

"No! I mean, that's OK." She tried desperately to change the subject. "They might be getting a divorce. They fight a lot."

Part 4: 1982–1985

Mr. Johnson sat on the edge of her desk. "How does that make you feel, Stephanie?"

"Sad, I guess. And kind of lonely. It's like they don't have time for me anymore. We don't do anything fun together. They just fight."

"That must be rough. Do you feel torn in two directions?"

He understood! "Yes," she said. "It's hard to know which team I'm on."

"Shall we let the project go?" he asked.

"Yes, please!" She felt grateful. She didn't know that it would affect her grade.

The Lancasters weren't overjoyed at Stephanie's first "C" but Mommy was kind about it. "I know things have been a strain on you lately—on all of us," she said, giving her a kiss. "You'll do better when things settle down again."

Settle down. Months later, Stephanie understood what Mommy had meant. "When things settle down" meant after they got the divorce.

Once Dan left, Artyce had to go to work. There were no openings for recent graduates with a degree in psychology. She signed up at an agency supplying businesses with temporary help and they ran her through a battery of tests. Thank goodness she had learned word-processing while she was doing her thesis and she could type fast. She could make $11 an hour and because she was a "temp," she had some flexibility in her schedule. Still, Artyce had much less time to spend with Stephanie than before and she hated having her daughter come home to an empty house. But there was nothing she could do about that.

Artyce went over and over in her mind how she could support the two of them without working outside the home full-time but she couldn't think of anything. The best she could do was to keep in phone contact with Stephanie and be sure Stephanie knew how to take care of herself.

Stephanie knew how to dial 9-1-1. She knew she wasn't supposed to use the stove and she knew where to turn off the main gas line if they had an earthquake. She knew which neighbors to call in an emergency and she knew to not open the door to strangers. She always called her mother promptly when she got home from school and sometimes two or three

Compelling Interests

times during the afternoon, to ask if she could play next door or whether they could order pizza for dinner. Artyce didn't mind the interruptions. She wanted her daughter to know that she came first.

Feeling guilty as a single parent apparently came with the territory, Artyce told herself. She reminded herself often that there wasn't really anything to feel guilty about. She had done everything a single parent could do, under the circumstances, and Stephanie was a responsible kid.

The pro-choice movement had suffered a major setback. Richard Michaelson, the doctor who had crusaded to get abortions legalized, whose medical testimony had indirectly impacted the Supreme Court justices who ruled on Roe v. Wade, had done a one-eighty. He wasn't doing abortions anymore and he no longer believed in them. In fact, if the reports were accurate, he was crusading as vigorously against them as he once had for them.

KASAL, the organization Michaelson had helped establish under its original name REPEAL, now found itself opposed to what he was saying and were frantically pointing out in their newsletters that he no longer spoke for them.

The women were especially agitated because Michaelson had the audacity to write a book which he claimed "exposed" KASAL. In it, he claimed that the statistics regarding the thousands of women dying from illegal abortions prior to 1973 were false. He claimed to have helped fabricate those figures, partly because of genuine concern for women—at the time, the end seemed to justify the means, he said—and partly because of the promise of a new and lucrative field for surgeons.

"That's absurd," snapped Cecile Tucker-Thomas, KASAL's director, to her staff. She hurled Michaelson's paperback, *How We Lied our Way to Legal Abortion*, across her office. "Richard knows perfectly well those figures were based on estimates. We didn't have any way to get accurate statistics then. No one was keeping records. But that doesn't mean our estimates weren't pretty close to the truth."

Part 4: 1982–1985

The other members of KASAL's board were relieved. Tucker-Thomas had been in on it all from the beginning and if anyone knew what had gone on, she did.

"There was a football player for Berkeley once who got turned around during the Rose Bowl and ran the wrong way with the ball," she said abruptly. Several members exchanged uneasy glances. *What did this have to do with anything?*

She saw the looks. "Michaelson is like that football player," she explained irritably. "On top of fighting the other team, I feel like I've got to send half our players to tackle one of our own men. What the hell's the matter with Richard?"

Ester greeted Julius one evening with a personal letter he accepted with interest, swinging his coat from his shoulder to the nearest wingchair.

"It's from Pat O'Connor," he told Ester. "We were in school together at Irvine. I haven't heard from him since—" He remembered the postcard but didn't want to refer to it. "He moved back to New York right after graduation." The sense of revulsion Julius had felt toward Pat when he'd read the card had long since dissipated. Pat had always been a bit crude. That was just Pat. In person, it was hard to dislike him.

Julius worked the envelope open with a finger and scanned the typed page quickly. "He's coming out for the conference. Wants to know if we can get together."

"What conference?" Ester asked, bringing martinis for them both.

He glanced up, said, "Thanks," took the drink and went over to the fireplace, pushing a chintz-covered ottoman out of the way with a foot so he could sit in the matching chair.

"KASAL—Keep Abortion Safe and Legal—their annual conference. It's in L.A. next month. Pat's going to be speaking on fertility control."

He read the letter again and chuckled. "He says 'I expect a real California welcome: just pop me in a hot tub and stick a joint in my mouth.'"

"We have the hot tub," smiled Ester.

Compelling Interests

"I'll have to tell him I haven't had a joint since the night of my high school prom."

A cocktail party at the Seventh Street Bistro Sunday night kicked off KASAL's conference, Legalization and Its Consequences. Julius wouldn't have recognized Pat, now fifty pounds heavier and wearing a suit, the red hair thinner, if he hadn't walked with the same rangy gait and smiled the same lopsided smile he'd had in college. And of course there were the distinctive red eyebrows, like bushy circumflexes.

It was Pat, in fact, who recognized him first.

"Julius Caesar! Mr. Meticulous! How're ya doing?" Julius felt a comradely clap on the back coming and steeled himself. He had forgotten the way Pat cuffed and tapped and nudged. The memories came back in a rush.

"I'm fine, Pat." He knew he sounded stuffy. His social graces seemed to have rusted through disuse. Why couldn't he summon the enthusiasm he had felt when he received Pat's recent letter? "How about yourself?"

"Happy and prosperous." He patted his stomach and then poked Julius in the side. "You haven't let down, have you, Julius? I bet you still play tennis three times a week."

"Handball," said Julius, "twice a week."

"And wipe down the shower walls?" Julius felt uncomfortably like Pat was about to announce it to the whole assembly as he had in college—"Hey, everybody, gather around. This guy—get it, *Guy*—wipes the moisture off the walls after he showers."

Instead, Pat was elbowing him familiarly. "Caesar, you're the only guy I ever knew who took time to dry between his toes. Me, I even brush my teeth in the shower to save time. So how's business?"

His question, tacked so abruptly on the end of his personal remarks, caught Julius off guard but he rallied quickly. Work was a welcome change of topic.

"I'm doing well. Quite well."

"I bet you are, eh?" Pat grinned, showing even teeth in a lopsided grin. He nudged Julius in the ribs. "What do you charge out here for slurping?"

Part 4: 1982–1985

"Slurping?" asked Julius.

"You know, suctions."

Julius looked at him distastefully. "Pat, I find that term inappropriate."

Pat grinned. "But descriptive, wouldn't you say?"

Laurel and Kim rode with Janice to the abortion conference Monday morning. Julius had given them unprecedented permission to close up shop, on the condition they attend.

The foyer of the Los Angeles Regency was so elegant Laurel felt like whispering. Their footsteps were silent in the deep carpets.

"I think we'd better split up," said Janice, while the other two peeled their nametags off the paper backings and patted them onto their shirts. "There are three workshops this afternoon that I really ought to go to and they're all at the same time." She pointed to the schedule in her workbook. "I really need to know more about complications."

"I'd like to hear the one on counseling," offered Kim.

"Laurel," said Janice, "could you cover economics and marketing for me?"

"I don't know anything about economics," said Laurel.

"Take notes," said Janice.

When she had located the room for the afternoon workshop and slipped into a chair at one of the long tables, Laurel glanced over the abstract on the talk. It was called "Enhancing the Bottom Line."

The speaker was a tall man, who seemed stooped less from his age than from embarrassment at his height. She tried to follow what he was saying, with the help of graphs which she dutifully copied for Janice, but she couldn't get into it. Something about financial solvency and creative strategies.

"We have to do the same things better and less expensively, the same things in different markets, different things in the same markets and different things in different markets," he was saying. Laurel struggled to suppress a yawn.

Compelling Interests

At last the group was filing out into the hall, toward a table with plates piled high with doughnuts. Maybe a cup of coffee would help.

Janice appeared. "Mine was helpful. What did you find out?"

He had said it twice. Laurel had forced herself to remember it. "He said, 'Increasing income and decreasing expenses is the name of the game.'"

"Yes?" said Janice, as if expecting more.

"That's what he said."

"Well, I know *that!*" she said, amused. "But how?"

"I took notes," said Laurel.

On Tuesday, Janice wanted to attend a workshop on infectious complications. "I swear it's not the same thing as yesterday," she laughed. "Laurel, please, please go to the workshop on harassment. It's really important but I just can't miss this one."

Laurel shrugged. She had come to the conclusion that the entire conference was a bore and she didn't care which workshop she attended. Maybe if she did Janice a favor, Janice would suggest Julius give her a raise. She had long ago left her sister's and moved in with her boyfriend, Roger, a lab technician at Seaside General. They shared expenses but even a small raise would help. *After all,* she thought, *increasing income is the name of the game.*

Right away, however, Laurel knew this talk would be different. The workshop was called "Anti-Choice Harassment and Violence" and there were six speakers. The room was packed.

"Is there anyone here who has *not* been the victim of anti-choice harassment this year?" one of the speakers, a woman in a green dress with a matching scarf around her neck, asked. "Anyone who has not had names yelled in your clients' faces, obscene signs carried where they offend and upset your clients?"

No one raised a hand. Whether all present had been victims or whether the non-victims were too timid to call attention to themselves, Laurel didn't know. Certainly, everyone in the clinic where she worked had been victimized.

Part 4: 1982–1985

"Last June," she continued, "the Supreme Court decided three abortion cases: Akron v. Akron Center for Reproductive Health; Planned Parenthood v. Ashcroft; and Simopoulos v. Virginia. In each of these cases, they reaffirmed a woman's right to abortion without governmental interference.

"They overruled attempts by anti-abortionists to require women to wait 24 hours after deciding to have an abortion so they could 'think it over.' They overruled so-called 'informed consent,' where women are forced to look at pictures of developing fetuses or of aborted fetuses. They overruled making pregnant women go through counseling by a physician. And they overruled mandating that second trimester abortions be done in a hospital.

"All of these strengthened our position and made it clear that any regulations which interfere with a woman's right to choose will be subject to judicial review."

Laurel's interest began to flag again. The legal stuff was as boring as the economic stuff.

"In Tennessee, these rulings triggered a daily harassment campaign that caught us flatfooted. With the lifting of restrictions on second trimester abortions, Memphis Center for Reproductive Health started an out-patient program in West Tennessee and there was a rash of violent actions taken against us.

"We need to anticipate enemy fire and recognize it for what it is. Our foes wear many disguises." Laurel flipped over a page in her notebook and poised her pen. This part would be important.

"Their attack on choice will sometimes masquerade as a bill to define when life begins or to refuse funding for abortions for poverty-level women. At other times it will appear as a state law or a city ordinance requiring parental consent for minors or the consent of a spouse or some kind of public disclosure of patients' names—or who knows what.

"The point is to be ready for it and to refuse to be intimidated. I don't need to tell you how critical this year's elections are in affecting the balance of power between the pro-choice and anti-choice groups. I won't go into that because we have a special workshop on that tomorrow. We face the potential loss of our right to choose.

"We need to enlist and train everyone in our facilities to register women to vote. It's easy, fast, and cheap. You can register patients and get them to sign petitions in a waiting room, in a counseling session, or in the recovery room. It will allow them to express their feelings when they are being picketed and harassed."

The speaker introduced a panel of abortion providers from KASAL and WomanPower—"non-partisan pro-choice lobbyists," she called them. But Laurel had all she needed. Register women to vote pro-choice. It was something she could get women to do in recovery that would make a difference.

When Legalization and Its Consequences was over, Julius took Pat home to Long Beach with him. At the end of the off ramp, Pat said, "Whoa, Caesar! Oil wells? In the middle of the city?" His humor was less embarrassing when they were alone.

"Sure," said Julius, more relaxed than he had been. "Long Beach was built over oil. Not much of it left now. I'm so used to the things, I don't even notice them anymore." He glanced at the laboriously working machines, insect-like in appearance—gray-green, on spindly legs, the narrow elliptical heads methodically dipping and rising.

"Which ones are yours?" asked Pat, giving Julius an amiable shove.

Julius didn't have to answer. He was turning into the curved driveway. The gravel crunched under their wheels.

"What's this? What's this?" cried Pat, looking at the expanse of lawn. "Grass? Where I live, the only people with over three square feet of lawn are in the Mafia."

They waited while the garage door went up. "Hold it, Caesar! What are those?"

"What?" Julius touched the brake.

"Those metal things in the grass—next to the sidewalk. There. Where the dirt is cut in a V."

Part 4: 1982–1985

"Pat, you loon, those are sprinkler heads."

Pat sat back in mock relief. "I thought they were triggers for land mines."

Julius smiled.

They tried out the handball court, they swam; Ester barbecued chicken for all of them out back. Julius stretched his legs the length of his chaise lounge and worked the barbecue sauce out from under his fingernails with a paper napkin. He felt great.

The weather was mild and there was enough of a breeze to have blown all the smog inland to San Bernardino. They were surrounded by a kaleidoscope of Ester's flowers. He had reduced Pat to gelatin on the court, the chicken had been perfect, the beer was cold—and he was out of Pat's reach.

"If only you had come a little later in the summer," said Julius, "when the Olympics are here; I could get tickets for track and field—Carl Lewis, Mary Decker. You sure you can only stay one day?"

"'Fraid so."

"What can I show you in one day? It takes a whole day to see South Coast Plaza, a day to do Disneyland or the planetarium. If you had a week, we could go skiing, sail to Catalina, see Scotty's Castle—Death Valley is beautiful at this time of year—We've got beaches, mountains, desert."

"Wish I could stay," said Pat, "but I miss my squaw and papoose."

"Papoose?" laughed Ester. "Must be heap big papoose by now!"

"Oh, that's right, you wouldn't know," said Pat. "Ginger and I divorced years ago. She got the kids. Penny and I have a 4-month old." He pulled out his wallet and extended it to Julius. "Look at that." The photograph showed a young girl in shorts, leaning against a tree, holding a baby.

"That's your wife? She can't be any older than your kids," said Julius.

"Eighteen," he said. "Four years older than my oldest." He worked the wallet back into his pocket. "I'll tell you, buddy, it's not easy starting over, but one big, toothless grin makes up for it all. You two never had kids, did you?"

"Never wanted them," Julius said shortly.

Compelling Interests

"I love kids," said Pat. "Oh, I grouse a lot about the dirty diapers and the night feedings—but having Penny and the baby to come home to makes life worth living."

They each mused on their own thoughts for a while.

Then Julius said, as casually as he could, "Pat, did I read something about your boss going anti-choice?"

"Michaelson? Yeah, about a year ago." He didn't seem to want to talk about it.

"On what grounds?" pursued Julius. "Did he get religious or something?"

"No, he's an atheist, as far as I know." Pat took a quick swallow of beer.

"Then what?"

"Oh, something about the new developments in fetology— ultrasound, hysteroscopy, radio immunochemistry, that kind of thing. He says it's been proven that the fetus is 'just a tiny member of the human community.'" He said it in a sing-song, disparagingly, and stood up. "Where's your little doctor's room?"

"Through the den, down the hall, second door on your left," said Julius.

He waited thoughtfully till Pat returned with a second can of beer. As Pat settled into the deck chair, Julius said, "I've struggled with the issue, too, Pat. I have serious doubts myself about second trimester procedures."

"What's the problem, Julius?" said Pat, louder than necessary. "You think all this new technology tells us something we didn't know before, something they didn't tell us at medical school? *I* know it's a baby, *you* know it's a baby. Big deal."

Julius let Pat's words fill a silence before asking quietly, "Pat, do you think—do you think they feel pain?"

"No, of course not! I don't know. Maybe. Maybe just for a minute or so. The late-stage ones. Not at 8 or 12 weeks. It's probably just like kittens, when you stick 'em in a sack, tie a rock to it and drop it in a pond. Didn't you do that when you were a kid?"

"No," said Julius.

Part 4: 1982–1985

When the silence became awkward, Julius spoke again. "*I know.* You ever tried waterskiing?"

"No, but I'm game."

"We'll drive up to Arrowhead in the morning. Our cabin's right on the lake. I'll have a guy I know up there run the boat and I'll teach you myself. There's a special way to do it, starting from the dock and using a split rope, so I can guarantee you'll get up first time."

It was Sunday morning. Ester was in the shower in the master bathroom adjoining his, and Julius, tapping his shaver on the side of his sink, steeled himself. Church was important to Dove and he knew she appreciated it when he attended with her. She wasn't going to like what he had to tell her.

"Dove," he said, as she stepped out, "I won't be going to Mass this morning. I've got some things to do at the hospital."

"Abortions?" she asked.

"Yes."

"On Sunday, Julius? Can't they wait a day?"

"I've got two that are into their seventh month. They've waited too long already."

They pulled out of the garage at the same time, his gunmetal Mercedes heading north, her maroon one heading south. As he drove to the clinic he knew he hadn't told her the real reason he was doing the late-terms on Sunday.

The real reason was all the picketers were in church.

Dr. Pat O'Connor was in the doctor's lunchroom at Manhattan General Hospital when Dr. Richard Michaelson showed up, a massive man with a full beard.

"Richard!" Pat cried in welcome, jumping up. He could count on his fingers the number of times he had seen Michaelson since his internship

Compelling Interests

under him in New York. His hand disappeared into the thick paw of his former mentor. "How are you? What brings you here?"

"I'm great, Pat. Sit down, sit down." They both took chairs. "I have a favor to ask of you." Michaelson had never been one for chit-chat.

"Sure." Pat picked up his hamburger again and took a bite, listening expectantly.

"I want to film one of your abortions."

Pat's heart skipped a beat. He assimilated this in silence for a second. Everything in him wanted to refuse, but one didn't refuse Richard Michaelson. Even if he hadn't felt that he owed this man his start in the practice, Michaelson's very presence made that unimaginable.

"Anti-abortion propaganda?" He tried to say it banteringly but his voice betrayed his nervousness, even to himself.

"Exactly," said Michaelson. "I want to film an abortion from the victim's point of view. Right through the uterine wall."

"How?" asked Pat reluctantly. He didn't really want to know. He really wanted to say, "Get someone else."

"Using ultrasound. I've got a theory I want to test out. I want the whole thing, from start to finish. You're familiar with ultrasound imaging, of course—a crystal sends out pulsing high frequency sound waves and a transducer collects the echoes—"

"I know," said Pat.

"I want a sector scan. We'll put the image on videotape. I'll stay out of your way as much as possible and I won't do it at all unless the woman involved agrees and unless she will not be talked out of aborting. I don't want to be a party to it unless it's going to happen anyway."

"I don't do abortions past twelve weeks," said Pat.

"Twelve weeks is what I want. May I?"

"I guess so." He tried to sound confident. "I don't see why not." That didn't sound much better.

"At twelve weeks, the nervous system is intact. I want to know if the fetus reacts to the instruments—pulls away, squirms—anything that would indicate it can feel pain."

Part 4: 1982–1985

"Don't tell—you don't have to tell me about it," said Pat uncomfortably. "Do whatever you want."

"Do you operate on Tuesdays?"

"I can."

"How about next week?"

"We've found the house!" Mariana exclaimed excitedly. "Oh, Tasha, it's *wonderful!* Can you imagine a three-story Victorian house smack in the middle of Long Beach? You've got to come see it."

It was a couple of days before Tasha was able to stop by the future maternity home. It was in the seediest part of the city, on a street with gutters full of trash. Set back from the road, the once elegant home seemed to be trying to retreat from the tract houses across the street.

Right next door, groups of men and small, unkempt children lounged in front of an apartment building, watching with curiosity as Tasha walked past from the bus stop on Atlantic.

There was a front yard of dead grass, a narrow pathway to the front steps, and an L-shaped porch from which three separate doors led inside. Tasha knocked at the first; when there was no answer, she tried another one.

Mariana opened the door, wearing an old flannel shirt and jeans, a bandana around her head, rubber gloves on her hands, and two of her children at her side. When they weren't in school they were usually with her.

"Come on in!"

Tasha stepped gingerly into a bare hall, with peeling wallpaper of an indeterminate hue, as Mariana went on, "I know it looks like a mess now but you should have seen it yesterday! We hauled five truckloads of trash out of here—empty boxes, broken furniture—"

She led the way through a kitchen with cracked Formica counters and an ancient, dingy range. "We'll use this room behind the kitchen to store things like rice and beans and there's a hook-up for the washer and dryer.

Compelling Interests

We're already getting donations of clothes and furniture—people just leave them on the porch because we have no place to put them yet.

"I'll have an office off the dining room." She opened the door of a small cubicle. "Oh, Tasha," she sighed, "there's so much to do." Another thought immediately perked her up. "Oh, did I tell you? We have a carpeting company that is donating carpeting for all three floors and they'll install it free!"

They started up the stairs. The banister was wobbly and the walls were badly in need of paint. "There are five rooms on the second floor, including the housemother's. We're going to have the tubs ripped out and showers put in instead. Pregnant women can't get in and out of tubs.

"And up here," reaching the top floor, "we'll have the moms who are keeping their babies. They'll each have their own room, with a crib in it. We have to have them on the third floor because it's the only one with a fire escape."

They stepped out on the balcony and gazed across the array of back yards full of clotheslines, lean dogs, and rusty bicycles.

"The Lord is so good," said Mariana. Her eyes were full of light.

Even before the house was ready for them, women began showing up at the door. "Someone down the street told me you might have a place for me. I'm pregnant and homeless—"

But an inspector's visit put an end to hopes that the women would be able to move in soon.

"Anything over two stories occupied by unrelated people requires installation of sprinklers in case of fire or we can't give you a permit to operate."

Mariana's heart sank. "I have four women ready to move in right away. They're all living with us—and we only have one bathroom."

The inspector looked marginally sympathetic. "My hands are tied," he said.

Part 4: 1982–1985

The lowest bid for a sprinkler system came in at $130,000. "How much do you have?" the contractor asked.

Mariana smiled. "Frankly, all I have is a nickel in my pocket—but I'll pray."

A week later, the contractor called back. "Have you come up with any more money?"

"No, but I'm still praying!"

"I'll tell you what," he offered. "I'll do it for $125,000."

Three weeks later, he lowered his bid to $100,000 and added, "I'll install it for you. I'm going to a meeting tonight for the pipe fitters union. I'll present the needs of your home to the members and see if some of them will donate their time a week from Saturday."

But when he called again, it was with discouraging news. "I talked to the union but there wasn't any response. I told them, 'Since there aren't any stables around nowadays, where are women going to have their babies?'"

Mariana laughed, but her heart was heavy.

"Anyway, I'm sorry. I did get some companies to donate five- and ten-inch pipe. It will be delivered there in a day or two. A couple of friends and I will do the work for you, evenings and weekends, but it'll take us six months."

Mariana thanked him and hung up. She felt overwhelmed—overwhelmed by this stranger's kindness, but even more with the enormity of what she had taken on. Her family of six plus four pregnant woman in a three-bedroom house for the next *six months?* Every day, it was a struggle to free up the bathroom long enough so Paul could have a turn before he went to work. Two of her kids were sleeping in the living room so women could have their beds. *What am I doing, Lord? I've made a mistake. I've promised women—and it's not going to happen. How did I get in so deep!*

The pipe arrived and at six o'clock on Saturday morning a truck pulled up and three men jumped out. Mariana was just greeting the contractor when another truck pulled up.

"It's the guys!" the contractor said. "They came after all!"

Two trucks were right behind them. Mariana was bewildered.

Compelling Interests

"Who are they?" she asked. At least twenty men—and one woman—were joining them in the big front yard.

"Journeymen!" said the contractor, grinning. "You guys didn't say anything at the meeting! You didn't tell me you were coming."

"But we wrote down the date and time," said the woman. "And we're here."

The journeymen worked all morning and when they broke for lunch, Mariana provided punch out in the front yard.

"We still need a trench to the street," the contractor told her thoughtfully, sitting on the porch steps.

"What do you mean?" she asked. "You told me you needed a trench and Paul dug a trench." She pointed to the shallow furrow.

He shook his head. "You don't understand. We need a *trench*. Six feet deep."

One of the men finished his punch in a single gulp and stood up. "I saw someone working a backhoe about a block from here—where they're building apartments. Let's go tell him we're volunteering our time—and see if he'll volunteer his time, too!"

They had all been sprawled on the porch or under the lone tree in the yard, grimy and tired. But at this challenge, more than half of them jumped to their feet. "Yeah! A backhoe! That would do it!"

The next thing Mariana knew, there was a large, decrepit machine bumping down the street toward them, the driver perched in the seat like a hero, with a host of cheering men striding alongside.

By six that evening, there was a six-foot channel linking the old mansion to the road and the entire sprinkler system was installed and ready to test. Mariana had to choke back tears of joy. "You're all wonderful," she told them. "I wish I could—"

"You just use this place for the Lord," said the contractor. "That will be our reward."

Part 4: 1982–1985

On her next visit to the maternity home, bringing an armload of canned goods from White Front, Tasha found the house alive with activity. A man was laying blue-patterned linoleum in the kitchen. Mariana was showing another workman which two of the three front doors she wanted walled up.

Upstairs, one of the rooms smelled of fresh paint and several women were holding fabric up to peach walls and discussing window treatments.

Across the hall, a group of junior high students studied another room and were arguing good-naturedly about whether purple walls would look too bizarre.

Mariana came up the stairs, breathless. "It's changed, hasn't it? We're naming each room after a fruit of the spirit—love, joy, peace, patience—you know—and a different church has 'adopted' each one. The women are from St. Cornelius and the kids are from Grace Lutheran. I think we're the only maternity home in the country supported by a whole community of churches, not just one."

The first pro-life pregnancy testing center opened before the maternity home was finished. Volunteers, after eight hours' training, would be working in pairs, testing urine samples, counseling, and showing pro-life videos to the women who came by. Tasha was one of them.

"The test itself is very simple," said the woman who headed up the training. "You mix five drops of urine and five drops of the solution on the slide and rotate it sixty seconds. It will become either milky, which means the test is positive, or grainy, which means the test is negative. Sometimes even that is hard to judge.

"Remember," she cautioned emphatically, "we are not medically authorized to tell the women they are pregnant. All we can tell them is whether the test came out positive or negative and refer them to their own doctor to find out for sure."

These days only the man with the rosary and the man with the posters patrolled the sidewalks in front of Dr. Guy's family planning clinic. The women who had counseled there were now putting their time in at the testing center.

Compelling Interests

Business was better than ever now that the anti-choice people were gone. The clinic was exceeding its quota and Janice often had to pull Kim off recovery to help prep patients.

Dr. Guy came infrequently now because he had so many other clinics to attend to—number 26 had just opened in Fresno. All three women took on many of his responsibilities.

Laurel didn't feel right doing things she knew nurses weren't authorized to do, but when she voiced her concern, Janice would say irritably, "Well, the doctor isn't here yet and when he gets here, you know he doesn't like to wait around. If they're in pain go ahead and give them something."

That same week, Laurel heard Janice tell Kim the same thing—Kim, who was only an aide. She heard Kim protest, just as she had.

"Good grief, Kim," Laurel heard Janice say in exasperation. "You've worked here long enough to know exactly what Dr. Guy would do. It's silly for women to wait for him to write them a prescription when we know what he's going to prescribe."

It had become standard now. Women six months or more pregnant were scheduled at his hospital in Compton for Sundays and he was there by seven A.M.

Beyond twelve weeks, abortion wasn't so simple. The contents of the uterus could not be suctioned out by hose or scraped out with a D&C. Those operations he did so routinely that he had them down to three minutes each.

After twelve weeks, the head was too large to come through the undilated cervix whole. First, the body had to be cut into pieces with a scalpel, up inside the woman where he couldn't see what he was doing and where it was all too easy to perforate the uterus by mistake. Then the head had to be crushed with forceps and none of the pieces of skull, as fragile as the shell of an egg, could be left inside to cause infection.

A nurse had to collect the parts as he removed them and be sure the entire fetus was there before depositing it in a plastic sack, sealing it and marking it with the woman's name and the age of the fetus. Nurses tended

Part 4: 1982–1985

to get squeamish at this; at some of his clinics, a few had refused to do it. He didn't blame them.

Beyond 24 weeks, there were two possible procedures. One was long and messy, called a hysterotomy. It involved giving the woman a general anesthetic and performing the equivalent of a Caesarian section. The fetus was removed from the uterus and placed in a container to be taken to the lab for analysis and classification. Usually, since no effort was made to clear its lungs or encourage its breathing, that presented no problems.

But it was major surgery, with all the attendant risks of any surgery and with considerable inconvenience both to the woman and to the doctor.

For Julius, as with most abortion providers, the procedure of choice for late-terms was saline abortion. His role in this merely involved inserting a long needle, similar to that used for amniocentesis, through the abdomen into the uterus and injecting a toxic salt solution. Sometimes the needle would stab the fetus and he could feel it wiggling like a fish on a hook.

Within 24 hours, usually at home, the woman would go into hard labor and deliver a premature baby. This had the double advantage of requiring nothing more of the doctor, either in the way of time or of unpleasantness, and of being certain. Babies hardly ever survived saline abortion.

The latter method was, however, shocking to the woman, who had to be prepared ahead of time. She would feel the fetus struggling for an hour or two within her uterus and see it after delivery, nearly the size of a full-term baby. Julius felt the shock had a certain value, in that the woman would be unlikely to put off an abortion so long the next time.

There were always women that waited too long. He could never understand that. Why wouldn't a woman who had lasted through seven months of a pregnancy wait another two and put the baby up for adoption? He had done hundreds of late-term abortions and they still didn't make sense to him.

One morning he performed an abortion on a 16-year-old black girl—in his hospital in Compton because the pregnancy was well beyond 12 weeks. The night before, nurses had inserted the laminaria, a kind of compressed

Compelling Interests

seaweed which would expand and dilate the cervix enough for the D&E the following morning.

On the table where he first saw her she seemed bloated and unattractive, her hair tangled and her face blotched with acne. She had been overweight besides being nearly six months pregnant and the nurses had reported her as extremely anxious and hard to anesthetize.

The abortion lasted longer than he had anticipated because when he got inside, he found out she was closer to seven months. If he had known that, he would have used saline.

He finished the surgery with great distaste. He was supposed to fill out and sign a death certificate for any fetus over 400 grams—about five months' gestation—but he had long ago ceased bothering with the forms. All the records were confidential anyway, they were no one's business except the woman's and she certainly didn't want a paper trail leading back to her abortion.

He left immediately, even though there were two other patients already prepped. No one on staff objected. He would let them explain to the women, tell them he'd had an emergency and have them reschedule.

The next morning when he dropped by the Long Beach clinic—late because he and Dove had had a joint counseling appointment she had insisted on—Janice said, "I couldn't reach you at home. You had several calls about a girl you did yesterday in Compton. Apparently she was hemorrhaging pretty badly. She's back in the hospital."

Before he could take a single case at the clinic, a nurse at his Compton hospital called and wanted him to see the patient.

"She's really bad," said the nurse. "I think she's dying."

They get emotional, he thought. *I'll prescribe antibiotics and have them keep an eye on her.*

But he drove over.

The 16-year old was comatose by the time he arrived and there was nothing he could do except, an hour later, call the coroner. The man sent out to investigate the death asked him questions and put checks in little boxes.

Part 4: 1982–1985

"Natural accident," volunteered Julius. "Expired after abortion. You can get her stats off the chart."

"Have you notified her next of kin?" asked the investigator.

"No." Her next of kin was her mother.

"Notify her," said the investigator.

Julius poured himself a drink and took it to the window. In the channel just beyond, his fiberglass sailboat bobbed in its dock.

"Ester, the Supreme Court should never have legalized late-term abortions."

"What are you saying, Julius? Don't you do them yourself?"

"Yes," he said, sipping the whiskey thoughtfully, "and I'm an expert at it—" He turned to face her. "But I struggle with their morality. It has bothered me for two or three years now."

"Why don't you stop, then?" she suggested. "You have plenty of business without the late ones."

He spoke musingly, as if he hadn't heard her. "I don't agree with the antiabortionists, that there's no difference at all between an embryo 15 seconds after it's fertilized and a fetus at 24 weeks gestation. I think there's a vast difference, a vast difference in every way."

He was gazing out the window again. "I really feel that the court erred when they made that judgment."

Ester didn't answer. Or if she did, he was too absorbed in his own thoughts to hear her.

Tasha was coming by the Victorian house on Martin Luther King Street on a regular basis now. It wouldn't be long before they could hold the long-awaited grand opening. Sometimes she insisted Mariana take time off and go home to her family. "Take a vacation," she urged. "I'll be here if anything comes up."

Compelling Interests

"Can't afford a vacation," grunted Mariana, then lifted her head to add, "What would happen to the moms while we were gone? Besides, Paul and the kids are always with me here when they're not at school or work. I see them all the time."

One day, Mariana handed Tasha a document. It read "CASE REPORT" and below that, "Examination at Forensic Science Center." There was the name of a female, Afro-American, with "Age 16, height 62 inches, weight 130. Hair black, eyes brown."

"It's a death certificate," explained Mariana. "Dr. Guy did an abortion on a 16-year-old and she bled to death." Tasha read the photocopied sheet again. It said, "Expired after abortion in hospital" and two boxes were checked: "Natural" and "accident."

"I know the girl's mother," said Mariana. "She's going to sue but Guy's been sued before. He always settles. Women are still dying from abortion, Tasha—but try to prove it! Doctors list infection or some complication instead of the real cause of death. There's no way the women who go to Julius Guy can know that he has multiple lawsuits against him or that his patients are being carried out on stretchers and rushed to hospitals every week."

Tasha's reaction was not what Mariana expected. She held the certificate in her hands and said, "That could have been me. Mariana, that could have been me!"

Tasha stared at the paper she held in her hands, then burst out, "Mariana, when the home opens, let me be one of the housemothers. Please. Or let me clean this house, instead of rich honky families'—sorry about that."

Mariana just laughed.

"Let me be a part of it. Mariana, if God is as interested in each of us as you keep saying, He can use me to help women who don't want to be pregnant. He must have had a reason for my going through it."

Mariana was serious again. "Let's pray about it, Tasha," she said.

Part 4: 1982–1985

Using the same sterile scissors that a physician uses to cut the umbilical cord of a newborn infant, representatives of the business, medical, and church communities sliced the ribbons of the Lifeline Mothers Home at an open house and dedication ceremony.

Three hundred people were on hand for the celebration, including two physicians, a minister, Senator Nate Marshall, and representatives of several corporations that had donated materials. St. Luke's Hospital had pledged a thousand dollars a month for the home's running expenses, yet the write-up appeared only in Lifeline's own newsletter, not in the *Southbay Journal.* Although notified, the editors had sent no one to cover the event.

Mariana, in a pale blue silk dress, brown eyes shining, summarized how the Lord had made the home possible. "To God be *all* the glory!" she said. "Our intent is to overflow this home with love and fill the house with Scripture so that the women who stay here will feel Christ's love for them."

Then she said she had a special presentation for someone who meant a lot to her.

"It was three years ago that my son Louie said to me, 'Shouldn't we do more than just pray?'" Mariana called Louie forward and smothered him in flowers and a hug.

"People!" called the teacher. "Get a grip here. We're starting!" The noise quieted as students took their seats. Stephanie slipped into hers just in time and flipped a lock of brown hair over her right shoulder.

"We've got a lot to cover today, guys," said Ms. Cox, "so listen up. Even you guys in the back—*especially* you guys in the back!" She arched an eyebrow significantly and the football players in the back row snickered and fell silent.

"Today we're going to discuss the unwanted pregnancy. I hope it doesn't happen to any of you but it could—even with birth control. Maybe for some of you, it already has. We're going to break into groups and role play in a few minutes, but I want to mention first that we are

Compelling Interests

very fortunate to be one of the first schools in southern California to have a school-based clinic on campus.

"The clinic is here to help you with any health needs, from a bunion to a bloody nose to appendicitis. We want you to feel comfortable talking to the nurse on duty anytime about anything. Ever heard of the book, *Everything You Always Wanted to Know about Sex but Were Afraid to Ask?* A little before your time, huh? Well, this is your chance. Any questions you don't feel you can ask your parents, anything you can't even share with *me,* you can ask the nurse. There isn't a thing you could tell her that she hasn't already heard.

"The clinic will have contraceptives available—condoms now come in all the colors of the rainbow, I might add, for you romantics—hot pink, baby blue, mean green. We're hoping to install machines to dispense them around the campus—yes, Gary, like Cokes!—but right now it's up to the school board and you know how *awful* some of those geeks think it is to let kids know that sex exists."

The students laughed at all the right places and Ms. Cox handed out a questionnaire. "This is real brief. It will be on file at the clinic so you won't have to take the time to fill out a bunch of forms when you go in."

Stephanie looked at the questionnaire. The first question was, "Are you sexually active?" The second was "Do you use birth control? If so, what kind?"

She glanced across the room at Justin. Since May, they'd been going around together. He had started walking her home from the bus after school every day and at first they would sit on the porch and have lemonade. They'd do a little homework and Justin would tickle her with twigs. Stephanie knew Mother wouldn't want a boy to come inside while she was away at work.

But one day there wasn't enough lemonade for two, so Stephanie went inside to make more—and Justin followed her. It seemed natural after that to let him in and they'd play Sorry at the kitchen table or roughhouse with the dog.

When they started kissing, it was only goodbye, at the door. Then it was hello and goodbye and a lot in between, on the couch. Yesterday, they

Part 4: 1982–1985

had gone into the bedroom. Was that being sexually active? Stephanie didn't think kissing counted. That wasn't really *sex*. They weren't going to go *that* far.

Joan Andrews looked up at the sound of a key scraping in the lock of her cell door. The matron had opened the door and was ushering a young woman through it.

"Here's one of your group," the matron explained kindly. "She's in a lot of distress. Guess it's her first time." She locked the door.

The woman she had put in with Joan stood shivering uncontrollably against the bars, partly out of fear, Joan guessed, and partly out of shame at having others recognize her fear. They and a dozen others had been arrested at the same Pittsburgh clinic but Joan didn't recognize her. There were always new ones.

Joan stretched out her hand and drew the woman to a seat next to her on her bunk.

"It must be my one *hundred* and first arrest," Joan offered companionably, "but I remember how it felt the first time."

"Joan," gasped the woman. "I'm sorry. I feel so weird. Claustrophobia. I've had it—" She stopped as if the words were choked off.

Joan put an arm around her. "You're shaking. You feel like jumping out of your skin. I know."

"Yes! That's it. My heart pounds, I break out in a sweat—look at my palms—I feel like I'm suffocating!"

Joan just listened.

"I get this insane desire—I don't know—to tear off my clothes and batter myself against the bars—"

"—And the worst part of it all," Joan finished for her, "is feeling humiliated for feeling that way, right?"

"Yes!"

Taking both the woman's hands gently in hers, Joan began saying a Rosary. Gradually, the woman calmed.

Compelling Interests

"I saw you in the doorway," she said at last, when Joan was quiet again. "You're Joan Andrews, aren't you?"

"That's right."

"'Joan never cooperates with the cops.' 'Joan doesn't pay bail.' 'She fasts in jail.' I've heard about you. I thought, *Spare me!* And now, here you are."

"Here we are."

"Do you really have a glass eye?"

"Yes. A horse kicked me—and years later, I got cancer and had to have it removed."

"Does it bother you now?"

"I have to be careful going downstairs." Joan changed the subject smoothly. "Are you thirsty? Here, take this." She passed the woman a half-pint of milk and a sandwich.

The woman glanced at her in surprise. "That's your lunch. Didn't you eat?"

"You eat," urged Joan.

"I'll eat it if you tell me about yourself. Tell me how you got started doing this."

So Joan began in her quick, soft voice, telling her first about the farm in rural Tennessee, about pitching hay and picking fruit and milking cows.

"My sister Miriam and I have a horse named Ruach," said Joan. "She's three-quarters thoroughbred and one quarter quarter-horse and she was sired by a gorgeous white stallion from the New York racing circuit. We had a whole herd of horses, with three thoroughbreds. I was training them. But we sold them when we needed money for our pro-life work."

Joan gave the woman a sidelong glance. "My two favorite things are horses and—matchmaking!"

"Do you have someone special?" the woman asked.

"No, not exactly. There is a man I care for but he wants me to stop rescuing babies. What about you?"

"No."

Joan's tired face brightened. "What kind of guy are you looking for? I've already matched up ten of my friends. I'd love to do the same for you."

Part 4: 1982–1985

"Well—"

"If he were a dog," pursued Joan, "what kind of dog would he be? A setter? A retriever? A Great Dane? A not-so-great Dane?"

They both giggled. "A beagle," said Joan's new friend. "With big floppy ears!"

"What kind of dog are you?" Joan asked. "How about something with beautiful eyes? Like a spaniel."

"If I were a spaniel and my husband were a beagle, we could have a Spiegel. And go into the catalog business!"

They were helpless with silliness, like a couple of fifteen-year-olds, when the matron came to the cell door with an announcement for the young woman. "You can go now. Your buddies have raised your bond."

Wiping away tears and breathless with laughter, the woman protested, "But I don't want to go!"

Joan patted her on the knee and nodded. "You go," she said. "You're not ready to refuse bond. Maybe you will someday, but not now."

"But you'll be alone here," she objected.

"I'm never alone," said Joan. "You go."

Richard Michaelson's filmed abortion was hardly top box office. Pro-life groups were buying copies and the Christian filmmaker who had produced it was sending free copies to members of the Senate and the House of Representatives. Cecile Tucker-Thomas told reporters she had no intention of watching what she knew was going to be "fraudulent and emotionally exploitative."

"The film concentrates on the fetus and ignores the woman. We *know women* can feel pain. How can a fetus feel pain before the hypothalamus is even fully developed?"

But Liz Tewskbury and Bobbie Porter watched it together because it was disturbing some of the women who had seen it and they were getting questions about it.

Compelling Interests

"Look at that!" Liz shook her head as Dr. Michaelson, in a white lab coat, pointed to a blurred gray shape on the screen next to him and intoned, "We see the child moving rather serenely in its sanctuary."

Liz rolled her eyes. "'The child!' Give me a break! It's just a fetus, for God's sake!"

"Its *'sanctuary?'*" said Bobbie. She made gagging sounds.

"The child's thumb is in its mouth," Michaelson was saying.

"He's telling the audience what to see! You can't tell which of those wavy lines is the fetus, much less see a *thumb!*"

"Now the abortionist inserts the suction apparatus which will tear the child apart."

Something long and pale seemed to appear and flash about, but it was indistinct—everything in the picture was jostling around now. "The child will rear away from it and will undergo much more violent, much more agitated movement as it senses the most mortal danger imaginable—"

"That's a lie!" burst out Bobbie. "How can he say that? It's only moving because the instrument is moving—like stirring tea leaves in a cup!"

After a few seconds of agitation, part of the darkish lump in the center of the picture vanished. "The lower extremities have already been lost—"

Liz jabbed the "off" button on the remote. "That's utterly outrageous! The whole thing is garbage! Nothing like that is happening at all. He's completely misleading them and he makes it sound so professional!"

"It's so obvious," said Bobbie. "No one will fall for it."

"They will," said Liz. "That's the trouble. He's a doctor, he's an authority figure in a white coat. Besides, anti-choice people *want* to believe a fetus feels pain. They'll see whatever they want to see."

Pat had just finished a routine surgery and was stripping off his gloves when he looked up to see Dr. Michaelson before him.

"Pat," his former boss began without preliminaries, "you've got to see this."

Part 4: 1982–1985

"What?"

"The ultrasound. Your abortion."

Panic clutched at Pat's stomach. "No," he said before he could stop himself.

"You've got to."

"I've got patients."

Dr. Michaelson didn't speak. His presence, as usual, was overpowering.

There was a VCR in the office. Sometimes the staff watched training films on it. Dr. Michaelson wheeled it into one of the side rooms and shoved a tape into it. Pat followed reluctantly.

Both tense, both standing with arms crossed, not speaking, the doctors watched. There was the uterus, a shadowy bowl. Inside, the fetus was clearly visible, on its back. Pat could make out the orbit of the right eye, the mouth, the ventricle of the brain, the ribs in silhouette, the spine. The placenta was a granular area above the fetus.

The recorded voice of Richard Michaelson was explaining, "We see the child moving rather serenely in its sanctuary. The child's thumb is in its mouth."

Now the suction tip appeared as a shadow at the bottom of the screen. Re-living the procedure, Pat felt the long metal wand in his gloved hand again, felt himself inserting it into the uterus.

"This is the lethal instrument which will ultimately tear apart the child," Michaelson's voice was saying. "The child will rear away from it and will undergo much more violent, much more agitated movement as it senses the most mortal danger imaginable. The heartbeat has speeded up, from 140 beats per minute to over 200."

Pat's heartbeat had speeded up, too. The suction apparatus—his own suction apparatus—appeared in the picture again, gray, aggressive. Probing, probing. It bumped into the child's thigh. Attached to thick tubing which led to the abortion machine beside the operating table, it clamped firmly onto the fetus. Pat knew that a pressure of 55 millimeters of mercury was being applied to pull the body inexorably out through the enlarged cervix.

Compelling Interests

"The body is being systematically torn from the head," intoned the voice of Dr. Michaelson. "The lower extremities have already disappeared in a typhoon-like series of echoes as the abortionist is exerting traction."

Pat found his palms sweating. His chest hurt. The child's head reared back and the mouth opened in a wide—yawn or scream, Pat couldn't tell which—and suddenly, half the child was gone. There was churning, the picture wasn't clear. Now the body disintegrated.

Pat felt faint. He tried to lower his eyes but couldn't take them off the screen.

"The head is too large to be drawn through the cervix whole. Now the abortionist introduces into the uterus a polyp forceps and he will attempt to grasp the free-floating head between the rings of the instrument—" Standing in a pristine medical gown before the enlarged image, the Michaelson on film demonstrated with a pair of silver forceps. "The head will be crushed, like so, and the contents of the head removed and then the bones of the head."

The forceps were invading the smeared, watery contents of the uterus. They searched out and locked onto the floating sphere. There was a silent crunch. Nothing but shards were left. The womb was empty.

"This is one of the 4,000 early abortions done every day—" the voice said. Dr. Michaelson clicked the machine off and turned on the lights. He looked searchingly at Pat. Pat had sunk onto a wheeled stool. He sat there, his head in his hands, for a long time.

Then he stood slowly, as if unsure his legs would hold him. "My God," he breathed. "My God." Without another word, he turned unsteadily on his heel, opened the door, and walked out of the room.

Dr. Michaelson waited a few minutes, retrieved his tape, and strode to the reception area. The nurse behind the desk was gazing open-mouthed at Pat's retreating back.

"The man's gone nuts!" she said aloud. "He resigned—just like that. He said he'd never do another abortion."

Part 5
1986

Laurel had been working for Julius Guy for five years. She had gone back to Omaha only once, just long enough to confirm to herself that she had done the right thing in moving to southern California. She and Roger were seriously considering marriage.

Her job at Family Services was pretty routine now, although it had enough variety to be interesting. When business was light, she helped Janice with paperwork. When it was heavy, Janice and Kim helped her prep patients. Once when things were really rushed and Dr. Guy was late, Janice told her to go ahead and start the anesthesia on two waiting women.

"I can't do that!" Laurel objected. "Only a doctor is authorized to do that."

"We're just saving him time. By the time it takes effect, he'll be here and he can get right to work. He's got 34 clinics and 250 patients a week at the hospital to run through. Let's give him a break."

"But starting the anesthesia—"

"I don't have time to argue with you, Laurel," said Janice irritably. "Just do it."

Laurel had prepped a D&C patient one morning. Dr. Guy was already there and was due to come in and give her local anesthetic when suddenly the girl grabbed Laurel's wrist and cried, "I've changed my mind!"

Compelling Interests

"What do you mean?" said Laurel, thinking frantically. "You can't do that!"

"I don't want an abortion! I don't want to do this!" The girl knocked Laurel's restraining hand aside and struggled to sit up.

Laurel ran to the door as the girl started to get off the table.

"Doctor! We have an emergency here!"

Janice was passing in the hall and sized up the situation immediately. She moved quickly to help Laurel block the doorway.

"Let me out!" the girl was shouting. "I want to go home!"

Janice spoke sharply. "Stop it! There are women here who *do* want abortions. You're scaring them."

She reached past Laurel and took the girl's arm. Laurel let Janice into the room, still blocking the door with her own body and watching nervously for Dr. Guy.

"You're all right," Janice was saying, more soothingly now. "Lots of women get a little apprehensive about the procedure. It's the most common procedure done in this country and it will all be over in a few minutes."

Dr. Guy was there. "What's the matter?" He didn't wait for an answer. "Get back on the table," he ordered the frightened girl. "Stop being such a baby. I've done thousands of these and no one has ever run out on me yet."

Timidly, her eyes downcast, the girl obeyed. She lay down slowly and Laurel could see that she was trembling. All three of them stayed, moving quickly and efficiently, and they took turns speaking directly to the girl, holding her attention.

But the minute the girl felt the cold metal speculum enter her, she started screaming and thrashing to sit up again.

"Hey! Stop it!" ordered Julius. "You can't move around! You're going to get hurt!"

"Let me go!" shrieked the girl. "Let me go!"

It took both Laurel and Janice to hold her down. Dr. Guy gave them a nod to indicate he would make it fast. He turned on the suction machine and in three minutes flat, he stripped off his gloves and announced, "All

Part 5: 1986

done. There, that wasn't so bad, was it?" and was gone before the sobbing girl could respond.

Janice, who worked the office and had never done any clean-up, helped Laurel throw the bloody linen into the laundry container and drop the instruments in alcohol before leaving without a word. Laurel stood by the operating table for a long time, holding the girl's hand and letting her cry quietly.

"It's okay," she said over and over, hardly aware she was speaking. "You're okay. It's all over now. You're going to be okay."

There were other patients she should have been prepping but neither Dr. Guy nor Janice interrupted her. When she finally helped the girl off the table and into bed in the recovery room, Laurel ached all over.

What's happening to me? she thought. *I don't like what I just did to that girl. I blocked the door. I held her down. I forced her to go through with it. I feel like an accessory to a crime.*

I want to get out of here and go for a long walk and think, she told herself. *I don't like who I'm becoming.* But there were patients waiting.

There wasn't time for the Guys to take a vacation. The waiting room was always full.

At Easter, Ester insisted.

"I want to go to La Jolla," she said. "Please, Julius. I've got to get away."

"Have the protestors been bothering you again?"

"No, but I think about them."

"There aren't many at the clinic, either," he said. "They've apparently got some kind of center for pregnant women and they need everyone to run it."

"Good," she said.

Once they reached La Jolla, Ester wanted them to stay there.

"I can't leave my practice, Dove. We couldn't keep up the payments on everything."

Compelling Interests

"You have clinics down here, too."

"But Long Beach is more central."

"Couldn't you commute to Long Beach a few days a week?" she appealed. "You could use the San Diego airport."

"No," he said gently. He wasn't even making it to all his clinics every week as it was.

She cried. So he bought her a house overlooking the beach and he promised to try it. He stayed in La Jolla three days a week, spending his nights with her, and he left Saturday night for Long Beach and Compton, coming back Wednesday—then Thursday, and finally, sometimes, not at all.

But it was all right, he told himself. She had joined the Country Club down there and found some tennis partners. And she had her epiphyllum.

He missed her but he felt better, knowing that she wasn't under the stress she had been under in Long Beach. With Ester happily settled in La Jolla, the stress was off him, too. He wouldn't have her nagging him about his drinking. He had enough demands at work; he didn't need that, he needed her support. But when he had tried to explain that to her, she had cried. She said she was becoming afraid of him—or afraid for him, he wasn't sure which, she got so emotional. Once, to appease her, he had gone with her to her psychiatrist, but as he had expected, it didn't do anything.

The time apart might help her get herself together. New friends, new interests—that would take her mind off trying to change her husband. Anyway, they could always call each other. If they could think of anything to say.

On March 26, 1986, after having informed the police and clinic staff of her intentions, Joan Andrews entered an unoccupied procedure room at the Ladies' Center in Pensacola, Florida, and attempted to unplug the electrical cord on the suction abortion machine—"disarm the murder

Part 5: 1986

weapon," as she put it. She was immediately arrested by waiting officers and carried to a van outside.

The judge let her out on a $20,000 bond. She went right back to the clinic, so he revoked her bond and ordered her to serve her sentence. Two guards came to escort her out of the courtroom—but Joan suddenly announced, "The only way I can protest for unborn children now is by non-cooperation in jail"—and she sat down in the middle of the floor. The guards had to carry her back to Escambia County Jail.

"This is our aim, and goal," she wrote home that week, "to wipe out the line of distinction between the pre-born and their born friends, becoming ourselves discriminated against.

"The rougher it gets for us, the more we can rejoice that we are succeeding. We must become aligned with them completely and totally or else the double standard separating the pre-born from the rest of humanity will never be eliminated.

"Thus I plead a case for complete and total vulnerability in court by refusing self defense and all legal argumentation for *self* protection. We only stand here in their stead, being substitute defendants by a compelling and painful logic. If it is a crime punishable by death to be unwanted, maybe it should be a crime, punishable by death, to love the unwanted and to act to protect them."

"Are you all right?" Tasha asked Mariana with concern.

Mariana sat unmoving, her hands in her lap, her head down.

"Mariana?" Tasha reached out tentatively and touched her shoulder.

"Now I know how they feel," said Mariana, so low Tasha had to lean forward to catch the words. "Now I know how *you* felt." Mariana looked up. "How many times have I stood right where you are and told women what you just told me." She pulled a Kleenex from the dispenser on her desk and dabbed her eyes, then gestured randomly with it.

"And they would cry, just like this." She looked up and tried to laugh through her tears. "They would tell me just what I'm telling you, that I'm

Compelling Interests

34, I already have four kids we can barely afford, that I don't want to go through this again."

Tasha moved behind her and massaged Mariana's shoulders gently. "And remember what you tell them? You tell them to wait. Just wait nine months. What you feel when you first find out you're pregnant will totally change when you hold your baby in your arms. Remember?"

Tasha was business manager of Lifeline Mothers Home. She had taken courses in accounting and she handled the bookkeeping, and did it well. At least on paper, she had a salary, although whether or not any of the staff actually received one on the first of each month depended on what contributions had come in. She seemed to have more self-respect than when Mariana had met her—she wasn't drifting aimlessly from event to event and from relationship to relationship as she had been.

There were also two fulltime housemothers. But it was Mariana everyone wanted to talk to. It was Mariana's opinion everyone wanted.

Mariana and Paul had mortgaged their home to help put the down payment on the maternity home. Just after Mariana found out she was pregnant, Paul was promoted to lead man in his company, which worked on the offshore oil islands, but Mariana confided to Tasha that she and Paul had talked it over and agreed to use the extra money for the "moms," even though it meant a *lower* standard of living for themselves.

Every Wednesday morning at the maternity home, Mariana and Tasha and the two housemothers, Irene and Carol, gathered with all the pregnant women for prayer in the sitting room on the second floor.

First they discussed the latest needs. "Mariana, we've been out of bread and milk for a couple of days," one girl pointed out. "I'll walk over to the store, if you'll give me some money."

"I wish I could," sighed Mariana. "We're out of money."

"But it's only the 18th!"

"God knows what we need," said Mariana.

Part 5: 1986

"Does he know we're out of baby powder, too?" asked a Cuban girl rocking a chunky baby.

"I've got some," said one who looked due to deliver anytime. "You'll need it sooner than I will. And could all of you please pray that this baby will *hurry up?*"

The others laughed.

"And," in a more serious voice, "Pray for me to know whether I should keep it or not."

A new resident said she was homesick and having morning sickness. The Cuban girl moved over so she could put an arm around her. "I felt like that, too," she said. "But now this is more like home to me than my real home."

Then they prayed in brief sentences, taking turns.

"Lord, we know you own everything in the world and you control all things. We ask you to provide the money you know we need to pay this month's bills."

"Father God, thank you for bringing me to this home and thank you for the friends I've met here."

"Lord Jesus, give us each a good day. Help us to do what pleases you. Strengthen Mariana and give her good judgment about each decision she has to make today. Help her to know which women to let come here. Bless all the women who come into the testing center today. If they are pregnant, let them know someone cares and will help them—"

Just then the doorbell rang and Mariana slipped out of the room, whispering to Tasha as she left, "It's probably the insurance man. He says we need more liability insurance. Pray."

So Tasha prayed aloud for God's will regarding liability insurance—but before she was through, Mariana burst back into the room, her face radiant.

"It's a church delivering a truckload of groceries! They told me there are *seven hundred* sacks of them!"

The prayer meeting was put on hold with a quick, "Praise the Lord!" and everyone rushed downstairs to help unload the truck and prove for themselves that God's provision included bread and milk.

Compelling Interests

Those who reassembled an hour later were in a great mood. They took turns thanking the Lord.

"I have a request," said one of the residents. "You remember Lorece? She had her baby and kep' it. I met her jus' before she move' out. She was doin' so well, the court give her other little boy back from the foster home."

"I remember Lorece," said Irene. "How's she doing?"

"Not so good. She say she back on drugs."

"Oh, no!"

"The court say they goin' to take her children away again."

"Let's pray for her!"

"That brings up something I want us to pray about," said Mariana. "Some of our moms have found it really hard to go from here to living on their own. Six months isn't enough time to learn how to raise a child and—well, just stay off the street. We need a place where women can live after they leave here that's close enough so they can still come to our classes and Bible studies and get help when they need it.

"Tasha and I have been going over the budget. I know humanly speaking it's crazy, but I want to pray about buying the apartment house next door."

"Right next door? The crack house?" asked Carol, pointing at the window.

"Yes," said Mariana. "They have six units. Mothers who wanted to keep their babies could move there and still feel like they're a part of Lifeline. They'd have built-in babysitters while they finish high school or train for a job."

"Can't hurt to pray about it," said Carol.

Tasha was jotting down the requests. Now she added one of her own. "Pastor Joe and his wife have been told they can't house pregnant women in their church anymore."

"Who's Pastor Joe?" someone asked.

"He's head of The Nest, that Pentecostal church on the west side. He and his wife adopted two of the babies born here before they started taking moms into their church. The city said the church isn't zoned for

Part 5: 1986

people to stay there—and it's unsanitary. But we're full and they have no place else to go."

Irene said slowly, "Wasn't he the one who was in the papers not long ago?"

"Yes—"

"What for?" asked Carol.

"He told his congregation to pray—when Justice Weiss was visiting Los Angeles—pray that he'd die."

"*Die?* Why?"

"So we could get someone on the Supreme Court who would vote down Roe. v. Wade. He sure got blasted by the press for it."

"Praying for someone to die—that seems a little extreme," said Tasha.

"I know just how he feels," said Irene. "He gets really emotional because he knows a lot of the women who have ended up in WEBA."

"What's WEBA?" asked the Cuban girl. Her baby had fallen asleep in her arms.

"Women Exploited by Abortion. It was started by Nancyjo Mann about four years ago and it's all over the world now. I think they had something like 15,000 members in the first two years," said Irene.

"Nancyjo had complications from a saline abortion and had to have a total hysterectomy when she was 22. She said as soon as the doctor injected the saline, she could feel the baby start to thrash around and it fought for an hour and a half. Then she went into labor and delivered a beautiful little girl, about five and a half months along. Dead."

"How awful."

"It was. She said the doctor lied to her. He told her she would have 'severe cramps' but it was actually twelve hours of hard labor."

Carol, the other housemother, had been listening. "Irene and I are both members of WEBA," she said, pushing her heavy blonde hair back from her forehead. "I had two abortions. The first time, I was single and I had a D&C. I slept through it. The second time, I was married and we had two kids. We couldn't afford another one. I went to a KASAL clinic and they did a suction abortion on me even though I was four months along.

Compelling Interests

"This time I was awake and I saw the nurse's face when the baby was sucked out. She looked really startled and she said, 'It was a boy!' Afterward, the look on her face and those words haunted me. I went through depression and guilt. I took drugs. I even tried suicide."

Irene said, "I was eighteen and I didn't even suspect I was pregnant. I went to KASAL because I had an infection and the nurse ran a routine pregnancy test. When she told me my test was positive, she made it sound like being pregnant was even more disgusting than having an infection. She talked me into an abortion.

"Everyone in the clinic kept telling me it was simple, I wouldn't feel any pain. That was the biggest lie. The doctor used these dilators that ripped up my cervix. It hurt horribly and they didn't give me anything for the pain.

"Then he stuck the vacuum aspirator inside me and turned it on. It had this piercing sound, like a fork grating across the bottom of a sink.

"The doctor kept smearing bloody bits of the fetus and the placenta on the sheet and telling me it was 'just a blob of jelly.' He said, 'See, there's no baby,' and I yelled, 'Of course not. You just ground it to hamburger!'

"How gross!" said one of the pregnant moms who had been knitting quietly.

"Then when he was all done," Irene went on, "he gave me this funny look and said, 'If your husband found you in this position, you'd probably get pregnant all over again.' I could have killed him."

Everyone was sober for a minute.

"We'd better pray," said Mariana. Half an hour later, when the prayer time ended, she excused herself and went down to her office. Tasha and the housemothers stood up and stretched and were about to leave, when one of the young women said, "Irene and Carol, do you ever wonder what the doctors did with—with—you know—"

"The fetus?" asked Carol.

"Yes. What happens to all those fetuses?"

"You really want to know? At some clinics, they throw them into a dumpster!"

"Yuck!"

Part 5: 1986

"I have an article in my room about a clinic in Chicago. I'll go get it."

"Get the article about the fetuses they found in Washington, DC," suggested Irene.

As Carol slipped out the door, Irene asked Tasha, "Did you read about them?"

"You mean all the ones in that storage box in Woodland Hills?"

"No, this was recent. Joseph Sobran wrote about it: some of them were eight inches long, without any heads. He said they'd had their blood drained out and they smelled like formaldehyde. He said one little girl still had part of her face. Her tongue was like a little white tab hanging out, and her eyes bulged."

The women were shaking their heads in revulsion.

Tasha asked, "Whatever did happen to the fetuses that man, Weisberg, had in the storage box in Woodland Hills? Weren't there over sixteen thousand of them? Last I heard WomanPower had some kind of court order to block their burial."

"The pro-lifers got permission to bury them last September or so," said the woman. "The court said it was OK as long as the county didn't hold any memorial service for them and if they removed all the mother's and doctors' names."

The other housemother was back.

"Here, I found them both. The one from Chicago is about the Michigan Avenue Medical Center. Joe Scheidler is a pro-life activist back there—he trains people to shut down clinics any way they can. Anyway, he and this Monica Miglorino who wrote the article found 43 plastic bags in a box in the trash." She held the clipping up so she could get better light on it and adjusted her glasses.

"It says, 'Each bag contained the mutilated body of an aborted baby, complete with placenta and uterine tissue.... Though many of the children were quite small, one could plainly see through the plastic their little arms, legs, hands, feet, rib cages, spinal columns, eyes (often out of the sockets), and sometimes even heads and faces.'"

At this, the pregnant girl leaped to her feet and headed for the door.

Compelling Interests

"I'll see if she's all right," offered Carol, following her out.

"Here's Sobran's article." Irene handed it to Tasha. "I won't read it aloud. It's even grosser."

Tasha read it silently. Sobran was describing a male fetus: "The lower half of his body is pretty much intact. From the waist up there is only the naked spinal cord, plus the right shoulder, arm and hand. His legs are spread apart, with the knees bent...you notice his genitals, his calf muscles and his feet. His toes are curled tensely upward, as if he died in the middle of a spasm. You could see and smell the fresh blood." Tasha looked up.

"Sickening, isn't it?" asked Irene.

"It sounds like the death camps in Germany."

Again they were silent, each thinking her own thoughts.

Then Tasha asked, "Are any of these doctors ever convicted of murder or manslaughter or anything for the late-term ones? I think some of the ones Weisberg had aborted were up to 7-1/2 months old."

"No one was convicted of anything," said Irene.

"I thought charges were filed against him."

"They had to drop all the charges," said Carol. "Under Roe v. Wade, abortion is legal all the way up until birth."

On the ground floor of Seaside General Hospital in Long Beach was the laboratory. All fetuses aborted up on the maternity floor were placed in basins and transported to the ground floor, where technicians weighed and measured them.

Two male technicians were there now, one of them Laurel's fiancé. Jamal was stretching a tape measure from the gaping hole where the head had been to the rump.

"How can I measure crown to rump when the head's gone?" he grumbled.

"Estimate," said Roger, without looking up from the rows of bottles on the stainless steel counter in front of him.

Jamal was quiet for a minute, measuring.

Part 5: 1986

"Bummer!" he said at last. "This one's too big, even without the head. Aren't they only supposed to be up to 11 inches? This one's 14. I can't put that down!"

Roger glanced over at his partner. "Well, sure it'll be too big if you stretch it out like that. Kind of compress it."

"We're not supposed to do that."

"I know, but if it's too long, what are you gonna do? Send it upstairs and tell the doctor, 'Put it back in?' Doctors can't always judge that accurately when the women are about five months along. And sometimes they do 'em anyway, hospital policy or no policy." He pulled a large jar toward him and unscrewed the top, wrinkling his nose as the smell of formaldehyde assailed him.

"You oughta see this one," he said. "Came yesterday. Must have been a hysterotomy because it's still intact. If saline had been used, the skin would be peeling off."

"Where do they go after we're through with them?" asked Jamal.

"Landfill. That's what happens to all of them, eventually. The doctors usually put the small ones in buckets and keep them in the freezer until the buckets are full, unless we're going to use the tissue later—then they come down to us. A truck comes once a month, hauls everything away and incinerates them with all the other infectious waste. Two thousand degrees will reduce anything to ash.

"Over 100 kilograms of infectious waste, a facility is supposed to have them burned. Clinics don't bother with that. They just bag 'em up in red plastic bags and toss 'em in a dumpster." Roger pulled over a stool and straddled it.

"We don't always burn them, either. Sometimes they do what's called autoclaving, which is a kind of steaming, to sterilize them. Autoclaving will melt plastic and stuff but it won't do anything to fetuses. It just makes them a bloody mess. Then they're compacted and hauled to the dump."

"Are there incinerators around here?" asked Jamal.

"Sure. Tarzana. Garden Grove. I've been to the one in Garden Grove. Big warehouse. Two smokestacks. Whole place was filthy and knee-deep

Compelling Interests

in soot. Smelled like—I don't know—musty like a basement but worse, like a sewer. They just punch a button and—presto, Auschwitz."

Roger reached into the jar he had opened and lifted something between his thumb and forefinger. He held it out, dripping, toward Jamal. They could both see the tightly closed eyes, the fine hair, the delicate mouth. "The doctor told me to write down 22 weeks for this one. That's closer to seven months, I don't care what he says."

He dropped it back into the jar disgustedly and wiped his hands on his smock. "I wish they'd stop sending us these."

In July, Joan wrote to her parents from Escambia County Jail, "The trial went very well. I'm sure you have already heard the news: I was only found guilty of a third degree burglary, and was acquitted of assault, and then was found guilty of two other remaining misdemeanors. It looks like I'll be here at least until September 24, and I hope I'll receive time served at that time. If not, it will not be an outrageous sentence, as was possible before. All is still in God's hands. Maybe between now and September 24 I will be released on personal recognition bond. It's not likely, but there is always a chance...I love all of you very much. I'm doing fine. God bless you, dearest Daddy and Mama. Love."

AP story by Bill Kaczor, *Pensacola News Journal*, 9 August 1986—"A woman convicted of invading an abortion clinic was kept in jail Friday after she again refused to promise she wouldn't repeat her crime...In rejecting post conviction bail, [Judge] Anderson said Andrews, who has been arrested more than 100 times in similar cases, was a danger to the community and the victims because it was likely she again would violate the law....The judge also said she doesn't have any ties to Pensacola and that the only reason she came here was to break the law."

Los Angeles reporters asked local attorney Liz Tewksbury to comment on Andrews' sentence.

"I'm relieved," said Tewksbury. "I just hope this increases the understanding that the law of this land must be adhered to."

Part 5: 1986

Joan went to court for sentencing on September 24. Escambia Court Judge William Anderson addressed her lawyer. "I was hoping you were going to come here today and say Miss Andrews has changed her mind about what she's going to do with her life. She and her supporters skip around the country spewing hatred rather than doing something constructive. It's a shame Miss Andrews has chosen to waste her life in prison instead of accomplishing something."

Florida guidelines recommended a year to thirty months for convicted burglars. Judge Anderson gave her five years in Florida's maximum security prison for women... . Later that day he gave four-year sentences to two men convicted of being accessories to murder.

FLORIDA CORRECTIONAL AT LOWELL, 24 October 1986—In a letter to her parents, Joan wrote, "I am sorry that I was not allowed to have a visit with you, Mama, when you came to the prison.

"When I was being brought back to my quarters, I tried to look for you. I was able to see part of the parking lot from the walkway the officer took while escorting me back, but I didn't see the family car, nor you... To think of you being only a few yards away. So close. I said my rosary when I got back to my cell and asked God to give you and John a safe trip home.

"Please don't worry about my weight...I have been eating normally except for my two days fasting per week...

"I love all of you so very, very much, and you are constantly in my thoughts and prayers. God bless you and keep you and may the Mother of God hold you close to her Immaculate Heart. All my love."

Syndicated column by Joseph Sobran, 28 November 1986—"It's hard to believe that if she had actually broken into a house and stolen a TV set, she'd have gotten five years. But Miss Andrews was trying to prevent abortions from being performed, as is her habit, so the judge threw the book at her...

Compelling Interests

"Miss Andrews is serving her term in a maximum security prison in Lowell, Fla. She is a surpassingly gentle woman, single at the age of 38... but the other inmates are tough, violent lawbreakers, and Miss Andrews has been told that she will be lucky to live through five years in the place. It's that violent...

"The judge who did the sentencing justified the stiff term by observing that Miss Andrews was 'unrepentant.' She would neither promise to stop doing rescues nor pay retribution to the abortionists. Granted, we want criminals to display contrition, and this mitigates our desire to punish them. But all this rests on the assumption that the positive law and the moral law are in alignment. Murder is both wrong and illegal. We expect the murderer to repent.

"But what if murder were legal? Would someone, then, who interfered with a murder by illegal means be expected to 'repent' in order to receive clemency?...Joan Andrews is evidence that an immoral law can't be workable. Legalizing abortion has made lawbreakers out of otherwise law-abiding people...but when such people act on their convictions, the legal authorities are expected to treat them as criminals, to incarcerate them with hardened criminals, and even to sentence them more harshly than criminals are usually sentenced...

"It is grotesque for an agent of the state to demand of her a display of conscience. Joan Andrews has shown her conscience in acts of courage and sacrifice. The state has shown no more conscience than an abortionist. It is her prosecutors and judges who should repent."

When solitary confinement and denying her Mass didn't break Joan, she was transferred from Lowell to Broward Correctional Institute in Miami, the maximum security prison for Florida's most dangerous female inmates.

When business at Family Services permitted, Laurel filled in as receptionist and paid bills. She was instructed to open all non-personal letters and use her discretion regarding them, answering all she could and

Part 5: 1986

signing Dr. Guy's name. She passed on to Julius only what needed his attention.

In May, she slit open a letter from the local Republican Party headquarters and found herself reading a letter more personal than she had expected.

"Dear Dr. Guy:" it started. "We received your donation in the amount of one thousand dollars and are returning it." She looked at the check, re-read the envelope, went back to the beginning of the letter and read it again. "—and are returning it. We do not believe that accepting money made through the performance of abortions is consistent with our party's stand on the sanctity of unborn life."

She took the letter to Janice and had her read it. "I opened this by mistake," she said. "What shall I do with it?"

"Give it to him," said Janice curtly.

"I wish there were some way I could seal it up so he won't know I read it."

Laurel left the letter in Dr. Guy's office, marking it "Opened by mistake." He never mentioned it directly but she found a scribbled memo the next morning instructing her to let him handle all his mail from now on. She noticed, as the days went by, that he was letting the letters pile up on his desk, untouched.

Joan glanced over at the woman who had been placed in the prison bus next to her. The woman was shackled with handcuffs attached to waist chains, which pinned her hands close to her sides.

"I won't make it," the woman was mumbling. "Broward is the worst! They call it Devil's Island! I won't survive even a year." She suddenly shouted, "*I'll take my own life first!*"

Joan waited until she quieted. "My name's Joan. What's yours?" asked Joan.

"Pat."

"What's your sentence, Pat?"

Compelling Interests

"Eight to ten. For murder. But I won't make it that long. Look at the quality of life in prison. I can't stand it!"

"With gain time," soothed Joan, "you'll be out in three or four. You can bear a few hard years, can't you, for a better life only four years ahead?"

"Prison changes you," said the restless woman darkly. "It makes you into an animal, a miserable creature. I won't live that way!" She studied Joan curiously. "How long have you been in?"

"Eight months."

"Then you know. You've been in as long as I have. It has changed you, hasn't it?"

Joan didn't answer. *Yes,* she thought, *it has changed me, but for the better! I am a better person now because of prison, through God's mercy and grace.* But she didn't say so aloud. Talking about her own joy to someone so miserable might be cruel.

The woman broke the silence one last time.

"What'd you get?"

"Five years."

"What for?"

"Trying to prevent murder."

"What makes you think you might be pregnant?" asked the woman behind the desk. Through the windows of the trailer, brought on campus to house the new clinic, Stephanie could see familiar groups of students clustered at lockers, laughing, talking, teasing. That was the real world. This, the one in which she sat so awkwardly, seemed alien.

"How long overdue is your period?" prompted the nurse again.

"About two weeks."

"Were you on birth control?"

"Yes—well, not really. Like, I had it but I didn't always—I didn't think we'd—"

"The pill?"

"Yes."

Part 5: 1986

"You need to follow the instructions exactly," said the nurse, "or it isn't effective."

"I know," said Stephanie miserably.

"Well, we'll go over that later," said the nurse. "Let's get a urine sample."

"I brought one this morning," said Stephanie. "The woman over the phone said to get it first thing in the morning."

"Good," said the nurse. She looked at Stephanie's chart. "Oh, yes, here—" She laced her fingers and looked Stephanie in the face.

"The results were positive," she said.

Stephanie felt numb—and small—and scared.

"Would you like to schedule an abortion?" the woman was asking. "How about next Tuesday?"

Stephanie's mind whirled. "Oh, no, I couldn't!"

"Thursday?"

"No, I mean—I can't be pregnant!"

"Honey, I'm afraid you are." The nurse allowed herself to look sympathetic for an instant. "It's still very early. The procedure is very common and it's easier than having your tonsils removed."

"But what will my mother say?"

"You don't need to tell your mother," assured the nurse. "We can schedule the procedure and get you excused from school. We have a van that can take you there."

"My mother doesn't believe in abortion!" said Stephanie.

"Your mother isn't getting one," said the nurse smoothly. "Are you ready for motherhood? Dirty diapers, the whole bit? Have you thought about what raising a baby will mean? You'd have to drop out of school. You'd probably end up on welfare and you'd be saddled with a child you'd always resent because it made you miss out on life.

"Besides," she patted Stephanie's hand, "it isn't a baby yet. It's just tissue."

"I don't know," said Stephanie. "My mother always said abortion was wrong."

Compelling Interests

"You don't have to be against something just because your mother is. Only you know what's best for you. It's your body, Stephanie. Shall we make it Tuesday?"

The bus headed for Broward drove all day. At one point, the woman struggled against her manacles so that Joan feared she was going to lose control of herself and become violent and hysterical but she finally fell into a listless stupor and stared out the window unseeing, closed off in her misery.

Broward. Unless God intervened, Joan would be spending five birthdays here, five Christmases. *If I spend all five years here,* she thought, *I won't get out till I'm 43. I wish they'd let me see Mama and Papa. I miss them so. And all my nephews and nieces.*

She thought back to her first kiss from a man, five years before. *I wish I could be married,* she sighed. *I want children so badly—lots of children, maybe adopted kids, handicapped kids—and I'm getting older and older. But at least I have known love and at least I have been held. And maybe that's enough.*

FORT LAUDERDALE, FLORIDA, lead editorial in *News/Sun Sentinel*, 29 November 1986—"Thousands of supporters of jailed anti-abortion activist Joan Elizabeth Andrews have been jamming radio talk-show phone lines, bombarding prison officials and Governor Bob Graham with calls and letters and planning huge protest rallies in an effort to get her a pardon.

"Their cause is unjust. Andrews is unworthy of their support, and their pleas should be ignored. Andrews, a Broward Correctional inmate, should not be shown any leniency...

"During commission of her crime, after her arrest and even after her trial, Andrews made it clear that she was on a crusade to protect unborn children, and that matters like people's private property and privacy rights and the law weren't about to get in her way. Originally sentenced to the medium-minimum security Florida Correctional Institution at Lowell,

Part 5: 1986

Andrews refused to follow orders or cooperate with prison officials, saying that to do so would be an admission of guilt. Because of that, she was sent to [Broward], a close-custody prison. There, she refused to be fingerprinted or complete her processing, so she has been placed in solitary confinement.

"Andrews may regard herself as some kind of martyr to a holy cause, but in reality she is just another of society's misfits who hasn't learned to respect other people's rights or to abide by the law. Governor Graham and Governor-elect Bob Martinez should resist the pressure for leniency and let Andrews serve her full term in jail."

As an interesting contrast, the lead editorial in the same newspaper on 2 December, 1986 defended a man accused of first-degree murder: "Roswell Gilbert says he killed his wife Emily in an act of mercy. Now he is seeking mercy for himself. He deserves it. Governor Bob Graham and Florida's six state Cabinet members should vote to grant Gilbert executive clemency Thursday."

Editorial in *Pensacola News Journal*, 30 November 1986—"Saturday's violent confrontation between police and pro-life protestors is an especially frightening development not because of what happened but because of what did not happen. As the level of violence and contempt for law in these pro-life marches escalates the chances of someone getting seriously injured or even killed greatly increases...That's exactly what is going to happen if these so-called pro-life marches continue to be led by professional, out-of-town protestors whose singular goal is to precipitate violent confrontations, attract publicity, and generate a never-ending list of jailed martyrs.

"This is a city of enlightened, tolerant, peace-loving people, who respect law and order as well as the right to peacefully protest. But when professional rabble-rousers and demagogues deliberately besmirch this city's good name and show their callous contempt for its laws, police officers, and judiciary, then the time has come to enforce the law to its fullest and punish those who deserve punishment."

"Broward," wrote Joan, "certainly looks more like one's idea of a real prison than Lowell did...you should see the landscape in which Broward is set. It's surrounded by desolate brush and land and the prison is isolated by itself in the barren wasteland.

"Inside the close-custody building everything looks stark and brutal. Death Row and the Reception and Orientation (R&O) quarters occupy one wing, and then behind two locked doors is the confinement lock-up of Disciplinary Confinement and Administrative Confinement (DC & AC) inmates.

"When I informed the R&O sergeant that I could not cooperate, things got a little ruffled for a while. A crew of staff came in. Finally the lieutenant in charge gave me a tour of the confinement wing to scare me into changing my mind. He kept saying, 'You'll be behind these locks for five years,' and 'This is a maximum security prison, not a jail... I have my roughest inmates in here...' I told him he had to handle the situation the way he saw best, but that I had to do what I had to do...

"Finally they had a big conference, while I waited out near the death row cells. Then the lieutenant and a sergeant took me to the medical building to be checked out by a psychiatrist to see if I was crazy...he turned to the two officers and answered their questions about my sanity by saying: 'No, she's not crazy nor mentally ill. She simply has very strongly held beliefs. She's perfectly normal.' And that was that."

There was a lot of graffiti on the walls, mostly obscene, but Joan was able to blacken out most of the worst. The floor was concrete. The cement-block walls of the cell were also polka-dotted and be-smudged with white and green toothpaste blotches where former occupants had stuck up pictures. This was against the rules, so Joan hadn't attempted to do so.

With her in the cell, she had her Bible, her breviary, and her rosary. She and another inmate read Scripture to each other and took turns praying aloud through their doors, and sometimes others joined them. It was difficult to hear for the noise.

Editorial in *Pensacola News Journal*, 7 December 1986—"Today's anti-abortionists are not arrested for peacefully marching in the streets. They are arrested when they commit crimes. The crimes they commit are no technical violations designed to challenge the law: they are crimes against people and property. When they are arrested, they are subdued with no

Part 5: 1986

more force than is absolutely necessary. When they are jailed, their rights are respected. And when they are sentenced, they are treated with just as much leniency as they deserve... They ought to take out every fanatic in the world and shoot him down like a dog."

Over Thanksgiving weekend, something new happened. Four hundred people gathered in front of the Pensacola clinic where Joan had been arrested eight months before. Joan's mother Elizabeth, 68, was one of them.

"We prayed and sang," she told friends in Lewisburg afterward. "The newspapers called it a riot."

It may not have been a riot but there had been a commotion when a truck tried to drive into the crowd. Some people remained in prayer. Others scattered. Elizabeth fell to her knees and felt herself lifted by a policeman at each elbow. Hoisting her in the air, they announced, "You're under arrest!"

The family priest was standing nearby.

"What should I do, Father?" asked Elizabeth, suspended in mid-air.

"You'll have to follow your own conscience," he replied.

"Then I'll cooperate," Elizabeth announced and as the police set her down, she let them escort her to their car in a more dignified manner.

Other members of the rally and vigil, seeing that Joan's mother had been arrested, knelt in front of the patrol car to prevent it from leaving. Mrs. Andrews leaned out the window.

"Let the car proceed," she told them. "This is an honor."

Something else happened in Pensacola that November. Several pro-life leaders met at Sizzler's Steak House to develop a strategy for blockading abortion clinics nationwide. They decided to call it Operation Rescue.

The waiting room of Family Services in Anaheim was crowded when Stephanie finally kept her appointment clutching her paperwork from the school nurse. She had re-scheduled it three times. She was barely aware that several other girls were in the waiting room already, some even younger than she was.

Compelling Interests

A woman in white came out to tell them all, "If you haven't signed this form, we cannot do surgery. This is a waiver absolving us of responsibility in the case of complications. The procedure is very safe, much safer than pregnancy and childbirth. Dr. Guy has been doing them for years and has had almost no patients who developed problems—but if you should have any bleeding or any questions in the next few days, please return to us.

"Note that on the green sheet we have given you, it stresses that we have 24-hour emergency care available. If you need help, please *do not* go to a hospital or to another physician. It will only cost you unnecessary money. We specialize in pregnancy termination and we have the greatest experience in handling the occasional post-operative problems.

"Often patients going to other doctors may be advised that they need a repeat D & C because of retained tissue, even if they don't. So *please* return to us and if we need to repeat the aspiration procedure, it will take only 30 seconds and we will charge you nothing. If you permit yourself to be admitted to a hospital, you will probably pay $1500 to $3000, which is totally unnecessary.

"Are there any questions?"

Stephanie couldn't think of a question that wouldn't sound dumb in front of all the other girls. Besides, she was trembling so much, she wasn't sure she could speak.

When at last she was called into the procedure room, she was having a hard time keeping back her tears. This was the scariest thing she had ever done in her life—and she was having to do it alone. Would Justin have come if she'd asked? Or—or her mother?

"Cold hands, warm heart," joked the nurse, settling her in the short gown on the gurney. "This shot will relax you and when you wake up, it will all be over."

I don't want to be here. I don't want to be here! Stephanie's mind pounded.

When she woke up, she felt nauseous, as if someone had slugged her in the stomach. A nurse was saying, "This one's bleeding bad." Then, seeing Stephanie was conscious, "Oh! Hi, there! You can go back to school whenever you feel ready. The bleeding will stop in a few hours."

Part 5: 1986

"Steffie," said her mother, knocking gently at her bedroom door. "May I come in?" A pause. "It's important."

"Okay, Mom." Stephanie's voice sounded muffled.

Artyce opened the door tentatively. "Can I talk to you?"

Stephanie shrugged, not looking at her.

No matter how often she reminded herself that this was a stage Stephanie was going through, that she had treated her own mother the same way, Artyce Lancaster still felt uneasy with her daughter. Stephanie seemed sullen. *She doesn't respect me,* thought Artyce. *I need to be more confident, more positive. I didn't respect my mother, either, when she was wishy-washy.*

"You're seeing a lot of Justin, aren't you?" she said aloud.

Stephanie didn't answer. She sat on her unmade bed, trying not to remember what had happened five hours earlier. Her stomach hurt and she knew she was still bleeding. The nurse had said it would stop.

"You know," her mother said awkwardly, "this is hard for me. My mother never talked with me about sex, but I think you have a right to know—"

Stephanie waited, not offering her mother a seat beside her on the bed, not making it easier.

"When two people spend a lot of time together—if they love each other—you need to be careful, honey. Sex should be saved for marriage." She licked her lower lip, groping for the right words. "It's an act that binds a man and woman together as one. It's not something you can do with just anyone—at least a woman can't."

She formed her shapely hands into a circle. "It's part of a whole context, a whole life of commitment and trust and—*you* know," she broke off, smiling at Stephanie, letting her tensed shoulders relax. "I know you're a smart girl and I know you and Justin will keep your feelings for each other under control—won't you?" The last words were pleading. She reached out to pat Stephanie's hand and Stephanie knew the one she was trying to reassure.

Compelling Interests

Stephanie looked her mother in the face and with an effort tried to bridge across the chasm into her mother's world. "Of course, Mom. We'll be careful."

That night Stephanie woke suddenly, aware that a pain had been growing inside her for some time. It was severe now, a demanding, unrelenting pain like nothing she had ever felt before. She had never felt so hot and her head throbbed. The bleeding, which the nurses had assured her would stop, must be worse—the sheets and her nightgown were wet and the hand she had had under her stomach when she went to sleep felt sticky. She must be dying!

"Mom!" she said, but it came out in a whisper. "Mom!"

Did she dare move? So scared that her breath was coming in ragged little moans, Stephanie worked her way cautiously to the side of the twin bed and tried to lower her legs over the edge. When her toes touched the carpet, she was afraid to put her weight on them. Instead, she pushed herself off and tumbled to the floor. She began crawling, doubled over, toward where the door should be.

There was something in the way, something big and hard, that shouldn't be there. She tried to crawl over it and as it toppled sideways under her weight, she realized in a rush of recognition that it was her rocking chair. In her pain and panic, she had crawled too far to the left.

Stephanie's long hair hung tangled in her face, some of it across her mouth, where fear had blended perspiration and a string of saliva. She curled up into a fetal position, holding her abdomen and whimpering into the darkness.

It was afternoon when she awoke again, this time to full daylight. She was in a hospital bed and her mother was in a chair by her side, looking intently into her face.

"Steffie? Are you feeling better?"

She didn't know. She stirred—and winced.

Part 5: 1986

Her mother's figure blocked out the light as she leaned down and put her cheek to Stephanie's.

"I was so scared, honey."

"So was I, Mom!" Her voice was weak. "I tried and tried to call you and I couldn't."

"The doctor says you lost a lot of blood but you're going to be all right."

"I was bleeding all over."

"I know. They had to give you a transfusion." Mom was the strong one for a change; this time her reassurance was genuinely for Stephanie.

Stephanie compressed her lips nervously. They felt dry. She still felt like she was burning up. Did Mother know?

As if reading both her thoughts, Mom poured her a partial glass of water, handed it to her with a straw and said,

"The doctors had to do a D&C, too, and you're going to be on antibiotics for a while. Apparently you had an infection from the abortion; the doctor didn't get it all." It was as matter-of-fact as if she'd known all along, but Stephanie knew that was impossible and her next words confirmed it.

"Honey, I didn't have any idea you were pregnant. I didn't know you were even—" she tripped over the words, "sexually active." She smiled ruefully. "Obviously!" Stephanie smiled back, wanly. They were both thinking back to their conversation only the day before.

"We're going to have to talk, Stephanie, but not now. I know you're not up to it. I wish—I just wish I'd known more what was happening in your life and how to help. Oh, Stephanie, you're only fourteen! You're so young for all this adult stuff! This isn't at all what I had dreamed of for you!"

Stephanie handed the glass back and as soon as her mother had set it down, Stephanie reached for her.

"I love you, Mom!" she said, pulling her close and gripping her tightly around the neck. "Please stay with me. I love you so much!"

In the weeks that followed, Stephanie waited for the lecture blaming her for what she had done. Little by little, she relaxed, realizing

Compelling Interests

that it wasn't going to come. Mother seemed sadder and she monitored Stephanie's activities more closely; she worked at better communication between them. But the anger was never directed at Stephanie. She turned it all outward.

The secretaries at Stephanie's high school were taken aback when Stephanie's mother showed up at the office, threatening to sue the school.

"You have no right running an abortion referral service on a high school campus!" she stormed across the counter. "I want to see the principal."

The secretaries hastily summoned him. Mr. Lowell appeared, pretending he hadn't heard the ruckus already through the thin walls.

"I'm going to hold you personally responsible for the fact that my daughter nearly died!" Stephanie's mother began, overriding the secretary's attempted introductions.

Mr. Lowell was all diplomacy. "Would you like to come in and tell me what's the matter?"

"I'm telling you what's the matter! My daughter nearly died from an abortion and she tells me that your staff sent her to get it!"

"Mrs.—uh—"

"Lancaster," offered Stephanie's mother curtly.

"Mrs. Lancaster, I'm sure no one on our staff would tell a student to get an abortion." He swept his hand toward the two secretaries, now looking very busy at their desks. "We wouldn't do that."

"My daughter wouldn't lie to me!" Mrs. Lancaster exclaimed, forgetting that Stephanie had told a whopper the day of the abortion.

"We have a pilot program on campus," went on Mr. Lowell, "a health clinic, which makes available to students information regarding a number of health-related issues, among them birth control and abortion—"

"What makes you think that sex is any of your business?" Mrs. Lancaster demanded, immediately turning bright red because she had said—no, shouted—the word in public. And to a man! "I don't send my daughter here to get 'information about birth control and abortion,'" she went on. "I send her here to learn things like algebra and chemistry! Who gave you permission to set up a clinic on campus to encourage kids to have sex?"

Part 5: 1986

"Mrs. Lancaster," smiled Mr. Lowell, acutely aware of his audience, bent unseeing over their work. "Nobody here encourages kids to have sex. We don't want that any more than you do. But what we *do* want—" and here he frowned, shaking a finger in her face, as Mrs. Lancaster imagined he would do to a naughty puppy, "we do want young people who are already engaging in sex and who aren't going to quit because some grown-up tells them to, to use proper precautions—to prevent the very kind of thing that happened with your daughter."

Stephanie's mother breathed heavily, her face red now with rage. "Now you're telling me it was *her* fault! Well, I am taking you to court, I am taking your so-called clinic to court and I am taking the abortionist to court—" she ticked them off dramatically on her fingers, "for Stephanie's medical expenses, for her emotional trauma, for malpractice, for—for damages, for any complications that may result from this in the future, for endangering the life of a minor—" She had no idea whether one could sue for all these things or not but by golly, she was going to try.

As it turned out, no lawyer would take her case.

"Mrs. Lancaster," one of them told her reasonably. "The law permits any woman to have an abortion, if she wants one."

"She isn't a woman! She's fourteen!"

"For the purposes of the law, she is considered an adult if she is pregnant and wants an abortion."

"That's outrageous! Just because she's capable of becoming pregnant doesn't mean she's mature enough to know the implications of a decision like that."

The lawyer shrugged.

Artyce went on, "It's criminal that at the time a girl needs family counsel the most, she is getting it from strangers who don't know her medical history, don't know her emotional make-up, don't know the family's moral standards. Stephanie was raised with solid values. Don't you think that knowingly violating those values will cause her mental conflict and anguish?"

Compelling Interests

The lawyer was shuffling the papers on his desk. Clearly, even at $100 an hour, he was ready to terminate the interview. But Mrs. Lancaster wasn't.

"Are these people who are so willing to advise other people's daughters regarding an abortion willing to assume financial responsibility for the complications that may result?

"No," said Stephanie's mother, standing up without realizing it, because the lawyer had, "to *them* she's only a referral or a case number. To me, she's *family*. *I'm* the one who cares"—punching her chest with her forefinger—"not them. *I'm* the one concerned about her and what happens to her." A new thought struck her. "And to my grandchild!

"My God," she said, her anger giving way to bewilderment, "the school made me sign forms to let her go to the zoo, sign forms to let her ride to a football game with friends." She brushed the invisible forms away from her face like so many cobwebs. "But they let her get *surgery* without my consent!

"What rights *does* a mother have?"

Unabashed, the lawyer held her blazing eyes with his.

"None."

PART 6
1987–1988

Artyce Lancaster was an angry woman. Stephanie was a sophomore now and they never discussed the abortion—not directly—but Artyce was never emotionally far from it. She took every opportunity to tell whoever she could that allowing minors to have dangerous operations without their parents' knowledge and consent was criminal. The enemy, she told them, was school-based clinics.

"School-based clinics 'solve' teen pregnancies," she told them, "about as well as gasoline 'solves' fires."

She would read to them from *WomanPower,* the monthly magazine put out by the organization of the same name. "'More teen-agers are using contraceptives and using them more consistently than ever before. Yet the number and rate of adolescent pregnancies continues to rise.'

"Even the people who push sex education and school-based clinics," she would add, "say that in areas where contraceptives are given to teenagers, teen pregnancies are significantly higher. According to the National Center for Health Statistics, teen pregnancies have tripled since the government started handing out contraceptives to teens."

She wrote multiple letters to every California legislator and called Washington, DC so often that she had memorized the phone numbers of the White House and the House of Representatives and even knew the names of a couple of the switchboard operators.

Compelling Interests

She became active in Stephanie's schooling, so active that Stephanie was embarrassed.

"Mom, it's not cool," she told her mother. "You're the only mother who's always in the office raggin' on some teacher or some textbook."

"I care about you," Mrs. Lancaster said firmly. "I pay taxes for you to get an education and I have every right to have a say about the content of that education." It was the same voice she used when she spoke at PTA meetings.

"To pay money for people to undermine every value and belief I've taught you over the years is just dumb. The principal and the teachers are accountable to us parents and to the taxpayers. We have a right to know what's going on and a right to do something about it."

"I know," said Stephanie, looking uneasy.

"No girl—*no* girl—should have to go through what you went through and no school board on earth has the right to make them."

Case closed.

ROCHESTER, NEW YORK—Joyce and Barry Burkett had gathered with other Unitarian-Universalists from far and wide for their national convention. For a denomination with an emphasis on harmony and unity, the tense controversy during day sessions and all-night debates was evidence that cooperation doesn't just happen; it may have to be hard-won.

Among the statements to come out of the meeting was a clear reaffirmation of a woman's right to determine whether or not to continue an unwanted pregnancy.

What was startling to Joyce was that the resolution went on to encourage something new and more than a little shocking to church members across the continent, dialogue with the opposition:

"Whereas the issue of abortion is morally complex, with people of strong moral and political conviction on all sides who share some basic values and want fewer abortions and healthy, wanted children and

Part 6: 1987–1988

"Whereas the current polarized environment is not conducive to open discussion...

"Thereby, be it resolved that individuals, congregations, and the whole denomination open discussion with those of different mind and seek opportunities for consensus on shared values."

Of course, Joyce reminded herself, *it's just a recommendation. We don't actually have to do it.*

But after they returned home to Long Beach, Joyce continued to be intrigued by the thought of dialogue with the opposition. What would it be like, sitting down with an anti-abortionist and discussing their differences? Was it even possible?

"Sit down with them?" scoffed a member of their local assembly when Joyce raised the idea after a Sunday service. "Sure! Right after they stop bombing clinics and yelling at pregnant women!"

A woman named Mary, balancing a piece of zucchini bread on a napkin in one hand and a cup of herb tea in the other, objected more sweetly, "I've tried talking to fundamentalists. They just quote a bunch of Scriptures at you. You'll never get them to listen to our side at all."

"But maybe," Joyce pointed out reasonably, "we could listen to theirs."

She thought about it some more, driving home with her husband. "Funny thing, Barry, I don't even *know* any pro-lifers. How do we go about finding some who might be willing to meet with us?"

"There's that woman who's written a couple of anti-abortion letters to the newspaper—Carol Tulaine, is it?"

"Carol Tulaine," said Joyce. "That's a good idea. I'm sure the newspaper will know how to get in touch with her."

At Lifeline Mothers' Home, housemother Carol hung up the phone. Four or five of "your people," the woman had said. What was it the Burketts were suggesting? A series of dialogues on abortion?

Compelling Interests

Dialogue, she thought. *That means no one tries to convert anyone. Can I do that? Can I chat about abortion as if it's just a subject of mutual interest and not a matter of life and death? Can I accept people who disagree with me on this?*

She didn't know. But maybe it was important to find out.

Who should I invite to represent our side? Pro-lifers covered a broad spectrum. A few wanted abortions outlawed without any exceptions and thought women who had them as well as doctors who performed them should be prosecuted as murderers. If there was a distinction between anti-abortionists and pro-lifers, these people were anti-abortionists. They would never come to something like this.

There were those, mostly Catholics, who objected not only to abortion but to all kinds of birth control. *I ought to invite at least one Catholic,* thought Carol. *After all, they were fighting this battle before the rest of us even knew there was a battle to be fought.*

Mariana should be included, of course, and Tasha, the business manager of Lifeline. She herself and Irene could represent women who had had abortions.

At their first meeting in the Burkett's cozy living room there were six pro-choicers and five pro-lifers. Joyce and Barry Burkett, the hosts, introduced the four other members of their church: a high school teacher, a young girl who worked as an aide at Family Services, an ex-priest, and a former Lutheran.

Joyce was a cheerful, bustling woman, Carol thought. Barry seemed more cautious, a stand-back-with-arms-crossed-and-see-how-it-turns-out sort of person. The ex-priest hardly said a word and appeared almost hostile. The teacher was a practical, salt-of-the-earth type and Kim Crnik, the young woman who worked at the clinic, was perky and earnest. Carol liked her immediately.

Then Carol introduced herself, Mariana, Tasha, Irene, and Stu, the contractor who'd put in the sprinkler system at the Home and who had stayed in contact with them.

Joyce read the challenge which had come out of their denomination's national convention. She explained that when she called the local newspa-

Part 6: 1987–1988

per to get a phone number for Carol the editor had been intrigued with the idea, too. He had suggested Joyce and Carol each write a letter to the paper, describing the experiment and what they each thought could come of it.

These preliminaries, with time out for refreshments, filled the evening. They had barely brushed the surface of the various facets of abortion when Joyce poised a pencil over her date book and asked whether the same day next month was OK for everyone. It was.

Walking out to their cars afterwards, Mariana said sadly, "I don't want to come next time, Carol. It's a waste of time. They took us out and played us instead of cards. We were the evening's entertainment. I'm too busy saving lives to have time for 'ecumenical dialogue.'"

Although she was the only one of the pro-lifers who didn't return, Mariana wasn't the only one uncomfortable with the process of "dialogue." Carol found herself less interested in finding commonality than in changing hearts. She told the others privately, "I'm afraid I'll come across as rigid and belligerent, that I'll confirm all their worst stereotypes of 'fundamentalist' and 'right-wing'—but how can there be middle ground? Either the fetus is a person and has rights, or it's not."

That Sunday, Joyce and Barry and the other Unitarian-Universalists who had come to the dialogue met to discuss how it had gone.

"I think it went well, considering," said Joyce. "They're as scared of us as we are of them. It'll take time. But we can't give up. When people get so polarized on an issue that dialogue becomes impossible, there isn't any hope of a solution."

The woman who taught high school agreed. "It would be stupid to jump right into the issue of whether abortion should be legal or not. We need to start with peripheral issues and maybe after we have learned to trust each other, we can dare to tackle the major ones."

Barry Burkett said thoughtfully, "Suppose this were a game and our arguments were cards. Which ones would we be willing to give up in order to play?"

The others looked at him and nodded slowly. Which cards were negotiable?

Compelling Interests

Tasha opened the discussion at the next meeting. She had done some research. "To me, as an African-American woman, this is about civil rights. The Dred Scott decision of 1857 said slaves were property and their owners could buy, sell, or even kill them. Roe v. Wade says unborn babies are property and their mothers can kill them. If I'd lived back then, it would have been just as hard for me to sit down and talk with 'pro-choice' plantation owners as to sit down with all of you. To me it seems unfair to give choice to the slave-owner and not to the slave!"

Carol had brought a new couple, Clay and Kristi. Kristi had gone through a traumatic second pregnancy after an amniocentesis showed that the child had Downs.

Clay told the group, "I wanted my wife to schedule an abortion. I figured she could always get pregnant again."

"I refused," said Kristi. "I told him I wanted the baby, even if it was retarded."

When she was born, Jenny Leanne had surprised them both. She was normal.

"What if we had aborted her?" Kristi asked, with tears in her eyes.

"She's the joy of our lives," added Clay. "I wouldn't trade her for anything."

"I don't have a problem with that," said the teacher to Kristi, "as long as *you're* the one who made the decision. If you had been the one who wanted the abortion, I think you should have been able to have one."

"What if the child *had* been retarded?" asked the ex-priest. "Shouldn't having a child like that be a joint decision on the part of both parents? Both will have to raise it."

Carol was surprised. The man she had felt was hostile made a good point. Her stereotype of pro-choice people was giving way to the realization that they were all individuals, just as pro-lifers were. But Tasha was objecting, "Who has the right to decide that a retarded child doesn't deserve to live?"

"Think of the child's life." Joyce jumped in softly before the ex-priest could speak. "Isn't it selfish to require a child to be born even if he may not have a fulfilling life?"

Part 6: 1987–1988

"Who can know if someone else's life is going to be fulfilling or not?" persisted Tasha. "We can't know that."

One of the Lifeline housemothers added, "Life shouldn't be conditional on our being wanted by someone or on someone else's evaluation of how happy we're going to be."

"I don't see anything wrong with that," spoke up Barry. "What about severe handicaps, where the child will have to be institutionalized all its life?"

Carol said, "There is a difference between 'quality of life' and 'sanctity of life.' Sanctity of life is unconditional. You have worth because you exist. You don't have to earn it by being beautiful or healthy or smart—or normal."

"If a child isn't wanted or if it stands a good chance of being abused, isn't it more pro-life to abort it?" said Barry. His voice was earnest but still respectful. *How* do *these people manage it?* wondered Carol. *Here we are blasting away at them and they're listening politely, not shouting us down. How do they keep their tempers—when I'm on the very edge of losing mine?*

Tasha was saying, "If you can kill a pre-born baby for being retarded, couldn't you kill any baby that was retarded? What if society didn't want people with club feet? Or old people? Or people with dark skin?"

Joyce leaped to her feet. "I think it's time for a break. I have two kinds of cookies in the kitchen. How many would like coffee and how many would like tea?"

The enemy was bigger than Artyce had first imagined. The enemy was sex education. *Girls didn't get pregnant when I was in school,* Artyce thought, *because we didn't fill kids' heads with this stuff. Kids don't need any encouragement to think about sex.*

One girl had gotten pregnant in her high school. Artyce hadn't known her personally but she had heard the rumors. The girl had been spirited away till the whispering had died down and presumably till the baby was born and put up for adoption.

Compelling Interests

What had formerly been done in secret, what had been shameful, what had been merely whispered about, was now spoken of openly and brazenly, even accepted.

Before sex education, teenage pregnancy wasn't a problem, she thought. *Not like today.* The statistics seemed to support her theory. The number of pregnancies, illegitimate births, and abortions was almost directly proportional to the amount of money spent on sex education. One ten-year study had concluded that for every $1 million of federal money given to family planners, about 2,000 extra teen pregnancies could be expected two years later.

She thought about it. *The more sex education we have, the more kids will decide to be sexually active,* she reasoned. *And if a higher number of kids are sexually active, even if they are using birth control, since it isn't fail-safe, a higher number of them will get pregnant.*

What was the solution? Keep them ignorant? Artyce thought long and hard on that one.

What would I have told Stephanie, if I'd known she and Justin were getting so involved? she asked herself. That was easy. *Don't.* Of course that wasn't enough and of course it might not have worked. But what if she had explained *why* kids should wait, why sex was a *marriage* act? There were plenty of good reasons for waiting. Physical and health reasons. Emotional reasons.

It was like playing with matches. You told kids not to play with matches but you also put the matches out of reach. That was the big problem. With a working mother and an empty house, sex hadn't been out of reach for Stephanie.

But that's beside the point, Artyce thought, shaking her head impatiently. *Schools aren't telling kids not to have sex. They aren't telling them to wait.* No, it wasn't the fact of public school sex education that bothered her. It was the content.

Once, while Artyce was washing up the cups after a meeting she had organized to talk to other mothers about the scandals of public school sex education, Stephanie came into the kitchen and stood silently for a moment.

Part 6: 1987–1988

"Mom?" she asked tentatively.

"Yes, honey?"

"You know what you were telling those women—about not understanding kids these days, why so many are having sex?"

"Yes?" Artyce kept working the dishcloth briskly around the inside of a teacup.

"You said it's—like, passion—you know, that they get carried away."

"Yes."

"That's not always it."

Artyce glanced at Stephanie. "What do you mean?"

"It isn't always like that. Some of my friends—well, they talk about sex and it's like—they plan it. It doesn't just happen. They know what they're doing."

Artyce stiffened. "You mean they say, 'I guess I'll just throw my virginity away tonight?'" The words had a bite to them.

Stephanie was quiet.

Artyce tried to control herself and went on, "I guess I really *don't* understand your friends, Stef. I mean, I understand getting carried away by passion more than I understand cold-blooded planning. Don't they realize what they're doing? What they're giving up? What they're risking?" They had been mother and daughter for a minute, but Artyce was raising a wall between them again.

"It's because this society's brainwashing them. Schools and billboards and TV and magazines that say 'Don't wait until marriage. Just wait until it feels right for you.' It's *wrong* and they're deceiving a whole generation with it."

Stephanie started to back slowly from the room. "It's just that it's—sex is no big deal anymore, Mom."

No big deal. Artyce picked up the last cup in soapy hands, which she realized were trembling. No big deal? She jerked the cup toward the faucet, hitting it. The handle came off in her hands. She stood holding the two pieces and felt her face flush with anger.

Compelling Interests

Stephanie didn't see it. She had retreated to the safety of her room. What was it about Mom these days? She was only working part-time now but she seemed to be gone more than ever and when she was home, she was on the phone or had groups of women in the living room.

There were rare occasions when Mom seemed to be trying to recover some of the closeness they'd had in the old days, but Stephanie found herself pulling away. She wasn't sure why. She missed the times they had spent together, reading aloud or walking on the beach. Was it just because she was a teenager that she held her mother at arm's length or was it because she didn't want to risk getting hurt again? Daddy had left. Justin had left. She felt betrayed and used. She just didn't want to let anyone get close.

No big deal. The truth of what Stephanie had told her was confirmed to Artyce a few days later by a speaker on James Dobson's radio program, Focus on the Family. James Dobson was an evangelical Christian with a doctorate in child psychology from USC and considered by many to be the 1980's answer to Dr. Benjamin Spock. Unless she had to be out of town at one of her speaking engagements, Artyce didn't miss his daily half-hour radio program that dealt with all aspects of parenting.

On this particular day, Dobson was interviewing a youth pastor who made the statement, "Sex is no longer relational. It's recreational."

That confirmed what Stephanie had said. The question, of course, was *why?* As she turned this idea over and over in her head, she wondered, *Is it true that kids are growing up faster than they did in my generation? Are they really asking different questions? Or are they asking the same questions kids have always asked—and getting different answers?*

If they were getting different answers, why were they? Surely sex education hadn't just appeared, full-blown, a curriculum which urged children to use birth control and a generation of school administrators who smiled benignly on children engaging in promiscuous sex, behavior which could result in a host of venereal diseases, even AIDS, not to mention more children. It was all part of a larger curriculum.

She had read somewhere that 40 years ago, the ten biggest problems in the public school included talking, gum-chewing, making noise, running in the halls, getting out of line, improper clothing, and not using

Part 6: 1987–1988

the wastebasket. Today the biggest problems in school were rape, robbery, assault, burglary, arson, bombings, murder, and suicide.

She started with Stephanie's textbooks, hoping to come across some clue to it all. Nothing much had changed since Artyce had been in school. Geometry was taught a little differently; science looked harder. But there was an indefinable something. Literature had fewer readings from the classics, more from contemporary works. These readings didn't seem to teach the same values the older ones had. The language was cruder. Writing assignments were more personal.

Artyce looked through several issues of the high school newspaper. The letters were free-thinking. Editorials sometimes got a bit graphic. There was an undercurrent of contempt for the ideas of adults, a disdain for authority. But maybe that was just adolescence. Kids had always been like that, hadn't they? Maybe not high school kids, but certainly in college, students were notorious for throwing over the traces of those who had come before them.

In health class, they were discussing different subjects. Alcohol. Marijuana. Tobacco. The textbooks didn't hesitate to discourage kids from smoking and getting high, Artyce noted. But when they got to sex, the attitude seemed to be "Kids will do it anyway." *What if we took that approach with drugs?* wondered Artyce. *Would we set up a clinic on campus to supply kids with clean needles?*

Then there was physical education. Stephanie's P.E. teacher had announced to the whole class that she was bisexual. Stephanie had reported this to her mother in a rare confidence.

Vaguely, Artyce knew that receiving this confidence without comment, keeping her opinion to herself, would have strengthened her relationship with Stephanie. She knew Stephanie saw her indignation on her daughter's behalf as condemnation of Stephanie's world. But Artyce couldn't help reacting with outrage.

"I don't care what that woman does privately," Artyce had responded tartly. "But she has no business telling impressionable students about it! If she can't keep that part of her life private, she shouldn't be teaching."

Compelling Interests

Artyce brought the subject up again at breakfast the next morning. She had thought it over and changed her mind.

"Even if she acts out her perversions in private, she has no business teaching children at all. A teacher is a role model. There's no way a person can be involved in homosexuality or adultery and not have it affect the values they impart to you kids."

Stephanie ate her cereal in silence.

"Just by telling you she's bisexual, she's telling you it's okay. She's telling you that all behavior is neutral and that irresponsible behavior is as valid a choice as responsible behavior."

The problem was bigger than sex education. The problem was public education.

Stephanie began carefully censoring what she reported to her mother. During Careers Week, Stephanie told her about the secretary and the flight attendant and the CPA who spoke to the class. She didn't mention the fact that her social studies teacher had also had a prostitute come to class and discuss her "career choice."

When one of Stephanie's friends, a girl her mother knew well and who often came to their house, confided after a class discussion of "lifestyles" that she thought she might be gay because she liked looking at other girls' "boobs" in the shower after gym class, Stephanie kept it to herself.

In a state-issued prison shirt with "J. Andrews" and her prison number, 151909, printed in ink over the left pocket, blue denim pants, white socks, and brown loafers, Joan Andrews sat cross-legged on the floor of her yellow-brown cell and addressed a letter to her friend and lawyer, using her knee to support her paper. It might have been more comfortable on her bed but on the lower bunk there wasn't enough light to write by and on the upper, which was closer to the single fluorescent tube in the ceiling, she couldn't sit up, so there was nothing solid to write on.

"I'm afraid the devil has been attacking me bitterly in here these last two months," she wrote. "It seems that all I want to do every waking mo-

Part 6: 1987–1988

ment is pray—and yet my prayers are so weak and distracted. I am sure it is emotional and psychological exhaustion, not physical, but it is hard to deal with. I trust God totally of course. Who could not! And yet, I can't seem to serve Him and be at least somewhat holy—though I certainly want to be. The problem is that I've allowed myself to succumb to unguarded thoughts. There is so much obscenity abounding, and it is all I hear."

Last night the noise had been so deafening, a lieutenant had threatened to put everyone on the confinement block into strip cells. When the noise continued unabated, the guards had started stripping cells bare—sheets, blankets, mattress, clothes, personal items, even toilet paper. That quieted most of the inmates.

Joan adjusted the piece of paper on her right knee, which was starting to hurt, and went on, "Please understand, I am not making excuses. At Lowell, the environment was just as oppressive, but I dwelled in God's grace and never knew such bliss and heavenly joy.

"I long for the joy and the peace I had in my spiritual life up until late November.

"Pray for my faithfulness to Him, that I may serve Him according to His will. He's here, but I can't find Him for my wretched sinfulness. Help me by your prayers to see Him and answer Him."

Joan put the paper and pen down on the floor and straightened her stiff legs. No one had gotten any sleep last night. Two women had resisted having their cells stripped and ended up in handcuffs. One of them, Yolanda, had to be put in leg irons and waist chains as well. She had wailed all night, complaining that there was nowhere for her to sleep; the concrete floor and the toilet seat were too cold.

After Joan had prayed for three and a half hours, pacing her cell as she often did and forcing herself to concentrate despite Yolanda's raving, she went to bed, trying to imagine how miserably cold it must be to lie naked on a metal bunk...

Tonight, after lights out, maybe the other inmates would be tired enough to sleep and Joan would be able to concentrate.

Compelling Interests

A bassinet now filled a corner of Mariana's office, which was barely big enough for the desk, the four-drawer file cabinet and the small library of books and videotapes on parenting it already contained. On her walls, pictures of babies now numbered in the dozens—black babies, white babies, brown babies—but plump and placid Grace Hernandez, with dark curly hair and sparkling eyes, was in a fair way to becoming the most celebrated and spoiled baby of them all. Everyone—the staff, the pregnant moms—loved Grace. They took turns holding her, playing patty cake, and spooning food into her mouth. Half the time Mariana had no idea where her daughter was, but, knowing she was safe, she would say with a laugh, "Someone's checked her out. She's our most effective teaching aid."

At Christmas, as she had for the past three years, Mariana sent out Christmas cards to all who had contributed time or money to the home. On the outside was a line drawing of a 3-story Victorian house, with a baby's face in each window.

Inside, it read: "This year's babies thank you for their first Christmas and we do too!" It was signed "Christian, Joseph, Chanel, Jonathon, Viamonte, Ashley, Andreas, Joshua, Carmen, Christopher, Ervin, and Ryan."

"I'm so glad you could stay for dinner!" the woman said cheerfully to Julius, setting two sacks of groceries on the counter. "It'll be ready in a few minutes."

She was a plain woman, perhaps 35, with a pleasant face and long thick hair pulled back with big combs. Julius finally realized where he had seen her. She had been one of his patients only a few days before. Now, however, she was wearing a green surgical gown with the strings dangling in back.

A husband and children materialized without a word and filled the kitchen chairs expectantly. The woman was still chatting to Julius, seemingly unaware of his uneasy silence.

Part 6: 1987–1988

"See what I got?" she said brightly to them all. She reached carefully into one of the sacks and drew out a brown, floppy-eared puppy. It wriggled with excitement and licked her hand. "I got two," she said. "They were on sale."

She set the puppies on the counter. One stretched out a wet nose to sniff the paper sack. The other spied the children, playfully splayed its legs and yapped at them, its head on one side. The children ignored him.

The woman opened the pantry door and instead of taking out an apron, was slipping her arms out of the surgical gown and hanging it on a hook, which left her in a loose green V-necked shirt and straight matching pants. Julius had worn the same thing when he operated on her.

He watched as she felt around in a pocket and pulled out a green paper cap. Humming, she pulled the cap onto her head, taking some time to tuck in her thick hair all around. She pulled clear plastic booties over each of her tennis shoes.

With a quick smile at Julius, she twisted the dial on her oven to 350. His uneasiness increased. This had to be a dream. He could feel the weight of the blankets and the cool satin of the pillow under his head. Why couldn't he make himself wake up?

Now she was at the sink, washing her hands, holding them high so the water dripped from her elbows; the next moment she was pulling on thin rubber gloves. "Almost forgot," she said, winking at him. "Don't want to burn myself." *As if surgical gloves could insulate her against heat!* Julius thought. She scooped up one of the puppies and carried it briskly to a turkey roaster by the sink. As she laid it inside, it placed a trusting paw on her arm.

"In you go," she said, setting the lid in place. She slid the pan into the oven and closed the door, checking her watch. Julius found himself handing her the other puppy. She put it, unresisting, into the microwave.

In his bed, Julius flung himself from his back to his stomach and buried his head in his pillow, but the dream continued relentlessly.

They were all at the table now. There was the clink of silverware and the sound of conversation... . Julius found himself at the head of the table and knew he had been appointed the honor of carving the puppy.

Compelling Interests

Mechanically, he sawed down through the crisp skin, clear juices running from the white meat and collecting at its base, and placed slices on plates that the woman handed around. She was saying something about how tender it was. Julius felt only mute horror.

He became aware that the other puppy, scalded red all over, its skin hanging in shreds, was lying at his feet, looking up at him with one bulging eye. Its right front paw was shriveled and its ribs showed.

Julius knew instinctively that the puppy couldn't get up. Still, he looked down at it in relief. This one had survived being baked! Despite its deformities, its eyes were friendly, even playful, and its tail wagged reassuringly. *He forgives us!* Julius found himself thinking as he broke through into consciousness. He was in La Jolla and Dove breathed peacefully beside him.

In the dim light of pre-dawn, the scalded puppy's friendliness, which had been briefly comforting, became horrifying. The whole dream appalled Julius. It was only five in the morning and he wanted whiskey. He lay still, refusing to give in to the craving, forcing himself to replay the scene in his mind, trying to disarm it, to neutralize its power over him. A phrase flitted through his thoughts: better dead than red. Or was it, better red than dead? *Macabre.* He shuddered, threw back the covers, and felt with his feet for his slippers. He would think about something else. Padding across the bedroom, Julius felt in a drawer for his jogging suit and pulled it on hastily in the dark. Down the stairs, through the living room.

He unlocked the sliding glass doors and stepped out into the La Jolla dawn, welcoming the cool air. Reality was dispelling some of the horror. The brick lampposts at the end of the driveway were barely discernable by the orange light from the pole overhead and the pillars of the house across the street were shadowy gray lines.

When he reached the lamppost, he leaned against it and stretched the tendons at the back of each leg, then began jogging easily down the cobbled street.

He ran to the end of the block. *Concentrate on breathing normally. Fill your lungs.* He ran down the hill, along the shore, measuring time by the frequency with which he passed the slender palm trees. At the railing

Part 6: 1987–1988

overlooking the rocks and a flattish island, he stopped, panting slightly. Beyond him was an empty park, ahead an empty sea—breathing evenly. Above soared a silent gull.

The whole world, Julius thought, *is like the inside of a huge gray egg and I stand alone in its air pocket.* Sky like an overarching gray shell, great gray breakers, gray gull, gray rocks. Now he noticed a tern down the beach, possessively dragging a Styrofoam cup along the sand.

He could not breathe as calmly as the sea. He could not produce within himself the serenity around him.

On the island he could just make out a rock—no, two—shaped like a stylized seal, smooth and bulbous and tapering upwards to points at both ends. He turned away for a minute and then looked back at the shapes. He had been mistaken. They were not curved up at the ends. They were lying flat. Looking closely, he could distinguish another shape, and another—over a dozen of the large slug-like formations. Even as he peered, another pointed head popped up silently against the lighter gray of the sea. They *were* seals.

The sea kept breathing, its waves now a bottle-glass green, and more birds wheeled, the pelicans and terns now brown. The seals slept as the tide rose. The sky was still gray, paler and more fragile than before. He could count 19 bodies, some dark, some light, some speckled.

Finally one lumped to the edge of the island, wiggled over it and poised, vertical, head down, before reluctantly letting go and disappearing beneath the cold waves. Then another slid into the water without a splash. Foam was now washing over the rock and whenever it did, the seals would lift their heads. One by one, like people zipped in sleeping bags, they lunged forward, first their front half, then their back half and flopped into the water.

Later in the day, when the girls in bikinis and the men in wet suits came, the seals would be gone. It was cold standing still. Julius turned and jogged back the way he had come. When he let himself back into the house and the bedroom, Dove was still asleep.

Compelling Interests

Artyce Lancaster never intended to start a national organization. She wouldn't have known how to go about it, for one thing. The idea would have been overwhelming. And she didn't have time. She only intended to educate herself on public school curricula and philosophy.

Once educated, the next step came without conscious thought. She told everybody she knew about what she was learning. In doing so, she struck a chord in the hearts of other frustrated parents.

"Students aren't just learning the subjects we learned in school," one told her. "The schools are undermining the home. They're teaching our kids not to trust us—their own parents—not to believe anything we say."

"Or any of our values!" added another. "My son was in a school play and he had to use profanities. He asked if he could say the lines without using God's name in vain and they gave the part to someone else!"

"It's OK to use God's name to blaspheme on campus, but try to get permission to use it to pray to Him or praise Him!" agreed a third. "Some of the Christian kids wanted to have a Bible study on campus and the administration said no, that was religion—but their teachers can have them meditate and chant mantras in class!"

"And play demonic games, like Dungeons and Dragons!"

"And make them talk about nuclear war and suicide and negative stuff like that all the time. My boys don't think they're going to live to grow up."

Artyce felt uncomfortable with some of the women who saw her as their champion. Some of them seemed so rigid in their fundamentalism that they were against their children reading any secular novels for English class.

Artyce considered herself a Christian and she knew she had pretty strict values, but she didn't see anything wrong with reading *Huckleberry Finn*. Still, these parents had a point, too. It wasn't right for the school to teach religion nor was it right for the school to belittle religion—whether it was Christianity, Judaism, or Islam. The state wasn't supposed to interfere, that's what the first amendment said.

Part 6: 1987–1988

Somehow, people were getting it backward. The state *was* interfering, saying the first amendment protected people *from* religion, but then teaching things that were religious—as long as they weren't Christian. It was all so confusing.

Artyce left all that to others. She couldn't fight on every front at once. She had to narrow her focus down to one issue she knew well, where she might be able to make a difference. She chose education.

From sharing with other mothers, she started to get invitations to address church women's groups and conservative political action cells.

Some of those who heard her, once they understood what she was claiming, that the philosophy behind public education was undermining traditional values, began pulling their kids out of public school. Some stay-at-home mothers took part-time jobs so they could send their children to private, religious schools. Others, surprised to find out it was legal, decided to teach their children at home.

Before she knew exactly how it had happened, Artyce had started a movement. Or rather, she expressed and clarified what a lot of women were already feeling and the movement grew out of that shared sense of anger and helplessness.

At first, Artyce used her own money to print up single sheets and then pamphlets presenting the facts and statistics she had discovered. Soon, however, people began donating their time or their money, helped collate pages, or brought doughnuts.

The donations enabled her to buy her own copy machine and a group met weekly in her home. When they outgrew the home, they met in a local Savings and Loan. They filed for status as a non-profit organization and called themselves Women for Traditional Values.

Letter from Joe Scheidler to Joan Andrews, 13 July 1987—"Nobody would think less of you, Joanie, if you signed the papers they want you to sign, took the tests they are requiring, started gaining time for good behavior... I believe you have suffered enough for the cause and that your statement, powerful as it has been, has been made."

What is the matter with me? Joan asked herself, wiping away her tears with the back of her hand. *I can't seem to pray, I can't concentrate, I've lost that sense of peace that always upheld me before—and I can't seem to stop crying. I cry when I read my mail and I cry when I look at my pictures of Jesus and His mother.*

Was the system winning? Were they going to break her after all? Her thoughts were like swirling leaves caught by an autumn wind. A fleeting memory of Papa's grave words, when she had asked him how people could go against their consciences: "I don't know how they could do that, Joanie." A glimpse of Mama's face. Miriam and Susan being dragged from a clinic doorway. Judge Anderson addressing her attorney: "It's a shame Miss Andrews has chosen to waste her life in prison instead of accomplishing something."

And now the words from Joe Scheidler, dear friend, fearless activist: "Nobody would think less of you if you signed the papers they want you to sign." Interspersed with these were the curses she heard daily, pressing in on her like a weight. Yolanda's wailing. The echo of steel doors clanging shut. I don't know, Joanie... It's a shame... Nobody would think less of you... Eternal rest grant unto them, O Lord...

This is our aim and goal, to wipe out the line of distinction between the pre-born and their born friends... We stand here in their stead... The only way to defend the innocent victims of a holocaust is to force the perpetrators to do to you what they are doing to their victims... If you're willing to die, what can they do to you?

They can break your spirit.

Joan lifted her face, letting the tears course down her cheeks. How could she give up? But how could she go on? Was the judge right? Was she wasting her life? Joe had said, "You have suffered enough." Was it only stubborn self-will that kept her here? Think of how it must hurt Mama to have her locked up, day after day—

Part 6: 1987–1988

Joan opened her eyes. Through her tears, a glint of bright orange caught her attention—so small she couldn't be sure what it was. It came from her window, which was painted over and covered with a large iron grate.

If she moved her head ever so slightly, she lost it. But there was something there, she knew there was. High up, out of reach from the floor, there was a spot on the window where the paint was chipped. She had noticed it about a month ago.

Carefully, gingerly, with growing excitement, Joan climbed onto her top bunk and peeked through the pinprick on the painted glass.

Outside, the sun was setting in a splendor of titians, russets, and golds. Joan blinked back tears of joy and clung to the window, balancing herself so she could drink in the brilliance. Even when she was too feeble, too distracted, too sinful, to hold on to God, He was there. He would not let her fall. She stayed until the sun had set and the colors faded, thanking her sweet Lord for this reminder of His love.

It was their 16th anniversary. Julius took Ester to the Aristocrat for the best Filipino food in Los Angeles. She wore a pastel dress that reminded him of the one she'd worn when they danced on the evening they met. But the romantic mood didn't last long.

"Remember our engagement party?" she teased him gently. "Shall I order *balut?*"

She wasn't prepared for his response.

"No!" he burst out. "I think that's a barbaric custom—eating an unborn bird—with the wings and the beak—and the feathers!"

She was taken aback at his vehemence. "It's just our culture," she said. "What's the difference if a duck is unborn or born? You love duck l'orange—"

"Stop it, Ester," he said, trying to control his voice. "I'm not kidding. I think it's a repulsive custom."

Compelling Interests

She lowered her eyes to the menu and let the subject drop. When the waiter came to take their orders she asked for steak.

They were in bed. Julius felt his wife's cool hands massage his back, then work their way restlessly over his body. He didn't move.

"Julius?" she asked quietly. "Are you still awake?"

"Yes," he said, reluctantly.

"Are you too tired again? It's been so long."

He stirred, turning toward her and putting an arm across her. She put her mouth up to his and kissed him hungrily. He felt panic.

"Julius?" They could both tell he was tensing again.

He kissed her neck but it wasn't a kiss of passion. His arm lay so lightly across her chest that she knew he had it suspended over her.

She sat up and flicked on the light. "Julius, tell me. Why are you like this? Is it me?"

He pulled away, moved back, thrashing in misery. He wanted a drink. He wanted to sleep. He didn't want to answer questions.

"Julius, is there another woman?"

That got his attention. "No, Dove, no! I adore you, you know that."

"'Adore' isn't what I want tonight. Don't you want me?"

He sat up too and she slipped a pillow between the back of his head and the oak headboard. He kissed her fingertips.

"What?" she prodded.

"I don't want to hurt you."

"You have something to tell me that will hurt me?"

"No, no, I mean—physically." It was so hard to verbalize it.

Her eyebrows shot up in surprise. "Hurt me? You mean sex? You don't hurt me."

He buried his head in her arms. "I'm afraid I will. You're so delicate, Dove. I'm afraid you'll break—that your bones will break, will crack—"

"It's OK," she soothed, rocking him gently. "I won't break. I won't break. It's all right."

But the next time and the next, it wasn't all right. He was more nervous than ever. He said he couldn't get any sleep, worrying about how fragile she was.

Part 6: 1987–1988

"Dove, would you mind—just for a while—if we slept in separate beds? Just till I get over this."

"But how are you going to get over it?" she fretted. "It's getting worse. You hug me like I'm a china doll."

"I just need some sleep," he said.

"If you need sleep, don't work so hard. You work all the time, Julius. You don't have to work so many hours. We make plenty of money and you don't have time to enjoy it. We don't go to the beach anymore. You could work maybe three days a week. That would be enough."

Finally, he agreed to a compromise. They would sleep apart but he would try to cut down his schedule and spend more time with her. And they would try counseling again.

He lasted two and a half sessions. Ester talked most of the first two hours and cried, telling the psychiatrist things that were so personal they made Julius even more reticent than usual.

The psychiatrist opened the third session with an expansive smile and gesture and said to Julius, "This time, let's hear from you. Tell me about your relationship with your mother."

"My mother? What's that got to do with anything? She died when I was six." He knew he sounded belligerent but he was tense and the whiskey he had had before leaving home, gulped secretly in the pantry because it was still early afternoon, hadn't been nearly enough to calm his nerves.

"Were you close to her?"

"I suppose all children are close to their mothers at that age." Then, "What do you mean, close?"

"How did you see her?"

"How?"

"Yes, how did you see her? Was she cruel, tender, loving, angry?"

"I don't remember anything that stands out one way or the other."

"Did you idealize her," persisted the doctor, "see her as perfect?"

"Maybe. Small children do, don't they?" Julius studied the doctor's serene face. "You have some kind of agenda here, don't you?"

"No agenda. There's no script."

Compelling Interests

"What? Do you think I'm getting my wife mixed up in my mind with my mother? Is that what you think?"

Ester looked concerned. "Julius." She put up a hand to calm him.

Julius stood up, shoulders hunched. "That's it, isn't it. You think my problem is that I'm making love to my mother. Well, it isn't! I know she's not my mother! She's my wife and I love her and I want—but I just can't.

"It's like little bones—like wherever I turn, there are little bones! I'm walking on them, trying to tiptoe so I won't break them and they're everywhere I go! My mother doesn't have a damn thing to do with this. Just tell me how I can keep from stepping—" He covered his ears.

"I can hear them crunching. All the time. Crunch! Crunch! It's like—like when I was sixteen and my dad and I went to Mexico. We drove overland from Puerto Vallarta to Tepic in a Land Rover, just crashing through the forest because there wasn't any road yet and there were these tree crabs. Millions and millions of them, all over the ground. You couldn't avoid them. And they sounded—" he shivered. "That soft crunch." He hugged himself.

Ester and the doctor were watching him, listening. He straightened up. "So it has nothing to do with my mother."

Ester turned to the psychiatrist. "He won't pull into the gravel driveway anymore. He parks on the street. The other day I was eating some kind of cold cereal and he couldn't stand the sound of my eating. He got up and ran out of the room."

"I think we can put you on some medication—" began the doctor.

Julius was breathing heavily. "I have to get out of here," he said. He was holding his elbows again. I'm sorry. I have to, I can hear them. I have to get away." Agitated, he bolted out the door.

Ester looked at the doctor with embarrassment. "That's what it has been like," she said. "He'll go back to work. Or he'll drink. When I get home, he'll be gone or he'll have passed out on the bed."

There weren't any more sessions together. Julius said he was too busy.

Part 6: 1987–1988

All over the nation, people were starting to break the law—people who had never been arrested before, people who would not consider jaywalking or dream of cheating on their income taxes. Few of these people had heard of Joan Andrews or realized they were following her example and answering her prayers.

When he came up with the idea of mass sit-ins in Binghamton, New York in 1986, Randall Terry was not proposing anything original. Grassroots participation on a large scale had long been the dream of the pro-life movement. But under Terry, the idea took root and his would become the name associated with mass rescues.

In late November of 1987, more than 200 anti-abortion protesters were arrested on minor trespassing charges during a peaceful sit-in that closed the Cherry Hill Women's Center in New Jersey for 9 ½ hours. The protest, dubbed Operation Rescue, drew more than 400 protestors. Organizers said the action, the largest sit-in ever held, was a warm-up for larger protests in major cities.

On the fourth of December, 250 were arrested in New York. Richard Michaelson and Pat O'Connor were among them. First by the dozens, then by the hundreds, then by the thousands, they blocked the entrances to abortion clinics, allowed themselves to be hauled to waiting police vans, only to be replaced by others.

Pro-choice activists, leaders of women's organizations, and officials of the clinic denounced the protest as a violation of women's constitutional right to abortions. Their best-known spokesperson, Cecile Tucker-Thomas, was quoted in newspapers all over the nation, saying, "I'm totally outraged at these kinds of terrorist tactics."

But the "terrorist tactics" only intensified.

The little group at the Burkett's was beginning to come to consensus—not on the life of the unborn, not on a woman's rights—but on a surprising number of related issues. They all agreed, for instance, that preventing a pregnancy was better than aborting one and that it was important to provide women facing problem pregnancies with options besides abortion.

Irene shared how she had felt talked into an abortion.

"No one offered me any alternative. They didn't tell me what could happen."

One of the women in the group spoke kindly. "You made the best choice you could at the time," she said. "It was OK."

Irene shook her head. "It *wasn't* OK! It was wrong. And I could have died!"

But she came back for the last meeting, where she helped draft a joint declaration outlining what everyone could agree on. Joyce approached the editor of the *Journal* again, asking if he would print this declaration. He was not only willing to print it but he wanted Joyce and Carol to write an article together summarizing what they felt they had accomplished. It ran Christmas Day.

"With our fifth joint meeting," they wrote, "we bring to a close our ecumenical discussions, feeling that we have achieved our original goal, which was to find points of agreement on abortion, despite our basic disagreement on its morality.

"At a recent meeting, there was a palpable sense of joy and relaxed warmth in a room that had seen seven months of anxiety, empathy, anger, acceptance, frustration and, finally, some fulfillment.

"We found it easy and natural to join, hand in hand, with a prayer of thanksgiving. Our experimental dialogue between people from the religious right and left had brought forth its fruit: a joint statement affirming that we do indeed share common ground, common goals and, to our mutual delight, common sense.

"It was that common sense that led us to talk about ourselves first, how the abortion issue has affected our own lives, rather than locking horns over whose side was morally right or wrong.

"In the areas where our groups differed, sometimes with considerable heat, we found that we could accept each other anyway, that we could still

Part 6: 1987–1988

respect and appreciate each other as individuals. We found that indeed we are individuals—not stereotypes, not the fanatics we had perhaps at first expected."

It ended with the declaration each member of the two groups had hammered out—weaker than the pro-lifers would have liked but quite a document, nonetheless:

We, the undersigned,

In response to a recommendation by the president of the Unitarian-Universalist Church that members of that body seek dialogue with those of other beliefs on current issues of mutual concern,

Having decided to initiate dialogue with pro-life Christians, some of whom may be considered 'fundamentalists,' on the subject of abortion,

And having met a number of times to share our views and air our differences with the goal of ultimately reaching consensus on aspects of the subject where consensus is possible,

Do hereby jointly offer the following declaration, as representing views on which we can all agree:

We approve the trend we are beginning to see in society, which is moving away from a self-centered and irresponsible attitude toward sex. We see this new trend reflected in television 'soaps' and in newspaper advice columns.

We urge an increased awareness to the negative sexuality presented in the media and advertising and call for a new level of public responsibility by these influential companies.

We affirm the power and joy of human sexuality, yet recognize that casual and exploitive sex devalues people and may cause physical and emotional problems.

We believe communication on issues related to sex should be encouraged between parents and their teenagers, as well as communication on the full range of other stresses on the modern young person. We believe abstinence should be encouraged as the best sexual option for unmarried minors.

We approve of having sex education classes for junior high school and high school students, as long as those classes are biologically factual without being so detailed regarding aspects and variations of sexual practices, that they only serve to titillate or imply advocacy.

We are concerned about the casual attitude some women have toward abortion. We feel that women should be discouraged from seeing abortion as a means of birth control.

We believe every woman with an unwanted pregnancy has a right to counseling which includes not only information on abortion but also on the possible medical and emotional risks during and following abortion and the availability of homes, financial help, prenatal care, etc., if she wishes not to abort.

This declaration reflects only the opinions of the individuals who have signed below and does not represent an official position on the part of the churches they attend.

The statement was signed by 20 people, representing 9 churches. At Joyce's suggestion, they donated the payment for the article to Lifeline Mothers Home.

Statement from the Office of the Governor of Florida, 26 December 1987—"Governor Bob Martinez today agreed to transfer Florida inmate Joan Andrews to the physical custody of Delaware prison authorities so she can serve the remainder of her sentence near her family. The Governor said humanitarian concerns during this holiday season led to his decision, although Andrews' request for clemency remains under review... The Governor said Delaware authorities have agreed to accept Andrews under an interstate compact that is used regularly to allow inmates to serve their sentences near family members in other states."

In a letter from Joan Andrews to Tom May, on December 26, 1987, from the Florida Correctional at Lowell, Joan wrote, "I was at Broward for Christmas, but early this morning, I was transported here. It will probably take several weeks at least to reach the Delaware prison at Claymont.

"I'll write only this one page because the lighting is poor. It's funny how different prisons vary—even the lock-up units. What is nice here is

Part 6: 1987–1988

the fresh air coming in through the cracked windows, and also the possibility to look out the window and see the sky and grass and trees. The windows are not painted out here.

"My Christmas was great! The priest came by and brought me the Sacraments, and I had a missalette, so after he left I read Christmas Mass. I had also read the Midnight Mass the night before. I was able to obtain two red plastic garbage bags the night before and I used these to cover my light fixture so that my room glowed. It was beautiful! I sang all the Christmas hymns from the missalette. Then when I was transported this morning at 4 A.M., I saw my first Christmas decorations. Even at that hour and on a minor highway, many of the little towns had their Christmas lights on. I got to hear one Christmas song on the vehicle's radio, too. It was a joy.

"I can't tell you how good it is to be away from Broward. Jesus certainly blessed me on His birthday."

Maybe this year will see changes, Mariana thought. There was already a subtle change in the attitude of American society toward babies. By the time Grace was a toddler, babies were "in"—although you almost never saw a pregnant woman on the street anymore. Prince Charles and Lady Di had a baby, Prince Andrew and Fergie had a baby, Cybill Shepherd had twins. Babies had been written into the plots of sit-coms such as *Family Ties* and *Growing Pains*.

Motherhood was becoming fashionable even among teenagers. Mariana found that when she spoke to high school assemblies now, girls romanticized motherhood and they all fell in love with Grace, who often accompanied her, adorable in a pink dress and matching ruffled socks, her dark hair a mass of curls.

Lest any high schooler become so enamored of the positive aspects of motherhood that she deliberately go out and get pregnant, Mariana hit hard not just on the negative aspects of abortion but on the difficulties of parenting. "Hold out for marriage," she would caution. "It will be worth the wait."

Compelling Interests

Wilmington, Delaware Morning News, 25 January, 1988—"The anti-abortion faithful gathered Sunday evening outside the Women's Correctional Center in Claymont in a homecoming ceremony for their captured angel. Joan Andrews, viewed by many as the 'Mother Teresa' of the anti-abortion movement, has been jailed there since Friday, following her transfer from a Florida prison.

"Andrews' incarceration has made her a symbol for the national movement, which has increasingly opted for direct confrontations. People in growing numbers are willing to face jail."

Two days later, Joan wrote to her sister, Susan—"The vigil here at the prison Sunday night was just tremendous. I was in lock and suddenly I heard shouts throughout the building of 'The pro-lifers are here! The pro-lifers are here!' My two cellmates were out in population and they told me later that everyone was really impressed by the vigil, and that they explained to everyone why the picketers were there and why I was non-cooperating, and that everyone was learning about the evil of abortion. They said everyone was in support.

"Next day the counselor, Miss Johnson, a very nice person, said that the prison could not allow the picketers to come back again. She said the prison would have them arrested. I answered, 'I don't think it matters if you have them arrested. They could join me in non-cooperation.'"

In March of 1988, lawyers for Joan Andrews sought a waiver of the rules of executive clemency so her sentence could be commuted to time served. Governor Robert Martinez and two of the other six Florida cabinet members supported the request, but this was one vote short of the required number of votes to get her sentence reviewed. The request was denied.

Artyce went to hear Phyllis Schlafly, a lawyer, syndicated columnist, and mother of six at a luncheon organized by local conservatives. Artyce's first impression of the poised and carefully-coiffed Schlafly was one of

Part 6: 1987–1988

humorlessness, even condescension, but with her opening words, that impression was dispelled.

"I want to thank my husband," she began, a twinkle in her eye, "for letting me come—I always say that and it always drives the feminists crazy."

The women in the audience chuckled. Schlafly spoke on what she called "child abuse in the classroom"—using school as a means of disconnecting children from family values, forcing them to role-play decision-making situations involving abortion, divorce, mental illness, nuclear war, death, and suicide.

"If you and your family were drowning," Schlafly cited as an example used by grade school teachers, "and you could save all but one of them, who would you save?"

She had written a book about it and Artyce, who bought a copy, was impressed with her research. It echoed some of what she had been objecting to about Stephanie's classes.

I could do the same thing with what I've been learning, Artyce thought. *Organize it, document it—I'll bet I could get it published.* She would have to cut back on her own speaking engagements and make this a priority, as she had when she wrote her college thesis, especially since she couldn't afford to work only part-time after this year. She had promised to pay Stephanie's way through college.

In mid-July, 1988, Operation Rescue went to Atlanta, where the Democrats were holding their national convention. Pro-lifers blockaded the doorways of every clinic in the city and 134 of the protesters were arrested before the week was out. They carried no identification and would not give their names when arrested. They made a powerful statement—they were as helpless and anonymous as the tiny beings they represented.

"First they ignore you," Gandhi had said of nonviolence campaigns. "Then they laugh at you. Then they crack down. Then you win."

Compelling Interests

But from the beginning, no one had ignored them. And no one was laughing. First the police fined and released them. Then they booked them. Then they cracked down.

"The Joan Andrews Case: An American Prisoner of Conscience"
by Patrick J. Buchanan, August 1988

"As we Americans draw up our annual lists of Soviet prisoners of conscience, perhaps this year we will consider one of our own.

"The prisoner's name is Joan Andrews. Now back in solitary confinement in the maximum-security Broward Correctional Institution in south Florida, she has served 23 months of a five year sentence, most of that time praying in a windowless cell...

"Six months ago, in response to press inquiries, and an aroused right-to-life movement for whom Joan Andrews is a beacon of courage, she was spirited out of Broward to Alderson federal prison in West Virginia, en route to Delaware where she could be near her sister. Joan thought it was a prelude to release; but when it turned out to be nothing of the kind, she asked to be taken back.

"On her return to Florida, some BCI guards had a welcoming party. Even though she never left police custody, Joan was subjected to an internal strip-search by five female and one male guard. It was 'like an attempted rape,' she wrote in an anguished letter to her sister. As she tried to protect her modesty, her clothes were torn off her; then she was held down while a 'cavity' search was conducted. 'A show of strength and contempt,' she writes, 'to teach me a lesson.'...

"Had this crude strip search been performed in a southern jail on Dr. Martin Luther King, political candidates would have raced one another to the cameras to demand King's release and a Justice Department investigation of his tormenters.

"This will not happen, because Joan Andrews' cause, the life of the unborn, is not today's trendy cause; and so it is that, for every day Dr. King spent behind bars, Joan Andrews has spent months.

Part 6: 1987–1988

"As the civil rights movement believed that laws mandating segregation were immoral, so Joan Andrews believes that court decisions and laws that permit abortions are immoral, and, hence, non-binding."

A groundswell of people on both sides of the abortion debate were lobbying for Joan Andrews' release. Mark Green, 1986 Democratic nominee for New York, and former California governor Jerry Brown, who called her incarceration a civil rights issue, were among them. Liberals for Life, Feminists for Life, the Right to Life League, Pro-Life Action League and the American Life League, among others, pressured the Florida cabinet to reconsider.

Governor Robert Martinez received 20,000 letters asking for pardon, commutation, or clemency for Joan. When a reporter asked Cecile Tucker-Thomas to comment on this fact, she retorted, "Joan Andrews is an individual legitimately regarded as a terrorist, who has tried to block the constitutional rights of the women of this country, who is uncooperative, who is facing other charges and who, if released, would continue to be a threat. To consider any kind of clemency is preposterous!"

Meanwhile, Joan was receiving support from another quarter. She received a handwritten letter that read,

Dear Joan Andrews, You have offered all to God and accepted all suffering for the love of Him—because you know that whatever you do to the least or for the least you do it to Jesus—because Jesus has clearly said, If you receive a little child in my name you receive Me.

We are all praying for you. Do not be afraid. All this suffering is but the kiss of Jesus—a sign that you have come so close to Jesus on the cross—so that He can kiss you.

Be not afraid—Jesus loves you—you are precious to Him—He loves you.

My prayer is always near you and for you.

God bless you.

Mother Teresa of Calcutta

Compelling Interests

Ever since it had opened five months earlier, Cindy Hodge had been a frequent sight at the new Sanger Clinic on Santa Fe Avenue.

Her son's school was two blocks from her house, and the clinic was three blocks beyond that. She walked Kyle to school, kissed him good-bye, and trudged on up the road, Petey in an infant carrier on her back and Darin in the stroller. For the last month or two, she had had to go slower. The imminent new arrival made her pant slightly as she pushed the stroller ahead of her.

About once a week, the Long Beach Police Station would get a call about "harassment," but what the proprietor of the family planning clinic called harassment usually amounted to nothing more than Cindy wheeling the stroller up and down the sidewalk, singing and praying aloud.

Sometimes when the receptionist came to work, she would find anonymous letters on the floor at the foot of the mail slot, letters threatening to bomb the clinic or burn it down. She had been worried at first but nothing came of it. The police promised to keep an eye on the place and they talked to Cindy a couple of times, sternly, but dismissed her as harmless.

Before he got put on night shift, Officer Michael Jaspers had responded to one of the calls. When he reached the clinic, Cindy was sitting on a large white-washed rock at the edge of the driveway.

"Ma'am," he' said formally, "this is private property. You'll have to move."

"They kill babies here," she said, looking up and squinting because the sun was behind him. The little boy on her back—he guessed it was a boy because he had on a little blue hat with an elastic band running under his chubby chin—was sucking his thumb philosophically.

"I don't know about that, ma'am," he said, "but we had a call from the owners of this place and you're trespassing."

"I'm protesting," she corrected him.

"You're allowed to stay on the sidewalk, as long as you keep moving and don't interfere with traffic into the building," he said. "If you cause problems, I'm going to have to book you." He said it gently, even affectionately. He had a soft spot for mothers and respect for people who were willing to take a stand, even a stand he had no particular opinion on and even though he was slightly irritated to be here.

Part 6: 1987–1988

There were so many more urgent calls—muggings, car thefts, drive-by shootings. Maybe his irritation was not so much with her for pulling him away from the real world, as it was with himself, for being glad she had.

As she read the first line of Birthright's monthly newsletter, Mariana gave a whoop of joy.

"Our prayers are answered," it said. "Joan Andrews is *free!*"

Florida officials had commuted her sentence and sent her to Pittsburgh, where she faced sentencing for a May, 1985 rescue. The judge there placed Joan on three years' probation. As she left the courtroom October 18, she was greeted by a crowd of supporters. With them, she attended Mass, giving thanks to God for her release. She joined a prayer vigil at the abortion center where she had been arrested in 1985.

At last, Joan was free to go home.

It was so good to see Mama and Papa—and Ruach—even if, with the phone ringing continually and friends and the media clamoring to see her, they hadn't much time together. After her brief visit, Joan began traveling, meeting with pro-life groups around the country.

Artyce should have been writing up the latest editorial for the Traditional Values newsletter, but she took a few extra minutes to read the newspaper over a second cup of coffee. She was glad she did.

It was just a paragraph buried in the local paper but it jumped out at Artyce. "Jane Roe," the 21-year old woman who had filed the original lawsuit in Roe v. Wade, had come out of the closet. Her name was Norma McCorvey and she said she had lied about being gang-raped. The fact was, she said, her boyfriend had gotten her pregnant.

Artyce ripped the article out of the paper and went to her bookcase. Where was that paperback by Richard Michaelson? He had admitted lying, too—there, on page 197. Cecile Tucker-Thomas and her comrades had used those very lies to pressure the Supreme Court.

Compelling Interests

Slowly at first, then with growing energy, she began to type. "Fourteen years ago, the U.S. Supreme Court legalized abortion for virtually any reason through all nine months of pregnancy. Now it turns out this legislation was based on a series of deliberate deceptions."

She stopped.

Deliberate? Those were serious charges. Could she back them up? She studied the clipping and reviewed Dr. Michaelson's statements again. She re-read *The How-To Book,* which she had located in Long Beach's biggest used bookstore.

There was no question about it. Artyce continued writing.

"Lie No. 1: The test case before the Supreme Court was itself based on a deception. Roe, a pseudonym for Norma McCorvey, 21, was a ticket seller in a carnival traveling in Georgia at the time. She claimed to have been gang-raped by three men, resulting in pregnancy. Her doctor refused to perform an abortion, which was illegal in Texas unless necessary to save the life of the mother, but he introduced her to two female attorneys who favored legalizing abortion.

"McCorvey challenged the constitutionality of the law by bringing a class-action suit against Dallas District Attorney Henry Wade. Although the cause of her pregnancy was not an issue in the suit, she circulated the story widely.

"This account was presented as fact as recently as the Fall, 1987 issue of *Life* magazine. In early September, however, McCorvey admitted to Carl Rowan on WASU-TV that her boyfriend had gotten her pregnant.

"Lie No. 2: When the Supreme Court justices, in all good faith, took the case, they called upon experts in the medical field to provide statistics regarding the effect of illegal abortions on women. Unknowingly, they swallowed a second lie.

"Statistics presented to dramatize the plight of desperate women gave a powerful emotional incentive to the passage of the ruling. One justice claimed he changed his vote at the last minute because his wife begged him in tears to remember the thousands of women dying from illegal abortions.

Part 6: 1987–1988

"Yet the claim that '5,000 to 10,000' women were dying yearly from abortion, according to a physician who promoted it at the time, was sheer fabrication. 'I confess I knew the figures were totally false,' writes former abortionist Dr. Richard Michaelson in his book *We Lied Our Way to Legal Abortion*. 'But in the "morality" of our revolution, the overriding concern was to get the laws eliminated, and anything within reason that had to be done was permissible.'

"The Center for Disease Control for the year before abortion was legalized showed only 39 deaths due to abortion. Even if, as now, the cause of death was disguised under resultant symptoms, such as hemorrhage or infection, the number was probably not over 500, estimates Michaelson.

"Lie No. 3: Not only were maternal death statistics falsified but those lobbying for legalization may actually have been responsible for some of those deaths that did occur. Many of the women who suffered and perhaps died at the hands of illegal abortionists were sent to them by the very people who insisted illegal abortions were dangerous.

"KASAL president Cecile Tucker-Thomas helped direct women to abortionists in Mexico and was paid for each referral. 'I only got $5 per woman,' she told a sympathetic audience at a National Women's Political Caucus meeting in 1985.

"Tucker-Thomas wrote a book designed to teach women how to deceive doctors into performing abortions on them. In what was known as *The How-to Book*, Tucker-Thomas discussed how to bring on a seeming emergency so that a doctor will perform an abortion.

"In her detailed and graphic chapter 'Abort Yourself,' Tucker-Thomas has a disclaimer stating that she is not advocating self-abortions, merely 'defining' the dangers and problems.

"She does, however, advocate fooling a doctor into inserting a loop as a contraceptive device *after* conception, which will cause a fetus to abort. She also advocates bringing a urine sample from someone who is not pregnant, so the doctor will assume the fetus is already dead and will clean out the uterus. She further advocates using liver to simulate blood so a doctor will think spontaneous abortion has already begun."

Compelling Interests

If someone gave a copy of the article to Cecile, Artyce didn't know of it. At least she wasn't summoned into court.

As a matter of fact, Cecile did see the article. Liz mailed her a copy of the Traditional Values Newsletter—she had gotten on the mailing list under an assumed name so she could keep a jump ahead of its members.

"This reminds me of what the Catholics were writing about us back in the sixties," Cecile told Liz over the phone the next time they talked. "Remember how they would give a blow-by-blow account of everything we were teaching? It spread our message to a wider audience than we had dreamed possible. Ms. Lancaster has done us a service. If the laws go against us," she pointed out, "women may need those ideas again."

It was a Tuesday evening. Senator Nate Marshall had taken off his shoes when he got home and was sitting at the kitchen table, drinking a Diet Orange Slice because he couldn't find any Pepsis, and reading the college football ratings. USC was ranked second. What do you know? The new coach was going to take the team to the Rose Bowl for the second year in a row. All they had to do now was get by Notre Dame and they'd have the National Championship, too.

It felt good to be on top again. It was where they belonged. He remembered the first time USC lost after their winning streak in the '70s. He and Marilyn had watched the game on TV and when the announcers gave the final score, Marilyn had sat in shock.

"They're not supposed to do that," she said. "They're supposed to win in the last ten seconds."

The phone rang. He could let the answering machine get it because it was probably for Marilyn—it always was. On second thought, maybe it *was* Marilyn. She was probably out shopping and was running late. He'd tell her to buy more Pepsis. He wanted something fully-leaded.

She's going to apologize for not being home to fix dinner, he thought, grinning, *and ask if she can pick up a barbecued chicken from Von's.* Marilyn hated to cook. He reached across the counter for the receiver.

Part 6: 1987–1988

It was a man's voice.

"Senator Marshall? I'm glad I caught you. This is Tim Carraway at the *Southbay Journal*. We're running a story about your wife's abortion and wanted to give you a chance to comment."

Marshall set his can of Orange Slice back on the table.

"You must have the wrong number," he said and hung up.

Almost immediately the phone rang again. Marshall's forehead furrowed.

"Yes?

"Senator Marshall?"

"Is this a joke?" asked Marshall. "Who did you say this was?"

"Tim Carraway. With the *Journal*. We met at the Republican convention this summer. I thought I'd better try to reach you at home. We're on deadline."

"Mr.—Carraway, is it? I'd be glad to help you but my wife isn't having an abortion. You know we're against abortion."

"Yes, sir, I know that."

"My wife isn't even pregnant. We stopped having babies twelve years ago."

"Yes, sir." There was a pause.

Tim Carraway asked gently, "Do you know where your wife is, Senator?" It sounded absurdly like the police asking after an errant teenager.

"She's out shopping," said Marshall. "At least—I think she is." He was briefly silent and Tim waited. "Mr. Carraway, I'm sure there is some mix-up. You've gotten information about the wrong Marilyn Marshall."

"Actually, Senator, she is listed at Irvine General as Mary Shea."

Marshall's head was starting to ache. "How can you think there is any connection between a Mary Shea and my wife?"

"A nurse recognized her, sir. Wasn't your wife's maiden name Shea? She had an abortion today." Carraway was all reporter again. "Would you care to comment?"

"No comment," said Senator Marshall and slammed down the receiver.

Compelling Interests

Daryl glanced sideways at his wife again, over the tousled head of their eldest daughter. Cindy Hodge was humming as she poked at the chicken sizzling in the skillet, her apron extended over the bulge which was Baby Hodge number four. She stepped briskly from stove to counter and back again, her floured hands holding more drumsticks.

"Move, Darin honey," she said to the child playing with pans at her feet, "I don't want to step on you."

Daryl knew he should feel relieved. Cindy hadn't been in such a good mood for weeks. Somehow, though, he still felt uneasy. They had had one of their worst arguments when he came home for lunch, parking the company tool truck out front like he did every noon. And they hadn't made up yet.

Cindy was a wonderful companion in many ways. Daryl used to enjoy coming home to her. What was it—being housebound with three kids under four? Was that what had begun to change her into this intense, even obsessive zealot for social justice?

When had they stopped sitting in front of the fire together, sipping hot cocoa and letting the kids crawl all over them? When had Cindy begun pushing the kids aside after dinner, with the dishes still on the table, to write her rambling, hostile letters to the family planning clinic? God would get them, she would write. They were going to burn in hell. *Maybe tonight will be different.* He hoped so.

I shouldn't complain about watching the kids, he rebuked himself. *She has them all day. She has a right to some time to herself in the evenings. I should help out more.*

He got up, uncertainly, Kyle's arms still around his neck. "Can I do something?" he asked.

"I've just got to make the salad," Cindy said cheerfully. "You can pour the boys some milk and put Kyle in his highchair."

He complied, still finding himself tensing and not knowing why. She hadn't brought up the subject of the argument again, even though it was screaming at them both from the front page of the *Journal:* Pro-Life Senator's Wife Aborts.

Part 6: 1987–1988

Daryl's face flushed with the same panic he had felt in the face of Cindy's fury at lunch, when the top slice of bread and some of the tuna had bounced off his plate as she set it violently in front of him.

"What right does Nate Marshall's wife have to kill her baby?" she had demanded. "He's a pro-life Republican! I voted for him! Doesn't he have a say in what happens to his own child? Doesn't she care about what this will do to his reputation? It makes him look like a fool! Why didn't he stop her?"

As his wife stormed on, ignoring her own sandwich and the scared faces of their little boys, Daryl couldn't tell if she was blaming Senator Marshall for not preventing his wife's abortion or whether she was defending him as an injured party. The words swirled about his head and confused him. Somehow, in it all, he just felt sorry; sorry for Cindy, sorry for Kyle and Darin and Petey, sorry for Senator and Mrs. Marshall, sorry for their aborted baby, sorry for himself and the marriage that seemed to be slipping away from him.

Tonight, however, Cindy didn't seem to be upset anymore and the evening passed pleasantly. She read to the three children, gave them their baths, and tucked them into bed, Kyle and Darin in the twin beds he'd bought from the ad in the paper and Petey in the crib, the bite marks still on the top rail where Kyle had gnawed on it when he was teething. Maybe next summer, thought Daryl, when the new baby needed the crib, they could afford to add on a third bedroom. More than likely, though, they would probably just curtain off part of their own room for Petey, especially if the new one was a girl.

He moved quietly behind Cindy, picking up toys and placing them in the big basket in the corner beside the couch. He knelt on the bathmat, wet from three dripping little bodies, and pulled the plug out by its chain. As the water level lowered, he gathered up the plastic boats and balls and swabbed the side of the tub with a sopping washcloth. He was pushing a wet towel over the puddles on the floor with a foot when Cindy appeared in the doorway.

"Daryl?"

Compelling Interests

He looked up. She seemed contented enough. Why couldn't he shake his uneasiness?

"Do you mind if I go out for a little while? Just a little while."

"Honey, if you need something at the store— You know I don't like you to go there after dark. Can't it wait till tomorrow?"

"No," she said, her lips tightening ever so slightly.

"Pampers?" he said. "I'll go get them."

"I'd like to go," she said and although he couldn't quite hear the steel, it was there. "I'll be right back. Petey's asleep and the other two almost are. I'm letting them listen to the Sesame Street tape."

He heard her pick up the keys from the top of the dresser and the front door closed gently. *If we had two cars, I'd follow her,* he thought. Immediately, he chastised himself for his suspicions. *She needs to get out now and then,* he told himself. *She'll be all right. What am I afraid of anyway, another man? When would a pregnant woman with three kids have time for an affair?*

Officer Jaspers, now on the night shift, was driving by just as Cindy stuffed the rags through the mail slot. The street was poorly lit by those terrible sodium vapor lights which saved the city money but made it impossible to tell the color of a suspect's skin or clothes. There was just enough light to make out a figure at the door of the clinic. He pulled to the curb and got out of his car.

"Mrs. Hodge?" Who else?

She jerked at the sound of her name and turned around.

"You aren't supposed to be hanging around here," he said, trying to sound firm.

"I was just—I had to—"

"Another hate letter?"

"Yes." She sounded relieved.

"Come on, ma'am. Go home." Wearily, "You aren't going to change anything."

Submissively, she got into her car and he followed her down Wardlow and left on Orange. As she stopped in front of a small apartment he assumed was hers, he drove on by, resisting an impulse to wave.

Part 6: 1987–1988

As soon as he was out of sight, Cindy put the Toyota in gear and made a U-turn. It was a lucky thing she hadn't lit the rags before she pushed them through the mail slot; the policeman might have seen the flames through the glass. She wasn't going to fuss with matches; she had found one of the thick candles Daryl had bought for emergencies after the Whittier Narrows earthquake. She would light that and shove it through the door. By that policeman's next cruise up Bixby, it would be too late.

She wasn't right back, but soon enough. She was agitated, excited, and she wasn't carrying any groceries.

Daryl's anxiety was a knot in the pit of his stomach. He forced his voice to sound normal, wishing he could keep himself from saying anything.

"Everything all right?"

"Fine!"

"Did you get the Pampers?"

She didn't answer but her face got a thinking look, like she was considering telling him a special secret. She looked almost like the girl he had married, four pregnancies and thousands of dollars of debt ago. Her expression was one of youth and anticipation and daydreams. For a dizzy second, he fell in love with her all over again. He took a step toward her.

"Can I tell you something?" she asked in a whisper, her face shining.

"Yes!"

She came to him, as close as she could get with the baby between them, came to him of her own accord for the first time in months, and took his hands in hers. Her weary eyes were alive as they locked onto his.

"I *did* it!"

"Did what?"

"I burned down the abortion mill!"

Daryl didn't sleep well. Once he thought he heard a fire engine and he wanted very much to call the fire station and ask about it but he knew he would blurt out that his wife had set the fire. If there was a fire. Maybe she hadn't really done anything, just talked big. Maybe she had tried and it hadn't worked—what did she know about burning down a building?

He still wanted to call the fire department. He wanted to apologize for his wife, for her convictions, for her instability. He wanted someone to tell him everything would be all right.

Compelling Interests

Cindy, meanwhile, slept through Petey's three o'clock feeding. Daryl got up and warmed the bottle without waking her; he was awake anyway.

Just before breakfast, the police came. Daryl had the water running and didn't hear the knock—the doorbell hadn't worked since they moved in—and Cindy, still smiling but more tightly than last night, opened the front door with the hand that held the spatula. Her other arm was around Petey, riding on her hip.

"Mrs. Hodge?"

"Yes." It wasn't a question. It was a statement. *Yes, I know why you're here. Yes, I did it and I'm not sorry.*

Two officers stood over her. "We have a warrant for your arrest. You are charged with arson at the family planning clinic on Santa Fe Avenue."

Daryl heard voices at the door. "Cindy? Is someone here?" *Please, please, don't let it be real.* In the kitchen, Darin banged on the tray of his highchair with a spoon and Kyle called, "Mommy, *brea'fus!*"

Cindy turned to him as he emerged from the bathroom, a towel to his apprehensive face. "It's the police," she said matter-of-factly, "here to get me for what I did last night."

Stunned, Daryl stood motionless. She handed him first the spatula and then the baby. He took them mechanically.

"I'm ready now," she said.

The officers stepped out of her way as she came out the door. She did not look back but one of the policeman flashed Daryl a quick glance before they escorted her to their car. The look was almost apologetic. It was a feeling Daryl knew well.

He stood rooted in the hallway, staring through the open front door.

"Mommy, brea'fus!" commanded Kyle from the kitchen. Darin was still banging.

Daryl realized slowly that he had a spatula in his hand. What in the world was he supposed to do with it? Cindy had always made the pancakes.

PART 7
1989–1991

This time Julius woke up with his own scream still echoing, his heart pounding, his silk pajamas clinging moistly to his chest. He switched on the lamp by his king-sized bed, afraid to look, afraid not to, and stared at his hands. The palms were damp too but it was only perspiration. As immense as that relief was, his heart would not quit slamming against his ribs and his breath came in ragged pants, as if he had been running. He looked over at the clock. *Only 2:30.* There were hours to go before dawn and he knew he wouldn't get back to sleep.

The night was silent. Ester was in La Jolla and even with the lamp on, the house beyond the reach of its light seemed vast and ominous. He wanted a Scotch—badly—but the bottle was light-years away, down the hall, down the curved staircase, across the tiled entry hall, up two steps into the carpeted living area, behind the bar.

I should buy a smaller house—or get a room at a hotel, he thought first and then, *Dove's got to come back!* But at the very moment he pictured Ester in the room a cold shudder went up his spine. There had been two women in the dream—

He wouldn't let himself think about it. He had a smaller bottle of Jack Daniels hidden under the sink in the master bathroom. Did he dare leave his bed to get it? Somehow even putting his legs over the edge of the bed raised specters. He remembered his brother teasing him about monsters that lived under beds and bored up through the mattress when he was asleep. It took every fiber of his being to reject that childhood phobia.

He stood up shakily and made his way toward the bathroom. His feet sank into the soft carpet and just as he was thinking, *No one can find me, because I'm not making any noise,* he found his mind responding in panic, *If there's someone else here, their footsteps are silent too.* He must have jerked his head around a dozen times before he reached the doorway, turning on the bedroom light as he passed it. Even though he had caused it himself, the sudden blaze of light startled him. *I do need a drink,* he thought. *My fear is feeding on itself. I have to break the cycle.*

There was less in the bottle than he had hoped but with it held tightly in his right hand, raised almost as if it were a weapon, he scrambled back into the middle of the bed, against the carved headboard, pulling his feet off the floor and tucking them under him.

A few pulls at the whiskey calmed his nerves and quieted his racing heartbeat. After several minutes, he felt himself begin to relax and he gathered his fears back to him like a hen her chicks, telling himself they were childish. It had only been a dream. There was no substance to it. He didn't know either of the women—

Something clutched at his heart again. Shivers ran through him. *Stop it!* he told himself. *The psychiatrist said we make our own dreams, that we re-create reality as we want it to be—and we play all the parts.* But he knew that wasn't true. He didn't *want* to be scared out of his wits and he definitely was not either of the—

No! He wouldn't think about them! He couldn't help looking at his hands again. He should have washed them while he was in the bathroom. Should he get up again? If he could summon the nerve to get up and wash his hands, maybe he could make his way through the house to the Scotch. He could turn on all the lights as he went. Who would care if the house was lit up like Christmas? It wasn't as if he had to be frugal with electricity.

He had been holding a knife. That had been the awful part in the dream, not the women. His hand still seemed to feel the handle. A knife or a sword. In the dream, he could tell from the way it gleamed that it

Part 7: 1989–1991

was razor sharp but he had not been able to stop himself running a thumb along its edge. That was where the blood had come from.

No, it wasn't.

Although in the dream, the terrible part had been the fact that it was he who held the sword, he who had the power, he who had to make the decision, now that he was awake he could think of that calmly enough, but the women—

He still could not think about the women.

Why?

The whiskey had given him the boldness to get more. He would go slowly, concentrating on holding the terror in check, and it would be all right. He could even take a weapon with him.

He had a revolver in the nightstand. He kept it loaded with the safety on. *Take a loaded gun with him to walk through his own house?* Reason returned in part. That was absurd! Every outside door was locked with a deadbolt, every window secured. There wasn't the slightest indication that anything was amiss in the house.

Except his mind.

There was the briefest flicker of a scene from the dream, like Halloween spider webs drawn across his face in a grade-school haunted house. There had been a baby.

Again, Julius shuddered. He had touched the baby. Wet with amniotic fluid, it had seemed—*he* had seemed—slimy to Julius' touch. Against his own will, despising it, Julius had lifted the squalling infant by one heel and dangled it aloft, gripping tightly lest it slip from his grasp.

The women... what was it about the women that his conscious mind was holding at bay with all its strength, but that his subconscious was infiltrating into his memory in wisps and snatches?

He forced the dream from his mind and went for the Scotch. The familiarity of each room as he passed it was comforting. Behind the bar was a nearly-full fifth. He brought it back to bed with him, moving faster than normal, trying not to.

And they were waiting, the memories. Both women silently, invisibly waiting for his return.

Compelling Interests

One woman had been haughty and impatient, standing with arms crossed. The other had been on her knees, imploring him, even clinging to the hem of his—had he been wearing his surgical gown? He felt again his distaste at her tugging at him. *Don't touch me!*

He knew now, of course, what it was. It was the old story of Solomon, the wise king who had to decide which of two women was the real mother of a disputed baby.

Somewhere in Julius' childhood, before his mother had died, she had read him that story from the Bible. It was amazing how clearly it all came back to him now. Two prostitutes had come before Solomon. Both had given birth to baby boys, a few days apart. One of the women had rolled over on her baby and suffocated it in the night and she had exchanged the living one for her dead one. Now they both claimed the living child. Why had this come back to him, out of the recesses of his past? *Perhaps,* he thought, *there was an illustration with it and the sword scared me when I was a child. This is probably just some primitive fear surfacing because I've let myself get so distraught.* That was probably it. He had seen the picture as an impressionable five- or six-year old and now—

And now, he was Solomon.

It was up to him to decide. Which mother was the real mother? Which one had a right to the baby?

The bottle was lighter now. It nestled among the covers to the left side of him. Just to be safe, he crawled to the edge of the bed and fished around in the nightstand until he found the revolver. He placed that beside him to his right. Now, nothing could threaten him. No dream could have any power over him.

He had to decide. Whose baby was it? The raucous screams of the shrew and the pitiful bleating of the supplicant were coming back to his ears. "He's mine!" "No, *mine!*"

What had the biblical Solomon done? The point of the story had been to show the depth of Solomon's wisdom. He had held the baby high, his sword poised, and proclaimed, "We'll divide the baby in two and you can each have half."

Part 7: 1989–1991

That's how Julius had stood—he remembered that part vividly. Everything else around him was starting to blur. He had stood erect on some kind of mountain, his surgical gown flapping behind him, except where the kneeling woman clutched it. He was Solomon, the all-wise. He was the man who solved unsolvable dilemmas. He was the clever one, the aloof one, the controller. And that's when the dream had become a nightmare.

Julius took a great gulp of whiskey, not caring that in his haste or his clumsiness some of it ran from each side of his mouth. He wiped his chin with a silk sleeve.

Solomon's cleverness had revealed the real mother. Just before the blade descended, one of the women had cried out, "Don't kill him! She can have him!" Mercy for her child's life trumped self-interest.

Julius had revealed the real mother, too. In one irrevocable gesture, he had slashed the child in half. And then he knew. He knew who the real mother was.

The woman pleading for mercy, screaming for him to spare the baby, even if she couldn't have him, was the fake. The woman who didn't care, who said contemptuously, "Divide him!"

She was the real mother.

That's what abortion was. The surrogate begging for the baby's life. The real mother demanding his death.

And he was the murderer.

Somehow his part in the death of this nonexistent baby, a mere figment of his own imagination, agitated him more than all the living bodies he had dismembered, all the skulls he had crushed in reality.

He had helped mothers murder their own flesh. Tens of thousands of mothers.

His hands ran red with unseen blood.

Cindy Hodge's face, pinched and troubled, looked wanly from the front page of the *Southbay Journal*. Her arrest for the destruction of the Sanger Clinic, still a blackened shell on Santa Fe Avenue, had stirred up a hornet's nest of opinion.

Compelling Interests

"Burning down a building doesn't change anything," Cecile said, not for the first time, to reporters who asked for a comment on the arson. "It doesn't stop a woman from having an abortion. She just goes somewhere else—and when she does get it, she's farther along in her pregnancy, so it's even more dangerous for her. Of course, the other side doesn't care about the woman anyway, so that's OK with them."

The *Journal* also interviewed Corinne Zinzzer of Birthright. "We deplore violence of any kind," she said. "But let's keep it in proportion. The pro-choice people are upset about violence to the building. They ought to be even more upset about the violence that went on inside the building."

It was obvious that no matter how much they publicly denounced Cindy Hodge, the right-wingers were grateful to her that another clinic was out of business, at least temporarily. One spokesman for an anti-choice group had even told his followers, "If God can't get a sane person to burn down an abortion mill, He'll get an insane person to do it," implying that God not only condoned that sort of outrage but orchestrated it.

Cecile flew south at Liz Tewksbury's request to hold a private emergency session of local WomanPower leaders. Bobbie Porter opened her home for the meeting and they invited about thirty of the most active women in the area.

Liz was smoldering. "We've got a problem," Liz told the group. "The enemy's pressure tactics are working. There's only one clinic left in Long Beach and that's one of Dr. Guy's. He's having to cover the whole area. We need some strategy to protect women's rights."

"The fundamentalists have two so-called clinics of their own," observed Bobbie. "A lot of women are getting confused and going to them, thinking they're legitimate."

"We oughta close *them* down," suggested someone.

"I like that idea," said Cecile. "But how?"

"I'll get the matches!" laughed Bobbie.

"No," said Liz. "It has to be legal. And it has to be final. Some kind of lawsuit."

Part 7: 1989–1991

"Sue them for deceiving women into thinking they do abortions there. They call them 'clinics,' you know—Lifeline Pregnancy Testing Clinics." Bobbie reached for the phone book to prove her point.

"You know," Liz said, "we *could*. We could close down those anti-abortion clinics if we had a test case. What they're doing is clearly against the law—calling themselves clinics, doing pregnancy tests— If we could just have a mole—"

"Don't look at me," laughed Bobbie.

"No, someone young—"

"Well, thanks!"

"I mean like a teenager, someone they wouldn't suspect, just to see what they're up to over there."

"How about one of my students? Practically any one of them would be good."

"Well, get me one. I don't even have to meet her. Just have her call me afterwards. All she has to do is go get a urine test—"

"Shouldn't it come out positive, so they'll urge her not to get an abortion?" one of the other women asked.

"Not necessarily," put in Liz. "I've heard that their scare tactics are all before they give a woman the results of her test. They'll show her pictures of dead fetuses and the whole bit—"

"No," a couple of women objected. "Have it come out positive."

"Okay," offered Cecile, "do the opposite of what we did in the old days. We used to have women bring urine samples from friends who *weren't* pregnant so doctors would give them D&C's without realizing they were aborting them. Have her take in a urine sample from someone who is pregnant and tell them it's hers."

"Would that matter if we made a legal case out of it?"

"Shouldn't. We'd keep the spotlight on them. Besides," Liz leaned forward conspiratorially toward the thirty faces and her eyes danced, "*Who would know?*"

Liz coached Robin, a university freshman, and gave her a small tape recorder and a paper bag with a bottle in it to take in for testing, pretending it was hers.

Compelling Interests

Robin wasn't acting when she knocked timidly at the clinic door and then let herself in. She was scared to death of anti-abortionists and she had steeled herself for their intimidation.

Only her admiration for Bobbie Porter motivated her to do this—that and the promise that it would count toward her grade in Bobbie's Intro to Women's Studies.

There were two women in the clinic, not much older than Robin. One sat behind a desk and had her fill out a form with her name, address, and phone number. She filled it out truthfully, as instructed.

At the bottom of the form was a multiple choice question: "If I am pregnant, I plan to ___ keep my baby, ___ find an adoptive family, ___ abort." As instructed, Robin checked "abort."

When she called Liz that afternoon, she said, "I'm not sure I got what you wanted—"

"What happened?" asked Liz. She switched the phone to her other hand and grabbed a legal pad.

"Well, they had me fill out a form and I gave them the—you know, the sample—"

"Yes?"

"There were two women there. One of them read over the form I'd filled out and took me to a little room. There was a desk in it with models of fetuses—

"Models?"

"Yeah, like for a classroom or something. They had a view of the uterus cut in half and the fetus inside—some real small ones that looked like shrimp and one that looked like a baby, all jammed inside—"

"What else did they do?" interrupted Liz.

"And twins," finished Robin. "Well, they turned on a VCR and asked me to watch a film while they ran the test. It was about a doctor, outfitted for surgery, and he showed the instruments they use in abortions and told how they pull—"

"So they made you watch this?"

"Yes. Then the woman came back and talked to me. She asked me what I would do if I was pregnant—who I would tell. I said no one, I'd

Part 7: 1989–1991

just get an abortion. She said a baby is precious to God and how could I kill my baby—she kept using the word 'baby.'

"I said I just wanted to know if I was pregnant, I'd heard they didn't charge for a pregnancy test—"

"When did she give you the results of the test—" Robin heard Liz break off and snort with disgust at someone else in the room, probably Bobbie, "The test only takes sixty seconds and they took half an hour to browbeat her!"

"Well, when I said my mind was made up, I was sure I would have an abortion, she had me watch another film. This one was really gross. It made me feel sick. I had to close my eyes."

"Then what?"

"Then she came in and said the results were positive. I asked if that meant that I was pregnant and she said she couldn't say that because she wasn't medically trained, but that I *should* see a doctor. She told me please to see one that didn't believe in abortion and she kept saying, 'Think it over. Come back and talk to us before you do anything you'll regret all your life.'"

Liz was taking notes as fast as she could with the receiver hunched up to her cheek. It was good, but it wasn't quite enough.

"Is that all?"

"Well, while she was saying all this—I was really scared, you know, because I felt like she was badgering me and everything—I kept asking, 'Am I pregnant? Can you just tell me if I'm pregnant?' just like you told me to. And finally—she was crying—she said, 'I'm not supposed to say this, but a positive test means you're pregnant.'"

"Did you get it—"

"It's all on the tape."

"Bingo!" shouted Liz. "You did great, kid! You got yourself an A!"

After Robin left the Lifeline Clinic, the woman at the desk told her assistant, "You can't tell her she's pregnant!"

"Well, she is!"

"Yeah, but we aren't—"

Compelling Interests

"I know, but what's the difference? 'Your test is positive' or 'You're pregnant.' They mean the same thing."

They would find out the difference. Liz sued on Robin's behalf, claiming that the clinic was practicing medicine without a license. Liz made sure that the reporters copied down Robin's words, buried in the lawsuit, "I was really scared because I felt like she was badgering me."

Joan Andrews had been out of prison five months. She had spoken at numerous pro-life gatherings and appeared on several television talk shows. Birthright invited her to be the featured speaker at their 1989 annual education conference in March. She had just turned 41 and prison had taken a toll on her. Joan's deep-set eyes were weary. Her dark hair, parted in the middle and tucked behind her ears, was streaked with gray. But she spoke with animation, her fingers speaking with her, and even 31 months of solitary confinement had not quenched her radiant smile.

In her talk, she didn't describe what she had been through. She didn't refer to herself at all. She appealed simply on behalf of the helpless, nameless little ones being killed.

She received a standing ovation.

The Supreme Court had ruled on the Missouri case, Cecile noticed, a test case the right-wingers had trumped up to give the new conservative-leaning Supreme Court a chance to reverse Roe. They had chosen Missouri to point up some supposed parallel with the Dred Scott suit of 1857, a suit Cecile thought totally inapplicable. The Dred Scotts of today weren't some unborn blobs of protoplasm. They were women pregnant against their wills.

In any case, the Supreme Court had not reversed Roe in so many words but had thrown the right to restrict abortions back to the states, turning the fight for choice on the federal level to fifty fights for choice on the state level.

Part 7: 1989–1991

Where lobbyists on both sides had trained their guns on Washington, now in each state, they had to do hand-to-hand combat. For just such combat, Cecile moved from San Francisco to Sacramento, to keep the California state legislature from making any concessions to the anti-abortionists.

In Los Angeles, Liz met with Bobbie and Robin.

"We have to make plans," said Liz. "Missouri was a great blow to reproductive freedom. There's a chance we'll lose everything we've worked so hard for."

"What will we do if abortion ends up against the law again?" asked Robin with concern.

Liz answered grimly. "We'll break the law."

Artyce hung up the phone and sat down to steady herself. She had heard of Liz Tewksbury but had never faced her in person. Now they had both been invited to be guests on the TV program Firing Line.

In less than three years, Women for Traditional Values had grown from one woman, Artyce Lancaster, to 100,000 women. It already had almost a third the membership WomanPower had laboriously gathered in twenty years. Every move WomanPower made, every statement that came out of the mouth of its president, Cecile Tucker-Thomas, was reported in the newspapers and shown on TV—WomanPower was a familiar name in every household—yet not one woman in a thousand on the street knew anything at all about Women for Traditional Values. It grew by word of mouth.

As membership multiplied, she had managed to computerize her mailing list and had had to get two extra people to help her read mail and answer phone calls fulltime. New members were joining Women for Traditional Values so fast, she had enough money left over after paying expenses to be able to pay each of them something for their time.

Artyce studied every piece of legislation that had to do with the family. Although her marriage to Dan had failed, and although she still had a lot

Compelling Interests

of unresolved anger left over from the divorce, Artyce was committed to marriage as a concept. She believed it could work, that hers should have worked, that the institution of marriage was sacred. She resented what she saw as attacks on marriage and the family.

The gratification she felt at having her manuscript, *What You're Not Supposed to Know They're Teaching Your Children,* accepted in the fall and published this spring had not yet worn off. Requests for the book and requests for her to speak about the book had been overwhelming.

She had spoken to political women's groups. She had spoken to groups of evangelical women interested in becoming informed on issues. But she had never locked horns in public debate with anyone who was pro-abortion.

Artyce had developed a popular skit she liked to use when asked to speak to conservative women's groups. She would lift the brim of an imaginary Stetson with an imaginary pistol and drawl, "They call us Tucker-Thomas and Tewksbury. We're—the Terminators."

The way she said it, she made them sound like a comedy team. It never failed to bring down the house.

She looked forward with a certain sadistic vengeance to an opportunity to tangle with Tewksbury.

Liz Tewksbury and Artyce Lancaster were scheduled to confront each other on the controversial program Firing Line, airing live on Friday night. Mariana and Tasha bought pizza for everyone and took it into the second floor TV room to watch.

"This should be a clash of the titans," observed Tasha. "Artyce Lancaster is the only person I know who might be able to stand up against Liz Tewksbury. I've never seen her debate before but I heard her talk on Focus on the Family about sex education in the public schools and it was devastating."

The moderator, a man, was introducing them. Both women were in their forties, both in suits—Liz's was scarlet—both attractively coiffed and manicured. Both were composed. Both were deadly.

Part 7: 1989–1991

Artyce was saying, "A woman has TB. Her husband has syphilis. Their first child is blind. Their second child died at birth. Their third is deaf and dumb. Their fourth has TB. Now she is pregnant again. Would you counsel her to abort?"

"I never tell anyone—"

"Come on, Liz," baited Artyce. "Stop waffling. *Would abortion be strongly indicated here as the wisest choice?*"

"Well, yes, to *me,* but I'm not—"

Artyce leaned forward, her eyes glinting. "Congratulations. You've just killed Beethoven." She sat back smugly.

"That's one case out of millions!" Liz protested. "But even Beethoven's mother should have had the right not to have to raise another—"

"Beethoven, Liz!" said Artyce. "The Fifth Symphony. Ode to Joy. Think what the world would have lost!"

"A woman has no obligation to carry a fetus to term for the world—"

Their voices, rising and heated, were riding over each other now. As the moderator tried to call time out for a station break, Liz snapped angrily, "Not every deaf, syphilic child grows up to be Beethoven!"

"Whew!" said Mariana, realizing she had been holding her breath, "they ought to call it Firing *Squad!*"

After the break, the two women were at it again, this time with Liz on the offensive.

"What about the woman?" she demanded. "What about the woman? Thousands of women died—"

Artyce shouted over her, "What about the millions dying now, that's what I'm concerned about—"

"Millions of—? That's ridiculous. Deaths from legal abortions are only a fraction of what they were—"

"A fraction? 1.6 million deaths a year—you call that a fraction?"

"That is the most specious— You know good and well I'm talking about the *women. Thousands* of women died from botched coat hanger abortions in back alleys before abortion was legalized!" Liz was beautiful in her fury, her dark eyes flashing, her cheeks flushed, her voice loud but controlled.

Compelling Interests

"Tewksbury," shouted Artyce, "that statement's a lie and you know it's a lie and KASAL knows it's a lie and WomanPower knows it's a lie—" Tewksbury was starting to retort angrily, "because Michaelson, who *founded* KASAL, said in print ten years ago that he made up those statistics to get abortion legalized—"

"Official statistics from before Roe v. Wade did not reflect the real picture," said Liz Tewksbury hotly. "Abortion was illegal! Who would report that their wife or mother or sister or aunt had died from a self-induced abortion? Those deaths were recorded as deaths due to—to infections or—accident or—*anything!* That's what we're trying to get away from—the stigma of—"

"Women are *still* dying and abortionists *still* don't report the deaths as due to abortion!"

As the moderator smiled and thanked each of them, signing off, Liz muttered in a low voice, "You can't have it both ways."

"That was intense!" Tasha clutched her chest and looked at Mariana. "I feel like I'm going to have a heart attack and all I did was sit and watch!"

At the TV station, Liz and Artyce were still smoldering. They were off the air, the moderator was shaking their hands but Liz was arguing, "You can't say illegal abortion *didn't* kill many women—and then turn around and say legal abortion still kills them!"

Artyce started to respond but the moderator was intervening. "Hey, ladies!" He made a T-sign with his hands to indicate "Time out." "Lighten up. You both did great. Maybe we'll have a rematch sometime, whatta ya say?"

In the weeks following the debate, Artyce kept studying. She told herself it was only fair to study what the pro-abortionists said about themselves but she studied their writings like a cat studies a mouse—looking for vulnerability.

Feminists traced their fight for reproductive freedom—with pride—to a woman named Margaret Sanger. In the 1920's, after working as a nurse in New York City's Lower East Side, Sanger was convinced that women should have the right to limit their families. For distributing literature

Part 7: 1989–1991

which advocated birth control, she was indicted; for opening the country's first birth control clinic, she was arrested, charged with "maintaining a public nuisance."

Artyce managed to absorb little of the primary point Sanger was trying to make in her books, that, like it or not, women were *going* to prevent the birth of unwanted children and that allowing them to use birth control was preferable to their risking their lives undergoing abortion.

Instead, Artyce focused on Sanger's most radical claims that overpopulation was the root of all evil, as if numbers alone accounted for increases in crime, disease, mental illness, illiteracy, prostitution, and poverty.

She loved to quote Sanger's belief that "the most immoral practice of the day is breeding too many children."

"Margaret Sanger was the sixth of eleven children," Artyce would point out. "In her book *Woman and the New Race,* she wrote, 'The most merciful thing that the large family does to one of its infant members is to kill it.'" Artyce would always pause and add sarcastically, "Beginning with Number Seven, I presume." She went on to point out that Sanger's solution to high infant mortality was to kill children.

Margaret Sanger had also been an early devotee of eugenics. "More children from the fit, less from the unfit—that is the chief issue of birth control," Sanger had said. "Birth control is nothing more or less than the facilitation of the process of weeding out the unfit, or preventing the birth of defectives or of those who will become defectives."

The "unfit," according to Sanger, were the physically handicapped, the insane, the criminal, and especially those "guilty" of feeble-mindedness, "that fertile parent of degeneracy, crime, and pauperism."

"It is a curious but neglected fact," Sanger had remarked, "that the very types which in all kindness should be obliterated from the human stock, have been permitted to reproduce themselves and to perpetuate their group....Sterilization is the solution."

Others in the eugenics movement had extended the definition of "unfit" to racial groups and they urged that birth control be distributed to limit minority populations. Every minority, at one time or another, had seemingly been targeted by some faction of the eugenicists.

Compelling Interests

In advocating population control as a means of producing a superior race, as Artyce often pointed out, Sanger was offering an argument which a paperhanger in Germany would use with great effectiveness a decade later.

Artyce was still only working part-time, to free her to travel and to debate. Stephanie was 17, old enough to fend for herself for a weekend now and then, Artyce figured. If only Stephanie would show some interest in all of this. It was so important and after all, Stephanie was more directly a victim of the feminist philosophy than Artyce herself was.

It puzzled Artyce. Didn't Stephanie care about the world she was growing up into? It was great to have WTV growing by such leaps and bounds, but it still frustrated Artyce that she couldn't convince her own daughter of the need to fight the battle against the feminists' deception and victimization of women.

Stephanie had been so strange since the abortion, as if she'd retreated into herself. *She never confides in me anymore,* thought Artyce. *She has crying jags and goes on eating binges but she won't talk about it.* Those people had destroyed her daughter's life. It just made Artyce mad all over again.

Recognizing that they were well-matched, both articulate and sure-footed in a debate, TV show hosts now often pitted Artyce Lancaster against Liz Tewksbury. In one of these confrontations, Liz argued that unwanted children would be abused children.

"So you're advocating murder as preventive medicine," Artyce mocked. "Why don't we wait till the child is born and *see* if the parents abuse it? If they do, *then* we can kill it."

Cecile watched that debate with friends. "Lancaster has the most absurd logic," she commented, smashing her cigarette butt into the ashtray. "She refuses to address child abuse as a serious problem. She just wants to be a smart-ass."

On one talk show, Artyce finally faced Cecile herself, the 65-year old "Dowager of Death," Artyce called her, the woman who claimed she had single-handedly ushered in legalized abortion.

Part 7: 1989–1991

That's something to brag *about?* Artyce sniffed.

Cecile stated majestically, "I have never advised anyone to get an abortion. If someone wants my opinion, I always ask, 'Do you think it's a baby?' If they say yes, I tell them I won't help—I don't help anyone destroy babies. With that mentality, they'll regret it all their life.

"But if they say no, I tell them 'Go ahead.'"

Watching the show from the executive desk in her office, Liz Tewksbury muttered, "Sock it to 'em, Seely."

"Mind games," Artyce was responding icily. "Since when has reality been determined by our attitude toward it? You can't change biological fact by an act of the imagination. What about those who don't think it's a baby at the time but realize that it is one after it's too late?"

"The whole issue will be moot anyway as soon as scientists release the 'morning-after pill,' RU-486," said Cecile. "The French scientist who developed it just received the Lasker Medical Research Award and the French Health Minister has ordered that it be made available to women in France—but our reactionary administration is blocking its release here. That would solve everything."

"Would it?" asked Artyce. "RU-486 is chemical warfare on the unborn. It doesn't prevent fertilization. It just dissolves the baby sometime during its first eight weeks of life. The drug is Mifepristone and it was developed by a company descended from I.G. Farben, which manufactured cyanide gas for Nazi death camps. By all means, let's make the death drug available to American women!"

"Who cares who developed cyanide gas?" said Cecile dryly. "Dow Chemical Company produced napalm for the Vietnam war. Does that stop you from buying Saran Wrap?"

To Liz Tewksbury's surprise and delight, Randall Terry and other leaders of Operation Rescue were tried according to RICO—the Racketeer-Influenced and Corrupt Organizations act—passed in 1970 to enable federal prosecutors to indict leaders of organized crime. After all,

Compelling Interests

Liz reasoned, in encouraging trespassing, they were organizing crime, weren't they?

They defended themselves, using the argument that a lesser law could be broken when a life was at stake. "If your neighbor's house was on fire, should the law against trespassing stop you from trying to rescue his children?"

The judge dismissed the argument as inapplicable and overruled Terry's attempts to introduce into the proceedings videotapes taken of rescues at which bones had been broken by the police—in one case, Terry claimed, the sharp snap was clearly audible.

The jury was out for four days. They returned with a motion to acquit, citing Terry's defense about the lesser law. The judge declared a mistrial.

American voters were polarizing, narrowing their political concern to a single issue: abortion. Each side had targeted legislators for defeat.

For the pro-choice contingent, of course, Senator Nate Marshall was a prime target. Despite his record on other issues, for which some of their people had helped keep him in office until now, he was outspokenly pro-life. His wife's well-publicized abortion had not changed that. Also, he had been instrumental in attacking the Women's Studies program at Long Beach University. In 1992, he would have to go, they decided.

But getting Nate Marshall out of office was easier than they had thought. After the 1990 decennial census, the predominantly Democratic state legislature reapportioned the senatorial districts. With a stroke of someone's pencil, Anaheim was divided into three parts. Each of these districts already had elected legislators.

Nate Marshall, 39, with two years left in his third term, had no district. He was out of a job. He was left with an office in Sacramento, an office in the heart of Anaheim, and two secretarial staffs with nothing to do. As neatly as that, politically, he had ceased to exist.

Part 7: 1989–1991

Stephanie enrolled in college the following fall.

"Cal State Anaheim?" repeated Artyce, when Stephanie told her what she had chosen. "Why there? And why do you want to live on campus? You could go to my alma mater, Long Beach University, and live at home. It's closer."

Stephanie didn't answer and Artyce knew immediately why she had chosen Anaheim. Long Beach University was closer.

One of the classes Stephanie took that semester was Introduction to Women's Studies, taught by a woman whose class was so controversial, she had been suspended from Long Beach University. Ms. Porter, who asked students to call her Bobbie, was a pleasant woman with short-cropped hair. In one of the classes early in the semester she assigned the writing of a running diary.

"I want you to record your sexual response cycle, including sexual feelings, attitudes, and activities," she explained.

"I'm single," one girl spoke up in a small voice. "I can't describe my response cycle. I don't have sex."

The class looked to the teacher, who was smiling encouragingly. "Our sexuality is more than just having sex," she said. "What turns you on in a man—or a woman? What makes you breathe hard and feel flushed? What do you fantasize about when you masturbate?"

The girl turned red. "I don't!" she said.

"Try it," suggested the teacher. "Put yourself in a setting where you feel relaxed—"

"I don't believe it's right!" gasped the girl in embarrassment.

"I'm sorry you feel that way," shrugged the teacher, still smiling. "Then why don't you write about why the idea of sex is disturbing to you? What did your parents communicate to you about sex, verbally or non-verbally? Did they get nervous when you explored yourself as a little child? Did they scold you for 'playing doctor' with a friend? Did they teach you accurate names for all the parts of your body except the sexual parts?

"What taboos were there that made you feel uncomfortable about being female or being sexual?"

The girl sat very still.

Compelling Interests

"Let yourself feel your true feelings," the teacher urged. She smiled sympathetically. "I hope you'll be able to overcome your inhibitions and to accept yourself more fully."

The girl never came to class again.

One day there was a visitor in class and Bobbie announced, "For too many years, women's reproductive organs have been kept a mystery. Most women don't know what their own genitals look like. Aren't you curious about yourself? It's your body! You have a right to know!

"We have a guest lecturer from the Women's Center who is going to demonstrate how to give yourself a pelvic exam. If women would examine themselves for lumps and discharge, they wouldn't have to go to male doctors every year."

The visiting lecturer, a tall thin woman with glasses, made some introductory comments and then, before Stephanie's shocked eyes, unzipped her jeans, pulled them down and stepped out of them. She had nothing on underneath. Calmly, she discarded the pants on the floor, sat on the edge of Bobbie's desk and lay back, spreading her legs. Stephanie blushed and looked away.

"I'll show you how to insert the speculum," she was saying, "and then you can each come up and take a look."

Behind Stephanie the voice of a student said evenly, "I'm a nursing student and none of my teachers have ever taken off their clothes to teach us anatomy. Don't you think this is a little unprofessional?"

As Stephanie turned to glance at the slim strawberry blonde who had just spoken, Bobbie answered, with a trace of amusement, "Don't you think women have a right to know what their own bodies look like?"

"Of course. I just find this particular method of teaching unnecessary—and offensive."

The teacher ignored her. "Would the rest of you like to come on up and look through the speculum?"

Stephanie felt that she would appear prudish if she didn't line up with the others. She wanted to know what her own insides looked like, even though she wasn't at all comfortable looking at someone else's.

Part 7: 1989–1991

The same student was vocal in almost every class. Stephanie learned that her name was Ann and that she was a senior, even though she looked about 25. She was apparently going around with Noel McAllister, a square-shouldered student Stephanie recognized from her history class, because she noticed him stopping by the door to pick Ann up after almost every class.

When Bobbie asked her students what "myths" their parents had taught them about sex, Ann said her parents had taught her "to remain a virgin till marriage and to be faithful in marriage." She didn't seem to think what they had taught her was a myth.

One day Bobbie spent nearly the whole hour talking about something called the Family Protection Act which had been introduced in Congress. She read from an American Civil Liberties Union pamphlet claiming the act was a serious infringement on women's rights.

Ann spoke up. "I'm *for* the Family Protection Act," she said. "It will protect the rights of women who prefer to stay home and raise a family."

Several students immediately interrupted. "What about the right of women to federally-funded abortions?" "What about lesbian rights?" "What about state-supported childcare centers?"

The teacher expanded on their objections to the Protection Act. She wrote on the board the number of the bill and the names and addresses of legislators who supported it and told students to write to them urging them to change their vote.

Again, Ann's quiet but persuasive voice came over Stephanie's left shoulder, "You have read arguments *against* the act—why don't you give us both sides? Why don't you read us the actual wording of the act?"

Stephanie always winced when Ann began to speak. Why did she have to be offended by everything? She sounded just like Mom.

In the meantime, Stephanie was learning so much she felt she had been in a cave all her life and was coming out into the world for the first time. She was much more aware than she had been of ways in which women were discriminated against, ways in which the patriarchal society she lived

Compelling Interests

in oppressed and exploited women. She saw her high school relationship with Justin in a new light. She saw now that he had exploited her, too.

Just before the last day to drop a class, Ann raised her hand and said, "Bobbie, I'm bothered by something on page 126 of our textbook. The book is encouraging women to help each other with what it calls 'menstrual extraction' up to nine weeks after their last period. If a woman hasn't had a period in nine weeks, she either has a medical problem or she's pregnant. In either case, she should see a doctor!

"Performing abortions on each other seems very dangerous to me. Wasn't the whole purpose of legalizing abortions to make sure that they're performed by competent people under safe conditions? I don't see how it is safe for untrained women to be performing home abortions on each other!"

"Women who practice menstrual extraction are not untrained," retorted Bobbie. "If they are familiar with the size and placement of the uterus, they won't risk aborting past the time when it's safe."

"There's a little warning at the bottom of the page," Ann went on, "that if the pregnancy turns out to be more advanced than they'd bargained for, they may have to 'resort to medical personnel who have access to the necessary equipment.' To me, this is saying that if the women botch the job, they may have to rush the woman to a hospital. By that time she could bleed to death! This seems to me to be practicing medicine without a license!"

The teacher wasn't smiling now. She said icily, "In previous discussions, Ann, you have made it clear that you are against abortions, per se. I think your emotional bias against abortion is affecting your opinion of this process."

Stephanie didn't see Ann in class again.

The U.S. Supreme Court's ruling on the Missouri case had thrown the issue back to the individual states. Some states ignored the opportunity to tighten up restrictions on abortion. Others, like Pennsylvania, took

Part 7: 1989–1991

advantage of it to protect the late-term fetus and the rights of parents to give consent to a daughter's abortion.

The next step, everyone knew, could be an overturning of Roe or a pro-life constitutional amendment.

The newspapers were full of dire predictions from the feminists regarding the chaos that would result if Roe were overturned. One Supreme Court justice had spoken of the change in mood throughout the country as a "chill wind."

Despite her hope at the prospect that Roe might someday be repealed, Mariana knew repealing Roe wouldn't put things back the way they had been before 1973. Women were used to the convenience. Doctors were used to the money.

"If abortion becomes illegal again," she told Tasha, "things will be worse for a while than if it had never been legal. What we do will be more critical than ever. We'll be swamped."

"It won't be illegal again," predicted Tasha. "Not entirely. I think late-term abortions will, once Americans understand them. But both sides are going to have to compromise. People like us who are against all abortion are going to have to recognize that sex happens and that birth control can fail.

"On the other hand, women who insist that abortion is a private thing will have to admit that abortion after the heart starts beating, at least, is taking life and that the state has a right to intervene in a private murder."

There was also a possibility that even if Roe were repealed, over-the-counter home abortion kits would make abortion such a private matter that there would be no way of controlling it.

There would be no clinics to picket.

Cecile, faced with the very real danger that women might lose all the rights she had fought to win for them, moved quickly from anger to weariness to a strange calm.

"Well, Liz," she said when Liz met with her in Sacramento to build the pro-choice lobby there, "we're about to become outlaws again."

Compelling Interests

"I think it's a mistake to talk about going underground before we've exhausted all our options in the political arena," said Liz.

"It's OK," said Cecile. "Legislation comes and goes. If we handle it ourselves, nobody can take it away from us. Besides, this time we have a far broader base of trained medical people to help us and a more effective network of lay people. We'll transport women from states where abortion is restricted to states where it isn't. And teach women to abort each other. Last time was just a dress rehearsal, Liz. We did it before. We can do it again."

"Menstrual extraction?"

"Sure. It's basically just a return to the old idea of the midwife, before women were supplanted by doctors. Midwives and herbalists have always been there with ergot or blue or black cohosh or some other natural abortifacent.

"We've got to get this information out now, however we can—videos, whatever it takes. We'll make these techniques as familiar as CPR. This is lifesaving, too, you know."

A home abortion kit, complete with manual, was pictured with a smiling woman in the *Southbay Journal.* In the accompanying article, the woman was quoted as saying, "Menstrual extraction is a technique that was invented by an elementary school teacher in San Diego twenty years ago, using suction. The beauty of it is, it involves items women already have around their homes or can get easily, like plastic tubing and canning jars.

"It has been tested on thousands of women and it doesn't cause any higher rate of infection or uterine perforation than medical abortions do. You just insert a small cannula into the uterus and squeeze an ampulla attached to it. There's nothing to it. The contents of the uterus are sucked out."

Within two weeks, Artyce was asked to join a panel of women on a talk show discussing the controversial kit. Two of the panel members had used it and both praised it highly. A pro-choice woman and an obstetrician joined Artyce in objecting to it as risky.

Part 7: 1989–1991

"I use it all the time," claimed one of the women brightly, "whether I think I may be pregnant or not. You can use it up to six or eight weeks after you've missed your period. You just get your friends in and do it together. It's really convenient for athletes and newlyweds and people going on vacation."

"Isn't it painful?" asked someone in the audience.

"Well, it felt stronger than menstrual cramping. But there aren't any side effects. It's great, whether or not a pregnancy has been implanted."

"You mean—a *baby?*" Artyce asked pointedly.

The doctor frowned. "There's a fifty percent chance that if menstrual extraction—and that's what we're talking about—is used to abort a pregnancy, it won't work."

The woman shrugged and smiled. "If you miss the product of conception, well, hey, you get together and do it again."

Artyce objected vociferously. "This is the feminist's answer to unsafe and illegal abortions? More unsafe and illegal abortions? The same women who fought for legal abortions, arguing that they would be safer, are now demanding the right to take this operation out of the hands of the professionals and train lay women to perform it on each other!"

The pro-choice panel member was nodding. "I think doing abortions on each other is terribly dangerous."

The obstetrician agreed. "Every time you invade the uterine cavity, there's a likelihood of infection. It's not as easy to do as its proponents would have you believe."

"If the feminists have their way," Artyce added, "we will have come full circle. Abortions will again be performed illegally by unqualified people, but this time in private homes where women gather as casually as if for a Tupperware party. This is progress?"

One of the two women defending the abortion kit tossed her head. "We know our bodies. We know what we're doing. Women can take care of themselves."

Compelling Interests

A nunchaku consists of two heavy hardwood sticks joined together at one end by a four-to-five inch chain or cord, somewhat like a short jump rope. When the chain is wrapped around a criminal's arms or wrists and the sticks are squeezed together, with surprisingly little effort the vice-like action applies enormous pressure and excruciating pain on sensitive areas. A nunchaku can crush bones and critically damage tendons and ligaments. For this reason, it is highly effective. For this reason also, for a civilian to possess a nunchaku is a felony.

In Los Angeles, where drugs such as crack can give a suspect superhuman strength, it may take four or five policemen to subdue a person who under normal circumstances couldn't press 150 pounds. When they are confronted with a level of violence and unpredictability which puts their own lives at risk, peace officers are not bound by the traditional policy of "sufficient force"—that is, enough force to control a violent suspect and no more.

In these exceptional cases, officers are allowed to use something called "pain compliance." Pain compliance, as it sounds, is the deliberate application of pain for the purpose of disabling a suspect and rendering him or her helpless. This may take the form of pressure in or behind the ears, at the base of the neck, in the nostrils or eye sockets, or reverse-wrist or finger locks. Or the use of nunchakus.

In Los Angeles, police geared up for a three-day assault, targets unknown, by Operation Rescue.

"Operation Rescue's *modus operandi* is to use passive resistance," Deputy Chief Welch told his squad. "When arrested, they go limp and have to be dragged one by one to the vans, requiring the maximum number of officers to take the maximum amount of time in removing them. In other cities, this has involved the use of manpower-intensive methods such as carrying them from the scene on stretchers.

"Our M.O. is just the opposite. In a city of over three million people, which has to handle 800 homicides, 2,000 forcible rapes, 26,000 robberies and 37,000 aggravated assaults per year, our department is stressed enough. We have no intention of spending an entire day outside an abortion clinic, tying up our best people and perhaps spending $100,000 carrying

Part 7: 1989–1991

non-violent offenders to vans. Therefore, we will deploy three hundred officers, two dozen of them mounted. We will wear riot gear and we will use pain compliance. Our object is to cause pain sufficient to bring about cooperation. Are there any questions?"

There were none.

On Saturday, it rained. By the time most of the rescuers got to the clinic in Los Angeles, the pro-choice vanguard was already in place, arms linked, each person carrying his or her mass-produced round blue and white sign, chanting slogans. Some of them skipped in the street in hungry anticipation.

Behind this vocal wall, blocked from view, were seated men and women willing to be arrested.

For Ann Lawson, seated deep in a doorway, with many rows of people in front of her, the decision had been a simple one. People shouldn't kill babies. She felt a sense of peace and even inevitability, that it had come to this.

Tasha, in great fear and trembling, was there too, on the front lines. She was scheduled for surgery in three days to remove a uterine tumor, which had been bothering her for weeks. She dreaded the additional pain the police might cause if they handled her roughly.

Besides that, she couldn't help wondering what her family back in Georgia would think if an unflattering picture of her appeared on the news that night as she was carried to a waiting van.

They didn't approve of Operation Rescue.

But this was the civil rights issue of the '90s and she could not in good conscience stand on the sidelines, any more than she could have stood on the sidelines in Selma or in Little Rock. Minority women were more victimized by abortion than anyone else.

At least her sons wouldn't be ashamed of her. They supported her stand. Raymond and Rodney were teenagers now and Tasha was proud of them. She had raised them alone since her mother had died and she had made sure the boys knew they would respect themselves only if they earned their own way in life.

Compelling Interests

She had taught them to respect women, too, and to take responsibility for their actions. Rodney had told her the other day, "Mama, I can't promise you I'm not gonna mess around but if I do, I'll take precautions. I'd be a fool to get a girl pregnant after you've told me what it does to them. If I do, you knock me upside the head!"

Except for this darn tumor, Tasha was very happy these days.

Crowds were surging back and forth, with Tasha caught, seated, in the undertow. She kept her head down and her arms and legs bent, so she wouldn't get stepped on. Suddenly, she felt someone kick her—hard—in the kidneys. The pain was so intense she didn't try to see where it had come from. Anyway, it could have been an accident. Everyone was so closely packed.

Artyce was there, grim. *Let the pro-aborts do their worst,* she thought. And they did. The wall of pro-abortionists stood between the media and the seated rescuers, so the cops and the reporters would never know that rescuers were being hit, punched, kicked and spat upon—even bitten. Artyce saw one man approach a seated rescuer and make loud, lewd suggestions. When the rescuer wouldn't respond or even look up, the man grabbed his wrist and bit it as hard as he could, breaking the skin. Then he stood back and said with satisfaction, "I have AIDS. Now you do, too." He worked his way through the crowd and disappeared.

Artyce was furious. Where were the police? Where were the camcorders? She had seen the police knock cameras out of the hands of bystanders so there would be no record of the real assault and the true aggressors would not be the ones arrested. It took every ounce of self-control she could summon to resist the violence welling up within her. She didn't dare look anyone in the face and if she opened her mouth, she would probably scream.

She knew the articles the next day would describe the scene, as always, as if the acts of hostility were mutual. It wouldn't be true and she must see that it didn't become true.

As the arrests began, Artyce realized that a fragile-looking, white-haired woman next to her was in pain. When she asked about it, the woman said, "It's arthritis. I should be in bed."

Part 7: 1989–1991

Artyce didn't ask the obvious.

The police came. Artyce recognized the LAPD Deputy Chief from the 6:00 news the night before. He was well-known as an evangelical, a popular speaker at youth conferences and Christian camps. He was also pro-life, yet he had vowed firmly to do his duty and arrest anyone who trespassed at a clinic.

Traitor! thought Artyce.

Now the Deputy Chief raised a bullhorn and read them some regulation against unlawful assembly. No one moved.

"Disperse or you will be arrested!" he commanded. The crowd at his feet only got better grips around each other and moved closer together.

Disperse, ha! thought Artyce. *Make me!*

Down the way, she could see the rhythmic up and down, up and down of Billy clubs descending indiscriminately on the crowd. Many on the sidelines who were using cameras were clubbed. She saw the police hook two fingers into one man's nose and jerk his head back, dragging him by it to the van. The pro-aborts cheered. "All *right!*"

"Woo! Woo! Woo! Woo!" they chanted eerie staccato war whoops. "*Get* 'em!"

Later, as the arrests began, the woman next to Artyce said as if to herself, "I want to get this over with." She called out to the police, "Arrest me, please." They ignored her. When one officer came close, she tried again.

"Lady," he said. "Go home so you won't get hurt."

"Put the handcuffs on," she insisted.

So two of them obliged her, cinching her wrists together with plastic cord. Artyce heard the bone crack, and at her shriek of pain, the pro-aborts applauded.

"My wrist!" the woman gasped. "I think you broke my wrist!"

"Poor baby!" said one officer.

"You asked for it," said the other, shrugging. They marched her off.

When the police reached her, Ann went limp. They refused to drag her. An officer pulled a can of mace from his belt and shot her full in the face. Choking, her eyes watering, the eyes and the lining of her nose burning, Ann stumbled to her feet and followed him to the car. Despite the pain,

Compelling Interests

the sense of peace she had felt from the beginning was almost palpable. This was a small price to pay to take a stand for life. If necessary, she had been willing to pay with her own.

Artyce was next. *Go ahead and hurt me, you pigs!* she dared them silently. *Give me something to sue you for!* They tied her wrists, jerked her by them to her feet and pushed her into a van. The pain only increased her resentment. At the end of the ride, she was led through a tunnel onto a huge football field—the Coliseum, someone said. It was still drizzling.

Somehow, despite the presence of a large number of cops, the scene looked to Artyce more like earthquake relief than a police station. Everyone was cold and wet. It was at least noon and they hadn't had food or water since five that morning. Streams of rescuers were joining them as one bus after another arrived.

In assembly-line fashion, the prisoners were each booked and cut loose. Artyce tried to rub feeling back into her hands.

Here the mood was different than on the front lines. Here, the officers were much gentler, almost sympathetic. More of them were women. One plump female cop joked with them as she cut their cords and motioned them to the field, "Singing or non-singing section?"

People *were* singing, Artyce noticed. As she was herded with the rest of her busload onto the field, she was surprised by the spirit of contentment and camaraderie that seemed to characterize the crowd, such a contrast to her own emotions. She still seethed and churned with resentment. All these people shared her revulsion about abortion, she thought. So how was it that they were not angry, as she was? Why weren't they shaking their fists and plotting revenge?

Instead, in their small huddles, guarded by police, they were giving each other backrubs, comparing bruises, and discussing their injuries in subdued tones or chatting happily as if they had run into each other at the supermarket.

Near Artyce was the woman who had arthritis, shivering miserably on a bench. Artyce nodded a greeting.

The woman leaned toward her and spoke in a near-whisper. "Well, I *did* ask for it—and oh, boy, did they give it to me!" She indicated her

Part 7: 1989–1991

swollen wrist and tried to smile through white lips. "There's a doctor in our group and he thinks it's a compression fracture. He gave me some aspirin."

"Are you going to be okay?" asked Artyce with concern. She took off her windbreaker and wrapped it around the woman. "Here. It isn't much but it might help."

"I don't think I've ever hurt so much in my life," said the woman cheerfully. "But I keep telling myself I can't hurt as much as my three-month old baby did when I aborted her."

Artyce was silent. She didn't know whether she wanted to hear about it or not.

The woman went on, "You know, sitting there in that rain, I felt I was doing something to right that wrong, doing something to make it up to my baby. Twenty-five years I've felt guilty about it! For 25 years I've dreamed that there was a beautiful baby girl just out of my reach. Today I feel as if I have reached her, as if she's right here with me." She tapped the chair next to hers and her eyes became watery. "It's OK. It's finally OK."

She turned to speak to someone else and Artyce sat for a long time, thinking about what the woman had said. She wondered for the first time whether Stephanie ever thought about the baby she had aborted, whether she felt sorrow over her loss, whether she grieved.

I have been so busy feeling angry and betrayed for her, I haven't thought about what she was feeling. Artyce remembered all the times Stephanie had stood silently while Artyce ranted on about some new atrocity perpetrated by the feminists. *Why wasn't I there for her?* she thought. *I thought I was helping her by going to battle to protect her—but I never once sat down and let her talk, or cry, or scream. I never once asked her if she still hurts inside or if she is all right.*

Artyce had a lump in her throat so big she couldn't swallow. Something within her was beginning to melt. A wall. A wall of rage and helplessness and guilt was breaking and for the first time in five years, Artyce felt the stirrings of compassion.

She felt compassion for Stephanie, deprived of one parent by divorce, the other by economic necessity, forced to make adult decisions much too fast, seeking affection from a boy to make up for the loss of the love of her father.

Silently, alone, despite the hundreds of small groups standing and sitting nearby, Artyce let herself forgive.

She forgave Stephanie for having had sex with Justin and for not confiding in her about their deepening intimacy and about her pregnancy. She forgave her daughter for not refusing the advice of the school clinic staff and of the abortion clinic staff, for allowing herself to be a victim. She forgave Justin for getting her daughter pregnant. She forgave the people at Stephanie's high school who had referred her for an abortion. She forgave the nurses who had ushered her in, lying to her that it would all be over in a minute, when it would never be over, never. She forgave the doctor who had sucked Artyce's grandchild into oblivion and made money from doing so.

She forgave all the children like Stephanie who were sexually active and having abortions. She saw them, too, with compassion—young people who were entering into adult relationships and often having to cope with adult consequences of those relationships long before they should have to.

At last, tears coursing down her cheeks, washing away the years of bitterness, she forgave the multitudes of women of all ages who were taking the lives of their babies. She forgave the feminists who created in them the mindset that it was OK. She forgave the Supreme Court justices who had believed the feminists and made it legal.

In a rush, like the banks of a river crumbling before a rising flood, the forgiveness gave way to repentance. *I have been wrong to hate,* she thought. *I have been wrong to judge. Oh, God, I am the one who needs to be forgiven.* Then, deep inside herself, Artyce knew that as she had forgiven others, God had forgiven her.

A load lifted. She felt, for the first time since Stephanie had been a little girl, a surging joy. She had told herself then, "I am standing on tiptoe at the very top of Maslow's pyramid." She could not say that now. The joy was real enough but beneath it was a layer of sadness, because her years of bitterness had driven Stephanie away.

Part 7: 1989–1991

Still, the relief and sense of freedom were so great that even regret could not fully overshadow them. She sat next to her new friend, took the cold hand which wasn't broken and began rubbing it gently. And together, with the others, they begin to sing "Amazing Grace."

Tasha panicked as two policemen grabbed her.

"I'll walk!" she said hastily. They paid no attention. One of them pinned her arms behind her. The other had what looked like a pair of sticks connected by a chain. Tasha could feel him wrapping this tightly around her wrists. Then he squeezed.

The most excruciating pain she had ever felt shot up both Tasha's arms, knocking her breath out of her in a terrified shriek. Dimly, as she felt herself starting to faint, she heard a volume of cheers and catcalls go up from the sidelines. As her body sagged, the pain doubled, so she fought to regain her feet, but the two men were dragging her across the rough, wet pavement. She was barely conscious of anything but the pain when they heaved her into the van on top of the other prone bodies—"just like Dachau," she had time to think, "except we're alive."

Shock, pain, confusion, embarrassment—her knee was in someone's groin—fear that she would smother, gratitude that the warmth of the strangers beneath her was countering her shivering, she was jolted by the arrival of two or three other bodies in quick succession. One was a 65-year old man whose pants had fallen down in the scuffle. He landed next to her, unable to cover himself.

Then the van door was slammed shut and the cacophony outside was reduced to a distant murmur. She felt the vehicle shudder as men jumped aboard and it started up.

The ride was agonizing. Her wrists burned and the slightest movement—her own or those of someone else—was unendurable. She had lost all feeling in her hands. Would there be nerve damage? Would it be permanent? She felt bad about the people beneath her who were groaning and gasping but there was nothing she could do.

Compelling Interests

When they stopped at last, they were lifted out of the van and set upright, still bound. They were being herded into a gymnasium, where hundreds of people were already being booked. The cords were cut off their wrists as they entered.

Two policewomen seated behind a table were asking each person questions, filling in forms on manual typewriters. "Name?" one asked of the man ahead of Tasha.

"Name?" asked the other woman, addressing Tasha.

"Baby Doe," the man in front of her said.

"Baby Doe," echoed Tasha in a whisper. She felt faint and she couldn't control her shivering. Her wrists hurt and the pain in her uterus felt like the contractions of heavy labor, but her arm hurt the most. Overweight, she knew her extra pounds had put added stress on her shoulders as she hung by them, struggling to comply with the police.

Two doctors, accompanied by a lawyer, were circulating among the rescuers, checking cuts and rope burns and listening to accounts of rough treatment. One of the doctors examined her shoulder. She let out an involuntary cry.

"Dislocated," the doctor was saying to the lawyer, who wrote it down.

"Your name?" the lawyer asked Tasha. Before she could answer, the doctor ordered, "Relax," lifted her arm and slipped the ball back into the socket. The pain was fierce but temporary. He took her other arm gently.

"For a black lady," he said—he was black himself—"you're turning mighty white. You'd better sit down." He led her to a row of bleachers a few feet away and the people on it moved over to give her a seat. He told her to put her head between her knees and for a long time, Tasha fought to stay conscious, not sure whether she was going to throw up or pass out.

At last she raised her head and started noticing the people around her. Many of them were sitting on the gym floor. A lot of them were shivering. Everyone was soaking wet and bedraggled.

There didn't seem to be the feeling of warfare there had been outside. On the whole, the police officers here were kind and solicitous. They

Part 7: 1989–1991

allowed the prisoners to share jackets or huddle together for warmth, to sing hymns.

If Tasha sat very still, the various pains were bearable. But gradually she became aware of another sensation. She needed to go to the bathroom. She told one of the policemen guarding them.

"Not yet," he said. She waited a long half hour and asked again.

"No."

When a new guard took his place, she asked permission again and again with increasing urgency and each time was denied.

One rescuer had jumped up on the bleachers and was quoting the entire book of First Peter from memory: "If you should suffer for the sake of righteousness, you are blessed! And do not fear their intimidation, and do not be troubled, but sanctify Christ as Lord in your hearts....To the degree that you share the sufferings of Christ, keep on rejoicing....When the Chief Shepherd appears, you will receive the unfading crown of glory..."

No one stopped him. In fact the police were listening as if in awe. Someone tapped one of them on the back and said, "Phone," but the cop shrugged him away. "Not now!"

"I've got to go to the bathroom!" insisted Tasha.

"Hang on," the cop said, mesmerized by the oration.

She had been enduring the discomfort for three hours now. Was this "suffering for righteousness"? If she hadn't felt so bad, she might have laughed aloud at the irony of it.

At last Tasha summoned all her strength and said in the loudest voice she could, "If I don't get to a bathroom right now, I'm gonna pee in my pants!" Several startled cops turned to look at her. Hastily, the nearest one called, "Anyone else need to go?" and led a contingent to the nearest women's room.

The man on the table had finished First Peter and was reciting Ephesians when Tasha came back, proud of herself. As he concluded with "Grace be with all those who love our Lord Jesus Christ with a love incorruptible," a hundred voices shouted "Hallelujah!"

A high soprano voice, alone at first, began singing, "My hope is built on nothing less than Jesus' blood and righteousness—" She was joined

Compelling Interests

by a great wave of voices. At last the voices died away as if by a signal. Someone—several people—everyone—began to clap, exclaiming again, "Hallelujah!" Now they were cheering Jesus. Tasha stopped clapping to wipe the tears from her eyes. No church service had ever been more moving. When it was over, strangers hugged each other—gingerly, because of the injuries.

There were still lines of new people coming in. One of those being booked looked familiar to her. He was a young man, Chicano, with a small, pointed moustache. As soon as he moved away from the table, Tasha made her way painfully up to him.

"I wonder why they don't use IBAR," he was saying to someone. "They just got a new computerized booking system. Between this place and the other one, there are about 750 people being booked and they're doing every one of us manually."

"Aren't you Mariana's husband?" Tasha asked tentatively. "I stayed in your house when I was pregnant." Pause. "I was the one who gave my baby to that couple in your church—"

Recognition lit up his face. "Oh, of course," he said.

"Tasha," she reminded him.

"Oh, Tasha, that's right. You work with Mariana, don't you? Paul Hernandez."

They shook hands.

"Isn't this incredible?" said Paul. His face was glowing. "Right on the front lines. Now I know what Mariana has been talking about."

They both knew Mariana would not leave the mothers' home even for a rescue. Others could do that. She was already rescuing fulltime. She would be in her tiny office off the kitchen, her desk strewn with papers, the wall covered with snapshots of newborn babies, answering the phone and figuring out how to keep the place open another month. Grace, now 4, would probably be upstairs on some pregnant woman's lap, insisting on hearing *Green Eggs and Ham* for the umpteenth time.

Tasha shook her head. "I just can't get over all these people taking time off work and coming here to get arrested to save babies like DeShawn. At

Part 7: 1989–1991

the home, all I see is women needing help and it seems like there are only a handful of people who care. But look at them all!"

"Your arm is bothering you, isn't it?" he asked. "Have you had one of the doctors look at it?"

"Yes. It's my shoulder. Were you hurt? I heard someone say that over half the people brought in are hurt—bloody noses, broken teeth, concussions—"

"They punched me in the throat. I'm going to feel it tomorrow," said Paul. "It doesn't matter." His eyes lit up again and his voice took on a warmth that made others around them turn to listen.

"I was sitting on the curb," he said, "right next to a mounted policewoman, watching everyone else get arrested. I asked them to arrest me right away but they were starting at the other end, so I was one of the last ones. I saw everything. I saw them drag one man headfirst through horse manure. I saw them break another man's glasses and knock his teeth out.

"But you want to know something neat that happened?" Paul exclaimed. "I'm allergic to horses! Terribly allergic. The last time I was near a horse I ended up in the hospital. I couldn't breathe. Here I was with this policewoman's horse right next to me—I mean, he was pressed right against me, I couldn't move away—and he was breathing on me. And I didn't get any symptoms at all."

Suddenly they realized someone was making an announcement through a portable loudspeaker. "If you give us your real names, we will release you right now."

A man shouted back, "We won't give our names until the charges against our leaders are dropped."

The cop with the bullhorn consulted briefly with another cop. "Those charges have been dropped," he said.

A number of people surged forward to give their names. Tasha had been arrested at ten. It was 5:30 or 6 by now—the scuffle with the police had broken her watch. She decided to give her name and go home. She was tired and contented; despite her apprehension, she had accomplished what she came to do. Besides, she had told the boys she'd be home by six.

"I'll stay here," said Paul. "Mariana will understand."

Compelling Interests

Those who gave their names were taken out back, divided by sex and escorted to buses.

"You will be released from Central Jail," a stout policewoman told them.

But not right away, apparently, Tasha realized. In jail, groups of 30-40 women were put in each cell, with a toilet in the corner, and they were given sandwiches of green baloney. Despite the pain in her lower abdomen and in her shoulder and wrists, despite her hunger and fatigue, Tasha felt a strange euphoria.

"I've never felt so free," she told Mariana afterward. "The feeling just swallowed me up. It was like I was in a womb—safe. I even cried, in spite of all my pain, because I felt so good."

The women took turns sitting on the steel bench or sitting or lying on the concrete floor, pillowing their heads on their arms. Tasha's tumor made her stomach ache. Each time she managed to fall asleep on the floor, a female guard would come to the bars and announce, "Come on, girls, let's go." The women would obediently troop after her, out the door and down the hall and into another cell. As Tasha put it later, the guards "played musical cells all night."

It went on like this till 2 A.M. "We were probably in every cell in the jail at one time or another," she reported to Mariana. "Then we were loaded into a third bus and driven to Sybil Brand Women's Institute. They let us have showers and make phone calls and gave us food and dry clothes.

"But they didn't release us till six in the morning. And do you know what we learned when we got out? The charges against Terry and the other leaders of Operation Rescue hadn't been dropped at all."

Tasha and Mariana stayed up late that night, talking. Mariana had a new dream. They had prayed the drug dealers out of the apartment house next door and it was finally up for sale. "The new moms that keep their

Part 7: 1989–1991

children could stay there for six months or a year. We could have classes in parenting and we'd be right next door if they have a question."

They needed $71,000 by the end of the month, half for a down payment and half for the first year's operating expenses. How much could Lifeline afford? At the moment, nothing—but if the Lord wanted them to have the building, Mariana and Tasha knew He would provide.

Although Stephanie didn't see Ann again that semester, she saw Ann's friend Noel McAllister every other day because they were in the same World History class. He was about Ann's age, maybe 25, tall and broad-shouldered. Behind old-fashioned glasses, his eyes were intelligent and gentle.

History was not Stephanie's strong suit. He was sitting next to her when she received a D on the first test and he must have seen her scowl.

"Didn't do too well, huh?"

She made a face.

"You might want to consider a tutor."

"It's all those treaties and things," she said ruefully. "That Maginot Line—I don't understand."

Noel closed his books and gathered up his things, walking with her out the door and down the steps, explaining to her as they went. They were halfway to the student union before he broke off and said, "Did that help?"

"Yeah, but I'm afraid I'll flunk the class anyway. I don't even remember what countries were on what side. World War Two—that's *ancient* history. Who gives a rip?"

He smiled. A couple of his teeth were crooked. "Well, I kind of do," he said.

She stopped and looked at him. "You really *like* this stuff? Whoa!"

He looked embarrassed. She looked at her watch.

Compelling Interests

"I'm going to be late. At least you explain things so I understand them. Every time I open this dumb book, I fall asleep. Before the next test, could you help me?"

"I'd be glad to," he said. "But maybe you'd better start a little sooner than that."

"Can we talk about it Wednesday?" she said. "I've gotta go." She dashed off, calling "Thanks!" over her shoulder.

They agreed to meet two evenings a week, just to go over what had been covered in class. When she told her boyfriend Leroy, he sulked. "Evenings are our time!" But she was insistent.

"Leroy, I've got to get at least a C in this class or my mom won't pay my tuition for next year. Don't worry, he's a geek."

Leroy grabbed her around the waist and pulled her to him. "Do we still have the weekends?"

"Sure."

"And Christmas vacation?" he said in a sultry tone.

She grinned and put her arms around his dark neck. "Yeah!"

Funny. She had felt a twinge of guilt calling Noel a geek. He was so nice to her, it didn't seem right to make fun of him behind his back. After all, he was giving up two of his evenings and refusing to let her pay him.

There was something else about him, too, something that attracted her. Stephanie couldn't put her finger on it exactly but he was different from other men. She felt comfortable with him but that wasn't it.

Safe. Maybe that was it. With Noel, she felt safe. And she didn't even know why she thought that was important.

One night she met him in the lounge with, "I got a B!" Noel's genuine pleasure in response was like a warmth seeping all through her. No man had ever been—well, proud of her like this. Not since Daddy left.

Part 7: 1989–1991

Finals were the third week of December. Noel went over the main points with her, tied them together, made it all come alive and make sense.

As soon as report cards came in, she waited till the room cleared and then went up to him. "We did it!" she cried, throwing her arms around his neck. He hugged her, stepped back, his face glowing, and poked his glasses farther up on his nose.

"I told you you'd like history!"

"Wait a minute," she snorted. "I didn't say I *liked* it!" *I like you*, she wanted to add, but she was too shy to say it.

"Want to try for double or nothing?" he asked. "Ready to tackle American History?"

"You're cruel," she teased. They walked over to the student union together.

"Think about it," he urged. He was serious now. Unspoken between them was the knowledge that unless she enrolled in another semester of history, they would no longer have an excuse to meet.

"Maybe I will," Stephanie said, now serious too and wondering at herself. They gazed at each other.

"Buy you a malt?" They had reached the cafeteria.

Stephanie came to with confusion. "Oh, I promised Leroy I'd meet him here—" There he was, in their usual booth, in the corner. "I've gotta go. But thanks anyway. For everything."

It was early January, one week into the second semester, just long enough, thought Stephanie, for the fun of coming back to old friends and starting new classes to have worn off.

It got dark so early now. Even the days were dreary. Stephanie went down to the lounge early, feeling restless. It was empty; everyone had gone to dinner. *I should have gone, too*, thought Stephanie. *Leroy will be mad at me again. But what's the use? Noel never comes to dinner.*

Compelling Interests

It was an odd thought. Why should she care if Noel ate dinner in the cafeteria? She always ate with Leroy and if Noel did come to dinner, he'd eat with that girl he was dating, the one that had dropped out of Women's Studies—she'd seen them together at lunch. The skinny one. Ann, that was her name. *They seem to have a good time together.* Something inside her felt wistful and lonely.

Anyway, she'd see Noel at seven, like she always did, when he came to the dorm. Why did she want to see him, anyway? What did she care about American History? And it wasn't like they had any relationship apart from a professional one. He hadn't given her his phone number. Since he didn't eat dinner in the cafeteria, he must live off-campus.

Why should I care where Noel lives or what he does?, she thought, impatient with herself. *What's wrong with me? I can't settle down to anything. I don't know what I want. We've known each other three and a half months! Why hasn't he kissed me or anything?* Stephanie frowned and reminded herself, *It's just a business relationship and besides, he's going with Ann.*

At ten minutes to seven she suddenly turned around and ran to the elevator. When she came down twenty minutes later, her heart pounding and her cheeks flushed, Noel was there and when she greeted him, she could see the surprise on his face. Instead of her usual jeans, she had changed into a skirt and blouse, leaving it unbuttoned so low that he couldn't help being aware of her as a woman. Her hair, which she often clipped back out of her way, was cascading in permed brown rivulets down her back. She was well aware that her hair was her most attractive asset.

Before now, she would not have thought twice about taking Noel's arm playfully as they walked into the lounge. Now that she wanted to, very much, she found herself strangely inhibited. She walked close to him and all her nerves were alive with awareness of her sexuality and her desire for him. But she wanted the actual, physical initiative to be his.

They sat side by side on an old Naugahyde couch. He had asked what the teacher had covered in class and she must have said something about causes of the Revolutionary War, because he began explaining it to her. She pretended an interest but her mind couldn't absorb his words.

Part 7: 1989–1991

She didn't know why she wanted him. Maybe it was only because he had made no advances. That confused her. Men usually wanted her and it gave her a sense of power. To have this one with whom she had spent several hours a week give her no encouragement sexually at all—was she losing her touch? Was her desire only a desire for conquest?

At one point he dropped his pencil and she leaned over to help him retrieve it.

"Stephanie," he said, straightening up, "you're making this very hard."

She felt a surge of triumph. He was flesh and blood after all!

"Frankly," she said, closing the book and tilting her chin saucily, "history is a drag. Let's go somewhere." Her heart was racing.

"Go somewhere?"

Was he dense? "My roommate's got someone over. Can we go to your room?"

"I don't live on campus. I'm about ten minutes' drive from here." *Aha, I knew it!*

He paused. She waited. Finally, to her relief, he said it. "Would you like to see my place?" His eyes held an expression she couldn't read—a tenderness that made her weak all over mingled with something like laughter.

She forced herself to sound indifferent. "Sure. Why not?"

"OK, my car's out front."

She was in her element now. She could afford to relax a little.

It was an old Mercury Comet. She wasn't surprised. As he let her in and shut the door for her, Noel said, "I should have asked you before. I don't know why it never occurred to me. I think you'll like my mother."

Stephanie, adjusting the seatbelt, sat bolt upright. "Your mother? You mean you live with your *mother?*"

He had gone around the car and was settling into the driver's seat.

"Your *mother?*" she repeated.

"Yup. Mother, father, and brothers." Turning the key in the ignition, he glanced at her, amusement tugging at the corners of his eyes and mouth. "You sound like it's a crime to be part of a family."

Compelling Interests

She was disconcerted and she knew it showed. "Wait, Noel. Never mind. I don't want to meet—I mean—"

Noel turned off the engine but made no move to get out. He wasn't teasing now. He hesitated, then said, "Stephanie, I know what you want. I'd love to give it to you, but it wouldn't be right."

Stephanie blushed, about to protest. He had seen right into her heart. It made her feel exposed and vulnerable.

He was still speaking. "It would destroy us both in the end. You know that. Sex isn't what you're really after."

They were both silent for a moment. Stephanie kept her eyes on her hands in her lap. She was embarrassed, she was insulted, she was hurt, but something about what Noel was saying was like water to her thirsty heart.

"Sure it is," she said but her voice was low and unsure.

"A part of life can't meet the needs of the whole person. The Bible says to put God first, and everything else will fall into place. Happiness is a byproduct of doing things His way." He paused. "I like you very much, Stephanie. That's why I want your ultimate happiness more than some transitory affair that might give us a few kicks for a while."

"Well, then," she said at last, "I guess I'd better go in."

He reached over to lay a hand on hers. "Pizza?" he asked. She looked into his eyes and read in them a desire as great as her own. This was as hard for him as it was for her.

Still, she made herself respond pertly, "I suppose *pizza* will make me happy. Right?"

He smiled. "Part of you," he said softly.

She couldn't have believed how much fun she could have spending an evening with Noel not being physical. They had frozen yogurt for dessert and walked around a mall and laughed at puppies in a pet shop window.

When they came back to the college, they walked to the dorm in silence. At the door, Noel took her hand, squeezed it, and left quickly.

Stephanie stood in the doorway, watching him go. She wanted to be held, to be loved. She wanted it painfully. But beneath her emptiness

Part 7: 1989–1991

there was beating a stronger pulse of genuine pleasure and fulfillment. No one else had ever treated her like that. Noel was a wonderful person! A lot like Daddy.

As the days went by, the memory of the evening with Noel touched such a deep chord in Stephanie that it scared her. Something inside that she had sealed off was stirring again and she wasn't sure what it was. She felt as if part of her—maybe all of her—had been dead and it seemed somehow dangerous to let it come back to life.

She hungered for more, wishing she could be with Noel all the time. And yet the risk of letting herself love and be loved, of being vulnerable to pain—was frightening and sparked warnings inside her which told her to flee.

It was Friday night. Noel was working. Stephanie's roommate was gone for the weekend and the dorm was nearly deserted. There was no homework she had to be doing.

Stephanie's buzzer rang; someone was downstairs to see her. She knew it would be Leroy and she went downstairs meaning to tell him it was over.

"Hi, Stef," he said. "All clear? Can I come up?"

"Not tonight, Leroy."

He arched an eyebrow. Everything about him seemed childish and boring. He moved toward her and said, "Are you sure?" Noel's words filled her head: "Sex isn't what you want, Stephanie"—but it was! Longing engulfed her. Leroy wasn't the one she wanted but Leroy was real and there and available. In her neediness, she grabbed at the nearest promise of fulfillment. She took his hand and led him to the elevator.

As the doors opened, she remembered something a friend had told her. "Women give sex to get love. Men give love to get sex."

Why had that come back to her mind now? And how was it she knew, when it was over, she would still feel lonely?

PART 8
1992–SOMETIME IN THE 21ST CENTURY

In total darkness, encased in sticky fluid, in an environment so hostile they could not survive in it much more than 48 hours, a billion microscopic torpedoes unerringly sought their single target. Each was 1/500th of an inch long, yet a thimble-full of them could have re-created the entire population of the world.

Struggling upstream, some perished in the acidic secretions. Others reached a barrier where two tubes led in opposite directions and many chose the wrong one. They too perished.

Those swimming up the tube to the right had to whip their tails even harder now, against a current of muscular contractions of the tubal walls, the beating of tiny, hair-like cells and the downward streaming of fluid.

In contrast to the frantic sperm, the ovum moved slowly, gracefully, regally from the right ovary down the fallopian tube. The ovum had been waiting within Stephanie's body since three weeks after she herself had been conceived, waiting in the place where ovaries would be before ovaries were yet formed.

The ovum was surrounded by over 5,000 cells which provided a protective halo around it, enabling the finger-like projections of the fallopian tubes to reach out and propel it downward.

Compelling Interests

In as little as two hours, several thousand sperm met the ovum, although many missed it by a hair, charging right on by. The rest bore energetically into the tough outer layer and clear, gelatinous membrane.

Of those, only one of the torpedoes successfully penetrated to the interior of the sphere. Plowing its way deep into the mass, lashing its tail and secreting from its "nose cone" an enzyme that dissolved the protective layers, the sperm fully penetrated the membrane. The sphere then sealed its outer surface so the thousands of torpedoes following would be blunted on impact and despite desperate attempts to be admitted, would fall away, useless.

Conception had occurred. The egg was fertilized. It now contained the full set of 46 chromosomes necessary for a new human life. Given the vast number of combinations possible between chromosomes, genes, and their infinitely small subparts, this exact combination would never exist again. Nothing would be added to this complete being from the time of fertilization until death, nothing except nutrition.

Twelve hours had passed since Leroy and Stephanie had sex.

Gently, slowly, over the next seven days, moving with deliberation down the fallopian tube, which provided nourishment and protection, the fertilized ovum began to stretch. About three days before it reached the uterus, it had grown to a mass of sixteen or more cells integrated into a mulberry-shared sphere.

At ten days, the mass of cells took control of its environment. It suppressed the body's early warning system, so that antibodies which would normally arm the body to resist invasion from a foreign presence, were not alerted. The presence was powerful enough to interrupt the rhythm of the mother's hormonal cycle to prevent ovulation and menstruation.

Now the cells were joining to form amorphous shapes—a bump here, a thickening there. They began to differentiate, some joining to become a kidney, others to form the liver or the brain.

Other cells felt for the great wall of blood vessels and capillaries which lined the mother's uterus and put out extensions that burrowed deep into it, releasing enzymes to assist in the "nesting" process.

Part 8: 1992–Sometime in the 21st Century

Where the cells dug in, the placenta formed to accommodate the embryo throughout its development in the womb. The mother's blood could not pass through the placenta. Instead, the new life produced its own blood, which was of a different type than hers. The umbilical cord carried the baby's blood into the placenta, re-oxygenated it, and returned it to the baby without mingling with the mother's blood.

Like the placenta, the amniotic sac in which the baby would grow began forming almost immediately. Filled with a warm, clear, and mildly alkaline fluid it served as a shock absorber, maintained a stable body temperature and provided extra nutrition.

Between the 18th and 25th day, at its core, a tiny, regular tapping began. The heart was beating.

During that first month, the embryo increased in size forty fold; billions of cells, as they were created, assumed their appointed functions, making muscle, blood, digestive system, organs. A "yolk sac" produced red blood cells until liver, spleen, and bone marrow became functional. Folds in the lower half of the face would become jaws, ears and internal throat structures.

All major structures were in evidence by the thirtieth day. All three of the major areas of the brain were demarcated. The important muscle groups were all in place. Primitive nerve fiber was beginning to spread to all parts of the body. Electrical brain waves would be measurable within the week. The mouth could open. Eyes, arms, and legs were beginning to appear.

In that first cell had been the genetic code for all that she would be: female, half-Caucasian like her mother, half African-American like her father, five-foot-three, brown hair, brown eyes. Her mother's high cheekbones, her father's slender feet, her mild dyslexia, her sense of humor, her 120 IQ—they were all there.

In the paired chromosomes was all her uniqueness. They held the date of her first and last menstrual periods. They determined whether she would need glasses or orthodonture or dentures, whether she would be susceptible to osteoporosis, whether she would be likely to develop

Compelling Interests

cataracts. The size of her breasts, the ease with which she would tan or gain weight, the texture of her hair, the shape of her nose.

Like a blueprint, the DNA was the imprint of this unique person—but there was a difference, a difference as profound as life itself. For this blueprint would not merely map the design and direction this "building" would take. It *was* the building.

When would this child be able to survive completely independent of the sheltering womb? Surely not at "viability," as doctors marked it, nor at birth, nor at toddlerhood, nor as a grade school child. Unlike animals, this tiny all-encompassing human being would be dependent on others well into adolescence.

The environment was friendly. A gracious host to the tiny guest, the mother's body adjusted and adapted. Her breasts began to swell and tauten to prepare for nursing. Her pelvic bones and tissues began imperceptibly to soften, preparing for the day, now eight months away, when the bones would yield and the muscles stretch remarkably to thrust the 7-pound baby through them into the soft lights of the delivery room.

Everything within the mother's body welcomed the presence of the child, deferred to it, cherished it.

Until she found out it was there.

As she carried her tray through the cafeteria halfway into her second semester, Stephanie felt a touch of nausea. *Oh, great,* she thought, *I bet it's the flu, just before spring break. That's all I need. Leroy and I were supposed to go to the mountains.*

A student who looked familiar was beckoning to her from a table.

"Stephanie!" she said, as Stephanie would have walked on by. "Ann Lawson. Women's Studies, remember? Sit down?"

Stephanie glanced over to the booth in the corner where Leroy and a friend were talking but Ann was pulling out a chair and Stephanie sat down without even meaning to.

"How have you been?"

"Fine." Stephanie was guarded.

"How did you do in the class?"

Part 8: 1992–Sometime in the 21st Century

"Got an A."

"I changed courses," said Ann. "I had some problems with Women's Studies."

Stephanie was silent.

"I guess my problem is with the whole philosophy of feminism. It seems so selfish."

"Women should have a right to do what they want with their own bodies," said Stephanie. "No one has a right to tell a woman what to do with her own body."

"No one has an unrestricted right to do what they want with their own bodies," pointed out Ann. "Men or women. There are laws against doing drugs and against suicide."

Stephanie didn't answer.

"That's why I don't understand the feminist position on abortion. We all have rights to life, liberty, and the pursuit of happiness. But if my right to liberty or happiness infringes on my baby's right to life—"

"It isn't a baby till it's born," said Stephanie. "Until then, it's just tissue."

"No way," said Ann. "Ever looked through a basic biology textbook at the stages of gestation? I suppose if women want to be sexually active, it's their own business. But if they get pregnant, there's another human being involved. Doesn't that human being deserve to be considered? You know, like they say, 'Unborn women have rights, too.' I'm really struggling with this, Stephanie."

Stephanie was torn. Ann was raising questions she had never thought of—questions she didn't want to know the answers to. Not tissue? It had to be tissue. If it wasn't just tissue, then Stephanie's own abortion five years ago— She couldn't let the possibility into her head. And what about now? Her period was late again.

Ann was saying, "Abortion isn't easy on the woman either—physically or emotionally. I feel afraid for women who have an abortion without knowing the emotional toll it takes. You can't interrupt any natural process without it having serious repercussions."

Compelling Interests

"I don't want to talk about this any more," said Stephanie abruptly, standing up.

Ann looked up, surprised, and saw that she was troubled. "I'm sorry, Stephanie. I wasn't very thoughtful. We can talk about something else."

But Stephanie was gone.

When Ann turned 21, she had inherited twelve hundred dollars. Her great aunt, with no issue of her own, had left $1,000 to her at her death and the money had sat in a savings account accruing interest. Every time she had been tempted to use the money for expenses in her nurse's training, something held her back. Her great aunt had been special; Ann wanted the money to go to something special.

The issue of abortion was heating up in the media but twice a week Ann stepped into a city within the city which seemed untouched by the controversy—a city that contained the generation most affected by it.

Cal State Anaheim, affectionately known as "Cal State Disneyland", was the largest university west of the Mississippi and female students provided a thriving and lucrative local abortion business. Several family planning clinics targeted them daily through advertisements in the *Cal State Clarion*.

At the beginning of the semester, Ann had decided to confront the *Clarion's* editor about these ads. She made an appointment with him.

"Mr. Mills?" He was no older than she was. "My name is Ann Lawson. I'm a senior in the nursing school and I'm interning in obstetrics at Anaheim Memorial. Why do you run ads for family planning clinics?"

He looked at her blankly for a minute, then gave her the answer she had expected. Ads helped pay their bills, abortion was legal.

"It may be legal, but it's wrong!" Ann said. "Abortion providers, as they call themselves, don't tell women all the risks, especially the psychological ones. They don't tell the woman that she is carrying a baby. They call it 'the embryo' or 'the fetus' or 'the pregnancy'—or even a 'parasite.' They tell her it isn't a human being."

Part 8: 1992–Sometime in the 21st Century

The editor listened politely but she could tell she wasn't making the slightest impact. Ann's shoulders slumped. She was aware of the clicking of keyboards and the smell of rubber cement. Two students near her were working briskly with large pages of graph paper, black and white photographs, and blue pencils.

"How much would it cost," she said at last, "to take out a series of ads, each one about four lines long?" She held her thumb and forefinger about a half-inch apart. "A different one for each issue. For the whole semester."

He calculated quickly. "About twelve hundred dollars."

Ann only hesitated a second. She had decided what she would do with Great-aunt Gwen's money. "All right," she said. "I want to buy a semester's worth of ads."

The first week, Ann ran ads urging adoption. The second and third weeks, she dealt with the dangers of abortion. The fourth week, she talked about post-abortion trauma.

Every ad was different. Every ad gave the phone number of the Lifeline Pregnancy Testing Center.

Stephanie tried not to see them but somehow the ads always jumped to her attention. Last week they had all been about God forgiving the sin of abortion. They had quoted from the Bible, verses like "Blot out my transgressions" and "Deliver me from blood-guiltiness." No matter how uneasy they made her, Stephanie always found herself searching them out.

But this week was worse. Each ad this week was titled "Methods of Abortion" and each one was different. Yesterday's had read, "In a D&C abortion, the doctor cuts the placenta and baby into pieces and scrapes them out into a basin."

Today's read, "In a suction abortion, the doctor uses a powerful 'vacuum cleaner' which tears the baby—" Stephanie hurled the paper across the table and stood up, shaking.

"That's *awful*," she said aloud. No one in the student union seemed to notice. "That's so awful!"

She looked around for a campus phone, lifted the receiver, and asked the operator for the editor of the *Clarion*.

"Jerry Mills," said a man's voice expectantly on the other end.

Compelling Interests

For a moment Stephanie could not compose herself enough to speak. Then she said, with an effort, "That's an awful thing to do!"

"What?" asked the editor with perplexity in his voice.

"Those—those *ads!* Those things you print every day about abortion. They're horrible! How can you do that? Don't you know—" her breath was coming in dry sobs now, "that some people have—have had—Nobody wants to know that!"

The editor was calm. "We aren't responsible for the content of the ads we run. We make space available for anyone willing to pay for it."

"Who paid for it?" Stephanie said, trying desperately to control the quaver in her voice.

"That information is confidential."

"Well, it doesn't belong in a school paper. Tell them to stop!" She hung up on him.

Thirty minutes later, Ann got a call at her room off campus.

"Ms. Lawson?"

"Miss. Yes?"

"This is Jerry Mills. We need to talk to you about your ads."

"What about them?"

"We've had some complaints that the ones running this week are too graphic. Some of our readers have objected. They find them offensive."

"*I* find them offensive," said Ann.

"Our editors have decided to pull the ads for Wednesday, Thursday, and Friday."

"Wait a minute!" said Ann. "Why is it offensive and objectionable to describe how abortions are done—and not offensive and objectionable to do them?"

"That's the way it is."

"What happened to freedom of speech? What happened to having to take ads to 'pay your bills'?"

"It's just three ads."

"Well, what can I say? You're not asking me, are you? You're telling me."

"That's right," he said.

Part 8: 1992–Sometime in the 21st Century

"This society is schizophrenic!" she said. "You can do it but you can't talk about it. A woman can take her own baby's life but if anyone else does, they go to prison! If a mother terminates her baby's life ten minutes before birth, it's abortion. If it's ten minutes after birth, she's tried for murder!"

The editor was saying something. "…in a minute, Gregg." Ann realized he wasn't talking to her, that he hadn't been listening. She controlled her anger with an effort.

"Mr. Mills?"

"Yes."

"I believe a woman has a right to make an *informed* choice. I'm sorry you don't agree with me." Gently, she replaced the receiver. For the second time that afternoon, Jerry Mills was left holding a dead line.

Janice heard it first, over KFWB on her way to work.

"They got him!" she said aloud, pounding the steering wheel with a fist. "The bastards got him!"

She pulled into the parking lot. There weren't any protesters outside. Had they heard too and called off their picketing or was she just early?

Her hand was shaking as she unlocked the front door and went upstairs. She started the day's routine mechanically but it seemed inappropriate now. She found herself doing inane things just to be doing something. She watered the plants in the waiting room. She brushed crumbs off the couch—someone had brought her little boy with her the day before and fed him crackers to keep him quiet.

Laurel and Kim arrived at the same time. Janice could tell by the way they were chatting as they came up the stairs that they hadn't heard. She met them at the door.

"They got Dr. Guy." She said bluntly, without raising her voice.

"What?" one of them asked, distracted from what she had been saying.

"They killed him. Broke into his house."

Compelling Interests

Both women looked stunned. Kim said, "Oh, no!" Laurel was asking, "How did you find out?"

"It was on the radio a few minutes ago. His wife found him in his recliner, shot in the head."

"I can't believe it," murmured Kim, sinking onto the couch. "They're crazy. They're all crazy."

"I knew this would happen," Janice said bitterly. "I knew it. They're violent people. I knew if they'll yell at women and burn buildings, they were capable of anything."

Laurel pulled herself together with an effort. "How do they know the anti-abortionists did it?" she asked. "Maybe it was a burglar."

"No way," said Janice. "Nothing was taken."

"He said they knew where he lived," added Kim.

Janice said bitterly, "The police called it a suicide but I don't believe it. Why would he kill himself? Because some Nazi types don't agree with what he does? That never bothered him. He has a successful practice and he'd just opened that new clinic in Santa Barbara.

"We would have known. He would have acted depressed or—or *said* something. There would have been signs."

They were silent for a while. *Maybe there were signs. He came late, he left early, he was always in a rush. He never read his mail*— Laurel brushed those thoughts aside. *He's just a busy man, that's all.* Was a *busy man*, she corrected herself.

"I can't believe he won't be coming in," said Kim, after a moment. Then, "Those poor women. Who will they go to now? This was the last family planning clinic in Long Beach. What will we tell them?"

"We'll refer them to the feminist clinic in Orange County," said Janice. "I'm going to turn on the phones and call down there. Maybe they haven't heard. They'd better be ready for a stampede."

The three of them listened to the news again at nine. "In local news, Dr. Julius Guy, whose abortion practice had drawn fire from fundamentalists since its inception twenty years ago, was found shot to death today at his home in Naples," said the announcer.

Part 8: 1992–Sometime in the 21st Century

"Mrs. Guy, who had recently separated from her husband, claimed that his behavior over the last year had been erratic and that he had been drinking heavily. She told police there were times when she had been afraid for her life. She was released after questioning.

"Pro-choice groups are reacting with shock. Despite the controversy surrounding the doctor, police are calling his death a suicide."

Janice switched the radio off. "I don't believe it," she said. "I'll never believe it was suicide."

It was a chaotic day. Laurel had to field phone calls when she would rather have locked up and gone home. The guard outside intercepted every car pulling into the lot and leaned through the window to explain to clients that they would have to make appointments through a separate medical group in Anaheim.

Worst of all, the two Catholic men came as usual. Janice shoved open the second-story window, nearly breaking it, and yelled, "I hope you're satisfied, you sons of bitches!" They looked up questioningly and went back to their pacing up and down the sidewalk. She knew she was verging on being out of control.

"I bet they're *praying* for me," she muttered.

Each hour Janice listened to the news and afterward vowed not to listen any more. There were more details now. The house had not been broken into. The gun, found by the chair, was a .22 caliber revolver owned by Dr. Guy and had only his fingerprints on it. He was dressed in silk pajamas and slippers. Two heavy white bath towels, one around the victim's head and another spread along the back of the chair, had absorbed most of the blood. No note was found.

WomanPower president Cecile Tucker-Thomas declared that if the anti-abortionists had not actually pulled the trigger, they had driven him to do it—"death by harassment," she called it. A reporter interviewed Janice and quoted her as saying she was "angry at the needless death."

"It's a tragedy for underprivileged, pregnant women everywhere," Laurel heard her say on the news that night.

Birthright president Corinne Zinzzer expressed "deep regret" at the news, although she admitted she had deplored what Dr. Guy did to women. She added, although it was cut out of all the newscasts but one and did not appear in print, that members of her organization had prayed frequently for Dr. Guy to change his mind about abortion but had never wished him harm.

"Ha!" snorted Janice, when she heard that.

Laurel felt herself strangely dissociated from the intensity of the reactions of the other two women on staff. She seemed to be in a kind of sleepwalker's trance and she thought she ought to feel guilty because she could not find within herself either Kim's grief or Janice's anger.

She felt only what could almost be called indifference. Dr. Guy's suicide seemed somehow fitting, somehow appropriate. It was to her a confirmation of the turmoil she herself had felt for months and at the same time a release from that turmoil. She knew how he must have felt; she identified with his last anguish—and she knew she could leave the clinic tonight with a clear conscience for the first time because she would never come back, to it or any other.

"It's time," Laurel thought when she woke up the next morning. "It's time to tell."

After Roger left for work, she dressed and had a piece of toast and enough orange juice to wash down her vitamins. Was there an approved way to do this? Was there protocol to follow or were there channels to go through? She didn't know. They could sort that out.

She took the light rail downtown and parked in front of the monolithic structure which was the home of the *Southbay Journal.* The lobby was carpeted, with a reception desk, potted plants, and separate windows like teller windows, to accommodate those who wished to place ads.

She stopped at a desk where a woman with glasses, her black hair coiled around her head, was on the telephone. The woman put her hand over the mouthpiece long enough to ask, "May I help you?"

"I want to talk to your news editor," she said.

"Local news?"

Part 8: 1992–Sometime in the 21st Century

"Yes."

"Tim Carroway. Third floor, to your right," said the woman. The elevators are over there."

Laurel walked past the elevators and took the stairs. She needed more time to decide what she was going to say.

On the third floor, she asked directions of the first man she saw and he motioned her to two others. "The younger one—sitting on the desk," he said.

Laurel approached him hesitantly. He and the older man were laughing over something.

"Mr. Carroway?" Laurel asked. "Could I talk to you for a few minutes?"

"What about?" He was courteous but she sensed that time off for joking with his peers was one thing; interruptions from outside were another.

"I worked for Dr. Julius Guy, the abortionist who just killed himself. I worked in recovery. I saw a lot of things I think you—I think people should know."

He was alert now. "Ben, can I use your office?" With the glass door shut, he pointed to a chair and asked, "Who are you?"

"Laurel Sandoval. I work at the family planning clinic on Pacific. The one owned by Dr. Guy."

"Do you know something about Guy's death?"

"Oh, no. I wanted to tell you some of the things that went on at the clinic. I started working there because I wanted to help women, especially poor women, and I really thought that providing safe abortions for them was helping them.

"But the women who came to Dr. Guy said he treated them like meat. A lot of them complained afterward that he was rough and rude with them. He only gave them five minutes each. He was proud of that—how fast he could get in and out. He never answered their questions. It was like an assembly line. Women woke up screaming—"

"Why are you exposing him now? He's dead," grunted Mr. Carroway abruptly.

Compelling Interests

"Because he isn't the only one. This kind of thing went on at the hospital where I worked in Omaha, too. I have friends in the medical field who have had the same kind of experiences with other doctors and clinics all over the country. Sometimes they do abortions on patients who aren't even pregnant. Dr. Guy always told women that their pregnancy test was positive, even when it wasn't. I saw some of—"

Mr. Carroway punched a button on the phone, interrupting her. "Ben? Can you come in a minute? I want you to hear this." He held up his palm to arrest her story momentarily.

The man Mr. Carroway had been laughing with stepped through the doorway.

"Ms. Sandoval? Ben Epstein, Managing Editor. Ben, she worked with Guy—the abortion doctor," Carroway told him. Mr. Epstein leaned back and listened, arms folded, as Laurel continued.

"He's made millions of dollars from abortions. He has—had—airplanes and a yacht and a ranch."

"Tell me more about the abortions on women who weren't pregnant."

"Everything was for money. Medicaid usually paid for it. We had a quota of abortions we had to fill or lose our jobs and the number went up every year. This year his goal was 3,000—and that was just at our clinic. He has 44 clinics. He did something like 12,000 abortions a year at his hospital in Compton. He told us—the women on staff—that once nearly every woman in America had had an abortion, the controversy would die down.

"He was really angry because the anti-abortionists cut down on his business. Sometimes we'd have twenty women scheduled and only ten would actually come in. They'd be scared off by the picketers or sometimes they'd read their handouts while they were in our waiting room and they'd back out.

"Dr. Guy told us we didn't have time to answer their questions or counsel them. We couldn't tell them what could happen. All we did was find out how far along they were, tell them when they were going to be through, get their money, do the procedure, and send them home.

Part 8: 1992–Sometime in the 21st Century

"Sometimes when they changed their minds, he would insist we talk them into going through with it anyway. I remember one time a lady was on the table and she was screaming. Janice—that's the director—blocked the door and yelled for Dr. Guy to come quick because the lady wanted to leave. He came into the room and made her have the procedure anyway.

"Several of them didn't want to go through with it after the laminaria had been inserted and he would tell them 'It's too late to back out now.' The laminaria is a kind of seaweed—"

"So he forced women to have abortions?" the editor interrupted.

"Yes. Lots of times women went into shock and we had to call an ambulance. One older woman turned blue. I tried to start an IV but all her veins had collapsed."

"What was your job there?" Tim leaned back in his chair and touched his fingertips together.

"A little bit of everything. I'm an RN and I was hired to prep patients and help out in recovery. I did office work, too. It got so busy, we had to hire a new girl who wasn't a nurse at all and Dr. Guy and Janice had both of us do things we weren't medically trained to do."

"Like what?" Now he was leaning forward, writing quickly.

"Like writing out prescriptions, starting the anesthesia, injecting the saline, diagnosing complications. Our office wasn't even supposed to do abortions past 12 weeks. That's why I wanted to work there instead of in a hospital, like I did in Omaha. But Dr. Guy ended up doing them way past 12 weeks. He didn't care. I left Omaha so I wouldn't have to put parts of babies back together like some kind of jigsaw puzzle and I ended up having to do it again. He'd just reach in and pull the legs and arms off with the—well, they're like tongs—and the fetus would bleed to death.

"Once there was this woman who must have been 18 weeks along. We saved her till last because she was so big and we knew she'd bleed and holler a lot and it would be a big mess.

"It took me and Kim both to hold her down. She was screaming and these tiny arms and legs were coming out and blood was going everywhere—on the doctor, on us. It was just horrible and it was so hot in there because of the lights.

Compelling Interests

"Anyway, Kim and I tried to clean up all the mess afterward. There was this big bucket at the end of the table to catch stuff. We had to take all the contents of that bucket—all the solid parts—and put it in formaldehyde. We couldn't find a jar big enough for that fetus, so we had to use two jars and label both of them.

"Kim ended up going into the bathroom and vomiting.

"I was standing there at the sink crying my eyes out. I said to Dr. Guy, 'My God, are we going to hell?' and you know what he said? 'Well, if we are, honey, I'll be there first waiting for you.'"

Laurel stopped speaking and sat as if paralyzed with the horror of the memory.

The editor finished his notes and looked up. "Can you type?" he asked.

"Sure. That was one of my jobs."

"Ben," he said to the man at the door, "what do you think?"

"I'll find her a terminal," Ben said. Then, to Laurel, "Give us what you know, what you personally observed, how you felt about it."

Tim Carroway broke in. "I'd like to investigate some of these claims. Do you have documentation—letters, interviews, names, dates, places?"

She nodded. "Just give me a little time."

If the pro-choice people were upset about Dr. Guy's death, it was nothing to the outrage with which they greeted the interview with Laurel and the articles which followed. Janice herself wrote a letter to the editor calling Laurel a traitor and a liar. A local WomanPower leader denounced the newspaper for its "tacky" treatment of someone deceased who couldn't defend himself. Roger, accusing Laurel of "creating hysteria," moved out.

But other letters began arriving, first a few and then, when the editors thought the fuss had died down, an avalanche of them. There were letters from those employed by family planning clinics confirming Laurel's claim that "family planning clinics have hired the back-alley abortionist to kill and maim legally."

Part 8: 1992–Sometime in the 21st Century

A nurse-practitioner in San Diego who had left a clinic there claimed that the clinic had a rapid turnover in doctors, all with medical malpractice suits filed against them. Shortly after the current one took charge, she wrote, the post-abortion infection rate had doubled.

Another nurse wrote, "I examined one lady who came for her post-abortion check-up complaining of vaginal discharge, fever, and lower abdominal pain. On exam, she had a large amount of purulent discharge and her abdomen was so tender she could barely stand for anyone to touch her. These symptoms are all indicators of an acute pelvic infection.

"I consulted the doctor who had performed the abortion. He told the lady that she had a benign uterine tumor and that she should have her uterus removed! I disagreed with him and he informed me that 'he was the doctor, not me.'"

There were letters from patients who didn't want their names used. A woman in Rancho Palos Verdes complained that her doctor had inserted an IUD when she was 12 weeks pregnant, causing not an abortion but the birth six months later of a baby with severe congenital defects.

Someone in the San Fernando Valley wrote that her doctor had not told her that she was carrying twins and the shock of finding out she had aborted twins was so great she had had to be hospitalized.

An 18-year old told of having had her uterus torn during a suction abortion on an 18-week fetus. She had to be rushed to a hospital where only a hysterectomy saved her life.

A woman in Riverside was angry because neither of the doctors who had done abortions on her had told her that the procedure might make her infertile. Now she was married and unable to get pregnant and she couldn't discuss the cause with her husband because he didn't know about the abortions.

The *Journal* had a policy against printing letters anonymously, but there were so many that the editor wrote an article in which he quoted from some of them.

Compelling Interests

The courts had finally ruled on the test case Liz Tewksbury had filed against the Lifeline Pregnancy Clinic: no testing center with a pro-life agenda could call itself a clinic or give women medical opinions or advice. That wasn't so bad, Mariana thought; they could take the word "clinic" out of their name and they could be more careful about telling women the results of their tests. But from now on, no pro-life testing center could give women pregnancy tests.

They were out of business.

Lawsuits having to do with abortion were becoming rampant. Husbands were suing wives for aborting babies they had conceived together, women were suing doctors and clinics for failure to disclose information regarding the possible effects of abortion and what exactly it was they were aborting. Operation Rescue had filed a suit against the Los Angeles Police Department for use of excessive force.

There were even some absurd applications of the Missouri ruling, which had declared that life started at conception. One woman insisted she was eligible for the carpool lane on the freeway because she was pregnant. A twenty-year old man claimed he should be able to drink legally because he was actually nine months older than his birth certificate indicated.

Finally, Mariana and Tasha were thrilled to see that a class action suit had been filed against WomanPower, KASAL, and family planning clinics in every major city on behalf of all the unborn who had been aborted between 1973 and 1991. Defendants included Cecile Tucker-Thomas, Liz Tewskbury, and all who had used the figures "5,000 to 10,000" or "thousands" when referring to women who had died of illegal abortions, presumably with the full knowledge that these figures were false.

Even more sensational was the lawsuit filed in Montana by a handicapped 18-year old boy, Brian Chen, against his own mother for aborting

Part 8: 1992–Sometime in the 21st Century

him by saline injection at five and a half months. In spite of "a conspiracy on the part of his mother and her doctor to deprive him of his constitutionally protected life," Brian had survived. Nurses had rushed him to the preemie nursery, where he was put on life-support.

Since his untimely birth, Brian had been deaf, hydrocephalic; he had cerebral palsy, one kidney had ceased functioning, the other was problematic. He had introduced medical evidence to show that his handicaps were the result of birth induced before his lungs and other organs were sufficiently developed to enable him to sustain normal life outside the womb. He also charged his mother with criminal negligence.

Chen's lawyer cited precedents where the unborn had successfully sued for injuries sustained in the womb. He pointed out that the unborn had the legal right to receive social security benefits and to inherit property and he asserted that these rights are meaningless unless the unborn also have the right to life.

The lower court had ruled against him, pointing out that abortion had been legal at that time and that heroic efforts had been made to save his life.

Chen's response, when this had been signed to him in court, was, "If it was legal to kill me inside my mother, why wasn't it just as legal to kill me as soon as I was out? I was the same baby I had been one minute before. Or does the Hippocratic oath give doctors the right to only one attempted murder per person?"

The court also claimed that, as a non-person before birth, he had no standing to sue.

Brian had appealed the case on the grounds that declaring attempted murder legal didn't make it legal, that the law was unconstitutional. The Chen case was headed for the U.S. Supreme Court.

Stephanie's hands were clammy. What if she *was* pregnant again? She *couldn't* have a child now. Leroy—well, she had no intention of even telling Leroy.

Compelling Interests

But she couldn't have an abortion, either. She never wanted to go through that again. Besides, what if the ads she read in the *Clarion* every day were right? What if it *was* a baby?

"No!" Stephanie said aloud. "No! Not again! I can't! I don't want this!" She swept the pregnancy kit off the counter into the wastebasket and wandered aimlessly around the restroom. *I'm so scared. I won't go through another abortion.*

I've got to think, she thought. Her chest felt tight and her breath was shallow, as if she'd been running. *I've got to sit down.* She could feel herself starting to hyperventilate.

Think. What were her options?

The very idea of abortion engulfed her in terrifying memories. What if she hemorrhaged again? What if she had to have a hysterectomy this time? Besides, she had nothing against this baby. She just couldn't have it now, that was all. It wasn't reasonable. She wasn't married and she had no interest in marrying Leroy, even if he would consider it, which he wouldn't. She had no way to support it, she didn't know the first thing about babies. Nobody expected her to leave school in the middle of the semester and raise a child!

What kind of job could she get anyway, with no experience and only a year of college? She didn't even know how to apply for a job. And what would she do with the baby all day while she worked?

She'd have to rent an apartment. How much did it cost to live, anyway? She couldn't expect her mother to take her in or pay her way. Maybe she could get Leroy to help—but he wouldn't take any responsibility for a baby. He'd think she was crazy for not just aborting it. Maybe she would be eligible for welfare. She could apply as "Head of household," like it said on the tax forms.

There was adoption, of course. After all, she had been adopted herself. That was probably far more practical. But that meant having people know she was pregnant.

It all seemed so alien to her. Her head ached. She didn't want to go back to her room. Her thoughts would just go round and round. She

Part 8: 1992–Sometime in the 21st Century

threw a jacket around her shoulders and headed for the elevator. She had to get out.

She must have been walking aimlessly for over an hour when a car pulled up beside her. She glanced up and realized that she had come full circle to the gates of the campus again—and the driver, just pulling out, was Noel McAllister. Of all the people she *didn't* want to see, he headed the list.

"Hi, Stephanie!"

Head down, she kept walking. She had no intention of telling Noel. She knew how strict his morals were and how shocked he would be.

He made a U-turn, eased the car forward and called to her again. "Stephanie! Get in!"

Was it the authority in his words or the genuine concern in his tone that made her obey? She climbed into the car without understanding why. *Could* she tell him? She had to talk to someone. She wanted to cry.

But, when he parked by the entrance to the dorm and demanded bluntly, "You've been avoiding me. What have I done?" she felt a surge of anger.

"Nothing! You haven't done anything. I've just been busy."

He put his hand on hers.

"Stephanie, don't give me that! Something's wrong. What is it?"

"You wouldn't care."

He sighed. "Of course I care. Why are you so darned recalcitrant?"

"You and your big words," she sniffed.

"Stubborn, then! Stubborn! What's the matter with you? I care about *you* so if something's bothering you, it bothers me. How can I help if I don't even know what it is?"

"You can't help."

"Stephanie, please don't shut me out! Does it have anything to do with me?"

She snorted scornfully. "No, I can *guarantee* you that it has *nothing* to do with you. That I'm *sure* of!"

"Then what is it?" humbly.

"None of your business."

Compelling Interests

"Why are you so miserable? Is it school? Your family?"

"No."

"Please. I'd like to help. I care about you!"

She burst out at last in a low, controlled voice, filled with desperation, "I'm *pregnant,* if you must know! Now will you lay off?"

He sat back, stunned. It was what she had expected but when he actually recoiled she realized that she had hoped he would put his arms around her and hold her instead. Her heart fell heavily.

"Are you sure?" he asked hesitantly, his head down.

Sarcasm boiled up again. Isn't that what men were always supposed to say?

"Of course I'm sure," she snapped. "Do you think I'm a complete dork?"

She fumbled for the handle of the door and thrust it open. "Don't worry about throwing me out. I'm leaving!"

At the last minute, he lunged across the seat and caught her hand.

"Don't go! Stay! Just let me—"

But when she tore loose and ran, blinded by tears, he didn't follow.

Stephanie went straight to her room. Why had she been stupid enough to trust Noel to understand? He was living back in the nineteenth century, when girls never dated without a chaperone and were still virgins on their wedding night! Of course he had been shocked!

In her mind she saw him again, his head down, both hands clinging to the steering wheel. He must have been appalled that he had so misjudged her, regretting that he had involved himself with her.

How could she have expected a man to care? Isn't that what Bobbie had warned them in Women's Studies? Men were the ones who rape women, men were the ones who abuse women and children.

Everything Bobbie had said was true. It was a patriarchal society and there was a double standard. Men could get away with anything but women—one way or another, women inevitably got caught. Women's lib couldn't change that. It was always the woman who had to pay.

Stephanie leaned back against her closed door, her jaw working, her chest heaving. Her features were brittle, expressionless except for the anger flashing in her eyes.

Part 8: 1992–Sometime in the 21st Century

Sex is no big deal, she had told her mother. But it *was* a big deal.

As her thoughts boiled and foamed over her, Stephanie jerked open her drawers and purses, then her roommate's. Leroy would never even know that he had begun one life and destroyed another.

Noel's anguished face came before her again. Noel. Was he like other men? Did he only want to use her? *It would only have been a matter of time,* she told herself. *They're all the same.* No, Noel couldn't cope with the real world. He probably couldn't even admit people *had* sexual needs.

Noel, Ann, both Christians—they were plastic, artificial. They had no idea what life was all about. They were characters in a play, repeating lines by rote, quoting the Bible. Their world was so simple, so unreal.

Stephanie found what she was looking for—some strong pain medicine prescribed for her roommate's sore back. Emptying the little bottle on the desk, she looked at the pills with satisfaction. This would give her the power to get revenge.

She could not punish an innocent baby—if it was a baby—because that was bad. But she could punish herself. They could not blame her if she punished herself. She would be out of their reach.

She filled her coffee mug at the sink and the water sloshed wildly as she carried it back to her desk, spilling down her hand. Within her, emotions sloshed wildly too, slamming back and forth from fury to an unbearable darkness and despair. It was as if everything inside her was being twisted and wrung.

She hated this crudely formed lump that was an unwanted part of her now. If only there were some other way to get rid of this thing within her, some way to leave it behind, undo the act that had caused it. She was its prisoner.

If she didn't die, she would be sentenced to bear this foreign matter for seven more months. It would go wherever she went. There could be no getting rid of it—not without going through what she had before and she couldn't do that.

On the table, the water in the cup was still. Stephanie poked the pills into patterns with her fingers, sat down and stared at them.

Compelling Interests

What would it feel like? A high? And then that jittery, sickening feeling someone told her you could sometimes get with pot? And then—? Her mind balked. Nothing, she hoped. Maybe a stretch of something unpleasant that her mind refused to see clearly and then nothing.

Nothing? How would she know when she was dead? Would her mind stop thinking, her body stop feeling? Even the good? She watched dust particles move in the sunlight, drew her finger through the light and saw them swirl and settle back to their slow drifting. Would she be dead to the dust and the light too? If only she could choose to be aware of some things and not others!

The capsules were there, waiting. It was up to her. Her hesitation was only cowardice. Hadn't she already decided? Why wasn't she going through with it?

Suddenly the sound of her buzzer pierced her nerves. She tensed, made herself relax. There was someone downstairs to see her. But dead people didn't have visitors. That was all over now. It rang again, longer, insistent. She waited a long time for a third ring but there was silence.

Again she thought of Noel, for once in his life at a loss for words, letting her run from him, not caring enough to follow or call her back. He was probably in the library now, engrossed in some book. He would get over her.

But if they had only known. She hadn't really meant it to be like this! She would have been so different, if it hadn't been for Leroy.

Leroy. Men again. In a burst of hate for them, she took the pills, first one at a time, then handfuls.

She sat still, wondering when she would feel different, wanting them to hurry up and take effect. But as the anger drained out of her, she was pricked with fear. Would she really die? Was there any way of turning back, if she didn't like what would be happening? She felt terribly alone, taking a road no one could share with her.

She had surrendered her destiny. It was out of her hands. She forced her mind to think of the reasons that made death necessary. Who cared about her, anyway? It was all their fault! They had brought her to this.

Part 8: 1992–Sometime in the 21st Century

They had closed every other honorable door. They, the ones who made the system and kept the double standard.

But the agitation grew. Was anything really bad enough to die for? What if tomorrow it turned out she wasn't pregnant after all?

How long had it been? Five minutes? It seemed so much longer. Was her mind changing, getting duller? Was she seeing just as well?

She had an overpowering desire to find someone and explain. Someone on her floor. Anyone. All she needed was someone to help—like Mom.

But what if Mom asked, "How can I help?"

How could she? Could she make Stephanie un-pregnant? Help her return to the impossible situation with no solution, to be back where she started? Give her platitudes to pass the dragging time until she lost consciousness?

Maybe she could write a note. Someone would read it, someone who might have cared, if he or she had only known. No, she was too unsettled to be able to organize her thoughts on paper. Jumpy. So they were working then. Her mouth was dry, her head a little light.

I'm scared, she thought. *But I can't panic. I knew I'd have to go through a rough part. I'll be okay once it's over.*

But her stomach did a hideous flip-flop.

Maybe I will call her after all. Call who? Mom. Of course. Mom.

What about Mom? She couldn't recall now why her mother was on her mind. She tried to form thoughts but they misted immediately and she couldn't grope her way back to make sense of them. Her eyes wouldn't focus now, either. They felt more comfortable closed.

She became aware that her roommate was in the room. She hadn't heard her come in. Stephanie wanted to speak but she could not form the words. Her thoughts felt thick and blurred. She did not even try to turn around. Her body would not respond.

Meagan was rummaging through her drawer, saying, "Have you seen my sweatshirt? Dave and I are going out for pizza and he's picking me up in two minutes!"

The words rattled meaninglessly in Stephanie's mind. She felt self-conscious and foolish. The room was swaying, even with her eyes closed.

Compelling Interests

Muddily, she heard Meagan say, "If Missy's got it again, I'll kill her—oh, here it is!"

The door opened. There was a pause. *She's noticed*, thought Stephanie. *She's coming back.* But at that moment the door slammed with an echoing retort. Meagan was gone. After a few minutes, Stephanie's head fell forward. She didn't feel it hit.

She woke slowly into a dense fog, sounds growing and receding. Things washed thickly in her head. She worked to open her eyes but it was too much effort. She was heavy inside but at the same time her body seemed to be weightless, suspended. There was no substance underneath her. She felt brief pressure on her wrist, then it was gone.

Gradually she knew a pain in her nose and throat and chest, a horrible taste in her mouth, a needle feeding into her arm. Another hospital! She was frightened. What had happened? Had she been hemorrhaging again? Was she dying? Then she remembered. She was *supposed* to be dying. But she wasn't supposed to be conscious of it. There must be some mistake. She let herself drift into sleep again.

Later she came to and remembered the capsules and the dust particles suspended lazily in a shaft of light, such a contrast to her own dark desperation. She was pregnant and nobody cared. *Nobody cares.* She went over each person in turn, once more. Her mother didn't have time for Stephanie's problems. She was too busy saving the world. Besides, Stephanie's first pregnancy had upset her mother so much. She couldn't tell her about this one. Her father? That was a joke. Leroy? Hardly. Meagan? That was a laugh.

Or maybe the pills—surely the pills had destroyed the fetus. Maybe she had solved her own problem! She wouldn't have to die, after all.

I should feel relieved, she thought. But she didn't.

There was a light knock on the door and Ann Lawson came in, her strawberry blonde hair tucked into a white nurse's cap. Seeing her, Stephanie turned her head away.

Ann paused, as if afraid to invade Stephanie's privacy, then said timidly, "Stephanie?"

Part 8: 1992–Sometime in the 21st Century

Stephanie looked listlessly at the wall. In the same hesitant voice, Ann said, "I just came to see how you are."

Stephanie spoke in a monotone. "I wish I was dead."

"Is there anything I can do to help?"

"Leave me alone."

"Are you sure?"

Stephanie didn't answer. She turned to the wall and after a few minutes, she heard the door close.

"You were having a nightmare," said a nurse's voice. "You called for your mother. Shall I contact her for you?"

"No," said Stephanie groggily. "No." Everything subsided into blackness.

Again she woke. She was crying. She was hardly aware of Ann at her side.

"Would you like something?"

"No pills! No more pills!" said Stephanie, conscious of the pain again, fresh and deep. "I'm sorry! I'm sorry! I meant for me to die, not you. I didn't mean to hurt you." She struggled against the restraints securing both arms and legs.

A cool hand was smoothing the hair away from her forehead, as her mother had done years ago, in another hospital. "Jesus, have mercy on her," said Ann's voice. "Jesus, help her!" And then, "You're all right, Stephanie. You're going to be all right."

Oh God!, thought Stephanie. *Are you there? Can you hear me? Help me! I hurt so much inside. I ache! I can't take anymore.*

She sobbed again. *Love me, God! I need you!* She fell asleep, the tears still wet on her cheeks and in her hair.

The hand must have been stroking her forehead for a very long time and Stephanie was aware that a soft voice had been singing into her ear for some time, too. The music was comforting and vaguely familiar.

Compelling Interests

"Amazing Grace." That's what Ann was singing. Stephanie opened her eyes.

"Good morning," said Ann tenderly. "Except that it isn't morning. It's three o'clock. How are you feeling?"

"Why are you here?" Not accusing, just curious.

"I care about you."

"Don't you have classes you have to go to?"

"I work here," said Ann. "Senior practicum 502."

There was a pause and then Stephanie asked, "Why should you care about me?"

"Because God does. You're worth caring about, Stephanie."

Stephanie didn't answer at first. Then she said, "I am not. I'm bad. I lived."

"What's bad about that?" Ann sounded surprised.

"I lived and they died. I killed my babies. I killed one when I was fourteen. Everyone told me it was OK. They said I'd get over it."

Ann was looking puzzled. "Were there others?"

"This one."

"You didn't kill this baby."

"You mean I'm still pregnant?"

"Yes."

"I didn't hurt it with the pills?"

"No. It's fine. Would you like to hear the heartbeat?"

Ann took the stethoscope from around her neck and placed one earpiece in each of Stephanie's ears. Then she positioned the head of the stethoscope just below Stephanie's navel.

"Tell me when you hear something." She waited a moment, then tried a new spot.

"There!" said Stephanie. "There's something like a 'tap-tap, tap-tap.' It's fast."

"That's it."

"It's a baby?" she asked wonderingly.

"Yes."

Stephanie listened. "*My* baby?"

Part 8: 1992–Sometime in the 21st Century

"Yup."

"It has a heartbeat already?"

"Yes."

"That's unreal."

"Stephanie, God counts every beat of your baby's heart. The Bible says He is forming your baby in your womb, that He knows this child inside and out and loves it, that He has permitted this pregnancy for a purpose—"

Stephanie listened.

Ann reached for a blue leather-bound book that was soft with frequent use. She opened it and read,

For You formed my inward parts;

You wove me in my mother's womb.

I will give thanks to You, for I am fearfully and wonderfully made...

My frame was not hidden from You,

When I was made in secret...

Your eyes have seen my unformed substance;

And in Your book were all written

The days that were ordained for me

When as yet there was not one of them...

She closed it gently. "That's from Psalm 139. The One who designed your baby designed you, too. He loves you and has a plan for you—and it isn't killing yourself."

"I always make a mess of everything."

"That's called sin, Stephanie. You weren't designed to run your own life, to have to figure it out by yourself. There's an Owner's manual." She lifted the book in her lap. "There's a way to do it wrong and a way to do it right.

"First we have to ask His forgiveness for doing it wrong. Then we give Him all the broken pieces and He gives us wholeness and a brand new start. He shows us step by step how to do it right."

"I want to do that," Stephanie said with a little choke. "I want to do it right, Ann."

"Tell Him that."

Compelling Interests

"Now? Like, right here?"

"If you're ready. Just talk to Him in your own words."

Stephanie reached out and Ann took her hand in her own.

"I'm new at this, God. I don't know how—" As Stephanie started, so did the tears. "I want to tell you how sorry I am for killing my first baby and for all the ways I've messed up and the things I've done wrong. I want to thank you for my new baby and that it didn't die and that I didn't die and that You gave us a second chance—"

She wiped her eyes with a corner of the sheet. Ann was weeping now, too.

"I want to thank you for Ann—and for Noel, even though I was mad at him, I'm sorry about that—I want to know how to do it right, God. I want to know how to be the woman You designed me to be.

"I'm kind of scared about this baby. I don't know how I can raise a baby. Show me what to do, God. If there is someone who will be a better mother for this baby, show me. I'll do whatever You want." She broke off and Ann moved to her side, pressing Stephanie's head against her.

After a few moment's silence, during which their teardrops mingled on the bed, Ann said, "Amen!"

That made them both laugh self-consciously and pull apart.

"I thought you were an old fuddy-duddy missionary or something," Stephanie said.

"I hope I am."

"But I *like* you."

"I like *you*. We're sisters now, you know, because we have the same Daddy."

Stephanie began to smile. She put one hand over the place where she had heard the tiny tapping and looked down.

"Wow!" she said. "There's a baby in there! I have a baby!"

Part 8: 1992–Sometime in the 21st Century

Next day the hospital psychiatrist cleared her to move back to the dorm. She was packing when she heard a man's voice at the open door of her hospital room.

"Stephanie?" It was Noel. He looked distraught and at the sight of her, he let his breath out heavily.

"I've been trying to find you for three days! You didn't answer your buzzer and then your roommate said someone had to call the paramedics and finally Ann called and said you were in the hospital. Are you okay?"

"I am now," said Stephanie, her face full of joy. "Oh, Noel, everything is going to be okay—and I'm going to have a baby!"

He searched her face. "That's what you told me," he said slowly, the puzzlement in his eyes asking what had changed her attitude toward her pregnancy. She came to him and put her arms around his waist and hugged him hard. "You *do* care," she said.

"I don't understand you. Yes, I care, but—"

"I thought I was all alone. But I have God and Ann and you!"

He took her into his arms. "You're never alone." He leaned down and kissed her and his lips were warm and reassuring. After several minutes, he traced the curve of her cheek with a finger and said, "Stephanie, please don't ever leave me like that again! You had me tied up in knots."

"I won't," she promised.

Stephanie was three months pregnant when Noel proposed. She told Ann all about it.

"He was so cute about it. He started out saying he doesn't believe there are any illegitimate children, just illegitimate relationships. He said this baby may be the result of an illegitimate relationship but that God is sovereign over its conception and has a purpose for its existence.

"Then he said he thinks God is calling us together. He said God has given him a love for me that grows stronger the more he prays about it and he has peace that this is the right thing. He says if we build our marriage on God, we'll have an unshakeable foundation—"

"I hope you told him yes, after such an elegant proposal," said Ann with a grin.

Stephanie laughed. "I told him I thought he'd been going with you all this time! I thought you two were together because he used to meet you after class."

"Our families are friends," said Ann. "We've known each other since junior high."

"That's what he said. Anyway, he says he wants to raise my baby with me. He says he loves children." Then, "Ann, tell me about my baby. What is it like now?"

"Three months?" said Ann. "Large eyes, button nose, fingers, toes. Even fingernails and toenails. She—he?—can suck her thumb. He can respond to touch or tickling, close his eyes, pucker his lips, make a fist. The lungs and brain and digestive system are all complete. All the tooth buds are in place. Everything from now on is just fine-tuning."

Artyce stood at the window, looking out, seeing nothing. She was remembering Steffie at the beach, a chubby 5-year old in a pink bikini, holding her hand as they walked side by side, barefoot, on the wet sand... "Mommy," Stephanie had said. "Look at the waves folding."

Look at the waves folding. Tears stung Artyce's eyes. Those early years with her daughter had been the best years of her life. *I was so busy trying to fix her world, I didn't even notice I was losing her,* she thought. *All those years we could have had together.* Not that it had been easy to get close to Stephanie after the abortion. She had held everyone off. *But we had shared so much,* she thought, swallowing a lump in her throat. Then, *I miss her.*

Was there any way to cross that gulf now, to say "I'm sorry I wasn't there for you." Was there any way to make up for lost time?

She wanted so much to try calling Stephanie again—but she had tried all through February and Stephanie never returned the calls. The two of

Part 8: 1992–Sometime in the 21st Century

them hadn't talked all semester, except when Stephanie called to tell her how much her textbooks would be, so Artyce could mail her a check. Besides, the telephone was so impersonal—

Just then, it rang.

Artyce picked it up, wiping away her tears and trying to compose herself. "Yes?"

"Mom?" It was Stephanie's voice. Artyce caught her breath.

"Stephanie? Oh, Steffie, I'm so glad to hear from you! I've been thinking about you!"

"Mom, I'm sorry. I'm sorry I hurt you."

"Oh, *I'm* the one who hurt *you!* I want to tell you—I'm so sorry I've been so blind all these years! I haven't been much of a mother."

"It's OK, Mom," she heard Stephanie say. "You were doing important things."

"They weren't as important as you. How *are* you?"

"I'm fine. I have some news." There was a perkiness to her daughter's voice that Artyce hadn't heard in ages.

"I'd love some good news."

"I don't know if you'll think it's all *good* news or not. I've become a Christian and I'm getting married. And you're going to be a grandmother in October!"

As soon as she said the words, Stephanie wondered if it had been a mistake. Her mother didn't answer right away. *I've blown it,* Stephanie thought. *I could have waited to tell her that. We were almost close there for a minute.*

She realized her mother was speaking again, more softly this time. "Oh, Stef!"

Stephanie didn't know what to say. She had been so worried about getting the news out that she hadn't planned what to say afterward. But her mother was still speaking.

"I've gotten straightened out with the Lord myself. I was doing some right things for the wrong reasons, with the wrong attitude." Then, "You're going to have a *baby?*"

"Yeah, Mom."

Compelling Interests

"That's wonderful!" The warmth and attention in her mother's voice was like something long-forgotten. She didn't sound all uptight any more.

"Wonderful?" Stephanie was amazed. "You think that's wonderful?"

"I *do* wish we could sit down together and talk face to face instead of having to be at opposite ends of a phone line." She paused and became sober. "Steffie, when you were 14, when you had—you know—"

"The abortion?"

"Yes, the abortion." It was the first time they had discussed it. "Well, you know how much reading I did afterwards about it—and I read that often an abortion can make a girl—" Her voice broke ever so slightly. "I thought maybe you—maybe I never *would* be a grandmother."

"Oh, Mom," Stephanie said ruefully. "I never meant for it to happen this way. It was a mistake."

"I know," said Artyce, her voice now muffled. Stephanie guessed that she was wiping away tears. "But the how and the when aren't as important as the fact that," she gave a small sniff and her voice was brighter, "I've got my daughter back and I am going to have a grandchild!"

This was the mother Stephanie had lost, the mother who was counselor and friend, the mother who loved her through everything, the mother she hadn't had since childhood. Suddenly, with a leap of her heart, she realized she couldn't wait to go home.

"Why did you take those pills?" Ann asked Stephanie, when she thought it wouldn't bother Stephanie to ask. "Were you afraid of going through another abortion?"

"Because I was afraid and because I didn't think anyone cared. And because of something I read in the school paper. They were these little—like sayings, three or four lines long. Every day. I didn't want to read them but I couldn't help it."

Ann searched Stephanie's face. "I put those in the paper," she said carefully.

Part 8: 1992–Sometime in the 21st Century

"*You?*" Stephanie stared at her. "That's what did it, you know—sent me over the edge."

Ann was silent at first. "I didn't know." There was an awkward silence. "Are you sorry?"

"Not any more."

"I used the money my Great Aunt Gwen left me. She was a wonderful person. She was a teacher and she counseled high school girls who had gotten pregnant. She used to say, 'The only difference between a baby before and after delivery is one of charm—who would kill a baby you could see?'"

"That's funny," said Stephanie dreamily. "I had an Aunt Gwen, too. Well, she wasn't really my aunt. We just called her—" She stopped. "She didn't by any chance live in Hawaii?"

"Yes, she did!"

"And she died in—let's see, 1973?"

"Yes! When I was six."

Stephanie and Ann looked at each other.

"My mother told me about her," Stephanie said, not taking her eyes off Ann's. "I'm adopted. Aunt Gwen brought me to the States right after I was born, a few months before she died."

"*You're* one of Aunt Gwen's babies?" Ann said, astonished.

"The last one, my mom said."

"But they were all Japanese!"

"All but one," said Stephanie.

Chief Justice James Weatherill Weiss stood at his window, gazing across Constitution Avenue toward Union Station at a Washington made hazy by falling snow. How many years had he been on the bench now? He felt as if he had grown up here, not just old. Who said turning thirty was a shock—or fifty? Eighty had been the one which sobered him—and that had been over ten years ago.

Two of his colleagues, who had been in their eighties when the new president was elected and who had been hoping for the liberals to gain

Compelling Interests

the White House and choose their successors, had died within weeks of each other and had been replaced by conservatives. The third had waited nearly a year as if to see whether he would die too, and when he didn't, he retired.

Of the seven justices who had voted to legalize abortion back in 1973, James Weatherill Weiss alone still served on the U.S. Supreme Court. Today, he would have the dubious honor, if he chose, of reversing his own decision.

There had been so many changes since 1973. In the Supreme Court alone—his home away from home—much had changed. Everything was computerized now. The year after Roe, the building had had its first facelift since the Court convened for its initial session in 1935. The coffered ceiling had been repainted, each decorative burnt-orange-and-ivory panel touched up laboriously with tiny brushes by men atop ladders. With new lighting and new gilding, the building had gleamed with its original luster for nearly two decades—and then needed painting again. Even the ancient, creaky old elevator that brought the justices from the parking garage had been upgraded.

But the same ancient, creaky justice still rides it, Jim thought, amused.

Since 1973, the court had heard many cases pertaining to abortion—and refused to hear many more, letting stand lower court rulings that kept husbands and mothers and especially the government out of the process.

In each of those cases which the high court had chosen to hear, such as Planned Parenthood v. Danforth, Thornburgh v. American College of Obstetricians, and especially the Akron case, with its multiple facets, the court had ruled against all attempts to modify Roe vs. Wade.

In 1989, however, Webster v. Reproductive Health Services had reflected the changing political balance on the bench when it upheld a Missouri law which made the unqualified assertion that life begins at conception. Webster allowed—it did not mandate—states to require that doctors determine whether a given fetus 20 weeks or older could live outside the womb, presumably so that they could refuse to abort a viable fetus. It also permitted states, if they desired, to prohibit the use of state

Part 8: 1992–Sometime in the 21st Century

funds, employees, or facilities for abortions unless the mother's life was in danger.

The public had hotly disputed whether Webster nullified Roe. In fact, as Weiss well and wearily knew, it did not, no matter what the justices had intended. Perhaps, had it been handed down in 1973, each state would merely have returned to its pre-Roe condition, whether liberal or restrictive.

But decades had passed since Roe. Abortion as a practice was well established. Apart from Pennsylvania and a few southern states, none had enacted laws anywhere near as restrictive as those they had pre-Roe.

The Chen case they would rule on today was an unusual one. A young man who had survived a saline abortion at 21 weeks was suing his mother and her doctor—now retired and living in Acapulco—for attempted murder and for damages sustained in the womb. As a result of the abortion, he was deaf and had multiple other problems, including one non-functioning kidney.

Weighing one pound even, Brian Chen had been rushed by a nurse to the preemie nursery, where he was put on life-support. "I just happened to notice he was breathing," she had testified. "If they take a breath, they're considered alive—but we don't usually check. We just put them aside until we're through with the mother—and they're never breathing by then."

Once it was apparent Brian was going to make it, no one knew what to do with him. His mother obviously didn't want him; she had wanted a girl. He was finally adopted.

But the case which could overturn Roe had been filed by the original "Jane Roe" herself. Norma McCorvey, now a Christian and pro-life, had admitted she had lied about being gang-raped. Her attorney in San Antonio had filed a writ on her behalf, petitioning the high Court to reverse the 1973 decision. Women harmed by abortion had provided class action sworn testimony and some were scheduled to be present and demonstrate at the Court. That case was due to come before the Court today, too.

We need to address the fact that legalizing abortion has not *helped women's health.* He'd read the statistics: abortion could cause infections, uterine ruptures, sterility, miscarriages in subsequent pregnancies, labor complica-

Compelling Interests

tions, premature births, even maternal death. There was a possible link to breast cancer. Psychological damage included depression.

The slaughter of fetuses after viability—able, however primitively, to react to pain—was to James Weiss unconscionable. Taking life, whether an innocent infant's or a criminal's, should be an act calling for the greatest wisdom on the part of all those involved—and the state, by rights, must be involved.

It is time to address the issue of the object of abortion, thought Weiss, pulling on the familiar robe. *Back in 1973, we didn't have the technology we have now. We couldn't see into the womb. We couldn't anticipate and even prevent birth defects. We couldn't do intrauterine surgery. We couldn't keep premature babies alive at twenty weeks.*

In Roe v. Wade, the Supreme Court had ruled, "The State does have...[an] important and legitimate interest in protecting the potentiality of human life... The appellee and certain *amici* argue that the fetus is a 'person' within the language and meaning of the Fourteenth Amendment... *If this suggestion of personhood is established, the appellant's case, of course, collapses, for the fetus' right to life would then be guaranteed specifically by the Amendment.*"

On January 14, 1988 the personhood of the unborn child had been declared, if not established. President Ronald Reagan had recognized the advances in technology and declared the personhood of the fetus in his Presidential Proclamation #5761: "All medical and scientific evidence increasingly affirms that children before birth share all the basic attributes of human personality—that they in fact are persons. Modern medicine treats unborn children as patients. Yet, as the Supreme Court itself has noted, the decision in Roe v. Wade rested upon an earlier state of medical technology. The law of the land in 1988 should recognize all of the medical evidence.

"I have asked the Legislative branch to declare the 'humanity of the unborn child and the compelling interest of the several states to protect the life of each person before birth.' This duty to declare on so fundamental

Part 8: 1992–Sometime in the 21st Century

a matter falls to the Executive as well. By this Proclamation I hereby do so."

This long and eloquent Proclamation paved the way for the overturn of Roe v. Wade and for a constitutional amendment to declare that the right to life extends to citizens from conception, rather than from birth—yet nothing had come of it.

Was the fetus more than "potential" life as far back as the fertilized egg? Weiss still didn't know. But he knew that declaring open season on America's unborn had not been the answer. Certainly aborting a full-term baby by delivering its body and then crushing its skull was an abhorrent perversion of what the justices had intended to allow. Rape and incest? Surely those exceptions should be determined on a case-by-case basis. *What we need,* he thought, *is not just to make abortion illegal—but to make it unthinkable.*

The teaching of abstinence? Better promotion of birth control? Stronger moral leadership? There was an answer to the skyrocketing illegitimacy—but it wasn't abortion.

Natural birth ought to be the rule and abortion the exception, he thought. At present, the nation was aborting one out of every three pregnancies. The pro-abortionists had almost succeeded in persuading women that giving birth was somehow dangerous and unnatural, something to avoid at all costs. Why, a mere three years after Roe, more women in Washington, DC had had abortions than had had live births.

A woman's own health was at risk when she aborted late, Weiss knew. It was at risk too when she aborted repeatedly—and that, to his great regret, applied to nearly half the women who had abortions.

After all, labor and delivery were natural processes for which the body prepared; abortion was not. It was an intrusion and an interruption, even a violent interruption, of the natural progression of pregnancy.

We never meant women to take it lightly, he thought. *We never meant for 98 percent of all abortions to be sought because pregnancy was an inconvenience or for women to abort multiple times. We were addressing the desper-*

ate woman, the emergency scenario. The women of this country have made a mockery of our compassion.

They have assumed more rights than Roe gave them, he told himself. *Women have argued that Roe v. Wade guarantees them an absolute right to privacy—although we stated explicitly, three times, that the Court refuses to recognize an unlimited or unqualified right to "do with one's body as one pleases."*

We made it clear, he thought with a shake of his head, *that abortion was destroying the life of a fetus. We stated plainly in the ruling that beyond a certain point the state has equally compelling interests in the mother and in the potential life within her, that the state then has a right to intervene to protect the life of her child.*

A woman's right to choose, his thoughts continued, *should be exercised, whenever possible, before conception.* Of course it was not possible to prevent every conception, even if you weren't speaking of rape and incest. There would always be unwanted babies—at least, babies unwanted by their natural mothers. But should being unwanted comprise a capital offense?

Would outlawing abortion prevent women from resorting to it? No, any more than outlawing any other crime prevented individuals from committing it. Whether legal or illegal, there would always be women who would risk their own lives rather than bear a child.

His thoughts lingered on his wife, three years in her grave. He missed her support, he missed her active interest in current affairs, he missed her wisdom.

Would she have counseled him again to "remember the women dying from abortion" if she had known that women would keep dying, that making it legal wouldn't stop that?

If only they had all known. If only they had known that child abuse, instead of becoming obsolete, would proliferate. It was five, six times what it had been. *And how could it be otherwise,* he asked himself, sighing inwardly, *when abortion denies the inherent value of a child's life? How could it be otherwise when it plants in the mind of a mother the seed idea of punishing the child for existing, an idea which might sprout two months, two*

Part 8: 1992–Sometime in the 21st Century

years, ten years after childbirth? How could it be otherwise when abortion itself is the ultimate child abuse?

He had meant well. He hadn't meant it to come to this. Carrying potential life to term was not an individual thing; there was more than one person involved. More, even, than two.

No, he thought, *none of us has an unlimited right to do what we want with our own bodies.* The selfish '70s, '80s, and '90s were over.

It's time to make our choices before we take actions that have serious consequences. It's time to assume responsibility for the decisions we have made. It's time for America to grow up.

He put his hand out and grasped the brass doorknob, not as sharply defined to his vision as it used to be, even with his latest prescription. He would vote this last time, Chief Justice James Weatherill Weiss thought, and then consider retiring.

Perhaps he had stayed in power for such a time as this.

Postscript

Compelling Interests is fiction but the backdrop, that is, the history of abortion in the United States since 1940, is not. It is thoroughly researched and can be documented. Even though this is a novel, almost everything in it really happened or is congruent with what really happened.

Some of the characters are real. Joan Andrews is a real person. Everything about her in this book is true and has been included with her permission. References to Mother Teresa, Phyllis Schlafly, Joe Scheidler, James Dobson, Margaret Sanger, WEBA, Randall Terry, and Operation Rescue are all accurate.

A widow from Maui really did fly to Japan and bring unwanted babies back to the States for American adoptive families. Her name was Charlotte Susu-Mago. She really was married to a Japanese man and they were interned together in a relocation camp with their infant son Douglas during World War II.

In response to her son's challenge to "do more" for the unborn, Rebecca Younger, an Hispanic wife and mother of four did try sidewalk counseling outside a family planning clinic in Long Beach, California. So many pregnant women eager to have an alternative to abortion responded that Rebecca did take them into her own home. Then, with Bonnie Beardslee,

Compelling Interests

she asked God for funds to buy a 3-story Victorian house for the women and fifty local churches did paint and furnish its rooms. **All author's proceeds from this book will go to the organizations she founded, New Life Beginnings and New Life Mothers Home.** Rebecca really did get pregnant with an unexpected fifth child who became a blessing to everyone.

A woman from Long Beach really did write an undercover "How-To" book suggesting women trick doctors into thinking they were having a spontaneous abortion so that the doctors would "finish the job." She and others did send women to illegal abortionists in Mexico and legal ones in Japan. The book was *The Abortion Handbook for Responsible Women* by Lana Clarke Phelan. I have a copy of the book and the transcript of a taped interview with Phelan, at which I was present.

Norma McCorvey, the original Jane Roe in Roe v. Wade, did change her position on abortion and did file a writ on January 18, 2005, petitioning the U.S. Supreme Court to reverse the ruling legalizing abortion

Although Justice Weatherill Weiss is fictional, when I ran the material about him past a lawyer who had worked as an aide for one of the Supreme Court justices who ruled on Roe v. Wade, the lawyer told me the description of Weiss sounded just like his boss.

A doctor really did say that in switching to abortions he felt as if he had drilled for water and hit oil. He really did say he had probably wiped out a kindergarten class.

An abortionist, Bernard Nathanson, really did help get abortion legalized in New York, later admitting in his book *Aborting America* that he had helped falsify statistics for the purpose. He really did become pro-life, and film a documentary ("The Silent Scream") of a fellow doctor aborting a 12-week fetus. When he showed this doctor the film, the doctor really did quit doing abortions.

Edward Allred, an abortionist, started with nothing, according to the *Orange County Register,* then set up a string of 46 clinics and became "a millionaire several times over." He owned a private plane, a 165-acre ranch stocked with quarter horses, and had dealings in land and cattle. He really did pride himself on his ability to perform an abortion in under

Postscript

five minutes, thus eliminating what he called "needless patient-physician contact."

The same Dr. Allred, who described himself as "one of the experts at doing second-trimester abortions," really did say, "I struggle with their morality... I have great difficulty with Roe v. Wade on second-trimester abortions. I do them and do them quite commonly... [but] I really feel that the court... erred when they made that judgment." He said this to a church congregation in 1984. I have his words on tape.

The death certificate of a 16-year old African-American who died as a result of a late (legal) abortion really exists and is one of many. Ambulances really were not infrequently called to the clinic in Long Beach which "Mariana" and I picketed. It still exists and still does abortions.

The Republican party really did return a contribution of $1,000 from an abortionist.

A lab technician in a hospital where aborted fetuses were kept in jars really did pick up a late-term baby by the neck and say "I wish they'd stop sending us these!"

The Special Mass at Stephen Martyr Church, the Legalization and Its Consequences conference, Operation Rescue's sit-in in Los Angeles and all the events outside the Long Beach abortion clinic really happened. A man who claimed he had AIDS really did bite a pro-life protester at a sit-in and say, "Now you've got it, too!"

A pro-choice activist really did throw a chastity belt in the face of a local legislator during a public meeting.

A woman who was not connected with any local pro-life group did burn down an abortion clinic in Long Beach.

The Unitarian-Universalists did encourage their members to "dialogue" with those of other views on issues. A group in Long Beach did have one of the first of these dialogues, on the subject of abortion, and did include local pro-life evangelicals. The resolution they passed is verbatim.

As for other characters, though fictional, some of them are based on composites of pro-life or pro-choice advocates. All articles quoted are from sources cited. There is no Long Beach University or Cal State Anaheim but

Compelling Interests

the assignments and homework I describe in their Women's Studies classes are representative of those in Women's Studies classes in other colleges.

Jessica Shaver Renshaw, March 27, 2006

To order additional copies of

Compelling Interests

Have your credit card ready and call:

1-877-421-READ (7323)

or please visit our web site at
www.pleasantword.com

Also available at:
www.amazon.com
and
www.barnesandnoble.com

Printed in the United States
70111LV00001B/169-186